no time
to say
goodbye

BOOKS BY KATE HEWITT

no time to say goodbye

KATE HEWITT

bookouture

Published by Bookouture in 2019

An imprint of StoryFire Ltd.

Carmelite House
50 Victoria Embankment
London EC4Y 0DZ

www.bookouture.com

Copyright © Kate Hewitt, 2019

Kate Hewitt has asserted her right to be identified
as the author of this work.

All rights reserved. No part of this publication may be reproduced,
stored in any retrieval system, or transmitted, in any form or by
any means, electronic, mechanical, photocopying, recording or
otherwise, without the prior written permission of the publishers.

ISBN: 978-1-83888-061-3
eBook ISBN: 978-1-83888-060-6

This book is a work of fiction. Names, characters, businesses,
organizations, places and events other than those clearly in the
public domain, are either the product of the author's imagination
or are used fictitiously. Any resemblance to actual persons, living or
dead, events or locales is entirely coincidental.

To everyone who has lost someone, and found a way to go on.

PART ONE

CHAPTER ONE

NATHAN

I didn't take the call. I'll never forgive myself for that, even though I learned later it didn't matter. It was already too late. I don't even know who the call was from—the police? A stranger?

I'd never know, but the time of the call still haunted me—11:42. Just minutes after the moment of my wife's death, according to witnesses. Apparently, someone was checking the time on their phone while a lunatic drew a gun and *shot* my wife.

I was in a meeting then, an important bid for a new build downtown; an eyesore of an office building from the 1960s was being demolished, and a European bank was moving their headquarters to Grand Street. They were shopping for an architectural firm, and they'd come to us—a smaller start-up, but with a handful of prestigious awards and a growing reputation for high-quality work.

I wanted that job. Badly. And so, when the blocked number came up on my phone, the buzzing faint but insistent, I swiftly swiped it to silence the call. Just a telemarketer, I thought, someone trying to sell me life insurance or window blinds. I shouldn't have even brought my phone into the meeting, but like most people in the New York business world, I took it with me everywhere, just in case the next big deal was a ringtone away.

I smiled blandly at the bankers and I refocused on the presentation my partner was giving about how the building would be eco-friendly, sourced with sustainable wood and other environmental materials. We had this. We *had* to have this.

I completely forgot about the call until half an hour later, after the meeting and the backslapping and the refills of coffee, the handshakes and the promises to be in touch soon. I glanced at my phone again as I headed back to my office, and I saw I had another missed call and also a voicemail, not from the unknown caller who hadn't left a message, but from The Garden School, Ruby's preschool.

Like any father's would, my heart lurched a little with alarm— not serious fear, nothing close to terror. Just that little needling of worry, closer to irritation than true panic, that Ruby might have got hurt, or had an allergic reaction. Perhaps she just needed Tylenol. They had to ask parents' permission for everything these days, although Laura was usually the one they'd call. She was always the one they called.

I listened to the voicemail in the elevator, registering the suppressed yet calculated irritation of Miss Willis, the lead teacher. "Mr. West? I'm calling you because no one has picked Ruby up from school today, and it has now been…" An ostentatious pause to check the time. "*Twenty-five* minutes since pick-up time." A carefully let out breath. "Could you please call me back as soon as possible? As you know, The Garden School has a policy of charging for every ten minutes after pick-up time."

Yes, twenty bucks per. I knew. I'd signed the agreement, inwardly fuming that a preschool that cost eighteen grand a year still had the gall to charge per minute.

Still, twenty-five minutes was a long time. Laura was never that late, and if she had been, surely she would have let them know? Let *me* know, although perhaps she wouldn't have, since I couldn't have done anything anyway.

I checked my phone again, but I had no missed calls or texts from her. Briefly I thought of the missed call from the unknown number—but who could it have been? Surely not Laura, not from her own phone, anyway.

The doors of the elevator opened and I strode to my corner office, brushing aside the cheerful greeting of my assistant, Jenny, as well as the curious stares of the dozen employees in our open-plan office; West and Stein Architectural had two floors in a building on Thirty-Fourth and Madison Avenue that was a bit too expensive for us, but we agreed appearances mattered, especially in our business.

I shut the door behind me, the phone clamped to my ear as I called Laura. There was no answer. For the first time, I started to feel properly worried, and not just that little pinprick of doubt, the *what if...* or *surely not...* that we all feel, as parents, as people.

The moment when you lose sight of your toddler in Target, or your wife is half an hour late coming home. You're worried, but you're not *really* worried. You don't actually believe that something bad is going to happen, or already has. Life is going to continue on the same, because it must. The alternative is impossible to contemplate, even as your heart rate speeds up just that little bit.

This felt different. This was an audible hitching of my breath, a frantic somersault of my heart, an icy plunging of my stomach. *Twenty-five minutes.*

I called The Garden School back, half hoping that Laura would have already come and collected Ruby, sure that she must have, but when Miss Willis came on the phone, she sounded alarmed rather than annoyed, which made me feel even more panicked, although I tried to keep myself from it. There was an explanation, a reasonable one. There had to be.

"No one has picked up Ruby, Mr. West, and it has now been nearly an *hour*."

"I don't know where my wife is." I blurted the words, like a little boy, ashamed and afraid, needing someone else to sort it out, tell me what to do.

"Then can you send someone else?" Miss Wills' alarm was seguing back into the more expected annoyance. This was the woman I knew—stern, a stickler for rules and details. "Your nanny?"

We didn't have a nanny, unlike just about every other family at the school, or even on the whole Upper East Side. Laura had never wanted one, although I'd always said we could use an extra pair of hands on occasion. On a lot of occasions.

I blew out a breath, impatience creeping up on my fear, even now. If Laura had just spaced, or forgotten the time, I was going to be as annoyed as Miss Willis. *But a whole hour…*

"I'll come," I said reluctantly, because there was no one else. I didn't know Laura's mom friends, not well enough to call anyway, and we had no family in the city. The babysitter we'd used was a student at Columbia who only did evenings, although more recently we'd let our oldest daughter Alexa be in charge on the occasions when we went out together, not that we did very often. "I'll be twenty minutes." More like forty, but everyone in New York pretended it only took twenty minutes to get anywhere.

I had just disconnected the call when I saw Jenny in front of my office, gesturing to someone behind her. I frowned, putting my phone down, and then I saw the policewoman standing there, her navy uniform a stark contrast to the light colors of the office—blond wood, white walls, Jenny's pink blouse. The policewoman looked like a streak of dark, a spill of ink. *Wrong.*

In that moment, those few awful, suspended seconds, it felt as if everything inside me had frozen—my blood, my heart, my brain. I simply stood there and stared, unable to move. To think. Not wanting to, because I knew any thoughts I had would not be good ones; they would propel me into the next moment, and then the next, and I wanted to stay right there, in a state of paralysed ignorance. If I didn't move, I didn't know. And I didn't want to know. Already, I realized that, with a bone-deep certainty.

Jenny knocked on the door, a matter of form, and then edged into my office. She was only twenty-three, fresh out of college, with aspirations to be a graphic designer. This was her first "real" job. She looked terrified.

"Nathan… there's a policewoman here." Her voice was soft as she bit her lip. "She… she wants to talk to you."

I think I nodded. I might have said something. Everything felt as if it were happening in slow motion, or underwater. There was a buzzing in my ears that made everything else sound muted, as if it were happening far away, to someone else. *Please, to someone else.*

The policewoman came in, looking far too serious.

"Mr. West?"

"Nathan, please." The words came out sounding oddly jocular, the verbal equivalent of a manly handshake. My professional voice that I used as a matter of instinct, or perhaps self-protection. *This is just a business meeting. That's all it is.* "What can I do for you?" I asked in that same tone, even though it sounded ridiculous. I knew it did, and yet I couldn't keep myself from it.

Jenny closed the door behind her, her expression still anxious, eyebrows drawn together in a crinkle. The moment spun out, suspended, endless, which was fine by me because I knew, I *knew* I didn't want to hear what this woman had to say, and as long as I could keep her from saying it…

I had a sudden urge to put my fingers in my ears, or throw my arms in front of my face. Anything to keep from hearing whatever came next.

"Mr. West, Nathan. I'm very sorry, but I have some difficult news to give you. Some very difficult news."

No. I didn't speak; I couldn't. I just stared at her, my body completely still and tense, my hands flexing into fists at my sides. I felt poised for action, as if I could start to sprint, but there was nowhere to go.

"Would you like to sit down?"

"No thank you." I sounded weirdly polite.

The policewoman nodded slowly, then spoke again, even though I didn't want her to. "I'm afraid your wife was involved in an incident on the subway this morning."

An *incident*? What did *that* mean? "The subway?" I repeated blankly. I shook my head. Laura never took the subway, or at least very rarely. She stayed on the Upper East Side, where our apartment was, as well as the girls' schools, the upscale supermarkets where she bought freshly ground coffee and organic everything, the gym, the library, the hair salons and nail bars—everything she could possibly want or need. She'd joked once that she hadn't been south of Seventy-Second Street in over three months.

"Yes, on the J Train, between the Bowery and Canal Street Stations."

A seemingly small detail, but such a crucial one. "Then it can't be Laura." I almost laughed with the sheer relief of it; I felt giddy with sudden, sure knowledge. "There's no way my wife would travel that far downtown." *The Bowery?* That was practically as far down as you could get, below Manhattan's grid of numbered streets and avenues, heading towards Wall Street, *miles* from our home. No *way* had Laura been on that train.

Yet even as I said the words, I felt their futility. Here was a policewoman, saying Laura had been in an *incident,* and only moments ago I had talked to Miss Willis, who had told me Laura hadn't come to pick up Ruby as usual. Two and two usually made an understandable four, but not this time. *Not this time.*

"I'm afraid we're quite certain it was your wife, Mr. West," the policewoman said. She was surprisingly slight for a law officer, with dark hair and gentle eyes. Had she been sent specially? She had the look of someone who knew how to break bad news, who would do it softly yet firmly... as she was now.

"How are you certain?" I sounded aggressive, but I couldn't help it. Laura could not have been on the J train in lower Manhattan. It was simply not possible. She didn't go downtown. She would have told me if she was doing something so different today.

In fact, she hadn't said she was going anywhere this morning, when I'd taken the girls to school... she'd mentioned no plans beyond the usual preschool run. Those precious three hours she had by herself. What did she do during those hours? I'd never really given much thought to them—or any other part of Laura's day—but I was as sure as hell that she didn't go all the way downtown.

"She had identification on her person that matched her appearance," the policewoman said, "and your details were on her phone."

I swallowed hard, said nothing.

"You are Nathan West, and your wife is Laura West?"

"Yes." Even this came out unwillingly.

"And this is your wife?" The woman's face was filled with compassion as she handed me Laura's driver's license. I stared at it disbelievingly.

Laura. Light brown hair, smiling eyes, freckles across her nose, a slightly crooked front tooth. "Yes," I said, and my voice sounded as if it were coming from a distance, from somewhere outside of myself, tinny and small. "Yes, this is my wife." I looked up, reality slamming into me hard as my mind suddenly sped up. "What's happened? Where is she? What kind of incident? What does that even *mean*?" The questions fired out of me like bullets, and I was too anxious, too terrified, to wait for any answers. "Well?" I shouted. "Can you please tell me what the *fuck* is going on here?'

The woman blinked, taking my anger in stride. "I'm very sorry, Mr. West, but your wife was involved in an incident—"

"You've *said* that already."

"She was shot by an unknown assailant in the subway car," the woman continued steadily, softly. Each word fell on me like a hammer blow. *Shot.* No.

"But she's all right..." I began, before trailing off. "Is she is in the hospital?" I tried again. "Where was she shot? How bad is it?" But I knew. I knew from the look on her face, from the fact that she'd already said this was very difficult news, the details she'd given without any assurance that Laura was okay, the complete lack of urgency about her, no need to get to the hospital quickly, no frightening addendum—*she was taken by ambulance* or even *she's in surgery now.* No more to the story.

Two and two made four again, and I couldn't stand it.

"Don't," I said abruptly, wheeling away from her. A pointless reaction, but I couldn't help it. I didn't want to hear. I wasn't ready.

The woman stayed silent, waiting for me to catch up.

I took a deep breath, staring out the floor-to-ceiling windows that covered two walls of my office. Far below, people scurried up and down Madison Avenue, phones clamped to ears, paper coffee cups in hand, shouldering their way through the ever-present stream of humanity. Everyone was so busy and important. No one knew what was happening up here. No one realized this was the end of everything for me. I was trying not to realize it myself. If I could just stay in this moment of ignorance forever...

The policewoman cleared her throat.

"Well?" I turned around, bracing myself, everything in me tense and expectant, knowing what came next.

"I'm afraid she is dead, Mr. West," the woman said quietly.

I knew it was coming, but I couldn't keep myself from crying out—a small, stifled sound—as I reached with one hand to grasp my chair and steady myself as if I might stagger. From the corner of my eye, I saw Jenny at her desk, looking pale and scared, her hands covering her mouth.

I realized the whole office was silent, everyone watching and waiting, my grief played out as if on a silent screen, from behind the floor-to-ceiling window. Could they guess what was happening? Did they know?

All I could think about was Laura, the fact that she was gone, just *gone*, a reality impossible to take in. My brain kept rejecting it, like a crumpled dollar bill from a soda machine. *No. That didn't happen. That simply didn't happen.*

"What..." The word came out in a breath, but then I stopped because I didn't even know what questions to ask, or if any of them mattered. Who shot her? Why? Why was she on the J train in the first place? What was somebody doing with a gun on the subway? Where were they now? Had they been caught? *How had this happened?*

No, none of it mattered. All that mattered was that Laura was dead. *Dead.*

"Do you have someone you can call?" the woman asked. "To support you...?"

I stared at her dumbly. Who was I meant to call? Laura's parents, so particular and polite, in Boston? We didn't get along at the best of times. My hippy-dippy mother, out in Arizona, "living her best life" now? Our few couple-friends, the kind of people we had dinner with on occasion, drinking too much wine and promising to do it again soon, but then it was always another six months before we did? *Who?*

My head was buzzing and I suddenly felt sick, my stomach cramping so hard and fast I had to double over.

"Mr. West..." Clumsily the woman patted my shoulder, and I shrugged her off. She stepped back, waiting for me to get hold of myself.

Slowly, with painstaking effort, I straightened. I was bathed in an icy sweat and I had to keep myself from shaking. Shock, I realized distantly. I was in shock.

"May I call someone for you, Mr. West?"

I shook my head. There was no one to call, no one to help me in this moment. My brain still felt frozen, each thought like an air bubble slowly surfacing up through the ice. It was hard to grasp any of them; they popped before I could even try.

"I need to get my daughter from preschool," I finally said.

CHAPTER TWO

MARIA

"Look at that."

Selma nodded at the television suspended from the ceiling in the corner of the room; on the screen, a news reporter with a somber look was standing on a busy street. A handful of people were sitting around, watching the news with only mild interest as they waited for their English class to begin.

Selma and I were doing our usual Tuesday volunteering at the Global Rescue Refugee Center in the Bowery, sorting clothing donations into piles—men, women, children, and those too worn or stained to be used. The last pile was by far the biggest.

"What is it?" I glanced at the ticker tape at the bottom of the screen: *Woman Shot on Subway. Assailant has not been found.* I looked away.

"Isn't that near here?" Selma said, sounding more curious than worried, and I turned back to the screen.

On the J train between the Bowery and Canal Street Stations… a single gunshot… assailant fled.

"It's right around the corner," she remarked, and I felt a fluttering inside that I didn't understand.

"Yes…" It was almost as if I knew, as if some old sense in me had awakened, attuned to tragedy, acquainted with grief. "Yes, it's very close."

I stared at the screen, waiting for more. Then a picture flashed up—a close-up of a driving license photo, blurry yet distinct.

Selma gave a soft gasp. "Don't we know her? Doesn't she volunteer here?"

I stared at the familiar face, the light brown hair, the smiling eyes, even though her mouth wasn't smiling, not for a license photograph. If it had been, I would have seen that crooked front tooth that somehow seemed friendly, in this world of straight, overly white teeth. Laura West's slight snaggle tooth had felt like a knowing wink, an arm around the shoulder. *See? We're alike, you and me.* Even though I knew we weren't.

"Yes," I said softly, as I resisted that sweep of loss, like an empty echo reverberating through me—old, yet familiar. So familiar. "We know her."

And I knew her best of all the volunteers, although I didn't fool myself into thinking that Laura West would count me as a good friend, or perhaps even as a friend at all. Conversations over coffee, the odd joke or shared confidence did not make a friendship, not really. It just meant more to me, because I had so little.

"She taught English, didn't she?" Selma asked.

"Yes." She'd been here just this morning. I'd bumped into her at the door as she'd left and we'd done an awkward little dance before she'd held me fast by the shoulders, making me tense just a little as she firmly maneuvered me to the side. *Sorry*, she'd said breathlessly. *I'm late for Ruby.* I'd nodded in understanding, still a little nonplussed, and she'd given me a smile of apology.

Take care, Maria, she'd said before hurrying away.

She always called me by name; she was that sort of person. We'd chatted frequently, nearly every week, although about nothing too important. I remember the first time she came up to me: *Where are you from? Bosnia, Sarajevo. Oh, I'm sorry.* A hand on my arm, a compassionate look. It was almost as if she knew.

"Laura West." Selma stared at the screen, her eyes wide. "To think she was here, alive, a few hours ago."

The thought made me want to shiver. Just a few hours ago, we'd been chatting.

"Poor woman." Selma shook her head. "She had children, too, didn't she?"

"Yes." I felt cold inside, numb and frozen. "Three girls."

One of the staff called those waiting into the English class, and after they'd filed out, I went over to turn off the TV.

Before I hit the button, I stared at the screen again; they'd moved onto a report about some business crisis, but in my mind I still saw the photo on the driver's license. *Laura West.* When we'd met, I'd noticed she'd had kind eyes. She'd asked me if I was married, if I had children—no to both, of course. She'd shown me a photo of her three daughters. The littlest one had reddish-gold hair and a gap-toothed grin. She'd been worried about them, about their little troubles, the love and fondness evident in her voice even when she spoke about their defiance and difficulties. Listening to her had felt like glimpsing another kind of life, one where warmth and love and family all loomed large. It was like listening to a fairy tale, but one that was real, and wonderful because of it.

The news program segued into an advert for rejuvenating skin cream, some sort of miracle cure. I watched the smooth, smiling face of a woman meant to be in her sixties, silver hair swinging jauntily as she strolled along a garden path, and for a second I saw my mother, her face as wrinkled as an old prune, wasting away. I turned the television off.

"It's very sad," I said to Selma. "Everyone here will miss her."

And so I told myself that would be the end of it. I'd put this little grief away with all the others, shut it all up and try not to think of it again. That was the only way forward—to exist. Walking through the wasteland one slow step at a time. For the last twenty-six years that had been how I'd lived; it was the only way I knew how anymore. But even as I told myself this, I pictured Laura West, how her nose crinkled when she laughed, how she'd always ask if I wanted a coffee, and again I felt that wave of grief. *Put it away, Maria,* I instructed myself. *Just put it away.*

Yet I could not stop thinking of her as I left Global Rescue and walked to the Bowery station where I would take the J train home, in the opposite direction as she would have, to Astoria, in Queens. I volunteered at the refugee center twice a week, during my days off, but the rest of the time I stayed in Astoria, working at a local hairdressing salon, run by a fellow Bosniak, Neriha.

When I got to the station, I saw it was closed; it must have been quite a few hours since Laura's death, but there were still no trains running in either direction. Bright yellow tape blocked off the entrance and a bored-looking policeman was guarding it, just in case. I stepped back quickly.

People were milling around, trying to figure out what had happened, or simply annoyed that the train service was disrupted. I heard a man swearing into his phone, complaining how he was going to be late "and all because some saddo probably threw himself in front of the train".

I walked away blindly, unsure where to go. I felt disorientated, as if I no longer knew my way, when I've lived in this city for nearly twenty years. For a moment, it was as if the streets I'd walked so many times were unfamiliar; the buildings rising so high above me felt as if they were closing me in, pressing down. I pictured Laura near here, walking towards her death, her bag swinging jauntily, having no idea. It all must have happened so quickly. I'd seen it too many times... it was nothing but the matter of a moment. Here, then gone.

Standing there on the sidewalk, people pushing past, twenty years fell away and I didn't know where I was. I struggled to breathe.

Someone grabbed my elbow, and I let out a little cry.

"Are you all right, madam? You looked faint."

I stared into the kindly face of a strange man, his dark face creased into a worried smile. I stepped back, pulling my arm away.

A deep breath, and once again I pushed it all down. Down, down, as far as it could go. "I'm fine, thank you," I said, and I walked on.

I would have to take the bus. I stopped again in the street, trying to remember where the bus picked up passengers. The bus system of the city had always seemed so inexplicable to me, a complex crisscross of routes that felt impenetrable but now must be navigated. I could figure it out, I told myself. I'd got all the way to America by myself, I could certainly get home to Queens.

In the end, it took nearly two hours and three bus transfers before I made my way to my apartment on 31st Road—a small studio I'd lived in by myself for the last six years.

When I'd first come to America, I had shared an apartment with four other refugees—two Bosniaks, a Serb, and a Croat, all put together by the state department's resettlement program, all fleeing the Bosnian War and its devastation on our lives. All of us from different cities, some of us speaking different languages, with different memories we needed to forget. Before the war, none of it would have mattered. Back then I couldn't have even told the difference between a Serb or a Croat, a Muslim or a Catholic, and no one I knew would have cared anyway. But after—and life feels as if it has always been an *after*—I spoke to none of those girls. I hardened my heart against all of them, because I did not know how else to be.

Now, in my little studio, I reheated some leftover stew—I always made a pot for the whole week and ate it every night. It was easier, when it was just for one. Usually I would sit at the tiny table, reading a book from the library—I preferred romance novels, fairy-tale froth my father would have despaired of—while

I ate. Even now I could picture the glass case of books in our old sitting room, velvet drapes drawn against the night, and how he'd have me sit on his lap as he told me how precious they were. *If you can read, Maria, you will never be alone.* How little he knew.

Tonight, however, I felt too restless to read, memories darting in and out of my mind like shadows I tried to dodge... the crackle of my father turning the pages of his newspaper, my brother's face, filled with fear. *Maria, did they...?* My mother's fluttering fingers, holding onto my wrist. *Promise me...*

To block it all out, I turned the television on, even though part of me didn't want to. I turned to the news and took my bowl of beef stew out of the microwave as I half-listened to a report on the economy, the reporter's voice a drone in the background.

Then, as I sat at the table, a woman faced the camera with another story, her expression appropriately sober.

"A woman was shot by an unknown assailant on a subway train today. The woman has been identified as Laura West, a mother of three who lived in New York and had been volunteering at a local refugee center." A terrible, telling pause. "It is not currently known whether she knew her attacker."

They flashed another picture of her on the screen, this one some sort of family snap, probably culled from Facebook. She was laughing on a beach, her arms around two children, their faces blurred out for legal reasons. I stared at the photo, her head thrown back, her smile wide as she embraced all life had to offer. So much joy.

Laura West. How many times had we laughed and chatted over the last year? We'd talked almost every week; she'd bring me a coffee during one of our breaks, milky and sweet as she knew I'd liked it. We'd sit at one of the little tables in the front hall and gossip—or rather, Laura would chat about her life and I would listen. I loved to listen.

It seemed impossible to me that she'd died, and so violently, even as some weary part of me was unsurprised. Wasn't this what always happened? Things ended, one way or another. They always ended.

Now, sitting alone, I recalled some of the many details Laura had offered up freely, imparting them almost carelessly. Her three daughters—Alexa was the oldest, Ruby the youngest, at just four. I couldn't remember the middle one's name, much to my regret. And her husband... Nathan, he was called. He worked too hard, he wanted a better life for his family, but it came at a cost. This had been said in a sorrowful tone, capped with a sigh. *He had a tough childhood... dragged around by his mom, his dad never in the picture. He wants better for our girls. I know that. It's just...*

She'd never finished that sentence. Now she never would.

The news changed to something else, something far away, and I forced the memories of Laura back down. I was sad, yes, I could admit that. I could allow it. But I had to push all the rest away, just as I did everything else.

Really, in the end, I hadn't known Laura West all that well, even if I'd always looked forward to seeing her, had called her a friend. The reality was, I had probably meant very little to her. Two women, caught up in the same place and the same time, chatting over coffee once a week. It wasn't as if I'd been really involved in her life.

Sitting there with the news droning on, I had no idea that I would become so involved, more than I ever could have imagined.

CHAPTER THREE

NATHAN

The next few hours were a blur of shocked pain and disbelief. I left my office, and the policewoman, and went to collect Ruby. It had suddenly become essential, absolutely *crucial*, to find my daughter—all my daughters—and keep them safe. It was the only thing that could both drive and anchor me now.

"I'm sorry, but we will need to talk to you again, Mr. West," the policewoman had said with a grimace of regret. "And you'll want to pick up Mrs. West's effects…"

I'd shrugged her words aside, not wanting to think about what they meant, Laura's things in some locker, languishing in some strange place. "You have my contact details," I'd said, as if I were talking to a salesman, and I'd strode through the office, not willing to meet anyone's eye. I was afraid their pity might break me. I would shatter.

"Nathan," Jenny had called softly. "What…"

I shook my head. They would hear soon enough. Everyone would. But, for now, I just needed to find my family… what was left of it.

I took a cab uptown because I couldn't bear the thought of the subway. Would I ever be able to take it again? Images of Laura on the train, a man with a gun… I realized there was so much I didn't know.

I didn't even know if it was a man who had shot her, or if he'd shot anyone else, or *where* he'd shot her. The head? The heart? I pictured her slumping in her seat, her body crumpling, and my stomach cramped again. I was imagining something from a horror movie, not real life. Not my life. Not *Laura*.

Yet somewhere out in this city there was a person who had pointed a gun at my wife. Who had shot and killed her—*why? Why were you even on that train, Laura?*

My thoughts swooped and reeled like a flock of desperate crows, finding no place to land. Nothing made any sense. My stomach cramped again. It hurt to breathe.

Miss Willis was struggling to decide whether to look concerned or irritated as I was buzzed into the entrance of The Garden School, a genteel-looking brownstone on Seventy-Eighth Street, the walls painted with colorful handprints and saccharine logos—*Happiness Starts Here. Bright Minds, New Beginnings.* Bullshit.

"Mr. West, it's been—"

"There's been an accident." I spoke tersely, focusing on Ruby who was standing behind her, looking wilfully woebegone, clearly feeling forgotten and wanting me to know it.

"An accident?" Miss Willis sounded skeptical.

"Yes, an accident." A sneer entered my voice; I felt, quite suddenly, *consumed* by rage. Did this sanctimonious woman actually *doubt* me? "Come on, Ruby."

"This really shouldn't happen again," Miss Willis persisted.

I whirled around, my teeth bared in a feral snarl. I felt the need to do violence, to smash or hurt something, make it break. I clenched my fists instead.

"Trust me, it won't."

Miss Willis opened and closed her mouth, her eyes wide, and I turned back around and stormed out of the school, my heart hammering, my blood surging.

"Daddy, why are you so cross?" Ruby asked, hurrying to keep up with me as I strode down the street, towards home. I'd wanted to collect Ella and Alexa from their school right away, just to get them home and keep them safe, but then I decided against it. I didn't think I could cope with all three of them at once, telling them the news, dealing with their individual reactions. I needed time to think, to figure out how I was going to handle this, or even if I could. As for Ruby...

I slowed my steps as I looked down at her—curly red hair, a throwback to my crazy mother, in ponytails tied with pink ribbons. Laura had tied those ribbons. Her fingers had touched them only this morning. I could picture her, humming under her breath, smiling down at our daughter. The thought sent a fresh shaft of shocked pain rushing through me, and I bent over, my hands on my knees.

"Daddy..." Like her teacher, Ruby sounded torn between irritation and alarm. "What's *wrong?*"

"Nothing, sweetie. I'm just a bit tired."

Slowly I straightened, the anger rushing out of me in one great whoosh, leaving something far worse in its place, something dark and vast and empty. Right then I saw a lifetime of moments such as this one stretching ahead of me, unbearable in their pain and poignancy, and I had no idea how to handle any of them. I didn't know if I could.

"Let's go home." I reached for her hand and started walking more slowly down the sun-dappled street, my steps lagging, each one laborious.

"Why were you so late? Where's Mommy?" At only four years old, Ruby was adorably, and sometimes annoyingly, precocious. She didn't miss a trick, something that usually made me feel both proud and affectionate, but now it just scared me. She was going to figure this out, or enough of it, and I wasn't ready for that. Not remotely.

"Mommy couldn't pick you up today." The words lodged in my throat. How on earth was I supposed to tell a preschooler that her mother was dead? That she'd been *shot?* And what about Ella, who was ten, and Alexa, currently a defiant fourteen? What was I going to tell any of them? How was I going to *do* this?

"Daddy…" Ruby's voice turned coyly wheedling, as she sensed a weakness. "Can we get ice cream?"

I opened my mouth to say no, we could not—of *course* we couldn't get ice cream when my wife was dead. No one did that; there had to be some implicitly acknowledged rule of the universe that you couldn't get ice cream, you couldn't do anything fun, when someone had just died. When you felt broken inside, as if you were nothing but shattered fragments. Of course we weren't going to get *ice cream*.

"Daddy? Can we? Please?"

I gazed down at my daughter's face—Ruby, our happy accident, her forehead crinkled up, her hands clutched together under her chin. She was even standing on her tiptoes. As I looked down at her, I felt as if my heart were twisting hard inside me and I thought: *She doesn't know yet.* And I realized that she could still be happy now, she could still have ice cream, and for that small mercy I was glad.

"Yes, Rubes," I said hoarsely. "Yes, we can get ice cream."

We ended up buying double scoops from an upscale gelateria on Lexington Avenue. Ruby was full of chatter, telling me about her morning at preschool, the games she'd played, the crafts she'd done, the princess costume someone named Chloe had worn and how she hadn't had a turn to wear it, which wasn't fair.

I let it wash over me, a soothing tide of normality; I savoured the way she licked her ice cream so carefully, eyes screwed up in concentration, and how her pigtails bounced. I didn't mind when she got a pink drip on her shirt; how could I?

"Daddy," she said, pointing to my forgotten cone. "Your ice cream is melting."

I stared down at it, the chocolate dripping over my hand, my stomach tightening so I knew I couldn't even take a bite.

"Sorry, Rubes," I said absently, and she started up with her chatter again.

My mind was beginning to race and seethe once more. I had to call Laura's parents. My mother. *Tell the girls…*

And what about the police? They'd said they needed to be in touch. They had questions to ask. I had questions I wanted answered. They'd mentioned picking up Laura's things…

"Daddy, you're not listening." Ruby sounded cross.

I opened my eyes that had fluttered closed without me realizing and stared at her bubble-gum-pink-smeared face.

"Sorry, Rubes, I'm listening. I really am. Chloe…"

"I wasn't talking about *Chloe*." She sounded disgusted. "I was asking about Mommy. Is she at home?"

I looked around the little gelateria with its spindly chairs and tiny tables of wrought-iron and glass, the tubs of colorful gelato in a glass case, pink and pistachio-green and white with swirls of scarlet. The woman at the counter, a twenty-something with two eyebrow piercings, gave me a smile. The moment felt weirdly normal; all I had to do was smile back, and yet I couldn't. I had the inexplicable and surely inappropriate urge to tell her my wife had just died, that she'd been *shot*. Perhaps in a few hours the news story that would come up on her Snapchat would be about Laura. I felt as if I could laugh hysterically at the impossibility of it, the utter ludicrousness, even as something inside me wanted to emit a primal roar of rage and fear. This was *real*.

"We should go." I lurched up from the table like a drunk, making the woman's eyes widen in alarm. "Ruby, come on. We need to get home."

"So will Mommy be there?" Ruby asked this so eagerly, it almost felt as if she knew somehow, as if she were testing me, waiting for me to disappoint her.

"No, she won't." Then, because I didn't know what else to do, I lied. "Not yet," I said.

*

Back at our apartment, everything was quiet, eerily so. Usually when I came home, the house was quiet, but it was a comfortable, lived-in sort of quiet, with a background hum of humanity—the dishwasher on, the creak of a bed or sofa, a distant murmur. Not this unnatural stillness, like a held breath, a waiting emptiness.

We'd bought a fixer-upper on Eighty-Third Street and Third Avenue in a pre-war building four years ago, when I'd started my own firm with my partner Frank Stein; it had three bedrooms, a dining and living room, a kitchen and a maid's room that I used as my study. Enormous by most Manhattan standards—and also in need of a huge amount of repair and redecoration.

The woman who had lived there had been ninety when she'd moved into a nursing home, and the place had last been decorated at least thirty years ago. We were doing it up slowly, because I wanted to supervise all the plans, and also cut costs where we could, and so far we'd only managed the kitchen, which Laura had insisted was the most important room to refurbish. So while that room was all gleaming marble and distressed oak, the rest of the house looked like something out of *The Brady Bunch*.

I walked in slowly, taking in all the once-upon-a-time insignificant details that now would be etched onto my memory forever: Laura's scarf, funky green and blue swirls, hanging on a hook by the door, waiting to be worn; her handwriting scribbled on the calendar in the kitchen. She had a dentist appointment next week. I breathed in, and I thought I smelled her scent—Jo Malone, something orangey that I gave her every Christmas. I imagined she was in another room, that she'd come in the doorway with a little smile, her eyebrows lifted, arms outstretched towards Ruby: *Home already?*

Ruby ran ahead of me, through the dining room, with its sliding pocket doors into the living room, that had a magnificent marble fireplace surround that had sold us on the place, as well as the long sash windows overlooking Eighty-Third Street. The walls were covered in a hideous olive-green flocked wallpaper that I couldn't stand but hadn't yet had time to get rid of, like so many other details of the apartment—the cheap bathroom suite in an ugly orange-brown, the army-green walls, the paint probably full of lead, in my study.

Ruby flopped on the sofa in front of the TV and then gave me a craftily beseeching look. She was always able to judge a moment, sense an opportunity.

"Can I watch *Peppa Pig?*"

"Yes, okay." I knew Laura had strict screen-time rules, but I hardly had the wherewithal to enforce them now. I turned on the TV, scrolling through the various streaming services we had, until I found *Peppa Pig*. Moments later, the cheerful theme music, accompanied by a snorting pig, echoed through the room, sounding ridiculous, especially considering the circumstances.

Everything felt ridiculous, offensive—the doorman's friendly greeting when we'd come in the building, the snick of my neighbor's door closing, someone beeping their car horn in the street below. How dare people go on with their lives? How could the world keep moving? All of it felt *wrong*.

In my head, I kept thinking *my wife is dead*, words on constant, awful repeat, thundering through me yet still not making any sense.

I left Ruby happily watching while I went back into the kitchen, unsure what to do now. Should I call someone? Start telling people? There would be a funeral, I realized. I would have to plan a funeral. How did I do that? I didn't even know where to begin. Death had always been something that had happened to other people. It had never touched me like this before… until now.

I sat at the kitchen table, feeling as if I should be doing *something*, but having no idea what. There was no manual for this situation, no navigation guide for these awful moments. There was just this emptiness, this awful silence... punctuated by *Peppa Pig*. I dropped my head into my hands.

In my jacket pocket, my phone buzzed. I didn't want to answer it; I knew I couldn't cope with more news, whatever it was. I was picturing Laura this morning, still in her pyjamas, the stripy top she always wore even though it was threadbare, and the loose bottoms in pale blue that had lost all their elastic at the waist.

She'd been loading the dishwasher with the dirty breakfast dishes as I took Ella and Alexa to school. I could see her perfectly, her hair in a sloppy ponytail, her smile relaxed as she told Alexa —who had been fuming about something as usual—where her math homework was: "On the sideboard, where you left it last night, sweetie. Look in the dining room."

Alexa had stomped off in a huff, muttering under her breath, but Laura had been unruffled. We'd exchanged a bemused glance and she'd rolled her eyes, still smiling; she wasn't fazed by our oldest daughter's teenaged angst, while I tended to let it irritate me, raise my hackles far too easily.

Except, I realized, I wasn't remembering that exchange correctly. I'd embellished it, turned it into a moment of affectionate solidarity when, in fact, I'd been almost as annoyed as Alexa, looking away without acknowledging Laura, jangling my keys loudly because we were running late and I resented having to take the girls to school when Laura could so easily do it, and it usually made me late for work.

That was how it had really happened, and I wondered, now that she was gone, how many memories I would try to reframe, casting everything in a sentimental, sepia tint because it was over. Our life rewritten in tiny, inconsequential moments—but it had been a good life, if not a perfect one, and I couldn't stand the thought of losing it, even as I knew I already had. It was gone. *Gone*.

My phone buzzed again.

I took it out of my jacket reluctantly, tensing as I read the text, from my partner Frank. *Just heard the news. So sorry.*

He'd heard? How? From someone at the office? Had the policewoman told them, or had they just guessed? Then a news alert came up on my phone, from the *New York Times. Woman shot on subway identified as Laura West, a Manhattan resident and mother of three.*

I swore, loud enough for Ruby's rapt attention to be broken. She looked at me all the way from the living room, wrinkling her nose the same way Laura did. *Had.*

"That's not a nice word, Daddy."

No, it wasn't, and she shouldn't have known it in the first place. I rose from the table, pacing the confines of the kitchen, fighting panic along with everything else.

I had to start calling people, before they found out from the damned internet. How had the story leaked? The policewoman had assured me it would be kept out of the media for now, right before I left, intent on getting Ruby. I had believed her.

My phone buzzed again, this time a message from Jane Sayers, half of a couple-friend of ours from Laura's publishing days. *Nathan, is it true?? I just heard the news about Laura and I can't believe it.*

Shit. Everyone was going to be messaging me. The news was out there, speeding through the internet, firing up social media sites, just hours after her death. I had to get to Alexa and Ella before they heard.

"Ruby, we have to go."

"But, Daddy, I just started watching—"

"We have to go!" It came out in a shout, and Ruby's face crumpled. She was so clever and precocious, I forgot how little she was sometimes. I took a deep breath. "Sweetie, I'm sorry, but… something's happened. We need to get Alexa and Ella from school."

"What's happened?" She scrambled off the sofa, coming to stand before me, her little face so serious. One pigtail had come loose and was lying limply against her head, the other one spring-ing out in a riot of red curls. I reached down and tried to retie the ribbon, but the material was slippery and I couldn't manage the bow. I left it in a tangled knot, ruined.

"Mommy..." I began, then stopped to let out a long, low breath. Saying the words out loud felt cruel, and I was afraid they would crack open my chest, split my heart right in half. "Mommy's had an accident." I fought an urge to laugh or scream, I wasn't sure which, because still I resisted the awful truth of it. *This couldn't be happening.*

Ruby frowned. "She's hurt?"

"Yes."

"Is she in the hospital? Are we going to visit her? Did she cut her head like I did at the playground and I had to have stitches?" This said with innocent relish; Ruby had loved having stitches, being the center of attention, allowed extra TV and milkshakes from the diner across the street.

"No, she didn't cut her head." If only. Briefly I closed my eyes.

"Daddy, don't *do* that." Ruby tugged on my arm. "I don't like it when you close your eyes."

"Sorry, sorry." I opened my eyes and reached for her hand. "Let's go get Ella and Alexa."

We took a cab even though it was only a few blocks away, because I knew every minute counted. How many kids in Alexa's class would be checking their phones? Did fourteen-year-olds read the news? Would teachers know? The school had a no-phone policy but according to Alexa every single student broke it. It could only be a matter of time, and not much at that.

We pulled up in front of the twin brownstones that comprised
The Walkerton School for Girls, one of the Upper East Side's best.
It had taken a lot of money, time, and effort to get both girls in
here, but it had been worth it.

Walkerton had the second best Ivy League acceptance rate of
all the city's private schools. Alexa had started in seventh grade,
Ella in fourth. It cost a mint, even with the financial aid we
received from the school, and Laura had had her doubts about
being part of such an exclusive social circle, but I was sure.

I wanted the best for my children, far better than I'd ever
had, being dragged along on my mother's zany adventures as
she tried to find herself and forgot me, time and time again, in
hippy communes and New Age centers, anonymous cities and
claustrophobic small towns. My daughters' lives would be different, I'd vowed when I'd first held Alexa as a squalling newborn
in my arms, and they were. They'd had the kind of opportunities
and stability I'd never had, and yet I couldn't shield them from
this, the worst thing of all.

Now I waited in the lobby while the receptionist went to find
Alexa and Ella in their classes, having looked both disapproving
and concerned when I explained, very briefly, why I was there. I
talked about accidents rather than incidents. I left the rest unsaid.

Ruby skipped around the room, gazing at the framed photographs of famous alumnae, artwork by students, entertained by
the novelty of the situation.

A few minutes later, Alexa and Ella came through the double
doors, clutching their bags and coats. Alexa's navy school skirt was
rolled up a couple of inches at the waist, and she had more makeup
on than she'd had that morning, but I hardly cared about that now.

"Dad, what's going on?" Alexa's hazel eyes—Laura's eyes—were
dark with fear.

Ella was winding a strand of blond hair around her finger,
looking surprised but not particularly curious, as always a little

lost in a world of her own, slightly removed from reality, as if viewing it from her own personal bubble.

"I'll tell you when we get home."

I thanked the receptionist and shepherded the girls out onto Eighty-Seventh Street.

"*Dad.*" Alexa sounded impatient. "I'm missing math. What's going on?"

"Something's happened," I said tersely. I wished I had a way to explain this that didn't feel wrong. "I said I'll tell you when we get home."

We were all silent in the taxi, four of us squashed in the back, Ruby scrambling over us because there was no space for her to sit.

"Ruby, get off," Alexa said irritably, pushing her sister away as she stared out the window.

Ella put her arms around Ruby's middle and pulled her onto her lap. We were breaking a million safety laws, but I didn't care. I just wanted to get home and start circling the wagons. I wanted to barricade the doors and keep the TV off and abandon the phones. Forget the world for a little while, and all its intrusions, and keep us all safe. Yet already I knew that was impossible.

As we entered the apartment building, I checked my phone and saw I had six unread texts, four missed calls.

No one spoke until we were back in the apartment, and Ruby had raced off to resume *Peppa Pig;* with expert ease, she turned on the TV by herself and pressed play. I let her.

"Come into the kitchen," I said quietly, and, both looking terrified now, Alexa and Ella followed me in.

I sat down at the little table by the window, which was always piled with papers and junk mail, never used for its purpose. They followed, their gazes tracking me.

"Dad…" Alexa's voice wobbled. "What's happened?"

"Alexa… Ella…" I took a deep breath, and then I cracked. It hit me, the reality of it, in a way it hadn't before, like a sledgehammer straight to the chest. Laura was *gone*. She was never coming back. I'd never see her again; she'd never hum in the kitchen, or tuck her icy feet between my calves when we were in bed. She'd never pull Ruby onto her lap and tickle her tummy. She'd never fold into me, her arms around my waist, her lips grazing my neck so I could feel her smile. Already I feared I couldn't smell her scent anymore; the house just smelled stale to me now.

My face contorted and I drew a deep breath, trying to organise my features into something small and sane. I pressed the heels of my hands into my eyes, willing it all back. Back, back, because where else could it go?

"Dad…" Alexa started to cry, dashing her eyes impatiently, not even knowing yet why she was sad, while Ella simply stared, wide-eyed and shocked at the sight of me looking so emotional. "What is it? Where's Mom?"

"Mom…" I managed the single word before I took another deep breath. I had to hold it together, for their sakes. "Mom's been in an accident." I didn't want to say incident. I hated that word now, so soulless and officious-sounding, like something on a report.

"What kind of accident?" Alexa's voice was high and thin. "Is she hurt? Will she be okay?"

I didn't answer and Alexa leaned forward, her fists clenched on top of the table, her eyes wild.

"*Dad*. Mom's going to be okay, isn't she?"

Still I couldn't speak, even though I knew I needed to. I was letting them down. Already, I was letting them down.

"*Isn't she?*" Alexa demanded again, the words a pleading screech.

Silently Ella reached over and held my hand. I didn't know whether it was a gesture of solidarity or comfort, but it broke me all over again. My ten-year-old daughter was stronger than I was.

"No, sweetie," I whispered, blinking hard, keeping the tears at bay. "No, she isn't."

"What do you mean…" Alexa's voice trailed off as she sagged back against the chair, her eyes like wide, dark holes, her mouth slack. Ella clung to my hand, squeezing hard.

"She… she's dead." I whispered it, for Ruby's sake, but also because it felt like the kind of thing I needed to whisper. Sacred somehow.

Silence echoed through the kitchen, a terrible, final silence. In the distance, I heard the catchy theme tune of *Peppa Pig,* followed by a snorty giggle.

"Daddy," Ruby called. "Can I have a snack?"

"No…" Alexa whispered the word, shaking her head, over and over again, harder each time, her expression dazed. "*No…*"

"I'm so sorry, Alexa. Ella." I turned to Ella, who had a vacant look on her face, as if she hadn't taken in what I'd said. Of course she hadn't. I hadn't even processed it yet; it kept slamming into me, leaving me breathless. Even now I was half-expecting, *waiting* for Laura to open the front door. I'd hear the jangle of her keys, the lightness of her step. *Sorry I'm late… Hey, why the long faces?* Her easy smile before she brushed a kiss on the top of Ella's head, a quick, comforting hand on Alexa's shoulder. Then she'd turn to the fridge, her hands on her hips, an almost comical frown on her face: *What should we do about dinner, guys?*

The memories, the wished-for reality, blew through me in an empty echo, the ensuing silence like a thunderclap.

Alexa lifted her tear-stained face. "How?" she whispered. "What happened?"

"She…" I closed my eyes, then opened them, remembering how Ruby hadn't liked it. I couldn't check out, not even for a second. Not now. Not ever. "She was… she was shot."

"Shot?" Alexa repeated incredulously. "*Shot?*"

It sounded ridiculous, like some sort of unfunny, obscene joke.

"By a stranger on the subway, some madman most likely," I said after a pause when my daughters were both clearly waiting for more. "They don't know who yet."

"They haven't caught him?" This from Ella, her voice trembling.

"No, but they will. Of course they will."

Alexa pushed herself up from the table, stumbling over her chair.

I half-rose, still holding Ella's hand. "Alexa…"

She just shook her head, turning from the room, from me. I watched her go, torn between wanting to keep her with me and knowing she needed her space. Alexa had always been an intensely private person, preferring to simmer or stew alone. Even as a toddler, when she'd hurt herself, she'd pull away from us, craving her own solitary solace. It used to hurt, and then it just became easier to let her go, as I decided to now, in part because I knew I wasn't strong enough to make her stay and ride that first wave of wild grief together.

Ella tugged on my hand. "But, Daddy…" She shook her head. "Who's going to take care of us?"

I tried to smile but didn't manage it at all. "I'm going to, Ella. I'm still here. You'll always have me, I promise."

"Yes, but…" She wrinkled her nose, clearly not wanting to state the awful obvious: *You're not Mommy. You don't cook, or clean, or even cuddle.*

Most nights, I came home after Ruby was in bed and Ella was in her pyjamas, reading. I'd give her a quick kiss before turning the light out—and sometimes not even that. As for Alexa, she barely talked to me anyway, spending her evenings doing homework, on her phone, or locked in the bathroom perfecting her makeup by watching YouTube tutorials.

I loved my girls, and I thought I was a good dad, if not always entirely present. I still showed up for most things; I listened when they spoke to me; I remembered birthdays and big days; I was *there*. Mostly. But I wasn't Laura.

"We're going to be okay," I told Ella, even though right now that felt like the cheapest and flimsiest of promises. "We will," I said more firmly. One day. Maybe. I couldn't imagine it now, but I had to offer my daughter some kind of hope, a promise that she could trust me to keep… if I could find the strength to keep it.

Ella burrowed her head into my shoulder. "I want Mommy," she whispered and then she started to cry, softly, a broken sound.

Ruby skipped into the kitchen, standing in the doorway, hands planted on skinny hips as she surveyed us. "Why is Ella crying?"

I put my arms around Ella and stroked her hair as I stared helplessly at Ruby. "She's sad, sweetie."

"Why?" Ruby's eyes narrowed. "When is Mommy coming back?"

Ella raised her head, sniffing. "She doesn't…?"

"Not yet," I said swiftly.

I gazed at them both, helpless, hopeless. Where were the parenting books, the helpful blogs, about this? Not that I'd ever read either, or even wanted to. I'd pretty much left all that kind of stuff up to Laura; she'd set the tone of discipline, enforced the rules, read all the latest advice and guidelines. I was, at best, back up, but, damn it, I'd been *good* back up. Hadn't I? Saturday-morning donuts, the occasional game or movie night, tickles at bedtime. I swooped in once in a while and felt good about it. Occasionally, I exerted my so-called parental authority: *Your mother and I agree…* But Laura was the one who gave me the words, made the rules, and I let her, because we worked that way. She never complained, and neither did I.

Yet now I was going to be responsible for all of it, all the discipline, all the hugs, all the housework and meals, the comfort and care, while I did my own grieving besides.

Laura…

I rose and swung Ruby up into my arms to distract myself from my own emotions; she was heavier than I remembered. When was the last time I'd carried her over my shoulder, tickling her all the while, the way I had with Alexa and Ella when they were little? *Good morning sunshine…*

"Daddy…!" Her squeal was part protest, part delight. "I want to know where Mommy is."

I couldn't avoid it forever, as much as I wanted to. Gently I set Ruby down on the ground and held her by her slight shoulders. "Mommy's not coming back, Ruby," I said. My throat was getting tighter by the second as I forced out the words. From behind me I heard Ella crying quietly.

Ruby stared at me hard, her lower lip jutting out. "Yes, she is," she finally said, sounding strident, and I had to shake my head.

"No, she isn't. I'm so sorry, Ruby. Mommy… died." It still felt impossible, to put those words together, incredible that I was saying them out loud. I wondered when they would ever start feeling real, making sense.

"Died…" Ruby looked confused. Could a four-year-old even understand what death was? What it meant? *Could anyone?*

"When someone dies it means they're not coming back," I explained. "They're gone forever."

She shook her head slowly. "But where do they go?"

I hesitated for a fraction of a second. Was now a time to start spouting off about heaven, a concept I'd never believed in but would surely offer some comfort now? I didn't know what the right thing to say was, as I knew Laura, and so I stuck with what I believed to be the truth. "They don't go anywhere, Ruby. They're just…" I shrugged. "Gone."

"That doesn't make sense."

"Their heart stops beating. They stop breathing." How else could I explain it? "They're not alive anymore."

Her frown deepened. "You mean like when I squash a bug on the sidewalk?"

I thought of that nameless assailant, someone who was still out there. He'd looked at my wife and he'd *shot* her. "Sort of," I whispered, and Ella let out a choked cry and buried her head in her arms.

Ruby's lower lip wobbled. "But I want her to come back," she said as tears pooled in her eyes and I knelt in front of her and drew her into a hug.

"I know, baby. So do I." I closed my eyes as I hugged her tight. "So do I."

CHAPTER FOUR

MARIA

The police came to Global Rescue the next day. It wasn't my day to volunteer, but I got a call while I was at work, asking me to come in.

"It's about Laura West," Cathy, the center's director, said. She sounded anxious and tired. "They want to speak to everyone who volunteers on Tuesday mornings. I'm sorry, Maria."

"It's all right."

I felt numb as I left the salon, apologising to Neriha, who shrugged it off as she waved me to go. The train was running again, and as it rattled along the track, I wondered if this was the car where Laura had sat. If perhaps this was the very seat.

I looked around at the various passengers, everyone lost in their own thoughts, their own fog, scrolling through phones even though there was no signal. Laura West had already been forgotten.

I knew how that went, how quickly people could forget when they chose to. Who thought about Bosnia anymore either? Who cared about that old story? Nobody, and I didn't blame them. I wanted to forget, too. The trouble was, no matter how hard I tried, no matter how hard I pretended that I had, I never could.

Cathy met me in the lobby. "I'm sorry to inconvenience you, Maria. This shouldn't take long."

"It's all right." I felt nervous, although I didn't know why. I had nothing to hide.

I had to wait twenty minutes before the police called me in to one of the classrooms which they used for teaching English and US Citizenship. They'd pushed all the chairs to the side, so there was only one in front of the table, two behind it. Two plain-clothes officers—a man and a woman—sat there, coffee cups in front of them. They looked tired.

"Thank you for coming in," the woman said. She had a neat ponytail of little braids and warm eyes. She smiled at me as she spoke. "What is your name?"

"Maria Dzino." I sat down, trying not to seem nervous.

"Hello, Maria." The woman's smile widened, revealing dimples. She looked kind, making me want to help her. "I'm Lisa, and this is Tom." The man, a blunt-looking guy with a buzz cut and blue eyes, gave me a curt nod. "We're here to ask some questions about Laura West, who was a volunteer here at the center?" There was a questioning lilt at the end of this statement, as if she wanted me to confirm it.

I nodded. "Yes."

"Did you know Mrs. West?"

"Yes, we chatted most weeks." I felt too shy to call Laura a friend now, even though I'd considered her one. What had I been to her, though? A casual acquaintance, surely nothing more.

"Did you notice anyone else here at the center talking to her? Taking an interest?" Lisa's smile was friendly, encouraging, while Tom gave me a level stare.

"Not really," I said. "She chatted to most people. She was that kind of person."

"Who else did you see her chat with?" Lisa asked, pulling a pad of paper in front of her. "Do you know their names?"

I pictured Laura moving around the center, smiling and chatting. "I don't know. Anyone. Everyone." I shrugged helplessly. "I didn't pay attention. I wasn't keeping count."

"I'm sure you could think of someone," Lisa said with an encouraging smile.

I wondered what she thought I could possibly know. Did she want me to say something incriminating, point the finger at some nameless stranger simply because he'd exchanged words with Laura once? Considering the situation, I was reluctant to name anyone, not that I could.

"It's often very busy here," I said. "People come and go. I'm sorry, but I really don't remember."

Lisa looked disappointed. "Did you notice anyone hanging around?" she pressed.

"No, not to speak of."

"Where are you from, Maria?" This from Tom, without Lisa's friendly tone or smile.

I tensed, wondering what on earth where I was from had to do with Laura, or their inquiry.

"Bosnia," I said after a moment.

He nodded slowly. "When did you come to this country?"

"2001." Weeks before 9/11, when they'd shut down the refugee scheme for months.

"And you used the Global Rescue Refugee Center yourself?" Tom said, although he sounded as if he already knew. Had they researched me? My skin crawled at the thought of these strangers looking through my files, learning about me and my life. "As a refugee, rather than a volunteer, yes?"

"Yes." I spoke stiffly; I couldn't help it.

"And you made friends here?"

"Yes." Of a sort, as much as I could. Friendship, along with so many other aspects of life people took for granted, seemed foreign to me now.

"And so you've been involved with Global Rescue since you arrived as a refugee yourself?"

Wary now, not knowing why, I nodded.

"So, for eighteen years?"

I pressed my lips together. *You can do the arithmetic.* "Yes."

"After all that time…" Lisa broke in, again with the encouraging tone, the friendly smile; I wasn't sure if I should trust them now, "you'd notice if someone was loitering around, someone who hadn't been before, very often?"

"It is possible," I admitted. "Although, like I said, people come and go. Some don't stay very long. They move onto other things."

"And yet eighteen years…" Lisa let the pause linger, stretch into something else. "That's a long time, Maria. I'm sure you know most people here, considering that length of time."

"I suppose." I stared uneasily at her, and then at Tom. Did they think I knew something? *Did I?*

For the first time, I let myself consider if someone from Global Rescue had in fact killed Laura. Followed her from here to the station, cornered her in the subway car, and taken out some imagined vendetta against her. It was perfectly possible; it even made sense, in a twisted, senseless way. I could understand why the police were questioning everyone, why they were wanting names. Why shouldn't there be a link? Why *did* a man shoot Laura, and no one else on the train? What if he'd been looking for her all along?

"So, you're sure you haven't noticed anyone hanging around here recently whom you don't know?" Lisa asked again. "The suspect we're looking for is approximately six feet two, with shaggy brown hair and blue eyes." She pushed a piece of paper towards me, and I saw it was a pencil sketch of the man who had shot her. A jolt ran through me at the sight of him, although I couldn't have said why. "Does he look familiar to you?"

"I… I don't know. It's hard to tell from a sketch."

"Of course it is." Lisa nodded in sympathy. "We hope to have some CCTV footage soon. But take a good, long look at it. Sometimes a small thing stirs a memory—a scar, or a mole…"

But this man had no scars or moles, at least not that anyone had noticed. I studied the sketch for a long moment. The drawing could have been of anyone, or everyone, with his ragged beard and unkempt hair. I'd see a thousand men like him come through the center, wearing baggy clothes, having vacant eyes. No one liked to talk about where they'd been, what they'd seen. What they'd done. He was no one, and he was every single man I'd ever met.

Still I took my time studying the sketch, more for Tom and Lisa's sakes than my own. As the lines blurred in front of me, there seemed, for a second, to be something familiar in his loose-limbed build, the jut of his chin, the peak of his eyebrows, but it was gone before I could catch hold of it. Had he been someone I'd talked to? Had I handed him a cup of coffee, helped him fill out a form? I had no idea.

"You see something you recognize?" Lisa asked. I was still staring at the picture.

"No, I don't think so." I pushed the sketch back across the table, giving them an apologetic look. "I'm sorry. I just don't know."

"It's okay," Lisa assured me. "It's worth a look, regardless." She paused. "For a second there, Maria, it seemed as if you recognized him."

"Yes, I thought there was something familiar, for a moment," I admitted. "But I'm really not sure. I couldn't give you a name or anything. I'm sorry," I said again, as if it were my fault.

"No worries." Lisa put the sketch away. "Like I said, it was worth a try. But if you do remember something, anything, you will tell us, won't you?" Lisa pushed a card across the table with her and Tom's names on it. "You can call that number any time, day or night, if anything comes to you."

"Okay. Thank you." I nodded and took the card, tucking it in my bag.

"Laura was the mother of three children," Lisa continued. "The youngest is only four."

"Yes—" I stopped; I wasn't sure why.

"She told you about them?" Lisa surmised.

I nodded.

Lisa nodded back, registering that detail. "We want to catch her killer, Maria. New York is meant to be a safe city for everyone who lives here. We don't want people to be scared to use the subway, or walk down the street."

"No," I agreed. Did she not think I felt the same?

"Everyone should feel safe here," Lisa continued. "Including people like you."

I tensed. "People like me?"

"I mean people who have come to the US to be safe. To have a fresh start. You lived in Sarajevo during the Bosnian conflict with Serbia?"

I swallowed hard. "Yes, I did."

"But you left the city in 1993?"

"Yes."

"And what happened then?"

"What does this have to do with Laura?" I asked, hearing the desperation in my voice. I never talked about the past. Never.

"We need to pursue all leads." Lisa gave an apologetic shrug. "What happened when you left the city?"

"I was detained for four months." I spoke flatly, sparing with the details. I didn't want to tell them any more than I had to.

Lisa nodded slowly. "You and your family?"

"Yes, my mother, my brother, and I."

"You were detained because you were Bosniak?"

"Half Bosniak." Bosniak, a Bosnian with Muslim heritage. And that had been enough to start a war. "My father was Muslim, my mother Catholic."

"And why were you released?"

"It was a prisoner exchange, just the women and children."

"And what happened after you were released?"

"I went to a city called Mostar, where I stayed with my relatives until the war ended, and then after, until I gained refugee status and came to America."

"It took a long time to gain that status?"

Three years from the point of application, when I'd been eighteen and able to apply as an adult. "It often does."

"What did you do during that time?"

I shrugged. "I went to school, and then I worked in a local shop."

Lisa nodded slowly, looking unsurprised, unmoved. She'd already known, I realized. It all had to be in my immigration records. "I'm sorry," she said quietly. "I understand talking about this might be troubling for you."

It wasn't troubling; I refused to let it be so. I refused to feel anything about any of that, but even so I resented her making me say it all. "May I go now?"

"Of course. You are free to go at any time, Maria. You are merely helping us in our inquiries. Thank you for coming in."

I nodded, not wanting to say anything more. I rose from my seat and started towards the door.

"If you remember anything," Lisa called after me. "Anything at all… you will be in touch, won't you?"

"Of course," I mumbled, and then I was out of the room, taking big gulps of air as if I'd been suffocating.

"Are you all right, Maria?" Cathy asked, looking concerned as she came up to me. "Let me get you some water."

"I'm fine." Just as I'd told the man on the street yesterday, just as I kept telling myself, all these years: *I'm fine. I'm fine.* What else could I be? No one would believe me if I told them the truth—that, inside, I think I am probably as dead as Laura West now is. That I have been for over twenty years, and by choice, because being alive hurt too much. Far better to be a ghost, drifting through my days.

"I'm sorry about the police," Cathy said in a low voice. "They don't realize how troubling it can be, to have police here, asking all sorts of questions. The man on the subway was most likely just some stranger on drugs. That's what everyone thinks."

I nodded slowly, wanting to believe her, even as I couldn't shake the uneasy feeling that something had been familiar about that sketch, that perhaps I had seen that man before. Here, at Global Rescue? Or on the street? Or was I just imagining that sense of familiarity, out of some sort of misplaced fear?

I left Global Rescue and walked back to the subway station, one foot in front of the other, head down. The day was clear and cold, the sky a hard, bright blue above. Mid-November, and the city was gearing up for Thanksgiving, a holiday I had never celebrated. The sense of expectation, like snow in the air, passed me by.

Back at the salon, Neriha merely raised her eyebrows and I shook my head. I had a customer waiting and I immersed myself in work, in the comforting and mind-numbing routine of washing, cutting, brushing.

I'd trained to be a hairdresser here in America, as part of a charitable program to help refugees gain new skills. There was something innately satisfying about it, taking the old and making it new. Creating beauty, even in such a small way. I always enjoyed the pleased smile of my customer in the mirror, as she turned this way and that, admiring the way her hair swung or bounced.

But today, as I snipped and chatted by rote, my mind drifted back to Laura West. I kept remembering bits of conversations we'd had over the last year, things I'd thought I'd forgotten but seemed to have stored somewhere deep inside. Ella was the name of the middle daughter. *She's so quiet. Still waters run deep and all that, I suppose, but I worry about her. She takes things to heart.*

And Ruby, the youngest, had been an accident. *A happy accident, we call her, although there aren't really any accidents, are there? I can't imagine life without her now. She knows her own mind, that's for sure. And she has a temper to match her hair. That's why we named her Ruby… she had a full head of it when she was born.*

She'd shown me a photo of Ruby, with her curly red hair and a determined expression; it had made me smile. She looked like a bright, sparky sort… like how I used to be—once, a very long time ago.

I thought about Ruby now. Did she understand her mother was gone forever? Could a child that small even begin to grasp what it meant? I pictured her curled up in bed, hugging a teddy bear, missing her mommy. It made me ache inside, stirring up an old sorrow that had been long buried. I didn't like the feeling.

"There." I put my hands on the shoulders of my client as I smiled determinedly at her reflection in the mirror. I did not want to think about old sorrows, or stir anything up. "Do you like it?"

"I love it," she answered, preening a little, and I stepped back, satisfied.

Laura West's murder, the police's questions, it had all brought the past bubbling up for me, but I needed to forget it again now, as best as I could. Every day was a lesson in forgetting, a sheer act of will. I'd done it before, and I could do it again. I *would*.

"Do the police think someone from Global Rescue shot her?" Neriha asked in a low voice once my client had gone and I was sweeping up whorls of hair from the floor. She'd seen the story on the news, and asked me for the details, which I'd given reluctantly. Neriha had been helped by the center as well, although she didn't volunteer there. She spent her free time at the Bosnian American Association here in Astoria and kept trying to get me to come along to their potluck suppers and quiz nights, but I always refused.

I shook my head as I swept the discarded hair into a dustpan. "No, they think it's probably just some homeless person or something like that."

But that night, back in my apartment, I turned on the news and waited for a report about the investigation. *It is still unknown whether Laura West knew her assailant, but investigations continue at the nearby Global Rescue Refuge Center, where she volunteered on a regular basis, and where she had been traveling home from when she was attacked.*

I sat back, hugging my knees to my chest, and thought about that sketch of the unknown man. What had been familiar about him? Maybe nothing. Or maybe he had come in to Global Rescue, once or twice. There were plenty of drifters, people who came through without staying or using the services. It didn't mean anything. It didn't have to change anything. After everything that had happened in my life, that was all I wanted—for things not to change.

And yet they would, very soon. Irrevocably. Wonderfully. And terribly. All of it together, and I had no idea.

CHAPTER FIVE

NATHAN

The morning after Laura died, I woke up to sunlight streaming through the windows as I stretched in bed, my toes seeking her presence, the feel of her smooth calves against my bare feet, the sleepy warmth of her next to me. Instead, all I felt was a cold, empty expanse of bed sheet.

I opened my eyes, and reality slammed into me all over again. *My wife is dead.* It echoed through me, just as terrible, still so unbelievable. When would it stop being a shock? Days? Months? *Years?*

Yesterday had been a nightmare from start to finish. Finding out… telling the girls… and then the phone calls. So many phone calls. Laura's parents, my mother, friends, colleagues, having to tell everyone what had happened, how much I still didn't know. The police had called as well, asking me to come in today, to answer some questions.

All afternoon and evening I had kept the TV off and refused to check my phone. There was only so much new information I could handle, but I knew I couldn't keep it all out forever. Not even for another day. I'd already told the girls they could stay home from school, although I wondered if the distraction would have been preferable.

Laura's parents were driving to New York today, to help out with the girls as well as the funeral, which was still to be planned. The police were expecting me this afternoon. Reality encroached even in that moment, as I lay in bed and felt Laura's absence like a physical ache, an emptiness inside me, an echo resounding through the room.

If I closed my eyes, I could imagine that Laura was in the bathroom, getting ready. I could almost hear her tuneless humming as she moved about, the whisper of her clothes as she put them on. I pictured her leaning over me, telling me to get up, giving me a lingering kiss.

Of course I was imagining a fantasy. I woke up before Laura every single morning, and the days of lingering kisses in bed were, for the most part, long gone. If anything, I would have been hurrying, slightly impatient, my movements clipped and precise, my mind already leaping ahead to the first meeting of the morning. Laura would have stretched in bed, snuggled down under the duvet again with a little sigh of contentment.

How can you get up so early?

I have to, I might have said, or, if I were feeling more charitable, *I've always been a morning person.* But a pinprick of irritation would have needled me. *I get up early because I have things to do.* I hadn't wanted Laura to go back to work when the girls were small; financially, with the price of childcare in the city, it hadn't made sense, and I wanted Laura to be there for the girls the way my mother hadn't for me. She'd wanted it, too.

But when Ruby had started preschool, I'd encouraged her to get something part-time, just a little bit to help with household expenses, and she'd prevaricated.

I don't want to go back into publishing. I barely earned anything as it was...

What then? I'd asked, feeling impatient, and Laura had shrugged. *Something more. When Ruby is a little older. It feels like too much right now. She's still so little.*

Too much? I remember biting back a sharp retort at the time. What was too much, I'd wanted to say, was the tuition bill for Walkerton. The mortgage on this apartment that we'd both fallen in love with. Walkerton might have been mostly my idea, but Laura had wanted this place. She'd picked out the marble countertop, the distressed oak in the kitchen.

And then there were all our other expenses—the trips to Cape Cod every summer to see her parents, which they insisted on paying for, until I wouldn't let them. The swimming lessons for Ella, ballet for Ruby, piano for Alexa, all outrageously expensive because this was Manhattan. Even a dinner out, with babysitting, ran to a few hundred bucks.

But I didn't want to nickel and dime Laura now; I just wanted to hold onto the memory of her moving about this room, the feel of her warm body next to mine in bed. When was the last time we'd made love? It suddenly felt important to remember, to imbue it with special meaning, but it had to have been weeks ago, a fumble in the dark when we were both tired. Nothing special at all.

I opened my eyes to stare at the ceiling, trying to banish both kinds of memories—the wished-for and the real. They all hurt.

"Daddy, I'm hungry." I turned my head to see Ruby standing in the doorway of my bedroom, her hair in a wild red tangle about her face. She was wearing a pink nightgown decorated with unicorns that was far too small for her, but last night she'd insisted it was her favorite and I hadn't had the strength or desire to argue.

Alexa had stayed in her bedroom through the whole evening, and when I'd checked on her, after Ruby was asleep, she'd been lying on her bed, her back to me, her voice muffled by the pillow as she'd told me to go away. Helpless, unsure whether to press, I had left her alone, feeling guilty for doing so. It was easier, but it still felt wrong.

Ella had stuck to my side like a silent shadow, although she'd agreed to reading a story together when I suggested one. I had no idea what was going on in her head, or any of their heads, even my own. *How do people survive grief? How do we keep going and going, like wind-up toys, marching forward when all we want to do is fall apart?*

Somehow we managed, one agonising, endless step at a time; the girls fell asleep, and I stumbled to bed, Laura's absence like a silent scream echoing all around me.

Now I beckoned to Ruby and she scrambled into bed with me, snuggling up against my back, a solid warmth.

"We can't have a Ruby sandwich anymore," she said in a small voice. That's what we did—Laura and me on the outside, Ruby in the middle, on far too many early mornings, when I'd resented the intrusion, rolling over and pulling the duvet hard over my shoulders in silent protest. *Never again.*

I turned towards her and gave her a clumsy, one-armed hug. "It's okay, Rubes. We can still have a sandwich. An open one."

"What's that?"

"One without a piece of bread on top." And even though it was so ridiculous, talking about sandwiches, that statement made my eyes well up. I pressed my face against her hair and did my best to keep the tears back.

I wasn't a crier. I never had been. Laura had teased me about needing to be stoic, a reaction to my mother's endless emotional theatrics, and maybe it was that, at least a little bit. But part of me just didn't see the point. Why let trivial things, whether moments or movies, affect me? Reach me? Why let anything?

Laura would cry at a Kleenex commercial or a sad story in the news, whereas I remained relatively unmoved even through the biggest tearjerker of a film. I think it had annoyed her sometimes, my lack of emotion, but I'd told her it was just the way I was, or maybe it was a guy thing.

Don't be so sexist, she'd say, laughing. *Guys can cry, Nathan.*

I felt like crying now, but I didn't. I held it back, because I had to. For Ruby's sake, and for my own.

"Do you like open sandwiches?" she asked and I bit my tongue.

I hate them. They don't make sense. They're messy. They fall apart.

"I love open sandwiches," I told her, my voice only just steady. I sniffed hard and then rolled out of bed, my body aching. "Come on, Rubes. Let's get some breakfast."

She looked up at me, all wide eyes and tangled hair. For a second I thought about tossing her over my shoulder, tickling her tummy. *Good morning sunshine…* I couldn't make myself do it. I felt too tired, too sad, as if I'd never say that again, never feel that light-hearted, that happy, if I ever had. Maybe that was a ghost memory too, a fantasy like the rest, the family life I'd thought I had, that I'd been taking for granted.

Had it even existed?

"Can we have pancakes?" Ruby asked.

Pancakes? Buying donuts was my special Saturday treat, not making pancakes. I had no idea how to go about it, but I felt as if I couldn't say no to Ruby about anything, not now. "Sure," I said wearily. I'd figure it out. I'd have to.

The kitchen was a mess from dinner the night before—takeout pizza, the boxes still on the table filled with half-chewed crusts, the milk left out all night, dirty dishes not even in the sink but at least somewhat near it.

Laura normally tidied up after dinner; in fact she *always* tidied up after dinner. I brought a few dishes from the table to the kitchen, acting as if I were doing my share. Occasionally, on a Saturday morning, I unloaded the dishwasher, feeling magnanimous. *What an ass.* It was a strange thought to have about myself.

"Let me just clean up in here," I mumbled to Ruby. "Then we'll figure out pancakes."

Ruby perched on a stool at the marble-topped breakfast bar, her chin propped in her hands, as I stuffed the pizza boxes into the recycling bin and poured the soured milk down the drain.

It was half past six in the morning and I was exhausted, feeling hungover even though I hadn't had a drop of alcohol. It seemed as if I was doing everything in slow motion, my limbs heavy and uncoordinated.

"Can I help, Daddy?" Ruby asked when I'd managed to load the dishwasher and the kitchen was semi-clean. Having Ruby help would make the whole exercise take longer, but I supposed that was the point. I knew Laura would have told me it was.

Time together, Nathan. That's all they want. They don't need the toys or gadgets or vacations. They just want us.

Had she actually said that, or was I imagining it? I couldn't separate the real memories from the wished-for ones, and I wondered if I ever would be able to.

"Sure, you can help," I said, and started looking through Laura's extensive collection of cookbooks for a pancake recipe. There wasn't one, at least not that I could find. Everything was ridiculously fancy—crepes Suzette with brandy sauce was the closest thing, and I certainly wasn't up for making that.

My fingers traced the crumpled pages, one with a smear of something on it, another with a line crossed out and scribbled over in Laura's handwriting. *Better with two eggs.* It was a recipe for a cake I didn't remember her ever making.

I ended up googling a recipe on my phone, as Ruby stood on a stool, swathed in a huge apron, determined to do as much as she could. Flour and sugar piled in soft white drifts on the counter as she measured everything, teaspoon by painstaking teaspoon, while I sagged next to her, one elbow on the counter, too tired to prop myself up.

"Can I do the egg, Daddy?" she asked, her face alight with eagerness. "Please? I'll be really, really careful."

"Okay." It was so much easier just to go along, to keep saying yes.

I handed Ruby an egg that she gave an almighty crack and then promptly dropped on the floor.

"Ruby!" My voice came harshly, a matter of instinct, as I moved my bare foot away from the mess of yolk. My daughter's face crumpled.

"I'm sorry, Daddy…" She gulped back tears but they came anyway, in gulping sobs, her little body heaving, and I put my arms around her.

"It's okay, sweetie. It's okay. I shouldn't have shouted. I'm sorry."

She sniffled into my shoulder as I patted her back, feeling utterly inept.

"What are you guys doing?" I looked up to see Ella standing shyly in the doorway, sporting an impressive case of bedhead, twining one leg around the other like a stork.

"Making pancakes," Ruby announced. "And *I'm* cracking the egg."

Wordlessly I handed her another one, hoping this one made it into the bowl.

"Can I help?" Ella asked, and again I was expansive in my agreement, because what else did I have to give them right now?

"Of course you can. Draw up a stool."

She did, and for a few moments, as Ruby whisked the batter, I felt a fragile sense of peace, as translucent as a bubble. I could hold onto it if I didn't let myself think too hard about anything, if I just concentrated on this moment—the sunlight streaming through the window, gilding my girls' hair in gold, the simplicity of adding sugar and flour, eggs and milk. *If I could just not think…*

"It's starting to bubble!" Ruby exclaimed as I spooned the batter into the pan.

"Can I flip it?" Ella asked.

"Sure, just be careful."

I held her hand as she started to flip it, but we were both startled by a screech from the doorway.

"What are you *doing*?"

I jerked around, and Ella's hand hit the hot pan. She let out a cry as I stared at Alexa, whose face was blotchy, her hair a nest of tangles, her eyes wild.

"Daddy, I'm burned!"

"Sorry, sorry, Ella." I hurried her to the sink, running her hand under cold water, as Alexa glared at us.

"You're making pancakes? You're actually making *pancakes?* Mom is *dead* and you're acting like this is a fun Saturday morning!" Her voice split in a shattered wail.

"Alexa, it's just breakfast." I tried to speak calmly, even though I felt on the brink of something—tears or rage, I didn't know which. My hand shook as I kept Ella's steady under the stream of water.

"Daddy, don't, it's *cold.*"

"The pancake's burning!" Ruby cried, and she reached towards the pan.

"Don't touch it!" My voice came out in a roar, and all three girls froze, eyes wide and wild as they stared at me as if they didn't know me. I didn't know myself. "You'll burn yourself, Ruby." I tried to speak more calmly, but I didn't think I managed it. I took a deep breath, feeling it shudder through me.

All three girls were still watching me warily—Alexa in a fury, Ella looking woebegone and scared, Ruby abject.

"Look, let's just all take it easy, okay?" I felt as if I could howl. "We're making breakfast, Alexa, that's all. It's not meant to be…" I trailed off, because I didn't know what it was or wasn't meant to be. I was just trying to cope, moment by moment, and clearly I wasn't doing a good job of it. Maybe I never had.

"Well, I don't want any," Alexa snapped, and then she stomped back into her room, slamming the door behind her so hard it felt as if the whole apartment rattled.

"It's ruined," Ruby said sadly as I lifted the smoking pan off the burner.

"It's okay, Ruby." I started to scrape the burned pancake off the pan. This, at least, was easy. "We can make another one."

A couple of hours later, it felt as if I'd scaled a mountain instead of simply making sure all three girls were fed, showered, and dressed. It was a school day, but no one wanted to go to school, and with Ruby and Ella parked in front of the TV, I decided to tackle Alexa.

She was in her room, sitting hunched on her bed, her thumbs flying over her phone. I knocked once on the door and poked my head in.

"Alexa?"

"Do you know what they're saying about Mom?" It came out like an accusation.

I tensed, because I hadn't expected that. I realized I'd been stupidly naïve in thinking I could shut the world out for a little while; of course Alexa still had her phone. I hadn't thought to take it off her, because Laura had always been the one to collect it at nine and make sure it was on the charger in the kitchen.

What had she read? Why hadn't I at least *thought* about that? All evening when I'd believed we were safe, protected from all the news flying around, Alexa had been handling it on her own.

I came in the room, closing the door quietly behind me. "What are they saying?"

Alexa's lips trembled as she glared at me, as if this were somehow my fault. Perhaps it was. "They're saying she might have known the man who shot her."

"What?" I stared at her in blank incomprehension, pooling dread. "No, she couldn't have…"

"They're saying she volunteered at some refugee center downtown." Alexa shrugged angrily. "She never even said anything about that. They think the man probably came from there. It's *trending* on Twitter."

Refugee center?

I shook my head slowly, reaching one hand out to the door to steady myself. "No. Mom didn't…" I trailed off, because why *had* Laura been on that train? And who had come forward, who knew her and knew that she volunteered at a place I hadn't known about, never heard of? *Where had all this information come from?*

I suddenly realized, with a sickening rush, how enormous my ignorance was. I'd been so consumed by grief, and having to tell the girls, I hadn't even begun to deal with the rest of it, all the implications, repercussions, everything. Laura was dead. That was all that had mattered. But of course it wasn't; it couldn't be.

"Look." Alexa flung out one hand, to show me her phone's screen. I moved closer so I could see it properly.

Woman shot on subway might have known her assailant. She was walking from a refugee center where she volunteered when she was attacked.

I took the phone from Alexa, scrolling faster through the headlines and then swiping for the full text.

Witnesses have come forward to share their accounts of the murder of Laura West on a New York subway train. After an unknown man drew a gun, West was shot in the head, seeming to be a specific target. "She was weirdly calm throughout it all," one witness, Maria Fratelli, 24, said, holding back tears. "Serene. She feels like an inspiration to me now."

The man who shot West was able to leave the subway train without being apprehended and is still being sought by the police who believe he might have come to know West through her volunteer work at a local refugee center. So far, police do not believe this is a terrorist act but rather a single man acting of his own accord.

I thrust the phone back at Alexa. An *inspiration*? I felt sick. "This is all sensationalism, just to sell papers," I told her numbly.

"It's all online for free."

"You know what I mean." My head was buzzing with the overload of new information. *What refugee center?*

"Do you think Mom was calm?" Alexa asked, her eyes glittering with tears, her chin jutted out at a defiant angle. "Do you think she knew him? Do you think she knew what was going to happen?"

"I have no idea, Alexa, but…" I shrugged. I didn't know anything, and I hated that.

"Do you think she wasn't scared of dying, like that woman said?" She fired the question at me. "Do you think she's gone to heaven?"

Heaven? "Alexa…" I began, and she glared at me.

"I know you don't believe in God and all that stuff, but Mom did."

I sighed, scrubbing my eyes. I'd always been upfront about my atheism, how I felt believing in God was like believing in the tooth fairy. Alexa knew that. Even Ruby knew that, although she insisted on believing in Santa Claus, despite my dislike of perpetuating such fantasies. My mother's hippy-dippy belief in everything from angels to auras had soured me on the supernatural.

Laura might have been a bit more agnostic than me, but not that much, surely. We'd never been churchgoers. We hadn't even had the girls baptised, much to Laura's parents' dismay. So why was Alexa acting like I was at fault here, while Laura was suddenly some saint?

Because she was dead. Because she needed to believe in something good, amidst all this.

I took a deep, steadying breath. Now was not the time to talk about this. Maybe Alexa needed the comfort of faith, of the concept of heaven, to get through this moment. I could understand that. I almost wanted it myself. Besides, I had so many other things to process. I hadn't even known Laura had volunteered at a refugee center. Why hadn't she told me? What sort of secret life had she been living?

"I'm going to talk to the police this afternoon," I told Alexa. "I'll know more then, about what happened, and, more importantly, what they're doing to find this man, because that's the important thing now, Alexa. In the meantime, please try to stay off your phone. It doesn't help, trust me." I leaned forward, trying to keep my voice gentle. "Whatever Mom did or didn't believe… how it all happened… even who did it… those are just details. They don't matter, not to us, because she's still gone. None of it will bring her back." I felt as if I'd just put a chisel to my daughter's heart and tapped once, twice. Now I started to see the fractures, hairline cracks all the way down.

Alexa's lips trembled and there was a wild glitter in her eyes. "Maybe you just don't want those things to matter."

"Alexa." I reached out, putting my hands on her shoulders, but she shrugged them off with an angry twitch. Still I met her eyes, tried to imbue her with a sense of certainty and strength I was far from feeling. "We'll get through this, I promise."

She let out of a huff of breath, angling her head away from me. I had no idea what the right thing to say was—if there even was a right thing. It had been a long time since I'd connected with Alexa, since I felt as if I could reach her. I tried to remember the days when I'd been her hero, when she'd scrambled onto my shoulders or snuggled next to me on the sofa. They seemed very far away.

"I'm sorry," I finally whispered, because I was. "For everything. I can't even begin to imagine life without Mom."

A tear trickled down her cheek and she dashed it away with one hand, but it was quickly followed by another.

"But we will get through this," I said, my voice as firm as I could make it. "We will. Somehow. Together." The words sounded ridiculously hollow. I felt as if I were reading lines from the script of a Hallmark movie. Cue the violins, the tremulous smile, the commercial break. I'd pull Alexa into a hug as the light faded to black…

But, no. That wasn't going to happen, not to us. Alexa pulled her knees up to her chest as she reached for her phone, her reddish brown hair—the same color as mine—hanging down in front of her face in an impenetrable curtain. "Whatever, Dad." She almost sounded bored, except for the catch in her voice.

I waited there another moment, searching for something to say or do that would bridge this brokenness, but then I realized that nothing would. Maybe, for a little while at least, we simply had to be broken. There was no instant fix to this. There might be no fix at all.

By the time Laura's parents were due to arrive after lunchtime, I felt as if the day had gone on forever, and all I wanted was for it to be over—this one, and the next, and the next after that. Time marching on, because maybe time would help us.

With Alexa in her room and Ella and Ruby still watching TV, I'd gone on my laptop to find out more, each detail seeming impossible to grasp, and yet sickening in its detail: Laura had volunteered at the Global Rescue Refugee Center near the Bowery station; a man had entered the subway car after her and drawn a gun. He'd pointed it at Laura and, according to some witnesses, she'd *smiled*. I'd never understand that. Then he'd shot her, in the head. She'd died instantly. The man had waved the gun around some more, and then the train had pulled into the station. He'd got off, disappearing into the crowds before anyone could say or do anything.

All those cowards in the subway car with her were eager enough to come forward now and tell their part of the story for the press. Where had they been when my wife had been shot? Why hadn't they *done* anything, sounded an alarm, created a distraction, *thrown* something at him?

My phone buzzed with another voicemail. I'd had three reporters calling me this morning, asking for an interview. How they'd got my number, I had no idea. They were tenacious, that was for sure. But I didn't want to involve the media. I didn't want my life—my family—to become a circus, a freak show, for public consumption.

I just wanted this to end, but it felt as if it never would. In the distance, I heard the buzzer sound. My in-laws had arrived.

CHAPTER SIX

MARIA

The police were not at Global Rescue when I returned there the following week. The story had already died down in the media, after an initial flurry of reports and talk shows. In the week since, there had been a school shooting in Texas, and a political scandal. People's outrage had moved on, as it always did, although there was the occasional editorial, a few seconds' snapshot on the news.

I tried to forget about it, but I still felt sad about it all. I still kept thinking about Laura, and about her family. Those three girls. The widowed husband.

What did it have to do with me? Something, it seemed, and not just because I'd been questioned, but because I kept remembering so many little things. She liked sugar in her coffee, but treated it as if it were some sort of guilty secret. I'd made her coffee once, before her class, and she'd ducked her head, giving me an apologetic smile.

I know I shouldn't...

Why not? It is just sugar. Something sweet.

No one where I live has sugar in anything.

Briefly I'd thought of the starvation months of the siege: sharing a small tin of meatballs between four people; digging up mouldy potatoes in other people's abandoned gardens; queuing for the better part of a day for a humanitarian aid package shared between neighbors, and—better than Christmas—a single bar of chocolate doled out in tiny, precious bites. I'd smiled at Laura and put two teaspoonfuls in, and she'd laughed, seeming delighted by my action.

I missed her, I realized. I hadn't even known her very well, but I missed her. Although perhaps I missed the idea of her more than the reality; perhaps I was embroidering her into the fabric of my life with a thread that had never really been there.

It was easy to do that, when you were alone. Without even realizing it, you made people more significant than they actually were. The postman who smiles and stops for a chat, the neighbor who occasionally asks how you are. When they are the only people you could call on in a crisis, you have to make it seem like more than it is.

Of course I had Neriha and Selma. Good friends, and yet they were still at a distance. They had husbands, children. I was on the periphery of their lives, not just by my choice, but by theirs. And for twenty-six years—since I was fourteen years old—that *had* been my choice—to be alone, to be lonely, because it was simply what I had to do, to get through each day. I didn't know how else to be anymore, with anyone, and I didn't think I ever would remember.

Perhaps that was why I fixated on Laura—because she was dead. She was safe. I could magic up a relationship where there hadn't been much of one. And I kept remembering details—snippets she'd said in our few moments of conversation.

Phones. It's all about the phones. Don't ever let them have phones, Maria.

I'd smiled and said nothing, because I could never imagine a situation where I would have to withhold a mobile phone, or anything, from my child. Every aspect of that circumstance was beyond the realm of possibility.

And Ella, so quiet, so good, yet still a worry to Laura. *She sees so much and says so little. I worry about her. I wonder what she's thinking, but she never likes to tell me.*

Yes, I knew how the quiet ones kept secrets.

*

Ten days after Laura's death, Cathy made an announcement to all the volunteers. Laura's funeral would be in two days, and she would be attending. Anyone who would like to come along could go with her.

I decided I would. It was my day off anyway, and I wanted to see Laura's girls. Maybe I could make sure they were okay, in some small way, although I had no idea how I would go about that, or why I felt I needed to.

"I thought it didn't involve us," Selma remarked when we met in front of the center, everyone dressed in dark colors. It was just after Thanksgiving, another cold, bright day.

"It doesn't, but I knew her," I said simply. "I'd call her a friend. I want to pay my respects."

There were four of us going—Cathy, Selma, me, and a man Laura had taught, from Ethiopia, who knew very little English. Cathy drove us in her minivan, and I watched the blur of buildings and cars stream by as we headed uptown, to a part of the city I'd never been to. I'd lived in New York for nearly two decades, but I'd always kept to my routes and routines—Astoria, the Bowery, occasionally a brief foray to the green market in Union Square. No further, because it felt safer to stick to the places I knew.

Now I watched out the window as the buildings fell away and the city opened up like a flower, surprising me with the huge green expanse of Central Park, the trees spreading their bare branches above it. I'd seen the park in films and on the TV, but the reality still enthralled me.

It reminded me of Veliki Park back in Sarajevo, with its endless, rolling green interspersed with statues and fountains, the mountains bisecting the horizon in a jagged line in every direction, breathtaking in their stark beauty.

We continued uptown, the park in the distance, elegant stone buildings lining Madison Avenue on either side. Everything felt bigger up here—the buildings, the sidewalks, the space.

"I'll let you all off here," Cathy said when we reached the church, "and then go find a parking garage."

All four of us looked at her a bit askance; none of us wanted to go in on our own.

"You'll be fine," Cathy said brightly, and wordlessly we filed out of the van, to stand in front of a large, impressive-looking church, its twin square towers pointing to the hard blue sky.

People milled about on the steps in front, dressed in sophisticated black; some of the women wore hats. It felt, strangely, like a wedding; no one was crying or wailing or showing their grief. I caught the eye of an older woman who was somber and tight-lipped; she looked away quickly.

A few journalists and cameramen milled about, a bit further away; it seemed Laura West's murder was still news. I avoided their curious gazes; one man was smoking as he waited, no doubt for the money shot of the grieving family.

I led the way, since no one else seemed to want to, climbing the steps and stepping into the cool dimness of the church. It smelled familiar—of incense and candle wax and dust. I had not been inside of a church since I'd gone to Mass with my mother as a child. My father had been a cultural Muslim, my mother a nominal Catholic, Mass reserved for Christmas and Easter or when she was feeling anxious.

The last time we'd went had been at the start of the siege, before it became too dangerous to cross town. I remembered kneeling, closing my eyes, offering a silent, formless prayer, no more than *please*.

I wanted to believe there was something bigger going on than the terror all around me; I still did. It all felt so empty and pointless if there wasn't, and yet life, time and again, had made me wonder. Doubt.

Now I walked to the back of the church and slid all the way down the pew. Selma and the others followed me, and we all sat quietly, waiting for the service to begin.

I'd been given a service sheet as I'd come in and I flipped through it, jolted by the photographs of Laura and her family on its thick, creamy pages: Laura and her husband at their wedding, looking young and a little scared, their smiles tremulous; on a recent holiday somewhere coastal and warm, a sailboat in the background on a placid sea, their children lined up in front of them—Alexa, the sulky teen who pouts instead of smiles, Ella, the dreamy middle one, gazing off into the distance, and Ruby grinning widely right at the camera. I felt as if I knew them, even though I didn't.

There was a message from the family at the back of the program, a thank you to everyone who had supported them through this time, and a request for donations to the Global Rescue Refuge Center instead of flowers. I read their names silently, my mind lingering over them: Nathan, Alexa, Ella, Ruby.

Cathy slid in to the end of the pew, and a few minutes later the service began. I felt another jolt as the casket was brought in, held aloft by six solemn-faced pall-bearers. It suddenly seemed so *real*, this presence of death, the complete absence of a person. It hit me like a fist in the chest, leaving me breathless. Then, following the casket, the family: a man with his head lowered, holding the hand of a little girl. *Ruby.* The other two girls walked behind him, staring at the ground, everyone subdued and silent. The girls were all dressed in starchy dresses of navy blue; they looked new and uncomfortable, too formal, even for this occasion. I felt their sadness like a palpable thing, a physical pain, binding us together.

I sat through the entire service, letting the words and music wash over me in a soothing tide. This wasn't just a way to remember Laura, it was a way to ascribe meaning to her life. She *mattered*. I felt that now, the necessity of it, when someone was gone. It didn't make it better, I knew, but it was still important.

Afterwards, we all headed downstairs to the church's fellowship hall, where there were platters of limp-looking sandwiches and large metal vats of coffee and tea. Everyone talked in low murmurs, not sure where to look. I wondered whether we should have come down; we didn't know anyone, and it was obvious that we didn't really belong in this small but well-heeled crowd.

Cathy, however, was determined to make a point of being there. After we'd sipped some lukewarm coffee from paper cups she headed towards Laura's husband Nathan, gesturing for us to follow, which we did, like a row of ducklings following their mama.

"Mr. West." She held out her hand which he took after a second's pause. "My name is Cathy Trainor. I'm the director of the Global Rescue Refuge Center. Your wife was a great asset to us. I'm so sorry for your loss." Each sentence felt as if it had been rehearsed, spoken by rote, although I was sure Cathy meant every word.

Laura's husband looked a little dazed, wearing a rumpled suit, dark circles under his eyes.

"Thank you…" he said after a moment, and then seemed unable to say anything else. His gaze moved over each one of us without any real interest. He was in shock, anyone could see that. Yet Cathy, for some reason of her own, persevered.

"Laura was so lovely, always bright and cheerful when she volunteered, chatting to everyone. We really appreciated her work at the center."

Nathan's gaze moved back over us in turn, this time more alert, before retraining on Cathy. "You all knew her," he said slowly.

"Yes… although I'm afraid not very well." Cathy looked back at us. "Maria probably knew her the best."

I stiffened as Nathan West turned to look at me. His eyes were very blue, piercing, even. They made me want to look away. "You did?"

"Yes," I offered hesitantly. "We were… friends. We chatted sometimes." My throat felt dry, my heart starting to hammer. Why was I so nervous?

"What did you chat about?" He looked lost, as if he didn't know what questions to ask. "What did she say?"

I hesitated, unsure how to answer. What did he want to know? Would it help him somehow, knowing she'd spoken to me, that I'd called her a friend? I could understand wanting to hold onto this thin thread of connection, before all was severed. "This and that," I told him. "The weather, or work… she chatted about your children…" I glanced behind him, to where the three girls were clustered by the platters of sandwiches, an older woman, perhaps a grandmother, holding Ruby's hand tightly.

"She talked about the girls? I didn't even know…" He shook his head slowly, still dazed.

"It was clear she loved them very much. She showed me a photo of Ruby, once." I didn't know why I said this. It felt too intimate, like an invasion, but Nathan West looked grateful.

"Thank you," he said, and I felt a wave of relief, that I'd done the right thing by telling him.

We left a few minutes later, after saying our goodbyes to Nathan West. He shook my hand, looking at me directly, his gaze once more so intent that I struggled not to look away. Then we headed upstairs and outside, and I breathed in the cold, fresh air in gulps as the tension that had knotted my shoulders for the last hour started to lessen.

I had paid my respects to Laura West; I had seen her husband and children. They were grief-stricken, but they would be all right. They had each other, as well as family and friends, a place to go home to, food on the table. They would survive, and even more than that. Eventually they would heal. They would flourish. And I had done my duty—if I'd ever had one—it was over now.

So I told myself, and I meant it as a reassurance, even if it didn't quite feel like that. Even if I still thought of them, still wondered, still missed Laura, and bizarrely, missed her family, even though they were strangers to me.

I thought it would all fade in time; it would have to. I had no idea that when I spoke to Nathan West in that chilly church hall, it was only the beginning. Of everything.

CHAPTER SEVEN

NATHAN

The day after Laura's death, I'd gone to the station to collect Laura's things and get some answers.

"Why haven't you found this man?" I demanded before the same two plain-clothes officers had had a chance to settle in their seats. I knew I sounded aggressive, and that it probably wasn't the best approach, but I was exhausted, angry, and fragile, my emotions bubbling away, seeping out like some noxious liquid no one wanted to touch.

"We are doing everything we can to apprehend the suspect, Mr. West," the woman, Lisa, said.

"The *suspect?* I think it's pretty cut and dried, isn't it? You've got umpteen witnesses who sat on their asses and *watched* while my wife was shot, and you've got the man waving a gun on CCTV. How is he only a suspect?"

Lisa's face tightened as she amended, "The man in question."

I took a steadying breath, knowing there was no point in getting their backs up, even as part of me wanted to reach across the table and grab them by their shirts. "So what do you know?"

"We're investigating a potential link to the Global Rescue Refugee Center, where your wife volunteered. Could you tell us about that?"

I shook my head helplessly, hating my own ignorance, shamed by it. "No, I can't. I didn't even know she volunteered there."

I could see that this surprised them; they exchanged looks, the sharp, blue-eyed Tom and the friendlier Lisa, caught on the back foot, just like me.

"She never mentioned it to you?"

"Obviously not."

Lisa frowned. "According to the director of the center, she'd been volunteering there for nearly a year."

I shrugged, because what else could I do? Why had my wife not told me she was volunteering? What did that say about her, about me, and about our marriage? I didn't know. I wasn't sure I wanted to know. "Do you think he came from there? The man who shot her?"

"We're looking through the CCTV footage from their lobby, to see if he's ever visited the center. At the moment, it appears he didn't visit it on the day of the attack, although CCTV from the subway station confirms that he came from that direction."

"The same direction as Laura."

"Yes."

"And you don't know any more? There have been suggestions on the news that he had been targeting her specifically…"

"That is a possibility," Tom cut in, his voice low and gravelly, a real man's man type of voice. "Although I wouldn't pay too much attention to what's in the news. Most of it is sensationalist." Which was what I'd told Alexa, yet I had trouble believing it now.

"Why would he target her, though?" I pressed. "There has to be some reason…" I couldn't help but grasp at straws, searching for answers when there didn't seem to be any. I wanted to make sense of it all, and I couldn't. I didn't know how.

"We don't know that he did," Lisa said quietly. "It could have been random, or he could have known her or just seen her. We're still pursuing the possible connection, if any."

"How are you pursuing it?" I asked, turning aggressive once again. "What are you *actually* doing now to find him?"

Lisa looked down at her notes, unfazed by my tone. "We're going over the CCTV of the Global Rescue Refugee Center, as that still seems the most likely lead, although you should be prepared for the possibility that he wasn't from there, that there was no link, and that your wife's murder was just a senseless act of violence." Her face softened in pity, but I wasn't having it.

"It *was* a senseless act of violence, link or not."

She nodded. "Yes, of course. I'm sorry. We're also circulating the artist's sketch of him, based on the CCTV footage and witnesses' recollections, as well as some photos of him from that footage—although unfortunately they're not very clear. But hopefully someone will come forward."

Hopefully? Was that all we had?

"Did your wife ever mention being followed by someone?" Tom asked. "Any unwanted contact…?"

"No, of course not." I sounded irritable, even petulant, but I couldn't help it. My anger had to go somewhere. "Don't you think I would have mentioned it if she had?"

"We're trying to help, Mr. West," Lisa said gently, and suddenly I deflated, my shoulders slumping, that tidal wave of grief poised to crash over me once more and suck me under.

"I'm sorry." My voice choked and I took a steadying breath. "I know you are. I just… I just can't believe this has happened. Why didn't anyone *do* anything? At least twenty or thirty people in that subway car, and not one person moved a muscle."

"He had a gun," Lisa reminded me gently. "People were shocked as well as scared."

"I know, but… how could he have got away? Just walked out…"

"Ran out, still waving a gun," Tom interjected. "And there were no transit police in the station or on the train at that time."

Even if there had been, it wouldn't have mattered. Laura would still have been dead. Yes, her killer would have been caught, but who cared? He was, in all likelihood, some strung-out nobody who had acted in a moment of insanity. How could I believe anything else?

I left them a short while later, and at the desk they gave me Laura's things. I took her battered leather bag, wincing at the bloodstains on it, horrible proof of what had happened. Although the police had been through it all, I wanted to see what was inside, to check if there were any clues, or even any messages—something for me, for the girls, even though the sensible part of me knew that there wouldn't be. It wasn't as if she'd known what was about to happen.

I ducked into a coffee shop near the station, ordering a black coffee before taking a table in the back. I put her bag on the table, running my hands over the soft, worn leather. I'd been thinking of getting her a new bag for Christmas, something from Coach or Burberry rather than this cheap knock-off she'd had for years. Why hadn't I done it for her birthday, or for last Christmas? Why had I waited? The thought angered me now, even as I recognized that Laura probably wouldn't have cared either way. She'd never been into brands, had laughed at my Gucci sunglasses.

I unclasped and opened the bag, staring into its dark depths. It was a mess of crumpled tissues and crumbs, as most of Laura's bags were. I took out her wallet, flipping through the cards. No surprises, and no money either, because Laura always forgot to go to the ATM.

Besides her wallet, there was a hairbrush, a tube of lip balm, and a crumpled brochure for the Global Rescue Refugee Center. I stared at the photograph of the uninspiring building on the front, a 1970s low build that had been squeezed between two brownstones. The kind of building that I would like to tear down, and build something new in its place, something both sophisticated and utilitarian, multipurpose and eco-friendly.

I flipped through the brochure, skimming the paragraphs about English lessons and classes in US Citizenship, help in filling out forms, dealing with health insurance, legal and banking services, job placement.

How had Laura even found out about this place? According to the police, she'd been teaching an English class there every Tuesday morning since last January. Why? And why hadn't she ever said?

Or *had* she, and it had slipped my mind? Uncomfortably I wondered if this could be the case. I'd often been busy and distracted in the evenings, worried about prospective bids, issues with new builds, zoning permissions, the cost of sourcing materials… it felt never-ending, always needing to stay on top.

I could almost picture the scene—the girls in bed, the two of us on the sofa, my laptop open as I did some work while pretending to watch some Netflix series or other with Laura.

I've started volunteering at a refugee center downtown. Every Tuesday morning, teaching English.

Huh. That's nice.

No, surely it hadn't happened like that. Surely I would have remembered; I would have *said* something. I would have asked why, or how it was, or if she enjoyed it. It would have penetrated my consciousness, rather than just being another detail I skimmed over.

In fact, as I thought about it, I realized if I'd listened properly, I might have resisted the idea. *Do you really want to spend your time doing that? What about Ruby?* What about working on the apartment, money pit that it was poised to be, or, better yet, getting a job as I'd suggested before?

Before the girls, Laura had been an editorial assistant for a boutique children's publisher. It had paid a pittance, but it still would have been something.

Sitting there, with Laura's bag in my hands, I knew that conversation could very well have happened, if I'd listened to her in the first place. If she'd told me about the refugee center, I might not have been supportive. I didn't trust my own responses, just as I didn't trust my ability to sift through the good memories from the bad. The real from the wished-for.

Too many times I'd been distracted, even indifferent, focused on work, on what I deemed was important. And it *was* important, because it paid the bills. It financed our whole way of life—the apartment, the schools, the vacations to Cape Cod to be with Laura's difficult parents. I might have worked too hard, but it had been for a reason.

Early on in our marriage, I'd told Laura about my upbringing. I hadn't wanted her to feel sorry for me, but I'd wanted her to understand. My mother's New Age schtick could seem endearingly goofy to the outsider; her tie-dyed T-shirts, flowing scarves, and crystal necklaces (white had healing powers, even I remembered that) were quirky and cute.

The reality, though, was that my childhood sucked. I never knew my father—never knew if he had ever been in the picture, or wanted to be in the picture, or even if my mother knew who he was. When I'd been old enough to ask, she'd dismissed him with an airy wave of her hand: *He's not important, Nathan. We need to live in the present.*

Except I never wanted to live in the present, since the present was moving around so much—my mother was on a quest to find herself, and I still don't think she has. She claimed she didn't care about money, so we never had any; she said "experiences" were more important than stability (or "stagnating', as she would have said with a shudder), and so I didn't finish a single school year in the same place. Possessions weren't important, so I never owned more than a suitcase worth of stuff.

All of it made me want my life, my kids, to be different. For them to have more opportunities, better options, and *always* to feel safe and secure. Laura's death made that last one feel less certain, but I knew I'd always do my damnedest to manage the rest—and so, yes, I worked hard. I wouldn't apologise for that, not even to myself.

But right now I felt the resulting lack like an emptiness inside me. When was the last time Laura and I had had a real conversation, one that didn't involve the girls' homework or who was picking up the dry cleaning? When had I last come home early and taken her into my arms for a smacking kiss? Or when had we lain in bed, legs tangled, lazy in the sunshine of a summer's afternoon? They all felt like a montage of moments that had never happened, and yet I knew they had. Once, they had.

Still, it saddened me to think that Laura might have told me something like that, or tried to tell me, and I hadn't listened. Even worse was the thought that she'd never told me, because she'd known I wouldn't have approved or even cared. Or because she didn't care about my opinion one way or another, since I was so busy with other stuff.

What kind of husband had I been? What kind of father? They were questions I thought I knew the answers to, but now I wondered, even though I was reluctant to. I was afraid to think too deeply about either of those questions, and worse, their answers. I didn't want to go back over my memories and examine them like scientific objects: exhibit A. Evidence for what? For the truth of what our life together had really been like lately?

The only other thing in her bag was her phone. I'd saved it for last, knowing it was potentially the most important. Now I swiped the screen; Laura had never put a lock code or fingerprint on it, something that had always annoyed me, just a little bit. *What if someone steals it? All your information… it's the latest iPhone…*

My fingers hovered over the screen; the wallpaper was a photo of us all at Cape Cod, partially obscured by various icons. I pressed the text message icon first, holding my breath, although I didn't know what I expected to find. The police surely would have alerted me if something questionable or worrisome had been on there.

As it was, most of the texts were from me, a few from Alexa, all monosyllabic. *Home at 6. Yes, I did. Can I stay longer? Did you pick up the dry cleaning?*

I scrolled through, looking for texts from other people, friends from school or work, or even from someone at the refugee center, but there weren't many, at least not recently. The last text she received from a friend from her editorial days was back in September, when we'd had dinner together, confirming the time.

I looked through the rest of the apps on her phone, finding out what she'd last bought on Amazon—a My Little Pony for Ruby's birthday—and how many steps she'd walked the day she'd died—5,541—but no real information. Her life held no secrets, except I was starting to feel as if I hadn't known her at all, and that scared me.

Of course I knew her, I told myself. I needed to stop being so melodramatic, so maudlin. I'd known her better than anybody. I'd known all her little vices—that she secretly bit her toenails, and how she hated the sound of cotton balls squeaking, and that she pretended to like smoked salmon to seem sophisticated. I *knew* her. And yet right then I felt as if I hadn't.

Finally I clicked on the photos icon, and my heart squeezed painfully as the first photo came up—a selfie of her and Ruby, faces smushed up together, both grinning from ear to ear. According to the date stamp, it had been taken the day before she'd died, on the walk back from preschool. I stared at it for another moment and then started scrolling through the others.

Most of the photos were of the girls—in the park, at home, while on vacation, goofing around, hamming it up for the camera, a few candid shots they didn't realize were being taken—one of Alexa laughing, looking happier than I could remember seeing her in recent memory. Laura had shown me some of them, but others had stayed on her phone, unseen.

I scrolled back to that first one of Laura and Ruby—probably the last photo ever taken of her. She looked so joyful, so *alive*—her hair falling out of its ponytail, her eyes glinting, the freckles on her nose. Studying her wide smile, I couldn't believe she was dead. I simply couldn't.

"Mister… are you all right?"

A hand came down on my shoulder, startling me out of my grief. I blinked in the dim lighting at the concerned face of another customer, an elderly woman. I realized that I was making a snuffling sort of sound, a kind of verbal weeping. My eyes were dry.

I shook my head, embarrassed, muttering I knew not what, and then, clutching Laura's bag to my chest, I stumbled out of the café.

Back at the apartment, Laura's parents were trying to be helpful, as they so often did, even if they weren't actually all that helpful. This was what they always did, whenever they visited; Elaine re-organised the kitchen, Paul gave me advice I didn't want. They tried to be overly involved, to seem as if they were so very helpful, but it was always on their very particular terms.

Wearily I listened to Elaine tell me how little food there was in the kitchen, how she intended to make roast chicken for dinner, which seemed like a lot of effort when none of us was eating very much and we didn't have the ingredients she needed, which put her out considerably.

"I thought you'd have poultry seasoning," she said with a sniff, sounding bewildered by such an oversight on our part. "I would have bought it otherwise."

I muttered some sort of apology, hardly able to believe I was doing so. I could already see what the evening would entail—

Elaine's endless fussing in the kitchen, and then the meal none of us could ever seem thankful enough for. Plus, I knew she'd harangue Ruby for not using her fork, or Alexa for mumbling, and everyone would be ordered to clean their plates, no leftovers, not even the Brussel sprouts. I wasn't sure I could stand any of it.

I'd never had a great relationship with my in-laws. I was always cautiously polite with them; we'd tolerated each other, for Laura's sake, and at family gatherings we'd acted as if we actually got along.

The truth was, they had always felt Laura had married down. They were Boston bluebloods, old money, country-club-type people; I was a scholarship kid with too much obvious ambition and a loony single mother who had told them the color of their auras during their one unfortunate meeting at Laura's and my wedding. It didn't help that Laura had been twelve weeks pregnant when we got married, something that they blamed only me for.

Over the years, it only got worse, although I did my best to suck it up. Paul and Elaine Taylor muscled in on my marriage in far too many ways—co-opting our vacation plans with suggestions of their own, trips we couldn't afford that were bankrolled by Daddy, even though they knew I couldn't stand that.

When we couldn't afford private preschool for Alexa—I was twenty-seven, just starting out—they told Laura they'd pay for it, without even asking me. She accepted, and then looked guilty, asking me if she shouldn't have. What was I supposed to say? *No, let's deprive our daughter for the sake of my pride.*

Still, it had always grated on me, over the years, to accept their handouts, for Laura's sake. She couldn't understand why I didn't want her father to buy us an apartment of their choosing, when I knew it would always feel like their home, not ours. Gifts always—*always*—came with strings, but Laura was so used to them dangling down that she never seemed to mind. But I did. I did a lot.

When I was thirty-two, I finally made my mark, designing an office building in San Francisco that won a lot of awards. Three years later, I started my own business with Frank, a friend from grad school, and we were lucky and driven and made it bigger sooner than anyone had expected. The money started coming in, and finally—*finally*—it was me who could afford the apartment, the school tuition, the vacations, just as I'd always wanted.

Admittedly, all those things stretched us a lot. Our credit card was usually maxed out, and the mortgage on our apartment was bigger than I liked or wanted to acknowledge. There was a reason we had only redecorated the kitchen, a fact Elaine seemed intent on commenting on repeatedly.

"How long have you been in this place, Nathan? Four *years*? I think there might be lead paint in the bedrooms... have you had the girls tested?" Yes, we had, and there were no concerns, but I hated the way she asked, as if she suspected we hadn't, as if we didn't even care.

Death by a thousand cuts, or really, sly sideways knife thrusts, right into the gut. And now, with Laura's grief such a raw, open wound, I didn't think I could take any more, not without saying or doing something I wasn't even sure I'd regret.

"I don't know if we're up for eating a proper sit-down meal, Elaine. Why don't we just get takeout?"

Her lips pressed together, her eyes flashing as she drew herself up, a posture I was well used to. "Nutrition is important, Nathan, and I doubt they'll be getting many home-cooked meals in the foreseeable future. Besides, I've already ordered the groceries."

I let it go; I didn't have the strength to fight these petty battles that always seemed to mean so much to my mother-in-law. Alexa was still angry with me, for some unknown reason, Ella silent, Ruby being clingy or having meltdowns in turns. No one knew how to *be*. No one knew how this was supposed to go.

I wanted to curl up on my bed and sleep for about a thousand hours; I wanted to drink an entire bottle of Jack Daniel's and forget everything, for just a little bit, but I couldn't. Of course I couldn't.

I couldn't even grieve, not that I knew how, because I was trying to manage everything—the girls, my in-laws, the small scattering of neighbors and friends who texted, asking if there was anything they could do, without entirely seeming to mean it.

And then, two days after Laura's death, the media found us. I walked out of our apartment building with Ruby, who had decided she wanted to go to preschool, only to stagger back at a blinding flash in my face. A camera.

"Mr. West, can you comment on your wife's murder?"

"What are the police doing for the investigation?"

"Did she know her killer?"

"Get the fuck away from me," I growled, shouldering past them, my hand clenched around Ruby's so tightly she whimpered. "Sorry, Rubes. Sorry."

I left them behind us, pulling her along.

"Daddy," she said severely. "You shouldn't *swear.*"

"I know. I know. I'm sorry." I glanced at her, looking so stern, like a school teacher. Like the fearsome Miss Willis. "How do you know about swearing, Ruby?"

"Mommy told me. I asked her what the f-word meant when a dirty-looking man saind it in the street. She said I should never say it."

"And so you shouldn't," I agreed. "And I shouldn't, either. I am sorry."

It was one of those many fantasy-memories that could have me doubling over and gasping for breath if I let it. I could picture Laura telling Ruby all about it—how serious Ruby would look, listening with every fibre of her being, and how Laura would answer, gentle and smiling, always patient. I could practically see her; if I turned, she'd be there.

I forced my mind away from it. I couldn't let myself think like that, dream and dwell on the impossible. It hurt too much, an emotional overdose that left me hungover and yet desperate for another hit. I didn't want to forget Laura, of course I didn't, but I couldn't bear to remember her… if I was remembering her at all.

A few of the mothers lingering by the school doors came up to me, murmuring as I brought Ruby in.

"We're so sorry… I can't believe it… is there anything we can do?" It was the usual litany, and I felt from them a morbid sort of curiosity mixed in with the genuine sympathy, and I even understood it. Hadn't I been like that once? *Look at those poor people. Thank God I'm not one of them.*

Now I was.

Miss Willis was all gushing sympathy when I came in with Ruby, putting her hand on my shoulder, looking deep into my eyes, a far cry from her demeanor yesterday.

"How are you, Nathan? We are so, *so* sorry…"

She never called me Nathan. It was a strictly Mr and Mrs type of place. I tried not to shrug off her hand as I gave her a quick, tense smile.

"We're okay. We're coping." Lies. All lies. "Let me know if Ruby has any trouble, anything at all, and I'll pick her up, okay?"

"Of course, of course." Miss Willis got down on her knees, putting her arms around my daughter in a way that left Ruby distinctly nonplussed. "How are you, sweetie? Would you like to play at the craft table today? I know it's your favorite…"

I couldn't keep from thinking this performance was for Miss Willis' benefit rather than mine or Ruby's. *See how caring I am. Such a good teacher.* Or was I just a cynic, hardening to everything because of my own bitterness?

I pictured myself in days, months, and years to come—angry and resentful towards everyone, sneering silently at the entire world because no one had suffered like I had. Like I was now. How could I keep myself from it? Did I even want to?

Over the next few days, that question became harder and harder to answer. Alexa remained angry, Ella silent, Ruby a handful. Ruby had returned to school, but Ella and Alexa weren't ready yet and the headmistress of Walkerton had agreed they could restart in the new year.

My in-laws made no signs of leaving, taking Alexa's bedroom so she had to sleep in with her sisters, and continuing with their exhausting version of being helpful.

They were determined to arrange the funeral themselves, with hymns and Bible readings they insisted Laura would want. They also asked if she could be buried back in Boston, even though it would mean a huge trek for us all after the funeral.

I allowed it all, more out of weariness than anything else. I knew Paul and Elaine were grieving; Laura had been their angel, their only longed-for child, after years of infertility. If this helped them, so be it. I couldn't even care about the funeral, something else to heap on to my guilt.

My mother, Nancy, flew in for it, offering her own kind of help— messages from angels, tearful hugs, and an irritatingly self-absorbed grief when she hadn't actually known Laura very well. We rarely visited her, and she hardly left Arizona, having decided to settle down when I was in my twenties. I think everyone breathed a collective sigh of relief when she was gone again, the day after the funeral, when we returned from Boston. She promised to come again soon, although I knew she wouldn't.

Over the years, I'd become used to my mother's brand of caring—effusiveness without sincerity, all gushing sympathy, gone in an instant. The girls continued to be bemused by her theatrics; although, for the first time, they seemed more interested in her strange pronouncements.

"Can you see Mommy's aura?" Ella asked, making me roll my eyes.

"Oh yes," my mother said, her voice reverent. "It's a lovely warm pink."

Ridiculous, but I let it slide, for Ella's sake, along with everything else.

The media were still hounding us, with phone calls and even text messages, pleading for interviews; a few photographers continued to loiter outside our building, and we'd learnt to leave with our heads tucked low, our hands flung out to ward off the invasive shots. *No comment. No comment.* We were celebrities, albeit reluctant ones.

I stayed away from the newspapers, from the musing editorials dissecting our pain to the updates or lack of them on finding Laura's killer, which thankfully tapered off after the initial rush.

Still, ten days after Laura's death, there were photographers at the funeral, snapping away, as we entered the church behind her coffin. I felt like walking up to one man who had a cigarette dangling from his lips as he lifted the camera to his eye and throttling him. I could picture my hands around his throat. I could *feel* them.

Finally, three weeks on, the media started to leave us alone; we'd become old news. Boring. And now I'd come here, to the doors of the Global Rescue Refuge Center, where maybe, just maybe, it all began.

The police still hadn't found any incriminating CCTV footage, although they continued to scroll through the endless hours of it; there was still no definitive link between this place and Laura's death.

And yet… I felt drawn here, to this surprising secret Laura had. To the people who might have known her. It was Tuesday morning, the same time as she had volunteered. I was desperate for answers, something to help me make sense of the senseless, even though the reasonable part of me knew that was most likely a pointless, hopeless task.

"Come on, Ruby," I said, and holding my daughter's hand, I walked inside.

CHAPTER EIGHT

MARIA

I saw him as soon as he came in. I was in the lobby, sitting at one of the little tables with an Armenian woman, Anahit, who needed help with some paperwork, trying to make sense of the jumble of crumpled sheets and receipts she'd given me.

I looked up as he entered, and my heart seemed to still in my chest. There he was, Laura's husband, holding his youngest daughter's hand. Ruby. Ruby and Nathan. I remembered their names, I remembered *them,* even though the news had dried up and everyone else had moved on.

I knew they hadn't. I knew how grief stayed and stayed, morphing into different feelings and shapes, like some kind of mythical monster. Just when you thought you'd got hold of it, it turned into something else and struck again. And I knew how it eventually slithered away and left you alone, left you with nothing, which was maybe worse.

He stood in the doorway with his daughter, looking both uncertain and determined, as he glanced around the busy lobby with its table and chairs, the small makeshift café in the corner, with vats of coffee and tea. Then he saw me.

I was looking straight at him, even though I knew I shouldn't have been, and our gazes locked for a second, like something clicking into place. Recognition flashed across his features and after a second's hesitation he started forward. I tensed, not knowing where to look.

Next to me, Anahit babbled anxiously; Cathy had hoped I might be able to understand her a little bit, since Armenian and Bosnian were both Indo-European languages, but that was like assuming someone could understand German because they spoke English. Still, I was what was available, and we both tried, waving our hands and doing charades in an attempt to understand each other, with limited success.

Nathan continued to walk towards me, clutching his daughter's hand.

"*Pogledajmo...*" I murmured, trying to focus on the papers in front of me.

"Maria, isn't it?"

I looked up, somehow still surprised to see Nathan West there even though he'd been walking straight towards me.

"Yes..." I glanced at Anahit, who was looking confused by Nathan's presence.

"Sorry, I'm interrupting." He ducked his head. "It's just, I remembered you saying you knew my wife. Laura West."

"Yes..."

"And I wondered if I could talk to you about her? For a few minutes?" He glanced at Anahit in apology. "When you're finished here, of course."

I hesitated, feeling as if I were about to take a step into deep, dark, swirling water. I could hardly refuse, and I realized I didn't even want to. Some strange, small part of me had been *waiting* for this, although I couldn't have even said why.

"Yes, of course. We'll only be a few more minutes."

He murmured his thanks and stepped back; as I bent over the papers with Anahit, I watched him wander around the room with Ruby, looking at the various photographs of events the center had held—community dinners, bingo nights, food festivals, and country dances. I hadn't been to any of them, although I'd always been asked.

I couldn't give Anahit much help, and we both decided to put it aside after another fifteen minutes; I was tensely aware of Nathan and his daughter for each one. After Anahit had thanked me and gone off, I stood up and made my way to Nathan. He was standing by the doors again, looking a little lost, and I could tell that Ruby was getting bored, kicking at the floor and tugging on his hand.

"Sorry to make you wait," I said.

"No, no, I'm the one who should be sorry, for barging in here." He shook his head ruefully. "I'm just trying to find some answers."

And so he came to me? Surely there had been other, far more important people in Laura's life. "I don't know if I can give you those, Mr. West."

"Please, call me Nathan."

I nodded but said nothing. Talking to him felt strange, yet not in an entirely bad way. Still, I was nervous. I couldn't remember the last time I'd had a conversation with someone who was essentially a stranger.

"Would you… would you mind going to get a coffee?" he asked. "I saw there's a Starbucks around the corner. My treat, of course." He spoke hurriedly, flushing a little.

Ruby glanced up at me curiously, her bright-eyed gaze roving over my face.

"Okay, yes," I said, even though I didn't usually say yes to things. "That would be good. Let me just get my coat."

I told Cathy I was leaving a bit early, shrugging on my coat as I rejoined Nathan and Ruby. Outside, the air was breath-stealingly cold and crisp; it was early December, and the city had already gone into Christmas mode, the streets and shop windows decorated with bows and baubles and fake, glittery snow, the sense of festive jollity seeming, as it always did to me, a bit too forced. *It's December, so we have to do this.*

I didn't really celebrate Christmas anymore, although I had as a child. Even my father had enjoyed the holiday, and attended *Ponocka*, the midnight mass on Christmas Eve, with us. I remember skipping home through the dark, excited for all that lay ahead—meals and family, presents on New Year's Eve, lights and parties and music. It all seemed so far away now, as if it had happened to someone else. In a way, it had.

We didn't talk as we walked the short distance to the Starbucks down the street, and Nathan held the door open for me as I stepped into the dim, coffee-scented interior.

"What would you like?" he asked. "Anything…"

"Just a plain coffee, with milk, please."

I stood silently behind him as he waited to order, clutching my bag to my chest. Ruby twisted around to look at me once more with the frank, unabashed curiosity of a child.

"Who are you?" she asked in a loud voice, and Nathan half-heartedly shushed her.

"My name is Maria," I said, smiling; my face felt tight, the smile stretching my skin in a way that felt akin to old joints creaking. "And I believe your name is Ruby."

Ruby's mouth dropped open. "How did you know that?"

"I heard your father call you Ruby, and also your mother spoke of you to me." I said it purposefully, knowing that this was why they had come, yet still feeling a ripple of trepidation at mentioning Laura to them, as if I were doing something dangerous or forbidden.

"You knew Mommy?" Ruby asked, her voice dropping to an awed whisper, and I nodded.

"A little bit, yes. She was…" I paused, "a friend."

Nathan ordered the coffees, as well as a large sugary donut for Ruby, and we moved to a table in the back.

"Thank you for talking with me," he said as we all sat down. "I really do appreciate it."

"It is no problem." I hesitated, gazing down at the milky depths of my coffee. "But I don't know how much I can tell you, Mr. West."

"Nathan, please."

"Nathan." It was unsettling to be so familiar with him. I smiled at Ruby, who was licking the sugar off the donut without taking a bite. "And Ruby. My brother used to do that." I nodded towards the donut.

"Make a mess of things?" Nathan asked wryly as he swiped inefficiently at the spilled sugar and crumbs on the table.

"Lick off the sweetness." I smiled at the memory, even though it caused me a pang of loss. I didn't usually let myself remember such things, the intimate details of a life once lived. A life that was long gone. "He liked the sugar on the *krofne,* which is like a donut where I come from, but with marmalade inside."

"I'm sorry." He shook his head. "I don't even know what country you are from."

"Bosnia. I grew up in Sarajevo."

"Oh, I see. I'm sorry," he said again, although for what exactly, I did not know. Perhaps he remembered the bombings, the devastation, the war crimes. Perhaps not. It reminded me of the first time I'd met Laura, and she'd said much the same thing. *Sarajevo. I'm sorry.* Was that what had become of my city?

I took a sip of my coffee.

"My mommy's dead," Ruby announced, watching me with wide eyes. Her lips and nose sparkled with sugar.

"Yes, I know. I am very sorry for it." I paused, feeling my way through the words. "You must miss her."

She nodded, gazing down at her licked-over donut, and my heart, lifeless thing that it was, gave a funny little jerk, like something had prodded it.

"Have you been in America long?" Nathan asked.

"Eighteen years."

"And you were... friends... with Laura?" He said the words as if he were testing them out.

"Yes, we were." I spoke firmly, because Laura had been my friend, whatever I had been to her. And yet... "But I did not know her so very well." I felt I had to say this.

"But she talked to you about Ruby? And the girls?"

"Yes, sometimes."

"I didn't even know she was volunteering at that center," Nathan said. It came out like a confession. "How could I not know something like that?" He sounded so broken by it, this seemingly small detail his grief had snagged on. "The police told me she'd been coming to Global Rescue for nearly a year," Nathan continued. "A whole *year*." He looked at me almost hungrily. "Did she ever mention to you why she came? Why she decided...?"

I hesitated, thinking back over the months of mornings with Laura, the conversations which had seemed so inconsequential at the time yet now were imbued with more meaning than perhaps they ever should have had.

"She told me it was something she'd been wanting to do for some time," I said slowly. "She said she wanted to make a difference..." A memory caught, and I spoke without thinking. "Not just to people there, but to herself. She wanted to do something more with her life..." I stopped as I registered the startled, hurt look on Nathan's face.

"Something more?" he repeated sadly, like a little boy. "Is that what she said? Do you think she wasn't happy with... with me?"

How could I possibly answer such a question? And yet more memories slid slyly in—how Laura hadn't liked how hard Nathan had worked, how she'd felt he cared about things she didn't think were important.

The school the girls go to… it's ridiculous. I don't have anything in common with the people there, Maria. A girl in Ella's class gave iPhones as party favors and they're only ten. I'd been speechless; I couldn't even imagine such a thing, such a life.

"I know you can't answer that," Nathan mumbled. "I'm sorry. I'm just so… Did she… did she… mention me?" He ducked his head, the question making him vulnerable.

"Yes…" I began hesitantly, and he leaned forward, his eyes bright.

"What? What did she say?"

"Nothing much. That you worked hard…" I trailed off, unwilling to part with more. Laura's comment had been accompanied by a twisted smile, a bitter tone.

Sometimes I think he doesn't even see me.

The words fell into my head; I could hear Laura saying them—when? A few months ago? I couldn't tell them to Nathan now. They would serve no purpose but to give pain, and perhaps I hadn't remembered them properly, anyway.

"You're remembering something," Nathan said.

"No." Without meaning to, I glanced at Ruby, and comprehension flashed across Nathan's face, hurt entering his eyes. "She said she wanted to give back something, because she knew she hadn't before." The words sounded trite, but I knew Laura had meant them.

"I don't know why she wouldn't tell me. Did she think I wouldn't care?" He was speaking more to himself than to me, and so I chose not to answer. What could I say that would help? "It's so strange," he murmured. "It feels as if she was living this double life, but I know it wasn't like that. I mean, she was volunteering, not… well, you know." He glanced at Ruby, who was licking her finger and dabbing it on the bits of sugar on the table before licking them off. "Ruby, don't, that's disgusting. Eat your donut."

"I don't like donuts."

"What?" Nathan sounded shocked. "Of course you like donuts."

"No." Ruby shook her head, folding skinny arms across her chest. "I don't. I never have. Mommy buys me ice cream."

"But…" Nathan looked crushed by this information. I felt a wave of empathy for him.

"Do you know, Ruby," I said. "I don't like donuts, either. My mother used to make the *krofne* I mentioned—the ones with marmalade in them—but I never liked marmalade. I wanted chocolate inside, and she never made those." I could picture her in the kitchen, lowering the donuts into the oil with a metal spatula, her apron around her waist, dark hair pinned up. Her tired smile. My throat grew tight, and then I pushed the memory away and it eased again.

"What's marmalade?" Ruby asked.

"It's like orange jelly."

She made a face. "Yuck."

I nodded solemnly. "Yes. Exactly."

Ruby grinned, and I gave a small smile back, this seemingly little exchange causing a welter of emotions to rise up inside me, an unexpected tide of feeling. Sorrow, joy, pain. *What if…*

But, no. I could never let myself think like that.

"Are you a Mommy?" Ruby asked, as if reading my mind.

"Don't be nosy, Ruby…" Nathan began, shooting me an apologetic look.

"No, I don't have any children." I spoke a little stiffly as I tried to smile at her once more. "No husband, either. I'm all alone." Not wanting to sound self-pitying, I made a funny face. "Boohoo."

Ruby grinned again. "You're funny."

"No one has called me that before," I said. "At least, not for a long time." As a child, I used to be something of a clown. It was so long ago, such a different life, that I could barely remember it now—the girl capering about the living room, putting on funny voices and faces, so confident in her ability to entertain. Who was she? A stranger now.

My father had always laughed indulgently at my antics, and my mother would shake her head, claiming he was spoiling me, but I think she enjoyed it too. Petar was so serious and studious compared to me, always in his books or at the piano; I thought they liked the change. I hoped they did.

"Do you have any family in this country, Maria?" Nathan asked quietly, and I shook my head.

"No, I came here alone, when I was twenty."

"That must have been hard."

"It was better than staying."

He hesitated, rotating his cup between his palms. "There are some reports about…about what happened to Laura… Have you read them?"

"Some," I said cautiously.

"Saying how she was peaceful right before… it's so strange. I mean, what do they even mean?"

What could I say?

"Daddy doesn't think Mommy is in heaven," Ruby announced. "He says she's squashed like a bug."

Nathan flinched, and then flushed. "I didn't mean…"

"Do you believe in heaven?" Ruby asked me, with the unsettling frankness only a child possesses.

"Ruby…" Nathan began, but I shook my head.

"It's all right. I do believe in heaven, Ruby. But I know not everyone does."

"Daddy doesn't believe in God."

"No?" I glanced at Nathan, who was still looking embarrassed. "Not everyone believes in God, either. It can be quite hard to, sometimes."

"Do you?" Ruby demanded, a bit rudely, and I smiled.

"Yes. At least, I like to think He is there." Even if there had been too many dark days when He had seemed all too absent. I turned back to Nathan. "I'm sorry I cannot tell you more."

"No, you've been amazing." He looked at me uncertainly. "You must know what this feels like, in some way," he said quietly, and it felt as if my heart writhed within me, prodded again, waking up even more. "I mean, if you lost people during the war…"

"Yes." I did not offer any more. I couldn't.

"So many people don't. So many people haven't experienced…" He shook his head. "Sorry, I'm not trying to compare. I don't even know…"

"It's okay," I cut him off, not wanting to have to answer the question he'd been trying to ask. "Grief is grief," I said after a moment. "It endures, just as love does. That much I know."

"Yes." He nodded, swallowing hard. "Yes."

"Daddy, I'm bored." Ruby drummed her feet against her chair.

"Are you looking forward to Santa Claus coming, Ruby?" I asked, in what was surely a vain attempt to distract her, as well as shift the conversation onto a lighter topic. "Will he come to your house, do you think?"

She looked at me suspiciously. "He comes to everyone's house."

"Ah, no, he doesn't." I smiled, shaking my head. "He does not come to houses where I grew up. There we get another visitor."

She looked curious now, and a bit confused. "Who?"

"Grandfather Frost. We called him Djeda Mraz and he is like Santa Claus, but he wears a blue robe and he lives in Russia. He and his granddaughter Snegurochka deliver presents not on Christmas but New Year's Eve. She is a beautiful snow maiden who wears a snowflake on her head."

"Like Elsa!" Ruby cried, and I looked questioningly at Nathan. "From the movie *Frozen*… do you know it?"

I shook my head. "Alas, no. But it sounds similar. Snegurochka was certainly cold, if not frozen."

"I didn't know any of that," Nathan murmured. "It's fascinating."

I shrugged, smiling a bit apologetically. "It's all somewhat new, I'm afraid. We celebrate on New Year's Eve because Christmas was forbidden during Soviet times. That is where the tradition comes from."

"Even more fascinating."

Ruby tugged on Nathan's hand, bored again, and he grimaced. "Sorry, I'm keeping you…"

"And I think I am keeping you." Very lightly I touched Ruby on the nose, brushing some grains of sugar from her. "You are like Snegurochka, Ruby, with snowflakes on your nose."

She laughed, delighted, making my heart feel like a balloon floating up inside me. When had I last made someone laugh? When had I last *tried*?

"I want to be Sneg-cha," she said. "Daddy, can I dress up as her for Halloween?"

"It's already been Halloween, Rubes, but maybe next year." He turned back to me. "I should let you go…" He sounded almost as if he didn't want to.

"Yes." I rose, dignified, trying not to feel the pointless wrench of leaving. I would never see them again now. It had only been a few moments, yet somehow they had touched me in a place I'd forgotten existed, just as Laura had. How foolish, to have allowed that to happen.

"Daddy, when we will see Maria again?" Ruby asked.

Nathan looked trapped by the question. "I'm not sure, Rubes…"

"I think this is goodbye, my little Snegurochka," I said, trying to smile. I felt far too emotional, the frozen parts of me breaking apart and floating away. "Or, as we say in my old country, *Zdravo*."

"Zer-avo," Ruby repeated, sounding proud of her new knowledge. "What does that mean?"

"It means goodbye."

Her lower lip wobbled. "But I don't want to say goodbye."

I shrugged helplessly, glancing at Nathan for direction. "That is the way of things, sometimes," I said when he seemed to not know what to say, either.

"Perhaps this doesn't have to be goodbye," Nathan finally said, sounding hesitant. "I'm sure my other daughters would like to meet you, and learn what you know of Laura. No one else knew about her volunteering."

I gazed at him without replying, because I didn't know what he was trying to say.

Ruby sidled over to me and slid her hand in mine. It was small and soft and sticky with sugar.

"Yes, Ella and Alexa should meet her," she said. "You can come over to our apartment."

"Oh…" I was not sure how to respond to this unexpected invitation, but Nathan jumped in first.

"Yes, why don't you come over for dinner? Then the older girls can meet you, as Ruby said. That is, if you want to…"

Did I want to? I was so shocked by the invitation that I couldn't respond for a moment. Most people had stopped inviting me anywhere years ago, because they knew I would say no. And I should have said no now, and yet…

"Yes," I said finally. "Yes, I would like that. Thank you."

CHAPTER NINE

NATHAN

"When will Maria come to dinner, Daddy? Tonight?"

"No, not tonight." I put my arm around Ruby as we sped uptown in a taxi cab; I still couldn't bring myself to take the subway.

"Tomorrow?"

"I don't know."

I was already starting to regret my impulsive invitation. I didn't know Maria at all. She was a complete stranger, even if Laura had known her, and yet… for the last hour, I'd enjoyed our conversation, and, more importantly, I felt as if she understood what I was going through somehow, perhaps because of her own experience, living through a war, although I didn't even know what that had meant for her. Still, there was a sorrow in her eyes, like a deep well, that drew you in. Ruby had clearly taken a shine to her too, and I thought the other girls would as well.

Perhaps it was her sense of stillness, the calm way she had about her. Or the sudden smile that lit up her face; her eyes were a beautiful blue-green, and I'd felt startled by their vividness every time I'd looked at her. She was a little older than me, but her skin was surprisingly smooth, or maybe it was just that her expression was so placid. She'd felt, for that hour, like a good force in my life.

But I still didn't know her at all, and I was wary about inviting a stranger into my home, into my life, even if just for one meal.

So, naturally, were my in-laws, when Ruby gaily informed them that she was coming over for dinner as soon as we got home.

"Who is this person, Nathan?" Elaine turned to me, already aghast, eyes narrowed, lips pursed, ready to judge and, of course, condemn.

"She's a friend of Laura's from where she volunteered, at the refugee help center downtown. I thought the girls might like to meet her, find out a bit about what Laura did there." When I said it like that, it sounded so very reasonable.

"But do you know her at all? Where does she come from?"

"Bosnia, but she's been in the US for nearly twenty years." As if that made her somehow more acceptable to them. Perhaps it did.

"But she's a *stranger...*"

"Laura knew her."

Although I'd had my own misgivings, Elaine's bristling concern made me more resolved to have Maria over. We'd exchanged contact details before saying goodbye, and so, that evening, when I had a rare moment of quiet, I texted her asking her if she'd like to come for dinner on Friday, in two days' time.

She responded within a few minutes, saying that would be lovely, and then I texted her our address. I realized I was looking forward to the evening, even as I suppressed a vague and instinctive sense of unease. Ruby liked her, I reminded myself, and children had a natural instinct for people. Besides, it was just dinner.

Elaine and Paul remained unimpressed by my decision—and, more frustratingly, they *remained*. They showed no sign of returning to their lives in Boston, and the night before Maria was to come to dinner, I found out why.

Ella and Ruby were asleep, Alexa holed up in my study with her phone, as always preferring to be alone, when they cornered me in the kitchen.

"Nathan, we need to talk about the future." Paul was using his serious man-to-man voice, the same tone he used whenever he wanted to talk to me about money. Stupidly, I thought he meant that they would be leaving soon. As much as I'd been relying on their help, I still wanted them gone. Ruby, Ella, Alexa, and I all needed to find our new normal, whatever that could possibly look like, and as hard as I knew it would be to get there.

"All right, Paul." I tried to sound friendly and affable, even though I was tense, tired, and still so emotional. Memories kept lurching up to grab me by the throat; just that afternoon I'd grabbed Laura's shampoo in the shower and the smell of it had nearly sent me to my knees. Even worse, I realized it was almost gone; one of the girls must have been using it. I wondered if I would ever be able to bring myself to buy it again.

"Why don't we sit down?"

So they weren't just telling me their departure date. Warily, I moved to the living room and sat on the sofa. Paul sat opposite me and Elaine hovered, clearly leaving him, as usual, to do the heavy lifting of the conversation.

"It's been nearly a month since Laura's death," Paul said, his voice catching a little. "And I'm sure you need to return to work, to get on with things..."

"Yes, eventually." I'd spoken to Frank and we'd agreed I would come back after Christmas, a little over six weeks on from Laura's death. I couldn't afford to take any more time off, and I thought the routine and regularity might help us all get back on an even keel. But I didn't see what any of that had to do with my in-laws. Surely they wouldn't still be here then.

"It would be very difficult, very demanding, for you to be a single dad to three young girls, Nathan." I never liked it when he used my name; it suggested a familiarity, an intimacy, that we'd never had.

"Would?" I repeated. "It is what it is."

"Yes, of course, but Elaine and I have been thinking... about what's best for you, and, more importantly, what's best for the girls. Those three lovely young granddaughters of ours have to be the priority for all of us."

Something about his phrasing grated on me. They were *my* daughters, and I didn't need reminding about how important they were. Of course I didn't. So I said nothing, biting my tongue to keep from snapping back, and waited to hear what more he had to say.

"And your job is demanding, in and of itself," Paul continued carefully. "The hours you work... Laura said you worked seventy hours a week sometimes." A note of censure had crept into his voice, although I doubted he'd meant it to.

"Sometimes," I allowed. "Obviously that will have to change now." Although I hadn't yet been able to think about how it could. The business still demanded my attention and time, a greedy mistress. And the bills were mounting up... household expenses, the mortgage, the next installment of school tuition due in January... I didn't know how I was going to manage, only that I would have to, somehow.

"Nathan, the girls need attention and care at this critical time," Paul said firmly, the words sounding rehearsed. "They need someone who can be there all the time—for school pickups and sick days, music and ballet lessons, playdates..."

I shifted where I sat, not wanting to betray my ignorance. Ella took swimming lessons, and Ruby did ballet one afternoon a week. Alexa had quit piano last year. I knew all that, but only just, and I didn't know where or when any of it took place. But I would find out.

"And not just those things," Elaine burst in, unable to contain herself, an evangelist for whatever they were going to spring on me. "But they need someone to be there for the afternoons when they're out of sorts... a listening ear... someone to give them a hug when they need it, make cookies with them..."

I thought of our disastrous pancake episode, and then pushed it to the back of my mind. "I can give them a hug," I said. It sounded ridiculous.

"But with your work, Nathan," Paul said quietly, giving me a sad smile, as if to show me how he understood. And he should have—according to Laura, he'd traveled four days out of seven throughout her childhood and had worked through many weekends. He'd been as much, if not more, of an absentee father than I had ever been.

"Plenty of parents work." I still didn't know what they were suggesting, but I was starting to guess. Were they going to relocate to New York? Or, God forbid, ask to move in with us? I knew they meant well, whatever they suggested, just as I knew I would say no. A couple weeks of Paul and Elaine had been hard enough.

"Yes, but in a time such as this? With no help, no backup…?" Paul shrugged, spreading his hands, as if to indicate the futility of it all.

I took a deep breath, trying to suppress my instinctive response of angry self-defence. They meant well, I told myself yet again. They were missing Laura too. And, it was true, I was going to have to find a solution to this rather large problem.

"I suppose I'll have to hire a nanny." Which was an expense I couldn't really afford, but I'd make it happen. Somehow, and without involving either of my in-laws.

"A *nanny*." Elaine couldn't keep the words from coming out in a cry of dismay. Which was ironic, because Laura had had a nanny when she was young, and Elaine hadn't even had a job outside the home.

"Someone to help, at least," I said, as if she had an objection to the word rather than the concept.

"But some *stranger*…"

Which made me think of Maria, for some reason. "I don't know yet, Elaine." I sounded impatient. "I'll figure it out." Soon.

"We have another suggestion." Paul leaned forward, elbows braced on his knees. "A way forward for everyone, and one Elaine and I both think will be best for the girls as well as for you."

"And what is that?" I couldn't keep from sounding chilly.

Paul and Elaine exchanged a tense look, and that was when I realized that they weren't thinking of moving in with me, or even just moving to New York. I braced myself for whatever they planned to say, but when the words came I still wasn't ready for them.

"What if the girls came to live with us?" Paul's voice was oddly gentle. "We have plenty of room, all our time available, and Boston has such good schools. We've already checked and there are places for all three of them at Laura's *alma mater*, one of the best girls' schools in the country. We've spoken to the headmistress and she'd be delighted to welcome them all. Some of the teachers who were there during Laura's time are still teaching. They remember her…"

I stared at him, hardly able to take in what he was saying. "Live with you," I repeated, my voice toneless. "Live in Boston."

"Yes." Paul met my gaze steadily, his chin slightly tilted, as if he knew what he was asking was wrong. It was indecent. *And yet…*

"There's a swim team for Ella's age," Elaine rushed in to fill the silence. "And a pre-kindergarten program for Ruby, half-days. They could each have their own bedroom. We were even thinking of getting a puppy…"

"A puppy?" I couldn't keep the scathing disbelief from my voice. "You mean a bribe."

"Nathan." My name was a warning.

I took a deep breath, willing the rage back, and worse, the hurt. They'd found my weakness, hell, they'd always known it, and they were exploiting it ruthlessly. Again. Once more they were offering my family everything I couldn't give them myself. Time. Space. Even a damn dog. "My daughters stay with me," I said flatly.

"I understand you saying that, wanting it, but think of them, Nathan," Paul urged. "You can't give them what they need right now."

"So this would be a temporary solution?" I asked in a pseudo-pleasant voice. "Or permanent?"

Once again they exchanged a quick look. "It would be important for the girls to have continuity," Paul said after a moment. "Consistency and stability…"

"Meaning you want to take them away from me forever."

"You'd still be their father," Elaine protested. "And, of course, you'd be welcome to visit any time—weekends, holidays…"

"I'd be *welcome*?" I'd be a guest to my own family? And eventually I'd be a stranger, and then I'd be nobody at all. I'd be the father who gave them away.

"This isn't an entirely novel idea," Paul said quietly. "Men in your position have made similar arrangements for centuries. It's accepted, it's understood."

I shook my head, unable even to begin to find the words. As if I wanted some *arrangement*. Didn't they realize that all the hours I worked, everything I did, was *for* my family? To provide for them, to care for them, to give them the opportunities and comforts I'd never had growing up, moved from trailer park to hippy commune to shabby apartment? If they took my girls away, did I have any reason for working at all?

And yet…

And yet, I was, to my own, everlasting shame, the tiniest bit tempted. Just a flicker, but such a terrible, damning one. It could be so *simple*. The girls would be loved. And they'd have things I knew I could never give them, no matter how hard I worked. I couldn't take Ella to her swim lessons, even if I cut back on my hours. We couldn't get a puppy. And I was so very tired…

I hated myself for thinking that way, utterly *despised* my selfishness. Yet I felt it anyway, the siren song of an easier life, or even just a life I could survive. Somehow.

"At least think about it, Nathan," Paul said, once again sensing my weakness, probing it like a loose tooth, checking if it will fall out with just another little push. "I understand why you might be offended by the idea at first, of course I do, and so does Elaine." A quick, quelling look for his wife, who was assuredly determined not to understand it at all. "But, for the girls' sake, please do consider it. Because ultimately we all want what's best for Alexa, Ella, and Ruby." He smiled then, as if to show how we were all in this together, when I knew we damn well weren't.

"The girls stay with me." I spoke flatly, my tone final because the fact that I'd considered their offensive proposal for even a millisecond both haunted and shamed me. What kind of father was I? *What kind of father had I been?*

"Don't say that yet. Please just think about it, Nathan," Elaine pleaded, sounding near tears. "Please. For the girls' sakes…"

And for theirs. I saw that so clearly, how this was a way of dealing with their grief and keeping Laura close. I felt a flicker of pity for them and their pain, but no more.

"I'm not going to think about it," I said stonily. "I'm saying no right now, a thousand times no. I'm not letting you have my children."

"They're Laura's children too," Paul said. His eyes were narrowed, his mouth compressed. He looked angry, but, worse, he looked dangerous. It occurred to me how difficult my in-laws could make my life, now that the gloves were so obviously off. They could plant seeds in the girls' minds, make them *want* to move. They could even sue for custody, and, hell, who knew, maybe they'd win…

"Paul, I'm never going to stop you or Elaine seeing your grandchildren," I said. *Much,* anyway. "But you can't *have* them. They're my daughters. They're all I have left. Besides, uprooting them from the only life they've known is hardly in their best interests. If you really want to do what's best for them, then think about that."

"Do you think we haven't thought very carefully about this?" Paul stood up, looming over me. He was six three, with a solid chest and a full head of white hair, and he scared me a little. He also pissed me off.

"Yes, I do think you've thought it through *very* carefully," I fired back. "You've thought carefully about how to find me at my lowest point, when I'm tired and overwhelmed and grieving, and how to slip the knife right into my ribs—"

"How dare you." Elaine's voice was a high-pitched hiss of outrage.

"How dare *you!*" I retorted, my voice surprisingly level. I felt strangely calm all of a sudden, an icy rage possessing me that kept me cold and clear-headed. "*Think* about what you've suggested to me for one second." I met both of their gazes; neither of them looked away. "How dare you," I repeated quietly. "How dare you."

"We won't stay here now," Elaine proclaimed shrilly as she drew herself up, determined to act in wounded affront, as if I was the one who had instigated all this. "We can't stay here, after you've treated us this way."

I let out a hollow laugh, amazed that, after all this, *she* was the one who felt offended. "Fine," I told her, knowing I was setting fire to my relational bridges and not even caring. "You know where the door is."

"Granny. Granddad. *Dad.*"

I turned to see Alexa standing in the living room doorway, her hair a wild tangle around her face, her eyes huge and dark.

"Why are you all *fighting?*" Her voice wobbled and then broke on the last word.

"Alexa, darling…" Elaine smiled sadly as she held her arms out to her, already playing the tragic victim. "I'm so, so sorry you had to hear this."

"Alexa, honey, it's all right." Paul gave her a comforting smile. "It's going to be all right."

She stared at them both in turn, searching for answers and wanting them to be the ones to give them. Not me. She didn't so much as look at me, at least not until Elaine had given her a hug. Then my daughter turned to me, hazel eyes narrowed to slits, and hissed, "This is *your* fault."

CHAPTER TEN

MARIA

The day of the dinner with the Wests, I was full of trepidation. I could not remember the last time I'd been to someone's house for a meal, not like this. Selma had had me over with her family a few times, and I'd reluctantly agreed, but this felt different. More important, somehow, even as I told myself it had to be less. Just a meal, as some sort of unnecessary thank you, with people who were essentially strangers.

I dithered all day about what to wear, what to bring, how to be. Eventually I settled on a nice sweater and jeans, nothing too dressy. I bought a bouquet of daisies, because I'd always loved their cheerful yellow heads, like smiling faces.

I took the subway from Astoria to midtown, and then the bus up Third Avenue, so I could see the sights, but, of course, it was already getting dark and I didn't see much. Still, I felt the way the city expanded, everything becoming wider, as if the buildings themselves could breathe better, and I could, too.

Nathan—it still felt funny, even in my own mind, to call him that—had told me his address, on Eighty-Third Street off Third Avenue. When I got off the bus, I felt disorientated for a second, unsure which way was which. The bus rattled off in a huff of fumes, and I turned around in a circle, clutching my daisies.

I started walking down the street, only to turn around when I realized I was going the wrong way. Finally, feeling a bit frazzled,

I came to his building, set back from the street with a square of meticulously clipped lawn in front of it and several little white picket signs reading *Please Keep Off the Grass*.

A doorman wearing what looked like a Prussian military uniform opened the door for me as I stepped inside the foyer, breathing in the scents of leather and furniture polish, blinking in the slight gloom.

"Name?" the doorman asked a bit abruptly, and I blurted, "Maria Dzino." He frowned. "I don't think we have anyone by that name here…"

"Oh, I thought you meant my name." I blushed, my bouquet of flowers pressed to my chest so I could feel their damp ends, even through my coat. "I'm here to see Nathan West."

"Right." He called up on the intercom phone, and I waited tensely, afraid even now that it might all be some sort of mistake. That Nathan West hadn't really meant to invite me to his apartment, for a meal. Then the doorman turned and smiled at me. "Go right up—the elevator on the left, fourth floor. The Wests' apartment is on the right side."

"Thank you."

The elevator was as elegant as the rest of the building, with a framed watercolor on the wall and a little leather bench. When the doors opened, I stepped out and saw that there were just two apartments on the floor—and Nathan was already standing in the doorway of the one on the right, Ruby poking her head out behind him.

"Maria." He looked tired, but he smiled. "I'm so glad you could come."

I thrust the flowers at him, a bit suddenly, because I couldn't think of what to do. "For you—"

"How kind of you. Thank you." He took the bouquet as he ushered me into the foyer. Although it was quite a large space, it was cluttered—with heaps of shoes and school bags, the one chair piled with coats, the side table covered with unopened mail. There was a burned smell in the air.

"Daddy burned dinner," Ruby announced. "He doesn't cook."

I smiled down at her, taking in all the endearing features I remembered—the curly reddish hair, the freckles scattered across her nose, the gap between her two baby front teeth. "I'm sure it will taste nice all the same."

"Unfortunately, I doubt it will," Nathan said as he ushered me into the kitchen, a huge room of marble and oak, gleaming granite and stainless steel. "But I did buy some more, although it's all ready-made. Ruby's right; I don't cook. Not yet, anyway." He smiled, but I saw how weary he looked, with deep creases by his eyes and running from his nose to mouth, a haggard set to his features, the unthinking slump of his shoulders. It had been a little less than a month since his wife had died, and I could see every one of those days etched on his face.

Ruby came to stand in front of me, her hands on her hips as she gave me a thorough inspection. I smiled at her, my eyebrows raised, trying to hide my nervousness.

"What have you been doing today, Ruby?" I asked.

"Watching TV. *All* day."

Nathan ducked his head. "I haven't had the usual limits on screen time recently..." he half-mumbled, his gaze on the containers in front of him.

"That is understandable."

"And Granny and Grandad left this morning," Ruby continued. "They were *cross*." This was said with something like relish, which I didn't understand.

"Ruby..." Nathan shook his head, a slight flush on his cheeks. "Don't..."

"You must miss them," I said quickly, to cover any awkwardness. "Will they come back and visit soon?"

Ruby shrugged. "Granny made me eat broccoli. I *hate* broccoli."

"But it's so good for you. It helps you to grow big and strong."

Her lower lip jutted out. "I don't care."

"It's hard to eat things when you don't like them," I commiserated, changing tack. I felt out of my depth already. What did I know of children? "But I'm sure your granny only wanted what was best for you," I added, feeling the need to stick up for vegetables, as well as her missing grandmother. Clearly there was a complicated dynamic there.

Ruby harrumphed and Nathan gave me a grateful smile. "Rubes, why don't you get Ella and Alexa? Tell them Maria is here."

"El-la! Al-exa!" Ruby bellowed, making me jump.

Nathan nudged her between her shoulder blades. "Go *find* them, Ruby."

With another harrumph, she trotted out of the kitchen, in search of her sisters. I glanced around, noting the personal little touches all around that had to have been Laura's: a wilted begonia on the windowsill, some photo magnets on the fridge—I recognized one, from the news. It was the same snap of Laura on the beach, but in this one I could see Alexa and Ella's faces. I saw a mug by the sink with *World's Best Mom* written on it in curly script, an inspirational quote taped to a cupboard, in what I suspected was Laura's loopy handwriting: *Start by doing what's necessary; then doing what's possible; and suddenly you are doing the impossible.*

"Would you like something to drink?" Nathan asked, startling me. I realized how nosy I must have seemed, craning my head around to look at everything. "A glass of wine?"

"Oh…" I hesitated, because this still felt so very strange. Were we friends? Acquaintances? *Strangers?* "Yes, thank you, that would be very nice."

"Your English is very good," Nathan remarked as he poured me a glass of red and handed it to me. I perched on one of the bar stools at the kitchen island. "Did you learn it while you lived in Bosnia, or after you came here?"

"I learned some when I was young. Most schoolchildren do. But mostly here." I took a cautious sip of the wine, enjoying the rich, velvety flavour. I drank alcohol sparingly, and I knew this one glass would go right to my head.

"Well, it's very impressive."

"Thank you."

A silence stretched between us, and I wondered where the girls were. I felt as if I had nothing to say to Nathan, and yet there was so much I wanted to, if only I could find the words, as well as the courage. But twenty years of silence, of suppression, had taken their toll. I couldn't even begin to try, and so I said nothing.

"You must be wondering about my in-laws," Nathan said after a moment. "The cross grandparents Ruby mentioned. We had an argument and they left in a huff. Not ideal."

"Emotions are strong in times like these," I offered cautiously.

"Yes, I suppose, although the truth is we've never got along." He let out a sigh, raking his fingers through his hair, which sprang up messily as he dropped his hand. "They've always resented me."

I wasn't sure how to respond to such a statement, and so I just nodded and took a sip of my wine.

Nathan turned back to the containers whose foil lids he was easing off.

"Sorry. TMI."

"TMI?" I was not familiar with the phrase.

"Too much information." He smiled wryly. "I just didn't want you to wonder."

"It's okay." I smiled uncertainly back, wondering if he had people to talk to, friends to help. Surely a family like the Wests had a whole community around them, people to bring food, offer to babysit, listen when any of them needed to talk. All the things I didn't have any longer, but I assumed everyone else did.

"Ella. Alexa." Nathan's voice took on an overly bright lilt as his two older daughters appeared in the doorway, Ruby pushing her way between them. Alexa was tall and leggy, her auburn hair loose about her shoulders and hanging forward to hide her face. Ella looked like a mini-Laura, with her near-golden hair, her round face and hazel eyes. She wore a dazed, distant expression, not meeting anyone's gaze, almost as if she were inhabiting some other emotional space.

I rose from the stool I'd been sitting on and smiled at them both. "My name is Maria. I'm so pleased to meet you."

Their gazes slid towards me without meeting my eyes and they both nodded their hellos, neither of them saying a word. I felt their grief like a palpable thing in the room, dark and heavy. It made me want to do something to relieve it, but how could I? I knew the weight of it. No one could take it away.

"I'm just going to blast everything in the oven for a sec," Nathan said, "to warm it all up. Alexa, can you get the plates? Ella, silverware?"

The girls moved silently into the room and did as they were told without looking at anyone or saying anything. They reminded me of ghosts, of myself, drifting here and there, halfway to being invisible. Yet right now, to my own surprise and wariness, I did not feel invisible. I felt very much alive.

"Let me help," I said, and I reached out to take a stack of plates from Alexa. For a second, as she handed them to me, she looked right into my eyes—her own were dark pools of pain before her expression smoothed over, turning blank.

I followed Ruby into the dining room, surprised at the difference between it and the kitchen. The walls were papered in cabbage rose wallpaper that was hanging off in peeling strips in some places, and the whole room had a musty, forgotten feel to it, cluttered with dark furniture, dusty velvet drapes in a dark green hiding the windows.

"We haven't got around to decorating this room yet," Nathan answered my silent question. "The apartment was a real mess when we bought it. We're doing it up slowly."

"If by slowly you mean not at all," Alexa interjected. "You did the kitchen and then stopped." There was a thread of anger running through her words, turning them into an accusation.

"Yes, well." Nathan tried for a chuckle, but it sounded more like a rasp. His eyes were pained, his smile forced. "We'll get there."

I laid the plates on the dining room table, Ella following me with the forks and knives, her head bent low so I couldn't see her expression, but I *felt* her sadness.

Oh, these children. They were burrowing into my deadened heart, slipping under its newly cracked shell, without even trying, and it scared me. Then I reminded myself that it could hardly matter, since, after tonight, I would most likely never see them again. That thought did not bring the relief it should have.

"I think we're ready," Nathan announced, as he brought in a tray with various containers of food—pasta and meat in sauce, vegetables with butter and cream, several salads. It was far too much, and his tone was too jolly, as if to make up for the girls' silences, for the sorrow they all clearly felt, enshrouding them in a grey mist.

We sat down and Nathan started serving, the only sound the clink of the spoon against the plates as he dolloped portions around. The girls didn't speak, not even Ruby, and as Nathan took his place the silence continued on, like a heavy, suffocating mantle draped over all of us, binding us together even as it kept us apart.

"Alexa, Ella." Nathan spoke again in a slightly manic way, too determinedly upbeat, his voice too loud. "Maria knew Mom from her volunteering at the refugee center."

Alexa glanced up, her dark gaze skewering me for a second before she looked away. Ella's glance was a bit more friendly.

"Were you friends with her?" she asked shyly.

"Yes," I said, feeling a bit like an impostor. Would she have called me a *friend*? And if she wouldn't have, what was I doing here? "She was very nice. Very kind." Ella's eyes filled with tears and she nodded, looking down at her plate. "She talked about you so often," I added. "She showed me photos. She was so proud of you all. I almost felt as if I knew you, just from the things she said."

"What kinds of things?" Ella looked up again, her expression one of desperate hunger for knowledge.

I hesitated, trying to remember the details, wishing I hadn't made it sound as if it had been more than it was. "Oh, lots of things. How you like swimming, Ella. You're on a team, aren't you? To race?"

"Not yet. Not till January." But Ella was smiling, shyly, and I felt as if I'd given her a gift.

"What about me?" Alexa asked, an aggressive, challenging note in her voice. "Did she say anything about me?"

Panic constricted my throat as I racked my memory for some elusive fact about Alexa that she wanted to hear. All I could think of was Laura rolling her eyes, telling me how Alexa wanted the latest iPhone, and how she wasn't going to get it. How difficult she could be, but how Laura was determined to wait it out.

"I'm sure she did," I said after a moment, when the silence had stretched on too long. "You like math…"

Alexa let out a huff of derisive laughter. "No, I don't."

No, she didn't, I recalled now. She struggled with it, and Laura was thinking about getting her a tutor. I cursed myself for the slip, wanting to try again, but Alexa had already dismissed me with a snort and a shrug of her shoulders, as if she'd just proved I was a liar. Perhaps I was.

I caught Nathan's eye and he gave me a sympathetic smile. *Teenagers,* his smile seemed to say, just as Laura once had.

"What about me?" Ruby demanded. "What did she say about me?"

My hands grew slippery on my fork and knife as I tried to think. What had started out so wonderfully now felt like something disastrous. Why on earth had I tried to impress them all?

"That's enough badgering Maria," Nathan ordered. "She's come here to be with us, not be asked tons of questions."

"I don't mind…" I began feebly, but Nathan was already giving his daughters a stern look in turns.

Everyone descended into a morose silence that felt worse than the questions they'd been asking me. As we continued to eat, I wondered if it would last the whole meal, and I realized I couldn't bear it if it did. I'd had too much silence, too much sadness, in my life already, and these girls were so young, so innocent. I wanted to make them smile; I wanted to help them somehow.

So I did something I hadn't done in years, decades. I turned to Ruby and asked, "Ruby, do you know the story of the boy who talked nonsense?"

Ruby looked at me with a mixture of interest and suspicion. "No…"

"It is a fairy tale from where I come from." One my father had told me, and I had told to others, acting out the parts, relishing the attention, encouraged by his gentle laughter, my mother's soft smile. *Oh, Maria, koka…*

"Where do you come from?" Ella asked, her voice so soft I strained to hear it.

"From a city called Sarajevo, in Bosnia. It's in Europe, across the sea from Italy, near Romania."

The girls all looked at me blankly, and determinedly, not knowing if I was being foolish, reckless, or worse.

I continued, "I thought of this story because it has three sons—just as you are three daughters. And the youngest son, Stefan, talked to animals as if they were people." I paused to gauge their interest, waiting to see if I should go on. No one said anything, but I could tell they were all listening, even Alexa, despite the curtain of hair that hid her face. There was a tense alertness to her that emboldened me.

"Why did he talk to animals?" Ruby asked finally.

"Because he loved them, and he was such a friendly, funny boy. But his poor old father didn't know what to do with Stefan. Such a silly boy, for who talks to animals as if they are people? And yet the animals loved him. When he came near, the horses whinnied and the pigs squealed and the cows rubbed their soft noses against his shoulder."

"What about his brothers?" Ella asked in her soft voice. "What did they do? Were they special?"

"Ah, were they special!" Quickly I expanded the story for both her and Alexa's sakes. "Mihailo, the oldest boy, was so clever and smart. The father decided he would be a priest. And Jakov, the second boy, well, if he wanted a particular item you had, he would offer you something for it, and whatever you took from him would be worth less than what you had. He was…" I struggled to think of the word. "*Vjest.* Crafty. His father decided he would be a peddler."

"What's a peddler?" Ruby asked.

"Someone who sells things," Alexa said, and then gave me a quick, darting look, as if seeking confirmation.

I nodded exuberantly, expanding to inhabit this role of childhood—the storyteller, the entertainer, the clown. It was like an old outfit I put on, only to find to my surprise that it fit me again, just as it always had, comfortable and worn in all the right places as I twirled about, stroking the fabric, savouring the fit. "Yes, you have it exactly. Someone who sells things. And what a profit he turned! He made money like a baker makes bread. His father was very proud of both of his sons."

"Not Stefan?" Ruby sounded put out, and I turned to her with a smile, daring to gently chuck her under the chin; her skin was petal-soft.

"Ah, Stefan! Stefan worked as hard as two men, and his laugh was the jolliest sound in the whole village. Ha! Ha! Ha! But this nonsense he talked, to animals and everyone! No one understood it. What was the father to do about that?"

I could tell I had all their attention now, and so I continued the folk tale from my childhood, embroidering details, taking my time, finding and keeping the flow as naturally as I had as a child, with the same exuberance and energy, neither of which I'd felt in decades, but which filled me like air in a sail, expanding and expanding inside me, making me feel as if I could float.

I told them about silly Stefan and his joyful nonsense, and then the grumpy old tsar whose daughter had had too much of books and learning, and only wanted to laugh and enjoy life, as she should.

I pretended to be the tsar in his fusty outrage, blowing out my cheeks as I exclaimed, "Wow! Wow! Wow!" every time his daughter, the princess, made some complaint or misbehaved, because she was tired of being shut up with her books. When Alexa smiled faintly the second time I did it, my heart sang. The third time, Ruby laughed. I glanced at Nathan, and saw he was smiling too, watching his daughters' reactions.

As everyone finished their dinner, I came to the end of the story, when the princess forced the tsar to hold a contest to see who could make her laugh, with a prize of three bags of gold. And then Stefan came to the palace and told his nonsense to the princess, who finally had a reason to laugh, and he even made the old tsar laugh too.

"And of course they lived happily ever after," I finished with a smile for everyone, a deep satisfaction stealing through my bones. "Because it's only a story, after all."

My words seemed to fall into the stillness and settle there, like snow.

"Yes," Alexa said after a moment, a hard edge entering her voice again, making me falter. "Only stories have happy endings." She rose from the table in a swirl of hair, and I bit my lip, wishing I hadn't ended it that way, afraid I had made it worse.

"Life has more shades than a story," I said quietly. "Happy and sad and everything in between." Or so it should. For others, it had no shades at all.

She gazed at me for a moment, and I thought she might say something, but then she simply shrugged and walked out of the room. Nathan watched her go, a frown puckering his brow, before he turned to me with a determined smile.

"Maria, that was marvellous. You're a born storyteller. What a gift."

"It has been a long time since I've told a story." I felt breathless from the exertion of it, the emotion and energy still fizzing inside me. Even Alexa's anger couldn't keep me from remembering that old joy. For a few minutes, it had felt as if I had come alive again, as if I were the girl I'd once been, the one I had buried so long ago.

"Will you tell us another one?" Ruby asked and I smiled and shook my head, trying to banish the lingering disappointment at Alexa's abrupt exit.

"Then I would be the only one talking! Why don't you tell me a story?"

Ruby pouted. "I don't know any stories."

"I'm sure you have some in your room. You could get one and then I could read it to you." Ruby's face lit up and she scurried off, returning moments later with a bright yellow book. "*Curious George*," I read aloud. "I don't know this one."

"You don't know *Curious George*?" Ruby said in disbelief. "I thought everyone did."

"Now I will find out."

As I opened the book, Ruby scrambled onto my lap, shocking me with her nearness, the solid warmth of her. Her head fit under my chin, her body pressed against me as her thumb found its way into her mouth. Shyly, Ella came over, to stand behind my chair, so she could look at the pictures in the book.

For a moment I could not speak; my vision blurred and I could not see the words on the page in front of me. If I could hold onto this moment forever, cup it between my hands, drink it in like living water, I would. Oh, how I would.

Gently, I put my arm around Ruby as I began to read.

CHAPTER ELEVEN

NATHAN

The apartment was quiet, the girls all asleep. Although the evening had started strained, with Ella so silent and Alexa in one of her moods, it ended on an upbeat note, thanks to Maria.

I sank onto the sofa, gazing unseeingly in front of me as I recalled the animation that had lit her features when she'd begun that folktale, as if she were drawing on some light from within. It wasn't until she'd told the story that I realized how sad she'd seemed before, a sorrow that was quiet and contained rather than wild and stormy, the way Alexa's was. The way mine felt, even if I tried to hide it.

Laura, why? How? What do I do with all this grief? How can I contain it? How can I go on?

Tonight, for a little while at least, I had almost been able to forget. Not really, not for more than a few seconds at a time, but those brief moments had been such a relief, such a *liberation.* Then I'd remember, and it felt like being pulled under, having to drown all over again, the grief sucking me down, making me gasp for air.

Still, overall, despite its ups and downs, it had been a good evening. I held onto that thought, let it bolster me. After Maria had read a story to Ella and Ruby, she'd risen from her seat and started to clear the table. To my shame, that had been a liberation, too—someone else was doing the work, if just for a moment.

My in-laws had helped, of course, but it had always been long-suffering, with pointed looks and drawn-out sighs, and I'd tripped over myself to thank them for so much as rinsing a plate. This felt different. Easier.

"Maria, you don't have to…" I'd begun, far too half-heartedly.

"I don't mind." She'd given me a quick, tentative smile. "It is nice, a table full of food and plates."

It took me a second to understand what she meant. "You live alone?" I'd surmised.

"Yes. For a long time." She'd bowed her head as she sidled past me, into the kitchen, where she set about scraping plates and bundling away the foil containers. I watched, transfixed and grateful, as she asked Ella to collect glasses and Ruby napkins. She made it a game, and soon the girls were racing in and out of the dining room with their "treasure"—crumpled napkins and dirty cups. I heard Ella giggle, the sound slipping out of her like an afterthought, and I realized I hadn't heard her laugh since Laura.

Since Laura. And there was a memory again, slamming into me. How many times would I have to take it, and try to stay standing? As Maria had cleaned up the kitchen, I knew I should help and yet I felt so tired that I simply sank onto a stool and watched as she moved around the space, briskly tidying away the mess I never seemed to get on top of.

The table cleared, Ella and Ruby had gone into the living room, sprawling on the sofa in front of the TV. I'd listened to the tinny theme song of some brainless kids show or other, the soundtrack to our lives recently. I told myself to go in there and spend time with them, or find Alexa and try to prise her out of her angry shell, figure out why she seemed to blame me for everything, but at that moment I felt too tired, too utterly drained, to do either. So I simply sat and watched Maria clean my kitchen.

"I'm sorry," I said after about fifteen minutes. I felt as if I'd been lulled to sleep by the simple presence of her, her movements so neat and efficient as she tidied everything away. "I'm being a terrible host." *And a bad father.*

"Not at all." Maria hung a damp dishrag over the oven rail. "I have enjoyed this."

"Cleaning?" I couldn't keep the disbelief from my voice.

"Cleaning a home." She'd looked away, and I'd wondered whether to ask her about her life, her past. I knew basically nothing—she came from Sarajevo; she'd emigrated to America. She was alone. Broad strokes, but what about the finer details? What had her life been like in Sarajevo during the war? Hadn't there been a siege in the city? How had Maria coped? I didn't even know what questions to ask.

I remembered seeing stuff about the war on the news when I'd been a kid, news stories of humanitarian aid packages, pictures of bombed-out buildings and piles of rusted cars, but in truth I hadn't been all that bothered by it. It had seemed so far away. Irrelevant, even, happening to people who didn't matter to me. It could have been happening on the moon. But Maria had *lived* through that.

It seemed unimaginable… as unimaginable as my wife being shot by a madman on the subway. Tragedy bound us together. Laura did.

"Still…" I'd nodded towards the now sparkling countertops. "You didn't have to…"

"I am happy to help. It is very little, after all."

"Did Laura say anything else to you?" I blurted. I realized we hadn't talked about Laura all evening, and it made me feel guilty. "Did she ever mention anyone or anything, someone who was bothering her, following her…?"

Maria had frowned. "You mean the man…"

The man. The man who killed my wife. My gut clenched hard and I felt that ever-present tide of powerless rage swell up inside me. *Why* hadn't the police found the bastard yet? Why did no one know anything, despite there being a subway car full of witnesses?

"Yes," I said flatly. "The man."

Maria reached one hand towards me, her fingers fluttering, her face crumpled in apology. "Nathan…"

"I'm sorry." I dug the heels of my hands into my eye sockets until I saw flashing lights. "I didn't mean to sound…"

"It's all right," she said quietly. "I understand." And I knew she did.

Ruby came in then, her voice a plaintive wheedle. "Daddy…"

Maria still wasn't looking at me. "What is it, Rubes?"

"Can Maria put me to bed?"

Maria turned back, startled. "I should go…"

"*Please…*"

"I don't mind if you tuck her in," I said awkwardly. "If you don't." I couldn't tell if she wanted to go, or if she felt as if she was intruding, and the truth was, I wasn't ready for her to leave. I didn't want to be alone.

"All right," she said softly, and something in me breathed easier as she left the kitchen hand in hand with Ruby, and I went to find Alexa, in what I knew would be a futile attempt to get her to talk to me.

She was still blaming me for everything, from Laura's death to her grandparents leaving, and I couldn't get her to tell me why. Her anger was like a shield, a defence against the person she'd decided was the enemy—me.

Still, I tried, if only half-heartedly, pausing in the doorway of her room. As usual, she was huddled on her bed, crouching over her phone, hair swinging down.

"Alexa…" She didn't even look up. I'd hesitated, not knowing what to say. How to reach her. This was Laura's territory, picking her way through the emotional minefields, defusing the bombs. "You okay?" I finally asked.

"Fine."

Of course she wasn't fine. No one was. I shouldn't have even asked; it was a stupid question.

"Do you have homework?" I asked, feeling like that was another wrong question.

"I've done it."

"Phone goes on the charger at nine," I said, and she finally looked up.

"Oh, so now you're enforcing Mom's rules?"

"They were my rules too."

She snorted her derision, and I wished I could have started the whole conversation over. Now I sounded like a nag.

"It's for your benefit, Alexa." Another misstep.

"Yeah, right. It's for *your* benefit, because you want to seem like you're a good parent when you're crap. Who are you trying to impress? *Maria?*"

I stepped back, winded by the vitriol in every syllable of that sentence. It was the most she'd said to me in weeks, and it hurt, a lot.

"Alexa…" I began, but I didn't know what to say. *Don't talk to me like that?* That would hardly help. "I'm sorry," I finally said quietly. "I am trying. I know it's not enough…"

If I'd been hoping for some sort of apology, a Hallmark-worthy *I know you are, Dad*, I didn't get it. I got another snort, and she was already back on her phone. I was tempted to snatch it from her flying fingers and throw it out the window, or grind it under my foot, hear the satisfying crunch of glass. Who was she texting? What was she saying? Who was comforting her in a way that I couldn't seem to?

I drew a steadying breath, knowing none of that would help, or maybe I just wasn't brave enough to actually do it and face her wrath. At least then she would be angry for a reason I could understand.

"Nine," I'd said at last, and I left the room, closing the door behind me a little more firmly than I should have, feeling like the whole conversation had been a failure.

Maria left a little while later, thanking me again for dinner, although I was the one who should have been thanking her for everything. I still didn't want her to go, and I fought the urge to make up a reason for her to stay longer, because I knew it would seem strange and there was no real reason for her to stay. Besides, it was nearly nine; I needed to wrestle Alexa's phone off her and Maria had to get all the way back to Queens.

"I'm glad you came," I'd said, and she'd smiled shyly.

"So am I." A pause as we stared at each other, the oddness of the moment making it feel impossible to navigate. "Goodbye," she said softly, and it sounded far too final, because of course it was.

"Maria…" I took a step forward, but she was already edging towards the door, and with a jolt of humiliation I realized how grasping and needy I must have seemed, this widowed, grieving man begging a virtual stranger to come into his life and make things better. Clean his kitchen and tuck his daughter into bed, even. Alexa was right. I *was* crap. "Goodbye," I'd said, and then she was gone.

Alone now, with the girls finally in bed, the kitchen thankfully clean and Alexa's phone safely on the charger, the apartment felt too quiet all around me.

In what was now another lifetime, on a night like this, I would have hauled out my laptop and done two or three hours of work—catching up on emails, going over building plans, or just surfing online for industry news.

Laura would have been pottering around, getting cereal bowls out for the morning, or sitting next to me watching something on TV. We wouldn't have said much to each other, but she would have *been* there. I missed her easy, comfortable presence with a deep, physical ache. And yet…

Other memories forced their way in, ones I didn't want to remember. My tut of irritation as I asked her to turn the volume down. The way she drifted around the apartment before asking me if I *had* to work. And my answer was yes, of course I did. The soft sigh of disappointment she seemed to make without realizing it, that I always pretended not to hear.

But it hadn't always been like that, I told myself. I hadn't checked out every single evening.

I grabbed the remote and started flicking through my account on Netflix, looking for the last movie we'd watched together, suddenly needing to know what it was. I scrolled through movies and series I didn't recognize, that Laura must have watched on her own. They surprised me—serious movies, docudramas, not the light fluff I assumed she watched.

Then I found it—an episode of a spy series that had been more my choice than hers. Staring at its lurid icon on the screen, I could almost feel her head on my shoulder, the lemony smell of her hair, her warm body pressed to mine, legs tucked up under her on the sofa.

Should we open a bottle of wine? Her voice light, teasing, and my response, a shrug, a smile. *Sure, why not? It's Friday.*

We'd drunk the whole bottle, cuddled up on the sofa together. Was I remembering it, or making it up? Wishing it had happened? Longing for it now?

Oh, Laura.

I rose from the sofa to pace the living room like something caged. Although I was glad my in-laws had left, at least their presence had acted as a buffer between me and my grief, just as Maria had.

Now, in these dark, empty moments, I had to face it, face the yawning loneliness all around me, and I couldn't stand it. I felt like screaming, or clawing at my skin, anything to end this agony, this endless parade of moments and memories racing through my mind, the fear and panic lapping at my senses.

The comfort I chose was predictable as well as pathetic—a large Scotch and a couple of sleeping pills, my usual night-time routine since Laura's death. I stretched out in the big bed, hating the empty expanse next to me, and let oblivion claim me, my only solace.

When I woke, it was to Ruby standing about two inches from my face.

"Daddy, why do you smell so bad?"

I rolled onto my back as I tried to blink the grit out of my eyes. My body felt leaden, my mind fuzzy. The alarm clock's red digits blurred in front of my eyes and I blinked again. 5:23 a.m. I should not have drunk that whiskey.

"Ruby..." My voice came out in a thick mumble. "You should go back to bed."

"I don't want to."

"It's early."

"Can I sleep with you?"

Wordlessly I lifted the duvet and she scrambled in next to me, fitting her small, warm body to mine. I wrapped one arm around her, pressing my cheek against her hair. She snuggled in closer.

"An open sandwich," she said, sounding satisfied.

"Right." My voice sounded rusty. I didn't want an open sandwich. I didn't want any of this. But this was what I had.

I tried to doze, but Ruby kept wriggling next to me, and then she started to hum some song from a kids' TV show, and by half past six I gave up my desperate attempt to grab some more sleep. Ruby, sensing her victory, rolled over to look at me.

"Daddy, it's going to be Christmas soon."

"So it is." Christmas was in just over two weeks, which seemed both crazy and awful. I couldn't imagine anything I wanted to celebrate less.

"We don't even have a tree yet." Ruby's lower lip jutted out mutinously.

With a rush of dread, I thought of the tidal wave of expectations that Christmas inevitably set—a tree, decorations, presents, stockings, food. That sense of expectation and wonder that Laura had seemed to manage effortlessly; she'd loved Christmas as much as the girls, while I, like with so much else, could take it or leave it.

I'd never celebrated Christmas as a kid. My mother claimed she didn't see the point of presents. *You should give freely whenever you wish,* she'd said, except she hadn't given presents any other time of year, either.

When I'd met Laura, she'd introduced me to concepts I'd only seen in cheesy films—leaving a cookie out for Santa, stockings heaped with what I privately thought was useless crap, a dining room table bowing under the weight of a meal no one could possibly eat all of. Her parents *adored* Christmas, and we'd spent several painful ones with them, while they'd lavished gifts on Laura, and looked at me like some inferior alien species for not really getting it. I'd always received a twenty-five-dollar gift card to Amazon, that Elaine handed me in a bow-wrapped box with a little shrug of shoulders.

I never know what to get you, Nathan, and since you don't really celebrate Christmas...

When our girls had arrived, I'd started to see the point a bit more. I'd got into the spirit of it, at least a bit. One year I had even dressed up as Santa. Still, over the years, Laura had pretty much done everything for the holiday; I usually swanned in on Christmas Eve with a Phillips screwdriver and a smile and spent half an hour putting some toy or other together and considered it a job well done.

I could not conceive of doing all of it—*any* of it—myself this year. I just wanted to pretend Christmas wasn't happening. And what about Paul and Elaine? We usually visited them in Boston for the week after Christmas. I doubted that was going to happen this year, but I suspected they'd still want some involvement, something else I didn't want to face.

"*Daddy.*" Ruby tugged on my T-shirt. "Can we get a tree today?"

"A tree…" It wasn't such an onerous request. We usually bought one from a lot a few blocks away, on First Avenue. That was my provenance, at least; I took the girls with me and, when we got back, Laura would have hot chocolate and home-made donuts ready. Ruby licked the sugar off those last year as well, I recalled. Laura would put on Christmas music while we decorated the tree, Ruby gleefully throwing handfuls of tinsel about…

My throat thickened and I had to close my eyes. It was going to be so different this year, even if I got the tree. Even if I tried to do it all, which I knew I couldn't. It was going to be different; it was going to be *hard*.

"Daddy…?" Ruby tugged on my shirt again.

"Yes, Rubes?"

"Can we go today? Pleeeeease?"

"Maybe." It wasn't even 7 a.m. The day, like every other since Laura's death, felt endless, something to slog through until I could drink my whiskey and go to sleep. Was this what the rest of my life was going to look like? I couldn't imagine anything else. I could barely picture making it to this evening, much less a week from now, a month from now, *Christmas*.

"*Daddy.*" Another tug; I had to strive to keep from sounding irritable.

"What *is* it, Ruby?"

"Can Maria come with us?"

CHAPTER TWELVE

MARIA

After spending the evening with the Wests, my apartment felt small and silent and empty. I drifted around the tiny space, resenting everything about it—the cheap furniture, the bland walls, the lack of photos or pictures or knick-knacks, anything to make it seem more like mine.

I knew it was my own fault, a deliberate choice I'd made years ago not to live in a space that brought up memories, or made me care—except it hadn't felt like a choice, just a way to cope. The reflection of my inner life, or lack of it. Now, to my own surprise, I disliked the fact that I might as well have been inhabiting a budget suite in the Holiday Inn for the last twenty years.

I was forty years old and I'd spent the last twenty-six years as a ghost. I hadn't known how to be anything else, but right then I wanted to feel alive again, the way I had when I'd told that story, brimming with emotion, with laughter.

Already I felt myself waking up, wanting more, and it *hurt*. It made me restless; it made me want things I hadn't even dreamed of. And it made me miss things. People. I sat in my little living room and pictured Petar at the piano, the music floating through the room. I saw my father lift his head from his book and smile in peaceful approval. I saw my mother come in, put her hand on my shoulder.

Had any of it really happened like that? It seemed so far away, so impossible. Then I pictured other, more recent things that felt just as impossible.

I recalled the warm weight of Ruby in my lap, Ella's hand on my shoulder. I remembered sitting on the edge of her bed, singing a Bosnian lullaby to her as her eyes drifted closed. It had all been so unbearably, achingly sweet—a life lived in a single evening, a *what if* that would never happen.

And now I was back to my real life, the reality of work, home, solitude, *loneliness*. It was what I'd had to choose; it was all I knew. And for the first time in over twenty years, I didn't want it.

So when Nathan phoned me the next afternoon, asking if I wanted to help them decorate their Christmas tree later that day, I said yes. Unthinkingly, hurriedly, only knowing I wanted to see them all again. Even if it still felt a little strange, a bit dangerous. Even if I wondered why they wanted someone like me in their lives.

"I get off work at five," I said. "Is that too late?"

"No, no, of course not. But only if you don't mind…"

"I don't mind." I spoke too quickly, embarrassing myself. It was obvious I had nothing else going on, but it seemed as if the Wests didn't, either.

"Who was that?" Neriha asked when I'd finished the call and went back to my station in the salon to tidy up. "A big date?" She was teasing; she knew I never dated. Never would.

"No, it was a friend." I paused, reluctant to admit who it was, but it was clear Neriha was curious and waiting for more. "Nathan West."

"Nathan West…" She frowned, the name not registering, and then her expression cleared before clouding again. "The man whose wife was shot on the subway, you mean? Him?"

"Yes."

She shook her head, looking surprised and a bit suspicious. "How do you know him?"

"You know his wife worked at Global Rescue…" She nodded, unimpressed. "He came by one day, wanting to talk to me, because he knew we were friends." I tested the word out, tasted it on my tongue. *Friends*. Yes.

Neriha frowned. "And you think that is a good idea?"

"Why shouldn't it be?" I sounded defensive.

"I just don't understand what he has to do with you."

I stiffened at that, because I didn't understand it either. Why did Nathan continue to invite me to his home, into his *family*? Surely he had people better placed, part of his own community, to help or spend time with them? "We're friends." I did not sound convincing, even to myself. How could we be friends?

"*Friends?*" Neriha arched one dark eyebrow. "Come on, Maria."

"What?"

"We're not friends with people like that."

I folded my arms across my chest, abandoning my half-hearted attempt at tidying up. "What is that supposed to mean?"

Neriha shrugged. "You know."

I didn't respond, because the trouble was, I *did* know. What did I have in common with Nathan West or his family besides grief? Their Upper East Side life, their private schools and moneyed vacations, the sense of privilege they didn't even know they had.

But what did any of that matter? It was just money. And yet, money aside, I knew I was still different, that I would always be different, no matter how much I might try to blend in. Unlike Neriha, a fellow Bosniak who immersed herself in the local Bosnian-American community, who preferred to speak Bosnian to English, and who found meaning in being with people who understood what she'd been through, I'd separated myself. I didn't *want* to be Bosniak, even though I knew I always would be. It was being Bosniak that had ruined my life.

It had always been this way in the Bosnian immigrant community: people who wanted to fit in, and people who didn't. People who wanted to remember and those who had to forget. People who had learned to hate, and people who were trying to love.

And then there was me—isolated and alone, because I didn't know how else to be. Because I couldn't bear the thought of opening myself up to anything—life, love, joy, pain. And yet here I was, wanting to see Nathan West and his children again. Perhaps the fact that he was so different made it safer, separate from my reality. It was never going to amount to anything, which was both a painful reminder and a needed reassurance.

I could hardly explain any of that to Neriha. I barely understood it myself. All I knew was I wanted to go to Nathan's apartment this evening and help decorate their Christmas tree. I *was* going.

It was snowing as I took the bus uptown, enjoying the sight of the fat, white flakes that drifted down, cloaking the city in gentle white, softening everything and turning it beautiful, hiding the ugliness.

The doorman waved me up without asking my name, which gave me a silly little burst of pleasure. I was *known.*

When I knocked on their apartment door, I heard an excited squeal, and then the sound of feet pounding down the hall. Ella threw open the door, with Ruby trying to elbow her out of the way.

"We got a tree!" Ella said, looking more animated than I'd ever seen her.

"I can't wait to see it." I stepped into the warmth of the apartment; already I was buzzing in a way I never was in my real life, simply by being here.

Ruby wrapped her arms around my knees, burrowing her head into my legs, and I laughed and touched her hair.

"Ruby, are you happy to see me? I am happy to see you."

Then Nathan came around the corner, looking hassled and tired, although he tried to smile. "We bought the tree... I'm just trying to put it up now."

"And it's *snowing* outside," Ella said, her voice full of wonder.

"Yes, look." I held out my scarf to them, the snowflakes that had been caught in the wool still glittering. "The first snow of the year."

"Did it snow where you used to live?" Ella asked as they pulled me along the hallway towards the living room.

"Yes, it snowed a great deal up in the mountains there. In winter we would go to a resort in Jahorina. You could ski, sled, snowshoe..." A memory flitted through my mind like a butterfly, skimming away before I could hold onto it—Petar pulling me on a sled, the snow deep and powdery and dazzling white. I was crying because I was cold, and so he pulled faster and I fell off, making me cry harder. Petar had picked me up, brushed the snow off my face, before carrying me the rest of the way home, pulling the sled with his other hand.

"Here's our tree!" Ruby exclaimed as I came into the living room.

The room was in just as sad a state as the dining room, with ugly olive-colored flocked wallpaper and brown-painted woodwork. A tree stood in the corner, listing heavily to one side.

"I need to get some twine," Nathan said. "Tie it on one side to straighten it..."

"And then we can start decorating!" Ruby exclaimed.

"Ah, the best part." I smiled at them all, filled with a fragile sense of bonhomie, as thin and translucent as a spiderweb, so easily broken and yet so beautiful.

"The best part is hot chocolate and donuts," Ella told me. "Mom always..." She trailed off uncertainly, and I smiled at her.

"Your mother made you hot chocolate and donuts? Lucky girl."

"Yes." She blinked rapidly. "Yes."

"And Daddy said we could have them today," Ruby added with a challenging look for her father.

Nathan gave me a quick, harassed smile. "Courtesy of Dunkin Donuts, I'm afraid."

"Well, that's all right, then."

But, of course, it wasn't. It wasn't the same, and both Ella and Ruby knew that, even if they were trying to make the best of it and be excited. I'd done the same as a child, when the electricity and water had gone off for weeks at a time, when there had been nothing to eat but tinned ham and dried prunes, when we'd tried again and again to make the best of it and laughed all the while, even as our hearts ached.

Until I couldn't do that anymore, because there was no best of anything.

"Where's Alexa?" I asked, and Ella shrugged.

"She's in her room."

"She doesn't want to decorate the tree," Ruby stated matter-of-factly.

Nathan gave me another grimace.

"She's in a bit of a mood." I nodded my understanding. "She might listen to you," Nathan continued hopefully. "If you wanted to ask her to come out…" He trailed off, ducking his head.

"I can try," I said after a moment, because I didn't know what else to say. I didn't want to try, and I didn't think Alexa would want me to, either. Surely she wanted to be left alone—just as I had wanted to be left alone, for years upon years. Yet how much had I missed, as a result? And I did not want Alexa to miss this, a seemingly small moment, but one that I knew would be important, could be a beginning.

"Come on," I said to Ruby and Ella. "Show me where her room is."

Looking both hesitant and intrigued, they led me to a door off the apartment's main hallway that was firmly closed. I knocked on it once.

"Alexa? It is me, Maria. May I come in?"

A grunt was my reply, but at least it was not a no.

Gently I pushed open the door and stepped into the room. It was dark, the light turned off and the windows, which faced the next building, letting in very little natural light, the view a brick wall just a few feet away. It was also a mess—a rumpled duvet heaped on the bed, clothes scattered over the floor, makeup across the bureau top. A stale smell of cheap perfume and unwashed body hung in the air.

"Ugh. I don't like it in here," Ruby announced as she backed away, making a face.

Alexa, huddled on her bed, threw her younger sister a malevolent look. "Who asked you?"

Ella slipped out of the room as well; I could understand why both girls avoided their older sister. Alexa radiated a sullen rage, from the curtain of greasy hair covering her face to her hunched position, her thumbs flying over the screen of her phone.

Out of habit, I picked up a school sweater off the floor and began to fold it, before changing my mind and putting it in the clothes hamper in the corner. "You do not wish to decorate the Christmas tree?"

Alexa gave me an unfriendly look before turning back to the phone. "No."

"Because it won't be the same?" I spoke calmly, and her lips trembled before she pressed them together.

"No. It won't."

"Of course it won't," I agreed, gentling my voice. I felt as if I were feeling my way through the dark, and yet at the same time meaning every word I said. "How could it? Nothing will ever be the same again."

Tears pooled in her eyes, turning them glassy, as she nodded.

Carefully I sat on the edge of the bed, wondering at myself and the wisdom I offered. Was I in any place—did I have any right—to try to comfort this child? Did I even know what she wanted or needed to hear?

"There is a saying in my country," I began after a moment. "*Hrabar čovek retko povreden u leđima.*" Alexa looked at me blankly. "A brave man is seldom hurt in the back," I translated quietly. "It is hard to go forward, into this unknown future that you didn't ask for. It is also brave."

Alexa shook her head. "I don't want to."

"I understand." I rose from the bed, deciding not too push too much, knowing this had to be in her own time. "But if you change your mind, there will be hot chocolate and donuts in the kitchen." I smiled and dared to pat her shoulder, amazed at my boldness. What was it about these children that allowed me to speak and act in ways I never had before? Was it how I saw myself reflected in their pain and bewilderment? Or was it that they fulfilled a need and deeply held desire in me that I'd never been willing or brave enough even to admit, that was now forcing itself out into the light, like some tender, green shoot? I smiled at Alexa and then left, gently closing the door behind me.

Back in the living room, Nathan had righted the tree and Ella and Ruby were taking decorations out of a cardboard box.

"Careful, Ruby," Ella scolded. "They're special."

"I know that," Ruby snapped, and then a shiny gold bauble slipped from her fingers and crashed onto the floor, splintering into a thousand tiny, glittering fragments.

"I told you!" Ella shouted. "You're so stupid!"

Ruby's face turned red with fury as her eyes filled with tears. "I hate you!"

"Girls!" Nathan's tone was ineffectual, his face bewildered.

"That one wasn't so special, eh?" I said as I stooped to brush the fragments into my hands; one caught and snagged on my thumb, drawing a tiny droplet of blood that I quickly dabbed away. "Look, there are three more in the box, just the same."

Ruby sniffed and peered into the box, while Ella glowered. "Mom bought those last year."

"There are lots," Ruby said. "Even more than three." She held up two more gold baubles, tear-streaked and triumphant.

"They're all special," I told Ella. "But some more than others, yes? Why don't you show me your favorite?"

Ella dug through the box before she found a pine cone sprinkled with red glitter. "I made this in preschool."

I took it from her and held it up to the light so the glitter sparkled. "It's beautiful."

"I made one too," Ruby declared, and started searching through the box.

"Yours is in the kitchen, Rubes," Nathan said. He sounded so tired. "You made it just last week."

Ruby ran off to find it, and Nathan smiled at me.

"Thank you," he said quietly. "Alexa…?"

"In her own time."

He nodded, and I wished I could have comforted him as I seemed to his children. He looked so sad.

"Shall I make the hot chocolate?" I asked after a moment, unsure if I was presuming.

Ella perked up. "Do you know how to make it?"

"I think I can."

"And what about donuts?" she asked hopefully. "So we don't have to get them from the store? Could you make them here?"

"Ella, Maria's here to decorate, not to cook…" Nathan began in his half-hearted way, leaving the decision up to me, as he often seemed to.

"I can make donuts," I said quietly. "If you want me to." The last thing I wanted to do was to try to take Laura's place in any way.

"You can?" Nathan looked startled, as if I'd just declared I could perform brain surgery. It almost made me smile.

"Yes, kroffie!" Ruby exclaimed as she ran back into the room with her precious pine cone. "Remember?"

"*Krofne,*" I corrected her gently. "Yes."

"But not with marmalade. Yuck!"

"Yuck," I agreed with a little laugh.

Ruby's face lit up. "Could you make it with chocolate inside?"

Could I? For a second I felt disorientated, as if I didn't know where or even who I was. Once I'd made *krofne* with my mother, and now I might with this little girl. A simple act, yet one laden with so much memory and meaning, time turning over on itself, a circle when I thought it had been a terrible, never-ending line.

"Maria?" Ella took hold of my hand. "Can you? Please?"

I looked down at her, blinking her into focus as worlds collided and then came apart again. "Let's go see what there is in the kitchen," I said, as Ruby slipped her hand into my other hand. As we started out of the room, I turned to Nathan. "Do you want to help?"

He gave a lopsided smile, his gaze sliding away. "I think the tree needs a bit more securing, so it doesn't fall down again."

It felt like an excuse, but who was I to say? I nodded, and the three of us left the room.

The kitchen was a mess, as it had been before, and I tidied it up as Ella and Ruby got out sacks of flour and sugar, spilling some in their excitement, so eager to begin this little adventure.

All the ingredients were there; Laura had clearly done lots of baking. There was a whole shelf in the walk-in pantry dedicated to it, and I ran my fingers along a stack of cupcake cases, the half-filled box of icing sugar, wondering when she'd last used them.

Had she baked with Ella and Ruby, as I was about to now? The possibility made me want to shiver, almost as if I could feel her presence, here in her own kitchen, a whisper of her breath as I closed the pantry door. What would she think of me being here?

Together we measured the flour and yeast, sugar and milk and water, Ella and Ruby both so endearingly intent.

"We need to let it sit," I instructed them. "Until it bubbles. Ruby, can you tell me when it bubbles? Ella, when it's ready, you can add the eggs."

"Can I add an egg?" Ruby asked eagerly. "Mommy always let me add the eggs."

"There are two," I assured her. "One for each of you."

They peered at the mixture, standing on their tiptoes, elbows on the counter as they gazed down at it. My heart stretched and expanded, cracked vessel that it was. It felt painful and good, like muscles that hadn't been used in a long while. It *felt*.

"Hey." I looked up to see Alexa standing in the doorway, winding a strand of hair around one finger. "What are you doing?"

"Making donuts." I smiled tentatively. "Do you want to help?"

Alexa looked at us all standing together, her eyes narrowing, and then wordlessly she turned around and left the kitchen with a swish of her hair. Ella and Ruby both glanced at me questioningly, and I pushed the unreasonable needle-prick of hurt I felt aside. Alexa was grieving, and I was nobody to her. A stranger still, and perhaps I always would be. These moments with the Wests—that's all they were. Moments. I had to remember that. I had to keep reminding myself.

Then Ruby grabbed my arm. "Look," she exclaimed. "It's bubbling!"

CHAPTER THIRTEEN

NATHAN

Christmas was quiet. I did my best, buying the girls each a couple of presents, although admittedly they'd picked them out themselves online because I had absolutely no idea what they would want, or even what they already had.

"Mommy didn't do it this way," Ruby told me accusingly, after she'd selected some glittery plastic ponies, and I had no answer. There were a lot of things Laura had done differently. Done better.

Our Christmas dinner was straight from Fresh Direct, ready-made side dishes and a ready-to-cook turkey, already stuffed and basted. Even that I managed to mess up; the turkey was dry, the side dishes microwaved for too long. Everything tasted rubbery.

Still, the girls all pretended to like it, which felt worse than if they'd complained. They'd started to pity me; they knew I was trying, just as they knew I wasn't measuring up.

"I'll do better next year," I told them, trying to inject some sort of enthusiasm into my voice. "I'll learn to cook."

My daughters deigned not to reply to those overly optimistic statements.

"You didn't get Christmas crackers," Ella said quietly.

"Yes, Daddy, why didn't you? We always have Christmas crackers."

Yes, we did—another tradition from Laura's family. For a second I felt as if I could almost see her at the other end of the table—her paper crown tilted rakishly over one eye as she read out one of the terrible jokes or played with the little toy included in the crown—a kazoo or a tin whistle, enjoying it all so much.

I missed her bubbly sense of expectation, even as I recognized I'd taken it for granted. So much for granted that perhaps I hadn't realized how it had been ebbing away, because now that I thought about it, that memory of Laura wasn't from last year; it was from when Ruby was a baby. She'd torn off her crown and started to eat it and Laura had rescued it from her with a laugh.

Last year… last year… what had happened last year? What had Laura been like? Why couldn't I remember? Why had I not noticed?

I turned back to my girls, blinking them into focus. "I'm sorry," I said. "Maybe we can have crackers on New Year's Eve."

"No one has crackers on New Year's Eve," Alexa said, rolling her eyes, and Ruby tugged at my sleeve.

"Daddy, why did you forget?" How could I answer that? "And why didn't Maria come?" she asked, her voice taking on the accusing tone she seemed to reserve for me, as she pushed her dessert—a chocolate cake that tasted bland and chilled—around her plate.

"It's Christmas, Ruby. She's celebrating with her own family."

"I thought she didn't have any family." This from Alexa, sounding suspicious.

I shrugged. "I'm sure she has someone."

"Can she come again?" Ella asked quietly. "She's nice. I like her."

"So do I." Ruby jutted her lip out, her eyes starting to gleam dangerously. A tantrum threatened like thunderclouds moving in, the latest manifestation of Ruby's grief that I couldn't handle. Last night she'd lain on the floor screaming for twenty minutes because I'd peeled a banana for her instead of letting her do it herself.

"I'll ask," I said, even though I didn't feel I could. Maria wasn't really part of our lives, even if the two evenings we'd spent with her had been the highlights of an admittedly crappy month and a half. I hadn't spoken to her since we'd decorated the Christmas tree, and I'd pretty much figured that was it. We'd never see her again. I didn't know how I felt about that, only that it was the way things were, the way they had to be.

After the mostly morose dinner, Paul and Elaine called and spoke to each of the girls in turn; it had been three weeks since they'd left and, after a frosty silence, just to make me aware of the extent of their displeasure, they were back, on their terms as always.

"We'd like the girls to come to Boston for the week after Christmas as they usually do," Paul said after they'd spoken to them all. The invitation was clearly for the girls, not for me.

"And you tell me this on Christmas Day?" I couldn't help but retort, even though I'd told myself I was going to be measured, even friendly. Sort of.

"I don't think we're being unreasonable. We'll come and collect them and bring them back. You won't be required to do anything."

"That's not the point, Paul." Although I wasn't sure what was. And, if I was cringingly honest, a week on my own did not sound like a terrible thing at this point. I was exhausted and overwhelmed by the constant demands and needs—Ruby's clinginess and tantrums, Ella's silence, Alexa's anger. Being by myself could be a break of sorts... a way to get on top of the house and work, at least.

"Have you sorted out childcare yet?" Paul asked in a tone that suggested he knew I hadn't. "You're going back to work after New Year's, aren't you?"

"Yes." And I hadn't sorted out childcare, although I'd at least made a start. I'd contacted a nanny agency and filled out an endless form, and then been chided by the director that I'd left this far too late to be able to get anyone of quality. I'd been too annoyed by her prissy, scolding manner to take it any further, even though I knew I had to.

"Nathan, this really seems like it's too much for you." Paul was pouring on the fake sympathy, which made me grit my teeth.

"I'm coping, Paul."

"But the girls deserve more than coping, surely?"

Laura had died just a little over a *month* ago. Did he really expect me to do more than cope at this point? "What are you trying to say?" I asked, even though I already knew and didn't want him to tell me yet again how my daughters would be better off with him and Elaine.

"We're here to help," Paul said quietly. He was still going the sympathy route, although it clearly grated on him; there was an edge to his voice he couldn't hide. "I know we haven't always seen eye to eye on a lot of things, but we're here to support you."

"By taking away my children?" I hissed, not wanting the girls to hear. I was standing in the kitchen, staring out the window at Third Avenue, covered in grey slush. So much for snow.

"For a *week*. To be able to spend time with them. To give you a break."

"You know what I'm talking about."

"Let's let bygones be bygones, shall we?" A steely note had entered his voice, and I let out a harsh laugh.

"Seriously? You classify that as a *bygone*?"

"What's your answer, Nathan?" No sympathy now.

I let out a long, low breath, my shoulders slumped as fatigue crashed over me. I was so tired, all the time. Ruby had come into bed with me at four this morning, and started chatting away at five. A week of uninterrupted sleep sounded pretty good right now, about the best thing I could hope for. Still, I resisted.

"I don't know…"

"We have a relationship with them," Paul persisted. "We have a right to a relationship with them. Laura would have wanted that. She always wanted to come to Cape Cod with us. Never missed a summer…"

Ah, those awful vacations to Cape Cod, where Paul insisted on paying for everything, and making sure everyone knew it. I finally put my foot down when Ella was a baby, even though it cost a mint. Money aside, the week was always an exercise in how *other* I was, when the family in-jokes about horse riding and country clubs were made with sliding, speculative looks I tried not to notice. Laura had a couple of ritzy cousins who looked at me as if I were some sort of alien species, tittering behind their hands when I betrayed my ignorance. No, I didn't know how to play polo. Who did?

A couple of years ago, I started leaving early, only staying the weekend, claiming the pressures of work. I think everyone was relieved, even Laura. She could have her family time and I could be free.

"Fine." I bit out the word, hating giving anything to my father-in-law. "When will you collect them?"

"We can come tomorrow, bring them back on New Year's Day. They start school on the third?"

How did he know that? I didn't even know that, although I probably should have. "Fine," I said again. "I'll let them know."

"We've already told them," Paul said, and he didn't even sound apologetic.

When I came back into the living room after the call, all three girls were there, waiting. I raised my eyebrows. "So Grandad told you?"

Ella nodded soberly. "Do you mind?"

I sidestepped the question with one of my own. "Do you? Do you want to go?" I felt oddly vulnerable in asking the question, afraid they were choosing my in-laws rather than me. And really, why wouldn't they? I was doing a terrible job at this whole single-parenting thing. I could admit that, and in any case, Alexa had already told me.

None of them answered; Ella gave Alexa a questioning look, and even Ruby, who always knew her own mind, looked lost.

With a jolt of guilt, I realized the position I'd put them in, making them choose. "Girls... Alexa... Ella... Ruby..." I shook my head slowly. "You can go. I don't mind if you go. I mean, I'd be happy if you did, although of course I'd miss you." The words stuck in my throat, but I forced them out, like jagged splinters, catching on everything. "Granny and Grandad are your grandparents, and they love you. It's okay," I assured them, and I couldn't miss the relief that broke over Ella's face like a wave. Alexa's shoulders hunched a little less, and Ruby smiled.

"They said they're coming tomorrow," Ruby said, and I nodded.

"I know."

It felt strange, packing their things that evening. The Christmas tree lights twinkled and the living room was a mess of torn wrapping paper, the remnants of our Fresh Direct dinner strewn across the kitchen. The prospect of an entire week alone loomed large, both a promise and a threat.

"Ella, don't you have any more underpants?" I asked as I hunted through her near-empty drawers. Damned if I'd send them to Paul and Elaine unprepared.

"You haven't done the laundry, Daddy," Ella said, without a single note of censure in her voice. It was just fact. "And some of them are too small, anyway. I need new ones." New underwear. Something I never, ever would have thought of, but, of course, these girls of mine were constantly growing—they'd need new everything eventually, and I'd have to be the one to provide it. Yet another thing Laura did that had not so much as rippled across my consciousness.

I put a load of laundry in and hoped there would be enough to see Ella through the week. Then I packed Ruby's stuff, and checked Alexa was packing hers, to which I got a silent shrug in reply, her back to me as she sat on her bed, hunched as usual over her phone. At some point I would have to pry that thing away from her.

"Is there anything you need?" I asked, a bit desperately. "Can I do some laundry for you?"

"I'm fine." The words were bitten off, hurled out.

I stared at the slender, rigid back of my daughter and wondered, yet again, why she was so angry with me. Did she really blame me for Laura's death? Was that a natural reaction, all things considered? Or had something gone wrong between us that I'd never even known about, and was I even *more* of a crap dad than I realized?

When I'd gone to the police station, Lisa had given me a card for Victim Connect, a charity that helped family and friends of those who had died by violent crime. A mother from Ruby's preschool had mentioned a grief support group for families offered at a nearby church. I'd more or less dismissed both things; I could barely handle life as it was, never mind adding another commitment to it. But now, six weeks on, I wondered if we needed that kind of support. If my daughters did.

In any case, it would have to wait until they returned from Boston.

"When you get back, Alexa," I said, hearing the desperation in my voice. "Maybe we could do something together?"

She turned towards me, scathingly incredulous. "*Do* something?"

"Whatever you want. Just… spend some time together." The words were stilted, painful. "I want us to get along." Which made it sound as if that was all I was hoping for.

Alexa stared at me for a moment, her eyes narrowed, lips pursed. "You never do something with me, Dad."

"That's not true." I couldn't help but be defensive; I hadn't been that bad, surely. "We went to the movies a few months ago…"

She rolled her eyes. "That was in the *summer*, and I didn't even want to see it."

"You didn't?" I felt lost.

"Whatever, Dad. You don't have to try so hard, okay? It's just embarrassing."

Ouch. "Why are you so angry with me, Alexa?" I asked quietly, and her eyes flashed for a millisecond before she closed herself up, like a shell snapping shut.

"Just go away, okay? I'm fine." She turned her back to me once more, and I stared at her helplessly, completely at a loss. After a few miserable moments, I did as she said.

Paul and Elaine showed up at ten the next morning; they must have left at the crack of dawn. We had an awkward exchange in the hallway, with a lot of shuffling and muttering, before the girls filed out and I brought their bags behind.

"I can take those," Paul said, shouldering two before I could stop him, but I held onto the third, a matter of principle.

"I'll say goodbye outside."

"We're double-parked," Paul returned warningly, and I had to fight the urge not to say something ugly.

Outside, Ruby clung to my legs as Ella gave me a quick, tight hug before climbing into the Taylors' luxury SUV, where Alexa already sat, her face turned away from me.

"Daddy, have you filled in my swim team form?" Ella asked anxiously. "I start as soon as I get back…"

"Swim team…" Vaguely I remembered something about it; it was in the plastic tray in the kitchen with myriad other school forms and letters I hadn't looked at. "I'll sort it out, Ella. Don't worry."

"It's important." She looked uncharacteristically anxious, and I tried to give her a reassuring smile.

"Don't worry."

"Daddy, I don't want to go." Ruby started with hiccuppy sobs, and I couldn't help but give Paul a pointed look as I prised her off me.

"You'll have lots of fun with Granny and Grandad. And I'll see you in a week…"

Yet as she clambered into the car, a visceral fear clutched at me; I had a sudden, terrible premonition that Paul and Elaine might not bring them back. Wasn't that what happened in custody battles, parents disappearing with children, all false promises and fake smiles? Possession was nine-tenths of the law, after all. What if this was it? How would I survive then? Because I realized in that moment that I needed my girls even more than they needed me. Even if I wasn't the best thing for them, I wanted them with me. I couldn't let them go, and yet I was.

"Be good, girls," I called half-heartedly, even though part of me didn't want them to be good. I wanted them to miss me, to act out, to show Paul and Elaine all the things I was dealing with. I tried to catch Alexa's eye, but she wasn't having it.

And then, before I could say anything more, they were gone, doors slamming shut and Paul revving the engine, pulling smoothly out into the street and leaving me behind in the frigid air and clouds of exhaust.

I stood there for a moment, already at a loss. For the last six weeks my life had revolved around my children—they'd been with me all the time, so I'd barely been able to go to the bathroom without someone knocking on the door. I wasn't sure I knew what to do, how to be, without them anymore.

Finally I went back inside; the apartment radiated emptiness. I closed my eyes, imagining that Laura was here, that we'd let the kids go for the first time on their own, so we could have a staycation by ourselves.

Can you believe it, Laur? A week of sleeping in. Takeout. Movies.

And we're going to watch at least one romcom. You promised.

Oh come on, action all the way.

I'll give you some action right now…

And, laughing, we'd chase each other down the hallway and tumble into bed, just like we'd done before kids, when we'd been young and silly, without a care in the world.

Except, of course, that had never happened. We'd never had a week without the girls, and even if we had, we wouldn't have done those things, or even had that conversation. We'd have come back inside, and I would have gone on to my laptop, and Laura would have drifted around the house, tidying up, feeling lonely. After an hour or so she would have roused me from my study, asked if we could go for a walk. I would have sighed and said okay, as if I were making a concession. Then we would have walked around the Central Park reservoir, hands deep in pockets, my fingers itching to check my phone. Laura would have made a few comments about the weather, the girls, what she'd read recently in *The New Yorker*. And I might have said something back.

That memory, real or not, was the way it would have gone. I knew it, with a thud of disappointment in myself. Why did it take my wife dying to realize it?

Shaking my head, trying to hold back that almighty tidal wave of grief, I started cleaning the kitchen, wanting to do something useful, but my heart wasn't in it. I kept imagining Laura; she felt so close, I lifted my head a few times, half-expecting to see her around the corner, coming into a room.

Hey, you've been at that for an hour. Come relax with me.

And sometimes I would have; a smile would have tugged my mouth as she reached for my hand. I would have rubbed her feet as she'd sprawled on the sofa, sun streaming through the window. That *had* happened. I was sure it had.

In the end, I left the kitchen still mostly messy and sprawled in front of the TV instead, turning on something mindless.

There were a dozen ways I could have used this time productively—tidied the apartment, caught up on laundry, checked in with work, dealt with the whole nanny, or lack of one, situation. All of those options felt overwhelming, impossible. I'd struggled on for six weeks and I *couldn't* anymore. I just couldn't.

I watched six episodes of *Ice Road Truckers* back to back before my brain started to feel like it would melt.

I stumbled up from the sofa, foggy-brained and blurry-eyed, pacing the confines of the apartment, so restless I could have slipped out of my skin. I told myself I could get a start on some of the renovations—strip the wallpaper from the dining room, since it was half peeling off anyway. Or I could paint the walls in the living room. Do something with the 70s-style bathroom, surprise the girls when they got back.

But of course I didn't. I didn't even finish cleaning the kitchen. Instead, I called Frank and asked him if he wanted to meet up for a beer.

"Nathan, it's so good to hear from you," he said in that slightly unctuous way he had of talking. I realized he was treating me like a client, someone who had to be handled. "Yes, sure, let's go for a beer. Where do you want to meet?"

I mentioned a bar in midtown, halfway between us since Frank lived in Soho with his high-powered lawyer wife Claire. They had no children.

"Thanks, Frank," I said, because I realized it was asking a lot, for him to come out the day after Christmas.

The bar was packed with half-drunk holidaymakers as I shouldered my way through the crowd and found Frank at the bar, sipping a draft beer. I slid onto the stool next to him and ordered one for myself.

"Nathan." He eyed me appraisingly, clearly not knowing quite how to treat me, which rankled, even though I understood it. My friendship with Frank had a foundation of mutual ambition and shared work; that had always been enough. In moments like this, though, I knew it wasn't. We hadn't seen each other since Laura's funeral. "How are you holding up?" Frank asked after a moment.

I shrugged. "I'm okay." What else could I say? *I'm falling apart, I want to howl, I've come to realize I've been a crap husband as well as dad?*

"Good." He sounded relieved. "And the girls?" This said reluctantly, because Frank and Claire had always been very firm as well as vocal about their desire never to have kids.

When Laura and I had had Alexa, things had invariably shifted between us; we were besotted with our baby, Frank and Claire not so much. Then we'd had Ella, adding insult to injury, and when Ruby had come along, a not-entirely-welcome surprise, we'd turned into this awkward, unwieldy thing, a family with far too many kids, especially by New York standards.

"It's hard for them," I told Frank. It felt disloyal to pretend that it wasn't, to gloss over my daughters' grief the way I could mine. "Really hard. Alexa, especially, I think. She's so angry, and I don't know why."

Frank looked shocked and even a bit embarrassed by my emotional outburst. *Way* too much sharing for him. Clearly he'd wanted a "fine", but I was sick of pretending. I hadn't been doing a good job of it, anyway.

"It must be tough," he murmured. "Do you have people to support you?"

I glanced up at him, unable to keep from noticing his choice of words—and having them sting. *Do you have people?* Meaning he was not one of them.

It was obvious what he wanted me to say: *Oh yes, lots. So many families and friends. We are totally taken care of!* At first it had felt like that, at least a little. A few preschool moms had brought casseroles, sent cards. Walkerton's PTA had arranged a schedule of meals, mostly ordered from Fresh Direct and delivered to our door, no personal interaction required. But all that had tapered off weeks ago, and nothing had taken its place.

No one had, I realized then, invited Ruby for a playdate, or suggested they take the girls somewhere fun for an afternoon. No one had sent a card or email or even just a lousy text, checking how we were. The radio silence, unnoticed in my own dazed and exhausted grief, hit hard now. Where were Laura's friends? Why weren't they stepping up? Was it because I'd never really known them, or because Laura had been detaching herself from them over the last few months?

I thought of the secret volunteering, the lack of texts from friends on her phone. I hadn't realized any of it. I'd had no idea what had been going on in her mind. *Maria* had known more than I had.

"Sure," I told Frank now, trying to smile. "A few friends." I could barely manage the lie, but he looked relieved, eager to drop the subject.

"Good, that's good. And you're looking forward to coming back to work? Next week, right?"

Wordlessly, I nodded.

"We need you back there, man. It'll be good to have you in the driver's seat again. You got the email about the Drexler bid?"

The bid we'd been making the day Laura died. I flinched as I nodded; I couldn't help it.

Realization flashed across Frank's features. "Sorry," he murmured. He didn't look apologetic, though, more like annoyed. Grief was an irritant to other people, I knew. It slowed them down, made them impatient. When you weren't experiencing it yourself, it was so very tedious to have to endure in someone else.

And part of me got that. I really did. I remembered when one of our admin staff at work had lost her mother. She'd asked for compassionate leave for three *weeks*, which seemed ridiculous to me at the time. I even remember thinking, *Come on, it's only your mom. She must have been at least eighty.*

Now I felt ashamed of my former self, even as I wished I could go back to that hardened, quick-moving version of me. Grief might be tedious for others, but for those feeling it, it just sucked. And I was tired of it. I was tired of feeling it, all the time, a never-ending drain on my life, my body, my heart.

Which was why I ordered another beer, and then another, and then a shot of Johnnie Walker. Frank matched me beer for beer, but when we got to shots, he backed off. *Coward.*

"Sorry, man, but Claire's waiting for me at home. And we're heading to Aspen tomorrow." He held up his hands in a don't-blame-me pose, shaking his head with mock regret. "Otherwise I'd be right there with you, absolutely."

Yeah, right. As if. I downed the shot in one; I was used to whiskey after six weeks of necking it as an anaesthetic every night, and it barely burned a trail to my gut. I held up my hand for another.

"Nathan…" Frank sounded more exasperated than concerned. "Don't get drunk."

"Why not?" I gave him an acid smile. "I don't have a wife waiting for me at home, and I'm not heading off to Aspen tomorrow." I slurred a little bit; I also sounded bitter.

Frank held up his hands. "Okay, okay. I'm sorry. I just…" He shook his head. "I'll see you in the new year? January second, eight-thirty sharp?" He smiled, wanting me to be excited about the prospect of work, and I just didn't have it in me. I didn't even have a nanny yet.

I nodded, not looking at him. "Yeah. Sure."

"Okay."

I watched him go, and then the bartender poured me another shot.

Things got a bit blurry after that. I had a few more shots, none of them helping, the bar, its crowd and noise, fading in and out.

At some point, a guy jostled me in the shoulder, and I shouted at him. I don't remember what I said.

The bartender came over. "Hey, buddy, I think you've had enough."

But I hadn't. I hadn't had nearly enough. I said something rude, I didn't know what, and then a bouncer came over, and I started to laugh, because *really*? I was going to get thrown out of a bar?

"My wife just died, okay?" I slurred, ashamed, even in my inebriated state, to play that pathetic trump card. "My wife *died*."

"I'm sorry for your loss," the bouncer said stiffly. "But there are rules, man."

"Fine, fine, I'm going." I threw a couple of twenties on the bar and lurched up from my stool, the room swinging wildly around me. I felt as if I could cry. People were staring.

I stumbled out of the bar, the cold air a slap in the face, but still not enough to turn me sober. A taxi sped by, throwing slush across my shoes, and then my stomach cramped, and I was violently sick all over the pavement. I ended up on my hands and knees, my insides turning out, people nearby exclaiming rudely as they swerved around me.

I felt a terrible, corroding shame. Was this what I had become? What I was *choosing*?

Somehow, I got a taxi back home, stumbling past the doorman, who remained solicitously blank-faced. Inside, the apartment's empty silence taunted me. The laundry I'd put on yesterday, still wet in the washer and starting to smell—all the clean clothes I'd forgotten to pack in Ella's suitcase. A spill of stale cereal across the kitchen counter, dirty bowls piled in the sink. In the girls' bedroom, Ella's too-small underpants lay on the bed, three pairs she couldn't wear.

I kicked off my shoes, started to undo my belt, and then I gave up, collapsing on my bed, too tired and weary even to cry. This was my life, and I felt as if I couldn't stand a second more of it, or of myself.

CHAPTER FOURTEEN

MARIA

"Thank you so much for meeting me."

I stared at Nathan West uncertainly and managed a nod. I was still shocked that I was actually here, in a coffee shop around the corner from his apartment building, talking with him... *why*?

He'd called me that morning, three days after Christmas, sounding exhausted and uncertain and alarmingly desperate.

"Maria... it's Nathan. I was wondering... well, I was wondering if you'd have coffee with me. I wanted to discuss something with you," he'd clarified hurriedly, as if I might actually jump to some inappropriate conclusion when, in truth, I had no idea what to think. "If you don't mind..."

"I don't mind." I spoke quietly, each beat of my heart painful. What did he want to talk about? Had he found out something about Laura's death? I could not imagine what he might have to say to me.

Nathan hadn't contacted me in two weeks, since we'd decorated the tree and I'd made *krofne* with Ruby and Ella. It had been a lovely evening; the memory of it had sustained me for the following weeks, as I went to work, to volunteer, and then home again, a numbing and familiar cycle. As the days passed and he hadn't been in touch, I'd resigned myself to never hearing from the Wests again. No, that was a lie. I hadn't resigned myself at all, and that was the trouble. I was waiting. Without meaning to, I was waiting for him to be in touch.

"I'm not doing well," he blurted, looking down at his coffee. His hair was sticking up in several directions and he hadn't shaved that morning. His eyes were bloodshot. He emitted, I couldn't help but notice, the stale, yeasty smell of metabolizing alcohol.

"It hasn't been very long," I reminded him quietly.

"I know… but it's not just that. I can't cope with everything. Anything. It's too much. All the time, it's too much. I feel like I'm a crap dad. I *am* a crap dad. And I'm going back to work next week… I have to. It's been six weeks already, I've got to work…"

I nodded to show him I understood, and he sighed heavily.

"My in-laws… well, it's complicated. The girls are with them now. And when they get back, I need to have childcare in place. Otherwise…" He paused, as if I should be able to finish that sentence.

"Are you going to hire a nanny?" I asked after a moment.

"That was the idea, of course, but the agency I found is so stuck up and they say it will take weeks, if not months, to find someone they deem suitable, especially over the holidays…" He shook his head. "Why does it have to take so long? It's like they *want* to make it difficult for you. Anyway, I was thinking… and the girls keep asking for you, Ruby especially, she's really bonded…" He trailed off, looking at me expectantly. I had no idea what to think. What he meant for me to think.

"They're lovely girls," I said after a heavy pause.

"And they're really fond of you. Already. I mean, I know this is a bit unexpected, and we don't know each other very well, and hell, it's a bit, well, *strange*… but it just occurred to me, you know, how all the girls seem to like you, even Alexa, and you know what she's like…" He hesitated, and I started to get a glimmer of what he was trying to say, even though I still couldn't credit it at all. "I know I have no right to ask you anything," he continued hurriedly. "And this might not even work, you might have no interest at all in something like this…" He stopped with another despairing shake of his head, needing me, as ever, to make the connection. The choice.

"Nathan," I said quietly. "What are you trying to ask me?"

He met my gaze, nodding once, as if coming to a decision. "I want to ask if you'd consider being a... a nanny to the girls. Nanny might be the wrong word, though. Housekeeper, super-woman, lifesaver..." He let out a shaky laugh and shook his head. "Tell me to stop whenever you want. I realize I'm being completely presumptuous. You have a job, I know that, a whole life, and we don't really know each other. It could be a temporary position if you'd rather, until I can work something else out..."

"A nanny," I repeated, hardly able to believe it.

"Am I crazy?" He gave an appealing look. "It's just, you get on so well with the girls. But I know I'm being presumptuous, offensive even. You have a job... at a hairdresser's, right?"

"Yes."

"So you probably don't want to leave that. Sorry, this was a long shot. It's just..." he trailed off again, shrugging, despondent now. "I suppose I thought it was worth a try..."

I shook my head, half to keep him from talking while I ordered my thoughts and half because I couldn't actually believe what he was suggesting.

Involve myself completely in their lives, day in and day out? For how long? My mind reeled with all the implications, the *images*—making dinner, baking with Ella, bedtime stories with Ruby, board games in the dining room, all of us like a family... but would it—*could* it—even be like that?

"I'm sorry," I said after a moment, because the silence had gone on for several taut seconds and something needed to be said. "This has surprised me. I need to think."

"Of course, of course..." He nearly tripped over the words. "I'm sorry for springing this on you. It must be strange... I know we don't actually know each other all that well, but the girls have taken such a liking to you. And I trust you..." He let that statement dwindle away, as if he knew he had no reason to trust me. No reason at all.

I took a sip of coffee, trying to compose my swirling thoughts. I was so shocked by his proposal that I couldn't get past the surprise, the utter unexpectedness of it. It had been over two weeks since he'd been in touch, and in truth I'd never expected to see any of them again. And now this... not just to visit once or twice, but to see them every day. To, more or less, mother his daughters. To order his home. I could picture it already, all of it, in sweet yet excruciating detail. I could see myself in that kitchen, tucking Ruby in every night, brushing Ella's long golden hair, somehow getting past Alexa's sullen sulks. Oh, I could see it. How I could. For the first time, I could see a future. My future.

And yet...

"I don't know," I said at last. "I'm... honored, of course. Very."

Nathan's face was already falling, disappointment turning the corners of his mouth down, clouding his eyes and slumping his shoulders, like something vital had just drained out of him. "Of course, I understand."

"I'm not saying no," I added quickly. "You've just taken me by surprise. I need to think. It is a big decision."

"Yes..."

"What would the duties be, exactly?"

Nathan raked a hand through his hair. "I don't even know. Just... being there, I suppose. Taking the girls to school. Picking them up again. Doing... well, doing what Laura did." He gave me a guilty look, as if he'd said something wrong.

"Yes, but the particulars? Meals? Housework? Laundry?" I supplied as gentle prompts. *All of it?*

"Yes, if you could. Would. Anything..." He shrugged, helpless, wanting me to take over. To step into his life and wave my magic wand. *Me.* It was so incredible, so outrageous, I wanted to laugh—or cry. How could I possibly fix anyone, especially this broken family, when I was nothing but a jumble of shattered pieces myself?

And yet...

Oh, and yet.

I was tempted. I was terrified.

I wanted, deeply and instinctively, to back away from all of this the way I would from a dangerous animal, a towering threat. If I came into their lives, if I let myself love those three sad-eyed girls... well, then none of this would be safe anymore. I'd kept myself apart for over twenty years. How could I contemplate now living my life differently, letting people in? I didn't even know how. I'd do it wrong.

You'd just be the nanny.

It felt like a safeguard.

"Take some time," Nathan urged. "Of course."

"Not too much time," I reminded him with a small, hesitant smile. "If you're going back to work next week."

He gave me a small smile back. "True."

I shook my head again, taking a sip of coffee. My mind was still spinning.

"If you like," Nathan said after a moment, "I could write up a list of duties. Make it... official. And, of course, I'd offer a proper salary, health insurance..."

I'd never had health insurance. I'd just avoided doctors, along with everyone else, but I was forty now and perhaps I'd need proper medical care.

"All right," I said. "That is a good idea. And perhaps I can get back to you... tomorrow?"

"Tomorrow would be wonderful. I'll send you the list by tonight. What's your email address?"

I shook my head. "I don't have email. I'm sorry." I didn't even own a computer, and there was nothing smart about my phone. There had never been any need for either.

"Oh. Right. Well, then, why don't I run it by your apartment? In Queens?"

I resisted the thought of him seeing my shabby little apartment. "That's too much trouble."

"It isn't…" But I knew he didn't have a car, and it would take nearly an hour to get to my apartment from here on the subway and bus. "Do you have time now, then?" Nathan asked. "I could write something up right now, if you don't mind waiting."

I hesitated, sensing his desperation, feeling my own uncertainty. The shock remained. "All right."

"Why don't you come up to the apartment and we can talk through it there?"

I nodded, and we left the café, walking in silence around the corner to Nathan's building, and then up in the elevator.

The apartment smelled familiar as I stepped into the darkened foyer—slightly stale, admittedly, but still a welcoming smell of people and life.

"How long are the girls with your in-laws?" I asked as I followed Nathan into the kitchen. I was starting to feel a little tense; I couldn't remember the last time I'd been alone with a man, and I hugged my bag to my chest, half-wishing I hadn't come up here. Already my heart rate was skittering, blood rushing in my ears. All around me, the apartment yawned, cavernous and dark and empty. No matter what he'd just asked me, Nathan was still little more than a stranger.

"A week. It's so quiet without them." He gave me a twisted, wry smile. "I thought I'd like the break, but I'm not sure I do."

I nodded, unsure how to respond. My heart was racing now, my mouth dry, a buzzing sound in my ears. I took careful, slow breaths, trying not to let Nathan notice.

"I'll make the list," he said, brushing past me so I quickly stepped back, my back hitting the edge of the island. "Sorry." Another quick smile. "My study is back here." He gestured to a door that led off from the kitchen. "But, if you agree, I'll turn it into a guest room, just in case."

"Just in case?"

"If there were ever any late nights…" He looked uncertain. "You could sleep over, sometimes, save you going back to Queens. But of course you wouldn't have to. It would just be a convenience…"

Sleep over? I pictured myself waking up to sunlight in the kitchen, a sleepy Ruby in her pyjamas. "That's very kind."

"I'll just be a few minutes. Make yourself comfortable."

As if I could. I decided I might as well tidy up while I was waiting, keep my hands busy.

As nervous as I was, already I knew in my heart, in my bones, that I would say yes. I couldn't keep myself from it, from longing for it, even though it scared me. To care about people again… to give them that power over me… I wasn't even sure I was capable of it, but for the first time in over twenty years, I wanted to try.

A plate slipped out of my hands and fell into the sink with a clatter, thankfully not breaking. I picked it up and rinsed it off and placed it in the dish drainer.

A few minutes later, I heard the buzz and whirr of a printer, and then Nathan came into the kitchen holding a piece of paper. "Oh, wow." He looked around the clean kitchen with a beam of pleasure. "Maria, you didn't even have to… but thank you."

I nodded, waiting for him to give me the paper.

He gestured to it. "Do you want to look over it now? Ask any questions? Then you can have a think…"

"All right." I felt nervous as I took the single sheet, Nathan's earnest gaze heavy on me. Quickly I scanned the few lines.

Take girls to school every day at 7:45 a.m. Manage housework and laundry as needed. Pick up Ruby from preschool three days a week at 12 p.m.; care for her on other days. Pick older girls up at 3:15 p.m. Manage after-school activities as needed. Make dinner.

Off duty from 6:30 p.m, onwards, and weekends unless needed; if so will pay extra.

The figure named at the bottom was a good deal more than I was making now.

"I know it isn't much to go on," Nathan said. "And we can discuss things in more detail as we go…"

"It's fine."

Of course, there was so much I didn't know, but I didn't think I could stand to nitpick through the details—would I be responsible for grocery shopping? Would I make breakfast? What did "manage after-school activities" actually mean? What I understood from this sheet was that, just as Nathan had said, I would be doing everything Laura did. I would be stepping into her empty shoes.

I raised the piece of paper in a gesture of thanks. "I will think about all this. And let you know tomorrow."

"All right, that's great. Thanks, Maria."

I nodded, not trusting myself to say more. I stepped around him to get out of the kitchen, and he followed me into the foyer, opening the front door for me.

"I appreciate this so much. Just thinking about it, I mean. You don't even know…"

But I did know. I knew how empty and aching his life was, because mine was too. And I knew how much he needed me, because I was realizing, to both my dismay and fear, that I needed him and his children.

I just nodded, and then I was outside the apartment, in the elevator, out on the street, breathing in lungfuls of cold, clean air as tears I didn't understand pricked my eyes. I didn't know whether I was sad or happy or something in between. All I knew was I felt far too much, and I hadn't even started yet.

*

That afternoon, I gave Neriha my notice. She stared at me in disbelief.

"You are going to work as a *nanny*? For that family?"

"It's a good opportunity, with good benefits. Health insurance…"

"Maria, in all the time I've known you…" Neriha shook her head slowly. "You've never done something like this."

"There was never the opportunity."

"But do you even *know* these people? Do you even know how to take care of children?"

"I know them a bit," I said defensively. "And I know enough about children. Besides, does any nanny know the family before she works with them?" I shrugged. "This is normal." Even if it felt like jumping off a cliff, letting myself fall and fall.

"What about your friends? Your community? You've been in Astoria for almost twenty years…"

"I'll still be in Astoria. I'm not moving, Neriha." And surely she knew I had no real friends. No real community. Yes, there were people in my life, like her and Selma, a few others, but they remained forever on the fringes. Perhaps they all assumed there were other people closer in, when there never had been.

"Won't you feel lonely?" Neriha pressed, and I almost laughed at the ludicrousness of such a question.

Lonely? I'd been lonely for twenty-six years. For the first time since the war, since everything, I had the chance not to be lonely. And, for the first time, I was willing to take it.

"I'll manage, Neriha. But I'm sorry to be leaving here so soon. The Wests need me next week."

Neriha shrugged, as if to say "it's your life". And finally it felt like it was. My *life*, rather than just drifting as a ghost.

That night, I texted Nathan, not brave enough to call and speak in person, telling him I would accept the position. He texted back immediately, saying I could start on Monday, the day after the girls got back. If I wanted, if it was okay, I could come over on Sunday afternoon to see them when they got back from Boston. I said I would.

I could hardly believe the steps I'd taken, the possibilities unfolding in front of me, and so fast. This was really happening. My new life was beginning. After all this time, I was finally coming alive, and it brought me both joy and terror.

PART TWO

CHAPTER FIFTEEN

NATHAN

"Welcome back, Nathan."

A solid handshake, the pleasing thud of my bag hitting my desk. A smile as I rolled my shoulders, something in me that had been clenched hard for nearly two months finally, *finally*, starting to relax.

I was back at work, and it felt good. After weeks of uncertainty and worry, I felt like I knew what to do, what was needed. I wasn't stumbling around forgetting things, feeling as if I were disappointing everyone. I gave Frank a firm smile as I willed him to forget my drunken evening of just a week ago. Life was different now; I was back in control. Maria had started officially yesterday, and so far things seemed to be going well, the girls adapting to her presence, and Maria proving herself to be quietly competent. Risky though it had seemed, I'd made a good choice. Now, for the next eight or nine hours, I could forget everything but this.

"Why don't you update me on what's been going on," I told Frank.

Jenny came in with a coffee and I smiled my thanks. I'd needed this. I'd needed this so much. To have my own space, my own life, again. To escape, if just for eight hours.

It had been strange, having Maria in the apartment all day. I'd spent a frantic couple of days transforming my study with its dark walls and cheap office furniture into a decent bedroom, just in case she'd need it for the late nights I might be working—fresh paint, a new bed and bureau and a small chair upholstered in ivory linen that matched the new curtains framing the single sash window. I was pleased with the result; the room was small but it was comfortable. When I'd showed it to Maria, she'd seemed surprised but accepting; I'd told her it was just a precautionary measure, and I hoped she didn't feel I was taking advantage of her generosity.

The night before Maria had started, I'd done a crash course online, trying to find out what a new nanny needed. I'd ended up on MetroBaby, a chat forum for well-heeled Manhattan moms. I'd had a jarring moment when I landed on the homepage and Laura's login details came up automatically. She'd never mentioned this site to me, but why would she? We'd never talked about things like that.

Unable to keep myself from it, I clicked on her account and read through her profile—mother of three girls, Upper East Side, was all it said, and that felt like both a relief and disappointment. I wasn't sure I wanted to nose around in Laura's private stuff. I didn't know what I'd find. Then I realized I could go through all the messages she'd posted. It hadn't taken long, because there was only one.

Does anyone else feel like there has to be more to life than this? I'm not talking about the drudgery of taking care of kids—housework, laundry, cooking, wiping dirty butts and noses. I get that, and it's okay. It's good. I just mean all this striving… the nice apartment, the premium parking space, the private schools, the five-star vacations… what's the point? I feel like there needs to be more, and I want to know what it is.

I read through the message three times, growing colder and colder as the words emblazoned themselves on my brain. This was what Maria had hinted at, and yet it was much worse, more real, seeing it there on the screen, knowing Laura had typed it. Felt it.

Had she really thought our life together was *pointless*? And when she mentioned striving, I knew who she was really talking about me. *Me*.

Curious now in a kind of horrified, rubbernecking sort of way, I'd scrolled through the responses, both infuriated and strangely satisfied by their general tone:

Are you seriously complaining about all those things? How about you count your blessings, bitch?

Nice life if you can have it.

Try yoga. Or just grow up.

I'd closed my laptop and sat back, dazed and reeling. It had never occurred to me before now that Laura might have been actually, *actively* unhappy. All right, yes, I understood now that I'd worked too hard. So did every business person in Manhattan.

And fine, I might have neglected our family a bit. A *bit*. I was trying to be better now. But this? This *emptiness* Laura had been feeling, the way she'd seemed to have been questioning everything we'd built our life on, how she'd been looking for something else? *And she'd found it at Global Rescue.*

Of course, I told myself, it was just one message. Maybe she'd been having an off day; maybe she'd been having PMS. It didn't have to *mean* anything.

I'd lurched up from the desk and started wandering around the apartment, pulling out drawers and riffling through their messy contents as if I were looking for something in particular. Some clue that just had to be there, because Laura needed to give me more than this; I needed to be able to make sense of it all, somehow. *Somehow.*

I yanked open medicine cupboards and bedside table drawers, plunging my hand into the mess of Laura's things in a way I hadn't been able to make myself do before. Then I riffled through the stack of paperbacks by her bed, and dug through the clutter of lip balms and old receipts in her bedside table drawer. Nothing called out to me. Nothing said, *This is who I am. This is what I was keeping from you. This is why.*

Eventually, the house even messier than before, I'd stopped, knowing it was all pointless. Senseless, just like her death. Why did I keep trying to discover a reason, find meaning in the way things had happened? There wasn't any. There couldn't be.

Feeling leaden, I went back to the desk and opened the laptop. I found the post about what to provide a new nanny, and I read through it doggedly.

Make a detailed list of all duties, children's scheduled activities, house rules, screen time guidelines, etc. Explain how all the appliances in your home operate. Provide a copy of your signed contract. Provide her with her own phone, if she doesn't have one, and credit card, MetroCard, etc, as needed.

Clearly I had my work cut out for me. I had no idea of the timings and locations of the girls' activities. I wasn't even sure what all the little icons on the washing machine meant.

By the time Maria arrived on Sunday to meet the girls, I'd managed to tick off most of that list. I'd bought her a smartphone and a MetroCard and opened a bank account for household expenses in her name. I'd even managed to find out when and where the girls' activities were, written on the calendar in the kitchen. I'd traced Laura's handwriting with my fingers, a loopy scribble. I'd come up with a daily schedule, and even a few house rules, although I felt as if I were cheating, pretending we had this normal, orderly life that no longer existed. Maria, I suspected, would see through my little charade instantly.

"The girls will be back in half an hour or so," I'd said a bit awkwardly. Now that she was here, in my home, it all felt a bit bizarre. What were Paul and Elaine going to think, that I'd hired a woman I barely knew to take care of my children? And yet I trusted her.

"Is there something I can do while I wait?" Maria asked. "Tidy up?"

"Oh, no, that's okay…" I'd blitzed the whole apartment that morning.

"Or perhaps you could take me through things?" Maria suggested. There was the barest hint of a smile in her voice. "The activities and schedule…?"

"Oh, yes. Right. Of course."

And so I did, outlining where the girls' schools and activities were, what food they liked for dinner, where the washing machine was. Maria listened silently, her expression composed and alert, yet also calm. She calmed me, somehow, and it was a huge relief to think she would be doing all these things now, not me, a thought which also brought the familiar accompanying dose of acid-like guilt.

Then the girls arrived, pounding on the front door, their voices the excited yelps of puppies. The look of astonished delight on Ruby's face when she saw Maria confirmed I'd made the right choice.

"You're here?" she exclaimed, and then burrowed into Maria's middle. Ella smiled, and Alexa looking nonplussed. I counted it all as a win.

Of course, my father-in-law wasn't quite so enthused.

"What the *hell*, Nathan?" Paul hissed angrily in the foyer as Maria took Ella and Ruby to the living room, and Alexa disappeared into her room with a firm click of her door. "You don't know her from—"

"We do know her. We've come to know her." I'd been hoping to avoid this exact scenario, but of course I hadn't been able to.

"She is a *stranger*, and you are intending to trust her with your children."

"She's not a stranger. And, in any case, this isn't your concern, Paul."

"It damn well is! Those three lovely girls are my concern." He pointed towards the living room with a shaking finger. "How can you risk their lives?"

His hyperbole annoyed me, although I tried not to show it. "I'm hardly doing that. And anyway, I would have to trust my children to someone. I know Maria more than I know some random nanny sent from an agency. Laura knew her, too, and called her a friend." I folded my arms. "And I don't need to justify my actions to you."

Paul's face was a dull, brick-red, his bushy eyebrows drawn down in a ferocious scowl. "I am *not* happy about this."

"Noted."

We stared at each other for another taut moment before Paul wheeled away, jangling his keys. "We plan to take the girls skiing over Presidents' Day Weekend."

Of course they did. I could already see a parade of holidays where I would never be invited. "We can talk about that later."

Paul nodded, still furious, and then he thankfully left.

Yet later, after the takeout pizza we'd had—Maria had offered to cook, but I told her that could start tomorrow—the girls watching television and the apartment eerily quiet, I'd realized yet again how little I knew Maria, and how I should probably address that before I handed off my family to her like a baton in a relay race.

I found her in the kitchen, the ironing board out, the girls' crumpled uniforms in a basket next to it.

"Oh…"

"I thought I would do this before I go," she said with a smile. "Ella said they needed uniforms for school tomorrow?"

"I should have remembered." Along with a thousand other things.

"That is why I am here."

Such comforting words, and yet they also made me miss Laura, not just because she'd done all these things, but because she'd been my companion and friend in a way Maria never would, no matter how much I came to know her. I sank onto a stool, fighting another wave of grief that threatened to pull me under.

For the few days I'd been so busy, I'd managed not to miss Laura so much. Now, in the cosy lamplight of a warm kitchen, the comforting hiss of the iron as Maria ran it over my daughter's clothes… I missed her as much as I ever had.

I cleared my throat, trying to draw my mind back to the present, and the task at hand. "I was realizing I don't actually know that much about you." I tried to pitch my tone friendly, but the look Maria gave me was guarded.

"What is it you wish to know?"

"I don't know." I smiled, trying to lighten the mood. Maria looked as if she were facing an inquisition. "You mentioned you grew up in Sarajevo?"

"Yes."

"And you had… a brother?"

"Yes." A pause. "Petar."

"Was he older or younger?"

"Older, by three years." Another pause. "He was very serious. Very studious. I was the funny one."

It was hard to imagine this quiet, contained woman as the funny one, but then I remembered how she'd come alive, telling that story about the man with three sons. "You liked telling stories," I surmised, and she gave a quick nod.

"Yes. A long time ago."

"The girls loved that story you told, about the sons. Ruby especially. I hope you can tell her others."

"Yes." Another nod; she was looking less wary, which relieved me.

"Do you have any hobbies?" I ventured. "If there is anything you like to do…"

"Hobbies?" She sounded mystified. "No. I have no hobbies."

"You like to read, maybe?" I persevered. "Or watch movies…?" This conversation felt painful; I didn't know what I wanted from her.

"Yes, a bit. Romance novels." She blushed at that. "Something light."

"Right."

"What about you? Do you have hobbies?"

I had to admit that I didn't. A few years ago, I'd played tennis and squash, been part of a wine-tasting club. When I'd gone into business with Frank, all of that had gone by the wayside. "Work is my hobby," I said, although, of course, that wasn't true. If anything, it was the other way around. Family was my hobby. Work was my life.

Maria must have seen something of this already, because she pursed her lips, her eyes turning shrewd, before she reached for another skirt from the basket and started to iron it.

"I can walk through the day with you tomorrow," I told her, deciding we might as well stick to practicalities. "Show you the girls' schools, the daily routine, where things are in the apartment. The next day I need to be back at work."

She nodded, brisk now, and I decided to try again.

"Do you miss Sarajevo?" I asked. As soon as the words were out of my mouth, they seemed thoughtless. A stupid question—of course she missed it. Her whole life had gone up in smoke there, as far as I could tell. What was I thinking, asking such an idiotic question?

"Miss it?" she repeated. "No." The word was flat and decisive.

"Not at all?"

She shook her head. "I don't miss anything," she said firmly.

"What about your family? You must have left family back in Bosnia?"

The silence that followed felt frozen. Maria continued to iron, her gaze of Alexa's tartan skirt spread out on the board. "No," she said at last. "No family."

"What about your brother?" I asked, puzzled. "Is he in America or Bosnia?"

"He is dead." She spoke tonelessly, her voice devoid of emotion.

"I'm sorry, Maria…" Too late—far too late—I realized I should have guessed this. "And… what about your parents?" I asked hesitantly, unsure if I was being nosily insensitive.

"Dead too." She looked up then, an almost defiant tilt to her chin. "My father was killed by a mortar shell in our apartment. He was reading the paper in the sitting room. We hadn't been able to go in there for weeks because it wasn't safe, but it had been quiet for a few days. There was a whistling and then…" She shrugged her shoulders.

I stared at her in horror. "I'm so sorry…"

"My mother died of pneumonia in a detainment camp in Vojno. We were there for four months."

"I…" I had no idea what to say.

"And my brother was tortured and killed by the Croatian Defence Council." She spat the words, her features twisting. "So there is no one left, besides my aunt and uncle, and I am not on speaking terms with them."

She stared at me for another moment, a hard look on her face, and then she resumed ironing.

I gaped at her, overcome by all these revelations. And I thought, in my self-pitying way, that I'd had the monopoly on grief.

And yet… her confession made me uneasy. What the hell had I done, bringing this woman into our lives? I really hadn't known anything about her, and I felt very aware of it now. How had all those losses affected her? What if she wasn't trustworthy, what if she became unhinged?

Then Ruby came into the room, holding her stuffed elephant by one worn ear. "I can't sleep. Maria, will you sing me another song?"

"Of course." The smile Maria gave Ruby was warm and easy; it felt almost pure. And as she slipped her hand into my daughter's, I told myself I could trust her.

After all, I had to.

Now, back in the office, winter sunlight slanting through the floor-to-ceiling windows, I pushed any thoughts or worries about Maria, and even about Ruby, Ella, or Alexa, firmly to the back of my mind. I didn't want to think about how Alexa still wasn't talking to me, or how Ella hadn't eaten her breakfast, or how clingy Ruby had seemed when I'd said goodbye that morning, still in her pyjamas, Maria tidying up the breakfast table.

I took a sip from my cup of coffee as I followed Frank into our conference room, determined to get at least this part of my life back on track. The girls would be fine.

CHAPTER SIXTEEN

MARIA

"Go, Ella, go!" Ruby was screaming as she jumped up and down next to me, both of us watching Ella cut through the water of the Olympic swimming pool. It was her first race as part of her junior swimming league, and she'd been even quieter than usual that morning, refusing to eat, full of a hard, focused determination.

My eyes stung in the chlorine-heavy air as I checked my phone, the latest iPhone Nathan had given me that I still didn't really know how to work, hoping for a text for him. It was Saturday afternoon, and he'd promised to make the race after checking in with work, but he wasn't here yet and it was almost finished.

This had become a more and more common occurrence in the three weeks since I'd begun working with the Wests. My duties had stretched and expanded to encompass more than had been written on that little list as Nathan immersed himself in work. And I'd let it happen, because I'd enjoyed being needed. Being wanted, even. Belonging. I'd willingly given up my job and volunteering at Global Rescue for this, and I didn't mind it at all.

It had felt amazingly easy, at the start. The look of incredulous delight on Ruby's face when she caught sight of me had been all that I'd needed, and more. So much more.

"You mean you're *staying*?" she'd asked over and over as she scrambled onto my knee. "You're staying for *good*?"

"Not staying, but I will take care of you," I said. "Yes." Nathan was in the foyer, exchanging terse words with his father-in-law, which I was trying not to overhear. "Is that okay, Ruby?" I asked.

"Yes!" This in a squeal that made me smile. "Yes, yes, *yes!*"

I'd pulled her close as she flung her arms around me. When had I last been so fêted? When, even, had I last been hugged?

Ella, naturally, was more cautious, and Alexa ambivalent, at the best of times. I'd told myself to expect that, not to try too hard at first. I let them have their caution; I understood it. I even felt it myself. Everything was still so strange, from the takeout pizza we had for dinner because Nathan had forgotten to buy any groceries, to the account he set up for me on the computer, so I could do the weekly shop online, something I had never done before. The girls crowded around me as I clicked on various pictures, asking for different snacks.

"Can you buy Frubes, please, oh please?"

"Twinkies, Maria! Please buy Twinkies!"

I didn't even know what those things were, but I'd laughed and said I'd think about it.

The strangeness had continued when Nathan tried to engage me in conversation, asking me about my family, about Sarajevo. This was chit-chat, something I'd long lost the knack of. When he asked me about hobbies, I had no idea what to say. And then when he'd pressed about my family… I hadn't wanted to tell him. Who wanted to hear? It always made things awkward, as people stumbled over their apologies, their blatant horror.

I supposed I thought Nathan might understand, at least a little, because of Laura, but he'd looked as stunned and dismayed as anyone else who has heard my story, and not many have, because I never want to tell it. I hoped it wouldn't change his opinion of me, to know my losses. He would not learn anything else. He'd backed off then, at least, perhaps realizing the futility of trying to get to know a ghost.

And yet I hadn't felt like a ghost when I'd tucked Ruby into bed that night, and she'd flung her arms around my neck and kissed my cheek. I'd felt very much alive when Ella, fresh from the bath, had asked me, shyly, so shyly, to help get a tangle out of her damp hair. Even when Alexa had slunk out of her bedroom and complained there was nothing to eat, and I'd been able to smile and tell her I'd buy groceries tomorrow… no, I hadn't felt like a ghost then, either.

And yet with Nathan I did not know how to be.

We stumbled through the routine of the next day, with Nathan showing me the ropes he was still grappling with himself.

"Daddy, my uniform is in *this* drawer," Ruby had exclaimed, rolling her eyes, when Nathan had been showing me where the girls' clothes were. "And I have ballet on *Fridays*, not Thursdays."

Nathan had smiled at me wryly, but with a glimmer of guilt. Beneath the good-natured teasing, there was a sorrowful note that twanged through all of us. *Laura would have known this.*

The next morning, Nathan had set off for work almost as soon as I arrived. I cleaned up the girls' dishes and helped them find their uniforms. Suddenly I was in charge, and I felt as I had when I'd first come to this country, catapulted into a strange, new world I knew nothing about, trying to find my footing and slipping all the time.

The girls liked to help me, at least; they held my hand, skipping down the street as they showed me the way to school. Although Alexa stormed ahead, pretending she didn't know me, all flying hair and catwalk stride.

"You *don't* have to pick me up after school," she tossed over her shoulder as she walked through the school's double doors. "I'm not a baby."

"*I'm* not a baby," Ella said with quiet dignity, and I smiled down at her, squeezing her hand.

"No, of course you are not. I shall see you this afternoon, and be glad of it."

After that, I'd dropped Ruby off at preschool, five minutes late, much to the huffy annoyance of Miss Willis, whom Nathan had warned me about. The other mothers had looked at me askance, with thinly veiled curiosity, exchanging looks with each other, eyebrows raised. No one spoke to me, but I did not mind.

I was back at the apartment by half past nine, and for a little while I'd busied myself, cleaning the kitchen, doing the laundry, making the girls' beds. I tidied Alexa's messy room a little, screwing lids on bottles and boxes of makeup, folding up sweaters, half-afraid to touch her things and seem as if I were poking and prying.

I peeked into Nathan's bedroom, unsure if I should make his bed or not, as I had all the girls'. Then I saw the rumpled duvet and creased pillows and decided I might as well.

It was strange, being in that room. I studied an artistic black and white photo of Laura and Nathan on their wedding day; she was holding her billowing dress down in the breeze, her head thrown back, laughing, as he reached for her hand. It was a moment of pure, uncomplicated joy, captured by a photographer without them even seeming to notice, all of it so foreign to me that I found myself studying it like a scientific specimen. *This is how people are, how they can be.*

I picked up the dirty clothes on the floor, and hung up a pair of trousers in the closet, pausing at the sight of Laura's clothes still hanging next to Nathan's—colorful skirts and soft cashmere sweaters, lots of boots and scarves. I caught the faint scent of her perfume, something orangey I remembered, and it filled me with sadness.

What was I doing here? How could I ever step into this family's life, attempt to help them, even if just in some small way? I was so unqualified. I was so unworthy. And yet I was here.

The Wests had taken over my whole life, what little there had been of it; five days a week, I left their apartment at nine at night or later and was back again by half past seven in the morning. Weekends, I'd started coming over as well, to manage their activities; I spent more time on the bus and train than I did in my own apartment.

A whistle blew from across the pool, interrupting my thoughts, and I looked up to see that the race was finished. Ella had come in third. She pulled herself out of the pool, her little body taut and dripping, and stalked to the bleachers where she'd left her towel.

"Did Ella win?" Ruby asked me, and I took her hand, leading her towards the bleachers.

"She did well."

Yet it was clear from the way Ella was hunched under her towel, her chin jutting towards her chest, that she didn't feel the same. Since joining the junior team, she'd poured all her focus and energy into swimming, with practices three evenings a week. As Nathan often worked late, I took her to all of them, usually with Ruby in tow, sitting a little bit apart from the other parents, listening to Ruby's steady stream of chatter.

I saw the way Ella tried so hard, how frustrated she became with herself when she didn't do as well as the others. I'd tried to talk to her about it, but she'd brushed me off. I'd mentioned it to Nathan, and he'd looked surprised.

"Ella? She's so laid-back. Laura used to worry she was a little too dreamy."

"She seems very focused about swimming."

Nathan had nodded, seeming almost pleased. "It's good for her to have something to focus on. I wish Alexa would find something, other than being angry with me."

I did not know how to answer that, and I wasn't sure it was my place, and so I'd said nothing.

"Good job, Ella," I said now, as cheerfully as I could. Gently, I put an arm around her shoulders, giving them a quick squeeze before stepping back, that little bit of contact still feeling unfamiliar and yet so important. "Shall we have hot chocolate at home to celebrate?"

Ella shook her head, wet hair flying and flicking Ruby and me with cold drops, her face closed, her mouth drawn tight. "There's nothing to celebrate."

"You didn't win?" Ruby interjected, and I gave her hand a quick, warning squeeze.

"I'm proud of you," I told Ella. "But we don't have to celebrate if you don't want to."

"I don't," she snapped and stalked off to the locker room without looking at either of us.

"Why is she so cross?" Ruby asked.

I shook my head and didn't answer. What could I say? Over the last few weeks, I'd immersed myself in the Wests' lives, but there were too many moments like this one when I felt as if I were floundering.

Only a few nights ago, Nathan had worked particularly late and I'd attempted to get Alexa to put her phone on the charger at nine, as Nathan had told me was the rule. She'd refused, rudely, and I'd been too timid and uncertain to press. Yesterday, in one of her sudden fits of temper, Ruby had told me she didn't need to do what I said. Ella had been refusing to eat breakfast for the last few days, and I could count the sentences Alexa had addressed to me since I'd started on one hand. So often, too often, I had no idea what to do with any of it, and yet I still wanted to try. I wanted to help.

"Wasn't Daddy supposed to come?" Ruby asked as we sat on the bleachers and waited for Ella.

"Yes. He must have got caught up in work."

"He always works."

"He is providing for you, Ruby. That is important."

"Providing?" Ruby's little nose wrinkled. "What does that mean?"

"Your clothes, your food, your house, your school. All of these come from your father."

"I don't live in a house."

"Your apartment, then." Her literalism made me smile, even as I worried about Ella. How long would it take for her to get over this disappointment? And why *hadn't* Nathan been here? He'd said he would be. I'd told him it was important.

Ella was silent on the walk back to the apartment; it was late January, the bleakest time of year, the world full of greys—slush and street and sky. Ruby skipped along, clinging to my hand, keeping up a steady stream of chatter I tried my best to listen to, while Ella lagged behind, head tucked low.

Back in the apartment, the emptiness rang out like a bell. Alexa wasn't home, which made me uneasy, and neither was Nathan.

"You said we could have hot chocolate," Ruby reminded me as she scrambled onto a stool. Ella drifted into the living room, curling up on a corner of the sofa, a pillow tucked to her chest.

"Hot chocolate. Yes." Perhaps once she saw the steaming mugs, the whipped cream and the marshmallows, Ella would soften a bit.

I glanced at my phone again. Nothing from Nathan. I wasn't all that surprised, considering how much he'd been working these last few weeks, but I was still disappointed, although I tried not to be.

Over the last three weeks, Nathan had become more and more absorbed in his work, so that by the end of the second week he was leaving before Ruby had woken up, and coming back when she was already asleep. It wasn't much better for either Alexa or Ella; he might say goodnight to Ella, or read her a story, but that was all, and he left Alexa to her own devices, quite literally, poking his head through her door for a few seconds, if that.

Yet who was I to condemn, or even judge? I was here to help, to make his life easier, not point an accusing finger. It wasn't my place or right, but I still worried. We'd stumbled into a rhythm, but it wasn't an entirely natural one. I'd taken over the shopping, the cooking, the cleaning, and—it felt like—a lot of the parenting.

And now Nathan had missed Ella's first swim meet, and that felt like a step too far. I needed to talk to him, but the thought of doing so filled me with fear. I didn't want to jeopardise what I had here, new and fragile as it was, and I hated confronting anyone about anything. Ghosts like me didn't argue.

"Hot chocolate is ready," I called to Ella as I gave Ruby a mug and a small pile of marshmallows, as she liked to sprinkle them on top herself. Ella didn't answer from the living room, and when I glanced in, she was in the same position as before, the pillow hugged hard to her chest.

"Ella." With Ruby decorating her hot chocolate, I ventured into the room and perched on the other sofa. "Are you sad because you came in third?" I asked. I'd never seen her look so closed off and despondent; the pinched, sullen look on her face reminded me of Alexa… which reminded me that Alexa wasn't here, and I had no idea where she was. At nearly fifteen she had a worrying level of freedom that Nathan had sanctioned, more out of weariness, I thought, than anything else. I knew I should speak to him about it, but I wasn't brave enough yet. "Ella?" I prompted gently. "Will you talk to me?"

"I wanted to be first." Her voice was low, the words barely audible. "I needed to be first." She clutched the pillow harder, her arms looking far too skinny wrapped around its velvety softness. I couldn't remember the last time she'd eaten breakfast, and she only picked at dinner.

"Perhaps you will be, another day. It was your first race, after all. There is lots of time."

"No." Ella shook her head, the movement sudden, violent. "No."

"Have some hot chocolate," I coaxed. "It's such a cold day…"

"*No*." Ella got off the sofa and ran into the bedroom she shared with Ruby; I watched her go, feeling as if I'd handled that all wrong, as if I should have known the right words when I so obviously didn't. Perhaps Nathan would.

An hour later, while Ruby and I were coloring at the dining room table, Nathan finally came home. He closed the door softly, as if he didn't want to be noticed, but Ruby was ever alert.

"Daddy!" She raced from the table to the hallway, and I listened to her babble her news. "I had *ten* marshmallows and Alexa *still* isn't home and Ella's *so* cross because she lost her race. She wouldn't even have her hot chocolate." Ruby seemed almost cruel in her succinct honesty.

I rose from the table and began putting the crayons back in their plastic tub.

"I'm sorry I missed the race." Nathan stood in the doorway, his hair and clothes both rumpled, a battered leather messenger bag hanging off one shoulder.

"Ella's in her room."

He raised his eyebrows at my somewhat pointed remark, but I pretended not to notice. Three weeks in this home and I still had not figured out how to act with Nathan. Most of the time, I tiptoed around him; our few conversations tended to be about the logistics of the girls' days, and how to manage them.

Nathan dropped his bag by the door and went in search of Ella, Ruby following behind.

"Ruby," I called to her. "Let them be."

She scowled at me, hands on hips. "You can't tell me what to do."

"I can and I am," I said firmly. I might not know how to handle Ella or Alexa or even Nathan, but Ruby was four. Her I would manage. "Come into the kitchen and help me start dinner."

One of the small, surprising joys of being with the Wests had been shopping and cooking for a family. I had eschewed the convenience of online shopping for the simple pleasure of handling fresh fruit and vegetables in the market, testing their burnished skins and firm texture. I'd even found a shop that sold Eastern European groceries down in the East Village, and pored over the selection of tins and packets I recognized from my childhood. The city I'd tiptoed around for twenty years, my head well down, was becoming my own at last, at least in this small way.

And so I'd made nourishing stews and warming soups, dolma and dumplings, kebabs and *tufahija*—apples boiled in sugar, stuffed with walnuts, and topped with whipped cream. Most things the girls had liked; a few they tried and shook their heads, pushing plates away. I had not minded.

Now I took some minced pork out of the fridge and set Ruby to putting a spoonful in the center of each parcel of dough, all the while half-listening to the murmured voices of Nathan and Ella down the hall.

"I'm sorry," Nathan said a few minutes later, when he came into the kitchen, looking abject. "I should have been there." I did not reply, because there seemed no need. "She's really broken up about coming third."

"It matters to her."

"Yes." He raked a hand through his hair, sighing deeply. "We're working on a new bid. It's taking a lot of time."

Again I could think of no reply. Already, after just a few weeks, I wondered if Nathan was always working on a new bid. Wasn't this what Laura had once said to me, with that disappointed look in her eyes? *He works too hard.*

I bent over the dumplings, pinching the dough together to make a neat seam. Ruby copied me, pressing the dough so hard, her fingers poked through.

"Gently," I reminded her. "Always gently."

"Maria," Nathan asked when Ruby had become bored with the repetition and gone off to play. "I was thinking… how would you feel about this becoming a live-in position?"

I looked at him in surprise. "Live in?"

"Yes, you could have the spare room. I know it's a bit small, but you're here so much as it is…" He shrugged, and I stared down at the dumplings. Part of me wanted to jump at the chance. To live here, in the bosom of this family… and yet I knew it would be an excuse for Nathan to work more, to be less involved, and I could not allow that to happen. "What do you think?" he asked. "It seems like it could make sense, and be easier for you."

"And easier for you," I could not keep from saying.

Nathan hung his head like a little boy. "Yes," he admitted. A beat of silence ticked by painfully. "Maria…" he said finally. "Are you disappointed in me?"

The question surprised me; I hadn't thought he cared or even noticed what I felt.

"I am worried," I answered carefully, afraid of presuming too much, stepping too far. "You are gone so much. Your daughters still need you. I cannot take your place."

"I know."

"All of them need you, in different ways."

"Yes." He nodded, but I could tell that he still didn't know what to do. How to make it better.

"Spend time with them," I urged. "Even when there is work."

"I try…" It sounded half-hearted. It *was* half-hearted; I'd seen it myself how much. How little. "Well, think about living in, at least. For your sake as much as mine."

I nodded slowly, not wanting to say more, even though I knew already I would do it. I could not resist.

"Where's Alexa, anyway?" Nathan asked.

"Out." I shrugged. "I don't know where."

Nathan frowned and glanced down at his phone. "She's been out all day…"

"I don't think it is good for her," I said, still feeling cautious. "All this freedom. It is too much."

"I know." He shook his head, his mouth and eyes both drooping at the corners. "Laura would have known what to do."

I nodded, feeling his sorrow like a wave rolling over us. "I'm sorry I do not."

"I ask too much of you already. I know that, even if I don't act like it. It's just easier… to work." His lips twisted wryly, his eyes filled with pain. "It's something I know how to do. I get it right."

I smiled sadly, touched by his honesty. "This is something you need to get right," I told him gently, gesturing to the apartment, his family. "And you can, just by being here."

"They need more than that."

"It's a beginning."

"I know." He sounded resigned, and for a second, despite all my understanding, all my compassion, I felt angry, and more than that, furious. Suddenly I was filled with a surprise rage; it grabbed hold of me the way a dog would with a bone or a bird, by the throat, shaking it hard. *Do you realize how lucky you are?* I wanted to demand. *You have three daughters, all healthy, all with you, all wanting your love. You lost one person. One. And yet you are willing to throw this all away for what?*

I took a deep, steadying breath, letting that unexpected surge of fury ebb away. It had no place here. I hadn't felt anything like it in a very long time, and it surprised me, the intensity of it, the way it had taken me over. This too, it seemed, was part of coming alive, letting yourself feel not just the joy, but the anger. The grief.

"Just try," I said, and the edge of that anger was audible in my voice.

Nathan stared at me for a moment, as I put the dumplings on a baking tray. "There's a grief support group that meets in a church near here," he said finally. "The church where we had Laura's funeral. I thought… maybe I'd take the girls there. See if it helps." He sounded uncertain, as if he were asking for permission or approval.

And so I nodded. "Yes," I said. "You should do that. That sounds like a very good idea."

Nathan nodded back, looking resigned, as if he didn't want to do it—any of it.

I wondered why he was not holding tight to his daughters, making the most of every moment, even as I understood why he wasn't: some things hurt too much.

CHAPTER SEVENTEEN

NATHAN

The air inside the church was warm and coffee-scented, a welcome change from the freezing temperatures outside, as I stepped through the double doors, Ruby and Ella clinging tightly to my hands, Alexa slouching behind me.

I'd been as good as my word for once and was taking all three girls to a grief support group for families. I'd debated whether to take Ruby, since she was so little, but she'd insisted on going, and with a threatened tantrum in the offing, I'd agreed. Besides, it could be good for her, even if when I'd mentioned it to them this morning, all three of my daughters had looked wary.

"Will they ask us questions?" Ella asked in a whisper. "Do we have to talk?"

"Only if you want to, sweetheart. It's just meant to be a help... to be with people who have been through similar things as you have."

"You mean people whose mothers were shot by some crazy guy?" Alexa interjected in a hard voice. "Wow, I didn't know there were so many of us."

"Alexa." I spoke quietly, but I felt a flash of rage towards my oldest daughter that I knew was utterly unhelpful. "Please don't speak that way, especially in front of your sisters."

"Why not? It's true." Her chin jutted and her eyes flashed, and even though it was only half past seven in the morning, I felt too weary for this.

Maria was bustling about in the kitchen; she'd moved in over the weekend, much to my relief. Ruby had been thrilled, Ella quietly excited, and Alexa, predictably, hadn't said anything at all.

"I think this could be a good opportunity for us," I said with far more determination than I felt. I didn't want to go talk about my feelings with a bunch of strangers, of course I didn't, but all the advice online seemed to say this could be helpful for the girls. "Let's try it at least once."

"And if we don't like it, we don't have to go again?" Ella asked, a bit too eagerly.

I sighed, the battle half-lost already. "No, sweetie," I said, because I only had so much fight in me. "We don't."

Now we stood in the empty foyer of the church, looking around askance. The last time we'd been here had been for Laura's funeral. The day was a blur, but I remembered walking into the church, behind her coffin, borne by six professional pall-bearers, dark and solemn in their black suits. I'd hated it all, the ritualistic formality as well as the terrible finality.

"Daddy, where is everybody?" Ruby asked, tugging on my hand. "It's so quiet."

"They must be downstairs, in the hall." More memories of wandering around assailed me, making small talk and sipping cold coffee, feeling like the host of a particularly horrible party. "Come on, girls. Let's go see."

Silently, we all headed downstairs. As we came to the bottom of the steps, I heard the murmur of voices, a sudden, unexpected laugh. Really? People were *laughing*?

Ella threw me a panicked look. Ruby clutched at my hand so hard it hurt, her little fingernails digging into my palm. And Alexa folded her arms and muttered something under her breath, undoubtedly rude that I chose to ignore, just as I'd chosen to ignore a lot of her behavior, preferring a tense truce of silence than to be continually rebuffed.

I hesitated now, torn between going ahead and doing something proactive and wanting to beat a hasty retreat home. What did you actually *do* in a grief support group anyway?

"Hello, you must be new."

All four of us whirled around to see a middle-aged, smiling woman coming down the stairs, holding a tray of white china mugs.

"We ran out of cups," she explained, hefting the tray aloft. "I'm Eloise. Come, join us."

Reluctantly, feeling as if I had no choice, I followed her into the brightly lit hall, a circle of occupied folding chairs in the middle. Everyone turned and watched us walk in; the girls kept their heads down and I tried not to look anyone in the eye. I was seriously regretting being there.

There was a flurry of introductions that washed blankly over me, and then Eloise explained that the girls went to a separate group in the room behind the hall, for children.

All three girls looked at me with various expressions of dismay—Ruby cautious, Ella terrified, and Alexa giving me a don't-you-*dare* glare that was icy enough to freeze marrow.

"Come on, girls," Eloise said cheerfully, before I could say anything. "There's hot chocolate and cookies." She shepherded them towards the back, one hand firmly on Ella's back, while I stood there, gormless and uncertain.

"There's an empty chair here," one of the women sitting in the circle called to me. "What did you say your name was?"

I hadn't yet. "Nathan," I half-mumbled. I felt like the new kid in school, an experience I'd lived through far too many times in my childhood. Already I was fighting an inevitable flush, my cheeks heating under the scrutiny of a dozen strangers, slinking to my seat.

Everyone introduced themselves again, slowly, so I could remember, but I knew I wouldn't. The chair creaked as I sat down and someone passed me a cup of coffee that I took with murmured thanks. *Now what?*

"So, Nathan, feel free to share your story or just what you've been feeling this week," the woman, Monica, who was clearly the leader of the group said in an upbeat voice. "Or just listen to others. There's never any pressure to speak here." This was followed by several murmurs of heartfelt assent that made me feel as if I'd joined a cult.

I smiled my understanding and buried my nose in my coffee cup, already counting the minutes, if not the seconds, until I could leave. This was so not my thing. What on earth had I been thinking, coming here?

"So, Ali," the leader said cheerfully. "You were sharing…?"

"Just that I'm still so angry," Ali, a middle-aged woman with brown hair and a pinched look, said. She had a tissue balled in one fist, her eyes glittering fiercely. Quickly I looked back down at my coffee, embarrassed by her emotion. "I thought I'd be past this by now. Aren't you supposed to move on?" Her voice broke, ragged with raw feeling, making me shift uncomfortably in my chair. I wasn't ready for other people's pain. I felt the same sense of bewildered discomfort I'd felt when Maria had told me about the loss of her family, in that terrible, flat voice.

"There's no timeline to grief," Monica said with an understanding smile. "If only there was."

"And it's not even linear," someone else broke in. "I've been angry, I've been depressed, I've accepted, and then I'm back again, right at the beginning, thinking how can this possibly have happened?"

Out of the corner of my eye, I glanced at the woman talking—she looked to be in her mid-thirties, with frizzy, sandy hair and an open, friendly face. Most of the people sitting in this circle of sadness were women, I realized. Besides me, there were only three other men, and we were all staring down into our coffee cups.

"That's true, Sarah," Monica said with an approving nod, like a teacher telling a student when she got something right. "Grief isn't linear. It's cyclical."

"So there's no end to it?" It took a stunned second for me to realize I was the one talking. My fingers clenched reflexively around my coffee cup. Why the hell had I spoken?

"It can feel that way, Nathan," Monica said in that same approving voice I decided I didn't like.

"It just goes round and round." Me again. "You never get past it." This was meant with a heavy silence; even in a grief support group it seemed someone could be the buzzkill.

"It does get better," someone ventured. "Sort of."

"Great." I sounded so bitter. "Something to look forward to, then." I really needed to just shut up. I was annoying myself as well as everyone else here. Was it possible to be expelled from one of these things?

"How long has it been since you lost someone, Nathan?" Monica asked gently. I could tell she was going to be the sort of person who used people's names too often.

"Three months tomorrow." I hadn't realized the anniversary was looming; now it felt as if it was pressing down on me. "Three fucking hard months." Now I was being really awkward. People shifted in their seats and I stared down at my coffee, took a defiant sip. Who cared? Wasn't this what these stupid groups were for? Weren't you supposed to be *honest*?

"I'm sorry for your loss," Monica said.

"You must say that a lot around here." Someone needed to stop me. I had no idea why I was being such a jerk, why the words kept bubbling up and out of me, but they just did. I couldn't have stopped myself even if I wanted to, which, strangely enough, I didn't. I was in the angry stage too, it seemed, and I hadn't even realized it. I thought I'd just been tired.

"Yes, I do," Monica answered with quiet dignity. I felt as if I'd insulted her. It really was time to shut up. "Would someone else like to share?"

I stayed silent as several people offered their feelings and experiences, still hardly able to believe I'd been such an ass. I listened to a woman who talked about donating all of her husband's clothes to charity, six months after his death from cancer. I thought of Laura's things in the closet, all over the house, and I couldn't imagine getting rid of any of them. Just the thought sent a visceral shudder of horror through me.

A home swept clean of Laura's things—her scarf not hanging on the hook by the door, her scribbled notes gone from the fridge—*no*. No way. I couldn't do it. I wouldn't.

But what if all the reminders were holding me back? And worse, what if they were holding the girls back? When was it right and healthy to move on, even if it was just a few limping steps? Surely not yet. I wasn't ready. None of us were.

I didn't speak for the rest of the session, and afterwards Eloise brought out a plastic platter of lurid-looking cookies covered with pink icing and refilled coffee cups while people milled around. Everyone clearly knew each other fairly well, gathering in tight knots, and chit-chat seemed impossible. Where did you start? *So who in your family died? Sucks, doesn't it?*

I drained my coffee, deciding I'd get the girls and make a quick getaway.

"Hi, I'm Sarah." The frizzy-haired woman sat down next to me, sticking out her hand with a friendly smile. "You're Nathan?"

I nodded and took her hand, releasing it quickly. "Sorry, I think I sounded like a jerk, in the group." I grimaced. "I didn't mean to."

"We've all been there. Coming to this group… it opens up something inside of you. You end up saying things you never thought you would."

"I didn't even want to come," I admitted, surprised at my sharing. There was something very open about Sarah's face.

At my admission, she laughed, a clear sound. "Nathan, none of us want to come. It's terrifying. It makes your skin crawl. To talk about what happened?" She mock shuddered. "No way. No. way."

Her understanding gratified me, like something clicking into place. *You get it. You really do.* "So why do you come, then?" I asked.

She shrugged, her smile fading. "Because the alternative is worse."

I thought of my self-medicating whiskey and sleeping pills, the oblivion of sleep that felt like my only comfort, other than losing myself in work and neglecting my children completely while Maria took over the entirety of my domestic life.

Yes, the alternative was worse, but I still didn't know if I wanted to come back here. "I don't know what the protocol is for groups like this," I said after a moment. "Are you allowed to ask why you're here, or is that considered rude?"

She laughed again, a soft sound this time, little more than a breath. "No, it's not rude. I lost my husband nine months ago. Pancreatic cancer, diagnosis to death was only six weeks. He was forty-one." She went quiet then, her face drawn into lines of sadness.

"I'm sorry." What else could I say?

"You?" She raised her eyebrows, waiting, as I hesitated. Laura had been on the news, and sometimes still was. I didn't want to be *that guy,* and yet I knew there was no escaping it.

"My wife was shot," I finally said. "By a stranger on the subway. They still haven't caught him." Lisa had called me a couple of times to update me on their progress, or lack thereof, but I'd given up hope. Three months was a long time with no leads. Finding the bastard wouldn't change anything, anyway.

"Oh." A wealth of meaning in that single syllable, as Sarah's eyes and mouth both rounded. Yes, I really was that guy. "I'm so sorry."

I nodded. "Me too. I guess that gets said a lot around here too."

"Yes, I suppose it does. You have daughters?" She nodded towards the back room where Alexa, Ella, and Ruby still were.

"Three."

"How are they coping?"

I shrugged. Would Alexa ever stop being angry? How much of that was natural teenaged angst, and how much was something far more troubling? And what about Ella, still upset over coming in third at her swim meet, as if that even *mattered*, considering everything else we were dealing with? She hadn't eaten much dinner tonight, even though Maria and I had both tried to cajole her. And Ruby... pinging between joy and wild grief, cuddling or throwing tantrums with equal amounts of passion. "I don't really know," I said. "Coping is the right word, I guess. Just."

Sarah nodded. "Sometimes that's enough." She rested one hand on my mine, no more than a light brush, before removing it. "For now. Give yourself time. I know it sounds trite, but it's true."

"You're six months past where I am," I said. "Does it really make a difference?" I didn't mean to sound harsh, but then I heard the disbelieving note in my voice and realized I did. Something flickered across Sarah's face, that open friendliness morphing into something quiet and struggling to be contained. "Sorry," I said. "I didn't mean..."

"It's okay." She spoke quickly, too quickly. "I understand. And it's true. There's no magic pill, no sudden switch and, poof, you're all better. I wish there was. But six months on from where you are? It is easier, if only a little. It doesn't always hurt to breathe." The words were stark and I understood completely what she meant. "Minutes and even hours go by when it's not dominating my thoughts. I don't have the urge to walk up to every stranger in the street and grab them by the shoulders, shake them and tell them, *do you know my husband is dead*? So, yes. It is easier."

My throat grew tighter and tighter with every word she spoke. "I don't know whether to say 'thank you' or 'I'm sorry'," I admitted with a raw laugh.

"I know." She smiled, and I smiled back, although it didn't feel like a smile. It was an acknowledgement of understanding. "Will you come back next week?" she asked.

Part of me still insisted no, even though I knew I would. "I guess I'll see how the girls did."

"Here they come now." The door to the back room had opened, and several children shuffled out, ranging in ages from Ruby's four to a boy with hunched shoulders and hair sliding in front of his face who had to be at least sixteen.

"They break them up into small groups by age," Sarah murmured. "And here's mine."

I hadn't realized she had children, but now I watched as the tall, rangy boy came up to her. His hands were jammed in the pockets of his skinny jeans, his chin tucked towards his chest.

"Can we go?" he asked in a barely-audible mumble.

"Yes, we can," Sarah said with a concerted attempt at cheerfulness; it heartened me that I wasn't the only one struggling with my children. She fluttered her fingers at me. "See you next week."

"So how was it?" I asked the girls when we were outside, the air freezing, the sky clear. "Did you have a good time?"

Alexa turned to give me one of her looks. "Seriously? A *good time*?"

"You know what I meant, Alexa."

"There was hot chocolate," Ruby said, skipping ahead. "With marshmallows. But I didn't get as many as Maria gives me."

"No one made me talk," Ella offered.

Alexa didn't say anything, and I decided to count all three as a win. Limping steps. That was what we were after, wasn't it?

Out of habit, I reached for my phone to check missed calls or texts, my stomach clenching when I saw the number that flashed up, indicating a voicemail. Lisa's cell. I recognized it by now.

I listened to the voicemail as we walked along, the girls engaged in a debate about how old the other kids in their group were, and macabrely, which parent had died.

"Nathan, it's Detective Lisa Worth. I'm calling because we've had some new information come in regarding your wife's assailant, and I'd like you to come into the station so we can update you. Please give me a call back when you can."

CHAPTER EIGHTEEN

MARIA

The morning after Nathan took the girls to the grief support group, just three days after I'd moved into their apartment, I woke up to find Ruby standing about two inches from my nose, her slight form barely visible in the dark.

"Ruby…!" My heart raced and I pressed one hand to my chest as a familiar, icy panic flooded my senses and then started to recede. "You scared me. What are you doing here?"

"Can I sleep with you?" Ruby was hugging her ragged toy elephant, her thumb creeping towards her mouth. "Daddy's already awake and I don't like being in his bed by myself."

"He is awake?" Blearily I saw the clock read half past four. What was Nathan doing up? And should Ruby really be in my room like this? I still felt shy about living here, always making sure to use the bathroom quickly, keeping my little room spotlessly tidy. I'd had no reservation about giving up my apartment in Queens; it had never been a home. But moving in here felt like a bigger step to me than perhaps it was to anyone else. I didn't want to make anyone regret it.

Now, with Ruby standing so plaintively in front of me, I hesitated, unsure if I would be crossing some unspoken boundary by letting her sleep with me, but then Ruby spoke again, her voice catching a little.

"Please?"

"All right, *koka*," I said. The endearment meant little chicken, and Ruby was like a fuzzy little chick, warm and soft next to me as I scooted over in my narrow bed and she scrambled in. She fit her little body close to mine, so I had no choice but to put my arm around her, anchoring her to me. She snuggled closer and after a few seconds she let out a deep, contented sigh, her body already softening in sleep. I closed my eyes, her hair tickling my nose, and breathed in the sweet, sleepy smell of her.

I used to do this, I recalled. I crept into my mother's bed and snuggled with her after I'd had a bad dream. I could picture it perfectly—the wooden shutters drawn against the city sky, the creak of the old floorboards as I tiptoed across the room. My father's faint snores, my mother's sleepy assent. Her solid arms around me, the precious feeling of safety, as if nothing could go wrong as long as I was there, with her.

I felt it now, the comfort of a human being next to me, breath and bone, warmth and love. I pressed my cheek against Ruby's hair as a newfound peace settled over me and I slept.

When I woke, startling awake as if someone had shaken me, it was half past six and the world seemed muted somehow. It took me a moment to realize why—it was snowing. I slipped out of bed as quietly as I could, causing Ruby to curl up into the warm space I'd left behind, and stood at the window, one palm pressed to the cold glass.

The city was cloaked in white, the sidewalks and streets nothing but pillowy drifts, and thick, fat flakes were still gently falling. Not a person or car was in sight; it felt as if the whole world was holding its breath.

"It's snowing!" Ruby's joyful cry split the stillness as she stood in the middle of my bed, her hair a wild red tangle around her delighted face. "Look at all the snow! Do you think we'll have a snow day today?"

I glanced back at the soft sweep of snow of the unploughed street, the lovely emptiness of it. "Almost certainly," I said. "But we shall have to see."

Ruby scampered out to find Nathan, and I dressed quickly and followed, plaiting my hair as I went. Nathan was at the dining room table, still in his pyjamas, hunched over his laptop, his eyes bloodshot.

"Good morning," I said, still feeling shy about being here, and wondering again why he'd been up at such a forsaken hour. Was it just work, always work, or something more?

"Daddy, it's *snowing*," Ruby exclaimed as she hurried over to him. "Maria says we'll have a snow day."

"Maybe," I reminded her. I moved about the kitchen, switching on the coffee I'd prepared last night before starting to empty the dishwasher, tasks that comforted me with their usefulness.

"We'll all stay home," Ruby continued joyfully. "We can go sledding. Daddy, can we go sledding?"

"I don't know, Rubes. Maybe." He ruffled her hair before shutting his laptop.

Ruby flopped on the sofa, already reaching for the remote; she was allowed one episode of something before breakfast, a rule Nathan had set down weeks ago, although he'd admitted that Laura had never allowed it.

Now he came into the kitchen, running a hand through his rumpled hair. "The police called me last night."

"What?" Suddenly the peaceful promise of the day, the vague, benevolent feeling that the snow somehow protected us, evaporated like snowflakes on my tongue. I turned to stare at him, one hand resting on the cupboard, unsure why this news made me fearful and yet knowing that it did. "What about?"

"I don't know exactly. They said they had some new information about Laura's... killer." He grimaced, and I tried to order my features as well as my thoughts. This was good news, certainly. A killer needed to be caught. Yes, indeed… and yet I felt anxious. What if it was someone to do with Global Rescue? What if it changed things?

"That is hopeful, surely?" I managed after a moment, knowing it needed to be said. "To find out something…"

"Maybe." Nathan shrugged. "Maybe they're just trying to appease me. I've given up a bit, with them, after all this time, and it won't make a difference anyway."

"Won't it?"

His face set hard. "She'll still be dead."

"Yes." There was no point denying it. "But knowing… finding justice…" My voice caught, surprising me. There had been no justice for me. Year after year, there had been no justice at all. How could I even believe in such a thing?

"Yes." Nathan sounded unconvinced. "I suppose. I certainly don't want this madman to do something like this again. But…" He paused, and I waited, my hand still on the cupboard. "I feel like we're only just starting to get somewhere, the girls and me. The grief support group last night… it was good. Surprisingly good, because I didn't want to like it at all. But talking about this stuff… it actually helps."

I could only imagine, because I never talked about *this stuff*. Not even once. I pictured my brother's agonised face. *Maria, did they…?* "I am glad, Nathan."

He let out an embarrassed laugh. "Sorry, I don't usually go all emotional like this. It's just… I don't want to take any backward steps, you know? When I feel like we're only just starting to find our balance."

"I'm not sure you can keep yourself from them, at least on occasion."

"You sound like you speak from experience."

I said nothing, because I could not even begin to know what to say.

"How did you get through it, Maria?" Nathan asked softly. "Losing so many people... suffering so much... how did you survive?"

I shook my head, the movement instinctive. Nathan's face was soft with compassion, his eyebrows raised in expectation. He wanted me to say something.

"I'm not sure I did," I said at last.

"What do you mean?"

I shook my head again. "For many years... I've felt like a ghost. I have been a ghost. That is how I survived." I turned away, feeling my face start to heat as my heart raced at admitting such a thing. "That doesn't help you, I know."

"I think I know what you mean," he said slowly. "But surely you don't want to be a ghost forever?"

I tried to smile. "I am not one now." Not quite. I was something in between, shifting all the time. I thought of Ruby snuggled warm against me that morning. Ella's hand in mine. Even Alexa, as much as she tried to resist and pull away. All three of them were bringing me back to life—a painful, necessary process I both feared and savoured.

"They asked me to come into the station today," Nathan said, glancing at Ruby lying on her stomach on the sofa, absorbed in her television show, chin propped in her hands. "So whatever it is, they must think it is important."

"Yes." I glanced outside, the snow falling even more thickly than before. "Do you think that will be possible, to go in today?"

"This is New York. Taxis will be out there within the hour."

But they weren't, and I was thankful for it. As I started to make breakfast, Nathan received texts about the schools closing—both Walkerton and Ruby's preschool. Subways wouldn't be open until at least noon. Drifts were piling up, and there was no sign yet of a snowplow. The world had stopped for a day, and I was glad.

I made pancakes, and during breakfast Ruby clambered onto Nathan's lap, Ella hovering nearby. Even Alexa seemed to have thawed the tiniest bit, although perhaps that was merely wishful thinking on my part. At least she was not rude.

"You won't be able to go to work, Daddy," Ruby said, sounding as if she were relishing the idea, one arm slung around his neck. "You'll have to stay home with us."

"I will, will I?" Nathan smiled and tickled Ruby's tummy, making her squeal in delight.

"Be *quiet*, Ruby," Alexa admonished, but she didn't sound as vicious as she normally did, merely half-hearted, poking at her food.

"Can we really go sledding?" Ella asked. Ruby had already mentioned the possibility more than once. I watched as Ella cut her pancakes into precise squares, something she'd started doing with most of her food, everything so very neat, and very little of it eaten. I worried, especially when I saw how her once-round face was starting to look lean, but I did not know what to do besides gently encourage her to eat. At least now she popped a syrup-soaked piece of pancake into her mouth, making me smile.

"Sledding…" Nathan mused, and everyone waited for his decision. I knew he was tired, that sledding was an effort on the best of snowy days. I recalled Petar, pulling me behind him, trudging through the heavy, wet snow while I cried because I'd got wet. I remembered how he had held me. "I suppose we can."

Ruby squealed again and Ella clapped her hands. Alexa looked surprised, as if she hadn't expected her father to agree. I hid my smile as I turned to the dishwasher with a stack of syrupy plates.

"Will you come with us, Maria?" Nathan asked and I turned back around in surprise, the plates sticky in my hands.

"Me?"

"Yes, you have to come," Ella said. "You told us you liked sledding. You did it with your brother."

I was pleased she had remembered. "When I was a child..."

"Please." This from Ella, who looked beseeching, her hands clasped together under her chin.

"I don't know..." I glanced at Nathan, uncertain whether he wanted me there. Wasn't this his special time with the girls? As ever, I was wary of presuming, of interfering. This was not my family, even though sometimes it felt as if it was.

"You should come," Nathan said firmly. "We want you there. It will be fun."

I looked at all three of the girls' faces, so open and expectant, even Alexa, and I smiled shyly as I nodded. "Very well. Thank you. I will come."

"Yay!" Ruby crowed, clapping her hands, and my smile widened, expanded. Right now I was part of this family.

An hour later we were out on the street, swaddled like snowmen in thick layers of Gore-Tex and fleece, hats pulled down low over our ears. Nathan had dug out two plastic sleds from the storage unit in the basement, and he held one while Ella clutched the other. Alexa stood a little bit apart, arms folded, expression closed, but at least she'd agreed to come. I hoped once we were speeding down a hill she would lose some of her surliness. Everyone was a child in the snow.

"Look, snow!" Ruby scooped up a soft pile, her face alight with the wonder of it—and it *was* wondrous, the world so still and silent, the snow thickly falling, so it soon coated our hats and coats in a dusting of white. The air was crisp and cold, and I could not hear so much as a single car in the distance. The city barely breathed; it felt at peace.

On a day like today I could believe the world was a pure place, that good was truly possible, that things made sense. I could believe and rejoice.

We walked to Central Park, the snow already halfway up to our knees, Ruby hefted on Nathan's shoulders. As we turned into the park, a few other hill-bound families joined us, and a feeling of camaraderie swelled up, children racing off, laughter echoing through the still park, the once-stark trees now heavy-laden with drifts of snow, boughs drooping under the weight.

As we reached the hill, the girls ran ahead, only Alexa staying behind, Ruby falling over in the snow but scrambling up again, joyously undeterred. Nathan offered me his arm as we started up and after a second's pause I took it; the snow was heavy and wet and it was hard-going.

At the top of the hill, I paused to catch my breath, gazing out at the snow-covered meadows, the reservoir an oval of white in the distance, the park an oasis of calm. Some children were already hard at work, pushing a sled down the hill to make a track.

"When will it be my turn?" Ruby asked, torn between excitement and impatience. "Maria, will you go with me?"

"All right," I said, laughing, although I couldn't help but look a bit askance at the steep hill. When had I last been sledding? Perhaps with Petar, when I was ten or eleven. I remembered the feel of the wind in my hair, my eyes streaming as I flew down.

"Daddy, will you go with me?" Ella asked, and Nathan gave his assent.

"What about Alexa?" Ruby asked, and Alexa shrugged, pretending indifference, looking bored.

"She can go with us," I said. "The sled is big enough if we squeeze." I glanced at her, my tentative smile a peace offering I longed for her to accept. "Do you think we can manage it?" She shrugged again.

Nathan and Ella went first, Ruby doing her best to give them a starting push. I reached down to help, my hand flat on Nathan's back, and then they were off.

As they started down, soon picking up speed, Ruby squealed in delight and even Alexa smiled at the sight. My heart expanded with thankfulness and joy. Such a simple moment, and yet it meant so much. I could live in this moment. I could happily stay in it forever, never moving, never changing. Just this, always, would be enough. More than enough.

"Your turn!" Nathan called from the bottom of the hill, his coat dusted with snow. "All three of you!"

I glanced at Alexa. "Do you want to go in the front or the back? Or the middle?"

"I want to go in the front," Ruby cried. "Please, because I'm the littlest."

"Alexa?"

"The back, I guess," she muttered, and so, clumsily, we all clambered on the sled—me first, pulling Ruby onto my lap, and then Alexa behind, her arms wrapped around me. There was no one to push us, and so I reached one hand out and pushed off.

Then we were going—slowly at first, and then faster and faster, the wind whipping by, the snow stinging my eyes, a shriek of both delight and alarm tearing my lungs as the world blurred by just as I'd remembered. From behind me, I heard Alexa laugh.

As we came to the bottom of the hill, the sled wobbled and we all tumbled off, into the snow that seemed to reach up and softly envelop us.

Ruby appeared over me as I blinked up at the sky, her face split by a wide, gap-toothed grin. "Can we go again?"

"Yes, when I catch my breath." I struggled up to a seated position and glanced over at Alexa. She was smiling faintly, brushing the snow from her hair. As I looked at her, she caught my eye—and held her smile.

Right then the past seemed to dissolve into fragments and I felt as if I could see the future, stretching out in a shimmering, golden line of promises. *You will survive. You will be strong. You will see why everything happened the way it did. It will be good.*

I was seeing it now, already, exalting in whatever curious twists of fate or guiding hand of Providence had brought me to this moment, covered in snow, with the unexpected sound of joy ringing in my ears, surrounded by happy girls.

"Again," Ruby said, pulling on my hand, and laughing, I let her lead me back up the hill.

We stayed out all morning, returning to the apartment with our clothes wet and our cheeks reddened by wind and cold. The snow had stopped falling, and the sky was a fragile blue, the city's busyness starting up again. Already Fifth Avenue had been cleared, a heap of greying snow piled by the gates to the park, taxis moving steadily downtown.

I wanted to hold onto the euphoria of our morning out, but, of course, you cannot hold onto such things. I felt it slip away like a shadow even as I struggled to keep it—by making hot chocolate, being generous with marshmallows, hanging the wet clothes on the radiators, the dripping sleds propped by the front door, all reminders of our happiness, that it had been real.

Nathan came into the kitchen, his cell phone in one hand. His cheeks were ruddy, his hair mussed, but he had a look of intent about him that already I knew well.

"The trains are running. I should go to work." He lowered his voice. "And the police station… to find out what they know."

"Yes, of course." I stirred the hot chocolate, the milk and cocoa swirling together, trying to keep that unwelcome feeling of anxiety from creeping in and taking over. *What was I afraid of?* What have I ever been afraid of? The answer, for twenty-six years, had been everything.

Nathan turned to get ready, and I began to pour out the hot chocolate. While the girls were still spooning the whipped cream from the top of their mugs, I heard the front door click softly closed.

"What shall we do this afternoon?" I asked brightly. "How about a board game?"

"Oh yes, please," Ruby cried. Ella nodded. She'd lost a bit of that pinched look she'd had lately, and she'd eaten all her breakfast this morning. Swim practice was cancelled that evening, something I was thankful for. Even with Nathan gone, today was still a reprieve of sorts. I could hold onto that, at least.

We set up Monopoly on the dining room table, Alexa even deigning to play, albeit reluctantly. I marvelled again at the simplicity of it all—the laughter, the excitement, the solid warmth of Ruby on my lap, playing an imaginary game with the Monopoly pieces as the rest of us rolled the dice and traded properties. Everything about it was sweet. Everything about it was fragile.

I felt its fragility as the game inevitably disintegrated into an argument, and Alexa slunk off to her room with her phone, Ella and Ruby sprawled on the sofa in front of the television while I cleaned up the scattered cards and pieces.

I felt it as I drifted into the kitchen and gazed down at the street, now freshly plowed and full of traffic, lined with deep furrows of grey-brown slush that sprayed onto the sidewalks as cars slid past.

I felt it as Nathan texted, as I'd known he would, that he was going to be late yet again.

I felt it as I stared out at the endless city streets and knew there was a man somewhere amidst that maze who had killed Laura West, and one day he would be found.

And I felt it as the simple joy of the morning faded into a far more familiar and amorphous fear and dread.

This wasn't my life. It never would be. As much as I longed to, I could not hold onto it; already I felt it start to slip away. Soon it would be gone forever, and in the end I would have no one to blame but myself.

CHAPTER NINETEEN

NATHAN

"We have a suspect."

The four words jolted me, because no matter what Lisa had said on the voicemail, no matter what had brought me to the station in the depths of a snowy day, I hadn't expected this.

"You do? Who is he?" My mouth was dry, my heart starting to hammer, although I didn't even know why. Just as I'd told Maria, this didn't change anything. It only felt as if it did. "Do you have him in custody?" I felt as if I were on some crime show. *Have you apprehended the assailant?* I didn't use words like that. No one did. Yet here we were.

"He isn't in custody," Lisa said, perpetuating the surreal feeling that I'd stumbled onto a TV show filled with bad actors. "But we are starting to develop a picture of who he might be."

"How…?"

"Some colleagues in another department alerted us." Which was a way of saying nothing.

"Alerted…?"

Lisa paused. "We believe he has recently entered the country, and that he was acting entirely alone."

I leaned forward, my fists balling. "So you think he does have some link with Global Rescue?"

"I didn't say that."

"You didn't say anything, actually," I snapped, giving vent to the fury that kept rising like a tide inside me, overtaking my common sense. "What do you really know about this... this *killer*?" It was starting to feel so familiar, this rage, like putting on a comfortable sweater. It fit, and it felt better than grief. "What the hell is any of this supposed to mean?"

"We're trying to give you some answers, Nathan," Tom interjected in his gravelly voice. I hadn't realized we were on a first-name basis. "We're all on the same side here, and jumping to conclusions doesn't help anyone."

"And what conclusions do you think I'm likely to jump to?" I said. "It's been three months, and you still have no answers." And I realized I wanted some, even if it didn't change anything. At least then I would know. Perhaps it would bring some sort of closure, if not actual peace.

"We wanted to share what information we do have," Lisa answered with dignity. "I know it's frustrating that it's not very much, but we are trying. We're going over CCTV records from Global Rescue as well as all the other cameras in a five-block radius, and the cameras on all the nearby subway lines. We've interviewed everyone we've deemed relevant at Global Rescue, and we're also reviewing all immigrant entries into the country over the last three months. All of this is very time-consuming, as you can imagine."

I sagged back against my seat, the fury that had been propelling me forward giving me purpose, leaving me in a rush. Nothing mattered. Nothing changed anything. Why did I keep hoping it would?

"Thanks for the update," I said dully. "I know you're doing your best."

"We called you in because we have another CCTV image of him," Lisa said, as if she were giving me a peace offering, or even a treat. "A clearer one. If you want to take a look...?"

Wordlessly, I took the black and white printout. It was of the back of a man's head as he walked down the street; he could have been anyone, although I recognized his clothing and even his rangy stance from the other pictures I'd looked at. "How do you even know this is him?"

"Based on the other CCTV footage we've pulled, the timing on this one works," Tom explained. "This was taken about halfway between Global Rescue and the subway station, in front of a jewelry shop, two days before the attack."

I glanced again at the picture, wondering if this man had had it in his head even then that he was going to kill someone. Kill Laura, even. It seemed so surreal, so impossible, and yet I'd been living with the knowledge for months now. When would I be able to accept it?

I was about to hand the photo back when something caught my eye.

Lisa, with her hand already out to take it, raised her eyebrows. "Nathan? Do you notice something?"

"Sorry…" I studied the image for another second—the man walking on a crowded street, people all around him, indifferent, busy. It didn't mean anything. Of course it didn't.

Because Maria was walking a couple of steps in front of him. Her back was to the camera, so I couldn't be sure it was her, but I thought I recognized her coat, the way she walked with her head slightly bowed. She had a patterned drawstring bag over her shoulder, the same one I'd seen her with before. Yes, it had to be her, walking right in front of the man who had killed my wife.

Coincidence? It had to be. Of course it did.

"Nathan?" Lisa prompted.

"Sorry, it was nothing," I said as I handed the photo back.

I didn't know why I'd lied. Perhaps because I didn't want them bothering Maria, bringing her in for questions. She would hate that, I knew it instinctively. None of this had anything to do with her. She just happened to be walking back from the center at the same time. That was all it was. All it could be.

By the time I got home after eight o'clock that night, after having put in a full day's work on the plans for the bank on Grand Street, I had managed to push the meeting with the police to the back of my mind, but it still lurked there, like something murky hiding in the dark, waiting to emerge.

The apartment was quiet as I entered, Ella and Ruby already asleep. I tried not to feel guilty about it; I'd been with them all morning, after all, and yet the simple purity of those snow-filled hours seemed a long time ago now, almost as if they'd never happened at all.

"Nathan?" Maria came into the hallway as I dropped my bag by the door, her face pinched with anxiety. "Did you see the police?"

Her question made me pause in a way it never would have before. Why did she care so much?

"Yes, I did." I could hardly credit I was being suspicious. I was being *stupid*. What on earth could Maria possibly have to do with any of it? Nothing. Of course, nothing.

One hand fluttered towards her throat. "And what did they say?"

"Not much. Just that he had recently arrived in the country."

"From where?"

Again I looked at her. Wondered, I didn't even know what. "They didn't actually say." I realized I probably should have asked. "They also had a new photo pulled from a CCTV camera, of him walking in the street."

"Oh? Did you learn anything from that?"

I paused, wondering if I should tell her she was in the photo. I felt guilty for suspecting her of anything, when there couldn't be anything to suspect her *of*. She didn't pull the trigger.

It was just that I was so tired, and so desperate for answers, as if Laura's death could be tidied up, wrapped in a bow, presented as a finished, understood thing. *This is how. This is why.*

Life didn't work that way. I knew it didn't; I'd accepted it a long time ago. I didn't believe in fate, or God, or some grand plan we are all part of, threads in a huge tapestry nobody could actually see. So why now did I feel this sudden, stupid urge to make connections, to find meaning?

"Nathan?" Maria prompted. She sounded a little nervous, and so, recklessly, I decided to tell her.

"Not really. It was only the back of his head as he walked down the street. But actually, weirdly enough, you were in the photo, Maria." I knew as soon as I said that I shouldn't have. Her eyes widened as she scanned my face, registering the tone I'd meant to sound offhand and was anything but. Now I really was a bad actor in some stupid show.

"I was?" Her voice was faint, but then grew stronger. "I *was?*"

"Yes, you were in front of him, walking down the street. Almost as if he were following you." I don't know why I said that; I didn't actually think it was true. Did I?

Maria's face paled, her blue-green eyes as huge as lakes.

"Nathan... do you actually think..." Her voice trembled, and I suddenly felt like the world's biggest jerk.

"I don't think anything, Maria." Clumsily, I patted her on the shoulder, and she flinched away. "I'm sorry, I didn't mean to sound as if I did. It was just... weird. It shook me a little."

She nodded slowly, and I couldn't tell if she believed me. "It is all very strange," she murmured, her face still pale, her hands fluttering at her sides as if she didn't know what to do with them. "You think perhaps he has something to do with Global Rescue after all? There could be a link?"

"I don't know." I was tired of talking about it all, of going around in circles, ending up nowhere. "I don't know. Maybe."

"Will the police… will they call me in, do you think?"

"I don't know." There seemed to be no end to my ignorance. "They didn't seem to recognize you in the photo, or at least they didn't mention it to me, and I didn't tell them it was you. Have you spoken to them before? They mentioned interviewing people…"

"Yes, early on. They questioned everyone who had volunteered at the same time as Laura." Her hands were now clutched in front of her, fingers laced tightly together.

"If they called you in, Maria, it would just be to ask you questions."

"I know." Her lips trembled as she smiled. "I know. It is just…" A pause as she struggled to find the words. "I don't like the police."

"Why not?"

"It is not just the police. It is… anyone like that. With… with power." She swallowed. "I have seen it abused."

"But this is America," I said, acknowledging as I said the words how naïve I sounded, how condescending. Terrible abuses of power happened here all the time. "What I mean is, I'd help you. I'd make sure…" I trailed off, aware how inept I sounded, along with naïve.

Maria stared at me for a long moment, her expression closed and fathomless. I had no idea what thoughts were veiled by her clear, blue-green gaze, and I realized I had no right to make any assurances to her at all.

"Maria, what I'm trying to say is, I don't want you to worry. They won't call you in anywhere." A promise I could hardly make, yet I still did. "And if they do," I added, because this was at least something I could genuinely offer, "I'd be happy to go with you."

She looked surprised, and still guarded, but after a few seconds she nodded. "Thank you, Nathan." She smiled, faintly, without it reaching her eyes, and then turned around and went to her room. I watched her go, feeling as if I'd offered so little, and she knew it.

*

By the time the grief support group rolled around the next week, the snow had melted to nothing more than a few slushy piles and I'd forgotten about the meeting with the police and that damned photo, or at least pretended to.

"Why are we going again?" Alexa asked in a bored voice as we walked the four blocks to the church.

"I liked it," Ruby chimed in. "They gave us cookies." And she'd bonded with Eloise, the leader of the children's group, which made me less reluctant to bring Ruby along. She was benefitting from it, even if Alexa didn't seem to be.

"What did you talk about?" I asked, sidestepping Alexa's question.

"What do you *think* we talked about?" Alexa snapped, flicking her hair. It was getting harder and harder to reach her; it seemed amazing to me that six months ago, we'd taken a selfie together on my phone, while walking to school. Alexa had been giving a big, cheesy grin, the likes of which I hadn't seen since.

I didn't even remember the moment; the sight of it on my phone, when I'd been flicking through photos as I often did, had shocked me. I'd stared and stared, as if it could offer me more than the simple fact of Alexa there, looking nonchalant and carefree, without the sullen darkness that surrounded her now like a shroud.

"We didn't actually talk," Ella informed me quietly. "But other kids did."

"And what did they say?" I asked, trying for a gentle tone, an encouraging smile.

Ella just shrugged.

"They said how it all basically sucks," Alexa said in a bored voice. "The End. What is the point of this, anyway?"

"Alexa, please. I'm trying." I smiled encouragingly at Ella, who looked away, her face drawn and pinched.

"Are you really?" The contempt in Alexa's tone made me cringe; it almost made me furious.

"Yes, actually, I damn well am," I snapped before I could manage to rein in my temper. "No thanks to you." Which of course made it worse.

Hurt flashed across Alexa's crumpled features, so quickly I almost missed it, and then she turned away. "Fine, then go to the stupid group on your own," she called over her shoulder, and she kept walking down the street, past the open doors of the church.

"Alexa…"

In response, she gave me the middle finger, without even turning around. I stopped there in the street, Ella and Ruby clutching my hands, as my oldest daughter was swallowed up by the darkness.

"Daddy." Ruby tugged on my hand. "Is Alexa in trouble?"

"Are we going in?" Ella asked, her voice wobbling.

I stared down the street. Alexa was gone. I could race after her, but what was the point? We'd just fight. She was almost fifteen; she'd be fine on her own for an hour. Maybe she'd even cool down a bit, and we could have a rational discussion later, or something close to it.

And yet I felt as if I were doing something wrong as I mounted the steps with Ella and Ruby, the church enveloping me with its comforting, coffee-scented warmth.

"We're just leaving her?" Ella asked anxiously. "Where will she go?"

"She'll be okay, Ella. Maybe she'll join us in a bit." I didn't believe that for a second.

"Nathan." Sarah smiled warmly as I took a seat next to her, having dropped Ruby and Ella off at their group. "How has your week been?"

"Alexa didn't come in with me," I blurted. I felt the childish need for reassurance. "She was angry about something I'd said…

I lost my temper." I shook my head, wondering at my parenting decisions. Why did I never know what to do?

Sarah's smile morphed into concern. "Where is she now?"

"Outside somewhere." To my horror, my voice actually wobbled. "I don't even know where. She just walked off, and I let her." I shaded my eyes with my forefinger and thumb, not wanting to break down in a grief support group, of all places—surely the right place for it, and yet I didn't want to. Not here, not ever. "I'm a crap father, basically," I told Sarah with an attempt at a laugh. "That's all you need to know."

"That's not true, Nathan."

"How would you even know?" It came out rudely, even though I hadn't meant it to.

"You're here, aren't you?" Sarah countered. "You're trying."

"That's what I told Alexa." I grimaced at the memory. "Angrily."

Briefly, Sarah laid a hand on my arm. "That's understandable. Look, why don't we go out and look for her? She can't have gone far."

I lowered my hand to look at her. "But the group…"

Sarah shrugged. "Is here every week."

"Ella and Ruby…"

"Will be fine. I'll tell Eloise you're going out. It's going to be okay, I promise."

"Considering you're here, how on earth can you make a promise like that?" I demanded, sounding more broken than angry.

Sarah shrugged again, a sad smile turning up the corners of her mouth. "I have to believe it's true. Otherwise, how do you get through each day?"

A few minutes later, we were outside, the night seeming darker and colder than before. I questioned my parenting ability yet again, that I'd let Alexa walk off like that. She'd been angry. She'd been hurt. And it was my fault, just as she'd told and shown me again and again.

"She was walking towards the park," I said as we set off towards Fifth Avenue. "But I don't think she would go in it. She knows the park can be dangerous at night." I couldn't believe I had to say the words. What the hell had I been thinking?

"Are there any other places she might go?" Sarah asked. "Friends nearby…?"

Friends? I realized I didn't really know any of Alexa's friends. A couple of them had come to the funeral with their parents, but we'd only exchanged pleasantries, and I couldn't remember their names or faces. None of her friends visited our apartment; everything seemed to be through social media. "I don't know," I admitted. "Probably not." Although maybe, who knew? Not me, obviously.

"All right, well, let's keep walking."

"She's been angry with me since Laura died," I confessed as we continued walking towards the park. I felt a sudden, unbearable need to admit to all the ways I'd failed. "She blames me for Laura's death."

"That's understandable," Sarah murmured, and I nearly stopped mid-stride.

"Is it?"

Sarah turned and caught sight of my shocked expression. "Oh, Nathan, I only meant that it's a common reaction in bereaved children, to blame the parent for the other's death."

"But why?"

Sarah gave me a sympathetic smile. "Because you're alive."

And Laura wasn't. And I knew, without any self-pity or judgment, that Alexa would have preferred I died rather than Laura. Of course she would have. Alexa and Ruby, too. Laura had been there, and too often I hadn't.

I couldn't change that. I couldn't rewrite the past or make it any better. I couldn't reframe all the memories that kept surfacing, reminding me of how it had really been—the sweet ones, which I savoured, and the cringing ones that made me want to have been better.

All I could do was try to fix the future, and lately I hadn't been doing that, either; I'd been hiding behind work, staying away because it was so much easier, when I knew my girls needed me, just as Maria had told me they did. Why hadn't I listened? Why hadn't I tried harder?

They needed me to show up—not just for a snowstorm, but for every day, day after mundane day, to just *be* there, again and again. And it would start with me finding Alexa tonight.

It took forty-five minutes of walking up and down the avenues with Sarah, checking in various cafés and coffee shops, before I finally found Alexa huddled in a diner on Madison Avenue, a can of Coke in front of her. It was five minutes to eight.

"Alexa…" I stood in the doorway, longing for the right words to say, wishing they came naturally. Sarah stood outside, giving us as much privacy as the public space could afford.

Alexa bent her head, her hair falling forward to hide her face. I walked forward. "Talk to me," I implored in a low voice. "Please. I'm sorry I lost my temper, I really am. But I don't understand why you're so angry, Alexa." Too late I realized how accusing I sounded, as if this was all her fault. "I mean, I understand about being angry," I tried to explain. "Trust me, I do. I'm angry, too. But… I want us to be in this together. For all our sakes. So we can move forward…"

Alexa still wouldn't look at me.

I felt impatience pick at the edges of my temper. "Alexa…" It sounded like a warning, even though I hadn't meant it to. I couldn't even get my heartfelt apology right.

"You've never wanted us to be in anything together," she said finally, her voice so low, I strained to hear it. "Ever."

"What is that supposed to mean?"

"What do you think it means?" She looked up, her face full of fire again. I hadn't reached her at all. "Mom wasn't happy with you. Why do you think she was volunteering at that stupid center? Because she didn't like being your stupid trophy wife. Because she wasn't interested in climbing some stupid social ladder, or having us all go to these snobby private schools that none of us even like. It's only you who wanted all of it. Any of it."

"Alexa…" I felt winded; it hurt to breathe. "You don't mean that."

"And what if I do?" she snarled. "What if you've got it wrong all along, Dad? You're playing the grieving husband, but what if it wasn't like that? I mean, do you even notice Mom is gone? Because you were *never even there.*"

"That is not true." My voice came out in a growl. I would not let my daughter tear my memories to shreds; they were damaged enough as it was. "Look, I know I wasn't always the best father. I know I probably worked too hard—"

"Probably?"

"For God's sake, Alexa, it was for you and your sisters—our *family*—"

"For God's sake?" she sneered. "But you don't even believe in God."

I shook my head slowly. "What does that have to do with anything right now?"

"You don't believe in anything. You don't *care* about anything," she cried. "Of course you don't care about God. You don't even care about *us.*"

And then she was gone again, pelting out of the restaurant and down the dark street, away from me.

CHAPTER TWENTY

MARIA

I was in the living room, a book on my lap, when the front door was hurled open and Alexa pelted into the apartment, her hair flying, her face streaked with tears.

I rose from the sofa, icy panic flooding my senses. "Alexa—"

"Leave me *alone*." She hurled the words over her shoulder before slamming into her room. I stood completely still, shocked and silent, listening to the sound of Alexa throwing herself on her bed, and then the far worse sound of her sobbing as if her soul was being torn from her body. I knew that sound.

I hesitated, unsure what to do. Where was Nathan? Ella? Ruby? Should I go in? How could I, when she so clearly wanted to be alone?

How could I not?

Don't do this, Maria, I told myself. *You cannot handle this. It is too much for you.*

From the kitchen, I heard my phone ping with a text. I walked to it slowly, the sound of Alexa's sobbing loud in my ears.

The text was from Nathan: *Hey Maria. Is Alexa back?*

How to respond? *Yes. She is upset.*

Okay. I think I'm going to let her cool off for a bit. I'm taking Ella and Ruby out—be back in an hour or so and then we'll talk. N.

I was not sure this was the right approach, but I did not feel I could say as much to Nathan, at least not over a text.

Alexa continued to sob. I stood in the hallway, my hand hovering over the doorknob. What could I do? What could I *say*?

I had no words to make things better, no magic wand to wave. I was just a woman—a broken, frightened, ghost-like woman.

But I was coming alive, and I knew that sound too well, and I could not leave a hurting girl alone. I reached for the knob, and I turned it.

The room was dark and cluttered, as it always was, because I was too hesitant to tidy it up properly. Alexa was on the bed, her thin back to me, her hair covering her face as her body was racked with sobs.

"Alexa…"

"Go *away*." A deep, whole-body shudder went through her and she curled up into a ball, like a baby, like someone trying to hide.

I sat on the edge of the bed, at a loss. There were no assurances I could give, there were no promises I could make. This was grief—raw, real, ugly, endless. I knew it. I'd felt it, until I hadn't been able to feel it any longer, and that was its own loss. The knowledge encouraged me, strangely—at least Alexa could feel.

I reached out one hand to touch her shoulder, her hands up by her face. I wasn't quite brave enough to do it, and that's when I saw. Three scored lines on her inner arm, not deep enough to mean it. *Oh, Alexa.*

Without even realizing what I was doing, I reached out to touch one, the pad of my thumb skimming along the raised, reddened flesh, before Alexa jerked her arm away, her face twisting in a mask of rage.

"What are you…" Her voice died away as she saw what I'd seen. She bit her lip, her eyes wide, her face blotchy. "It was an accident at school."

Three neat lines, like tic-tac-toe?

I shook my head, everything in me soft and sad. "No, it wasn't, Alexa."

Her anger turned to fear, which made me sadder. "Don't tell Dad, Maria. Please."

I took her wrist again, and she let me. I ran my finger over the lines, each in turn, my touch gentle. Silently, Alexa watched me, waiting to see what I would do.

I wondered how long she had been cutting herself, doing anything to end or at least blunt the pain.

"Maria…" Her voice was hesitant. Another minute passed; I was still holding her wrist. Then, wordlessly, I dropped her wrist and held out my own, rolling up my sleeve. Alexa stared at me in confusion and then she looked down.

Mine was deeper, because I'd meant it.

Alexa looked up, silent questions in her eyes like stars. She glanced at my other arm, and so I held it out too, pushing up the sleeve so she could see both scars. Twenty-three years old now, made a year after the war had ended, when I had felt as if I could endure no more.

The lines were no more than pink seams in my skin, slightly raised, on each wrist. That was what happened to scars—at least the ones on the outside. They faded. They healed as best as they could, while other parts of you did not.

"Why…" The word was a whisper. Alexa reached out to touch one of my scars, but then she drew her hand back.

"Because at the time, it felt like the only way. But it wasn't. I promise you, it wasn't."

She looked up at me fearfully. "Were you trying to…?"

I hesitated, and then I nodded. "Yes."

"Why…?"

"Because it hurt so much." I would not burden her with any of the details. I did not want to think of them myself.

"But you didn't…"

"No, it turns out it is quite difficult to do that." Neither of us wanted to name it. "For which I am grateful." Although I wasn't at the time—I wasn't for a long time, not even until now, when I had these girls in my life. I brushed my fingers against her lines. "I understand this, Alexa," I said softly. "Sometimes you feel as if you will burst with the pain. Your body cannot hold it. But this…" Another brush, feather-light. "It is not the right way."

She made a choked sound. "Then what is?"

What answers did I have to give? What ones had I found? "To let yourself keep loving," I finally said. It had taken me so long to realize this, to risk it. "As best as you can."

A tear trickled down her cheek as she looked down at our bare arms, marked by scars. "I don't know if I can."

"Why, *koka*?" I spoke gently, as if she were my little chicken, as if she were as small as Ruby.

Alexa shook her head. I could feel her withdrawal, like a cooling in the air. She pulled her arms away, yanking the sleeves down to cover the scars. After a moment I did the same. I would not push.

"I won't tell your father yet," I said quietly. "But you must, Alexa. This is not a secret to keep."

"I can't…"

"And you must stop." I gestured to those three lines again. "For your own sake. It is not good."

"You won't tell him, though?" she asked, sniffing.

"No." I was reluctant to make any sort of promise. "But will you?"

Alexa sniffed again and nodded. "I'll try," she said, and I let that be enough, at least for now. She turned away from me, wiping her sleeve across her eyes. "Thanks, Maria," she mumbled, and my heart lightened, then filled. This was hope—this darkened room, this slight girl, these scars.

I touched her shoulder once, and then I rose from the bed. I let her be, going to the kitchen, moving around the apartment as I tidied up aimlessly, my heart both full and sad.

I had never thought my own pain could help someone else's. I had never thought my scars were anything but that—signs of my own woundedness, marks to bear, a life to endure.

But this… this possibility that it was *because* of those scars, I could reach Alexa… I could help Ella… I could love Ruby. I could love all of them; I could give them something I hadn't even realized I'd had. *Me*. The thought was intoxicating, overwhelming, wonderful. It gave purpose to my life in a way I had never dared hope for.

A little while later the front door opened, and I heard Nathan come in with a drooping Ruby—it was an hour past her bedtime—and Ella. I went into the hallway, my heart still so full.

"Maria." Nathan smiled tiredly. "How is Alexa?"

"She is okay." I did not know what else to say, how to explain. A new thought had occurred to me, filling me with sudden, fearful alarm. What if Alexa told Nathan about my scars? What if it made a difference to him? He might think I was unstable, untrustworthy, too damaged to be of use. And what if I was?

"Good." He rested a hand on my shoulder, the feel of his palm warm and solid. "Thank you."

"It is nothing." Not true.

"I'm just going to put Ella and Ruby to bed."

"Okay." I watched in some surprise as Nathan helped Ruby on with her pyjamas, and then read her a story. I could not remember the last time he had done such a thing. I hovered in the hallway while he tucked them in, kissing them goodnight. When he came back into the living room, I was sitting on the sofa, my book unread in my lap.

Nathan sat down opposite me with a sigh. "I'm sorry for offloading Alexa onto you. She was so angry with me…" He shook his head, his gaze turning distant. "She said some things… true things, probably." A shuddery breath. "But I knew I couldn't deal with it. I'd get angry again, and I'm tired of being angry."

"It was all right. I spoke to her." Without realizing it, I traced the graven line of my scar through my sleeve.

"You did?"

"Yes. A little bit. I think… perhaps… it helped."

A smile broke across Nathan's face like a wave, like sunshine. "Thank you, Maria. I don't know what I would do without you."

My chest warmed along with my cheeks. I looked down at my book. I felt full—my heart, my soul, everything.

"Alexa said some things," Nathan said in a low voice, with a glance at his daughter's closed door. "About Laura…" He stopped, and I waited. I did not feel I could ask for more. "She said Laura was unhappy with… with me. With our life. And I have to admit, in these last few months, I've started to wonder, to think that maybe she was, at least in some way." He glanced at me, looking like a little boy. "Do you think she was?"

How on earth was I meant to answer that? I thought of Laura's frustrated sigh, her downturned mouth. I could not burden Nathan with those things now; they were so little anyway. "I did not know her well enough to say," I offered at last. "But she did not seem very unhappy." That much I knew.

"Thank you," Nathan said after a moment. "I always knew she didn't like me working so much, but I thought it was a price worth paying. I thought we wanted the same things but now I don't know. I don't know anything." He shook his head, despondent. "And I hate second-guessing it all. It makes me feel as if I didn't know our marriage at all. As if I didn't know *Laura*."

"You cannot let the present rewrite the past," I said slowly. "You loved each other. That is a truth that time cannot change."

"Yes, we did, but…" Nathan shrugged helplessly. "I just keep going around in circles. Tonight was the first time things actually felt normal, for just a little while. I took Ella and Ruby out for ice cream with another family from the support group, and we actually *laughed*. Just a little. And then I felt so guilty… as if I'd forgotten Alexa, as if I'm betraying Laura. Does that make sense?"

"Yes." It sounded like grief in one of its many forms, always twisting its shape, turning into something else. Had I felt guilty for laughing, for surviving? No. I'd felt envious, for those who had died. But that was not something I could tell Nathan now, not when he'd laughed and I had held hope in my hands, like a butterfly about to take wing.

"There is a word in my country," I said instead. "You do not have it here, but it is a word that I think is good for you. *Dilbere*." I let myself linger over the syllables.

"What does it mean?"

"It is often translated as dear or darling. I have even seen heart-throb, but it means so much more than that." I paused as I felt my throat thicken and I thought of those who were my *dilberes*, ghosts alongside me. "It means 'the one who carries your heart'," I said softly. "And that is true for you and Laura. She carried your heart, and you carry hers. When you laugh, when you seem to forget, when you grieve. You will always carry it." My throat grew even tighter as I registered the sheen of tears glossing Nathan's eyes.

When he spoke, his voice was hoarse. "*Dilbere*. Yes. I like that. Thank you, Maria."

I nodded, feeling even fuller than before. I had helped Alexa; I had helped Nathan. I had offered more of myself than I ever had before, and it had been accepted.

That night I was full of hope, buoyant with it, lighter than air. I didn't realize that, like grief, hope has many shapes, that it can twist and turn into something else.

I thought this was a beginning, when in fact it was an end, which was then a beginning in itself. Right then, I saw the future in a long, shimmering line, when it was forever a circle, twisting around and around on itself, never ending, never going anywhere.

CHAPTER TWENTY-ONE

NATHAN

That evening that Alexa stormed off and Sarah helped me and Maria told me I would carry Laura's heart; that evening felt like a turning point. It shifted something inside me, making me turn from the anger and the tiredness and even the grief, and start to feel something else. Something small and fledgling and good, like a seed planted in surprising soil.

Was my lowest point when Alexa ran out of that diner, after hurling so many hurtful words at me? Her accusations had rung in my ears, clanged in my heart. *You don't even care about us.*

I told myself she didn't mean it, and next to me Sarah had murmured the same, but I didn't believe either of us. There had been too much truth in Alexa's words, even amidst the exaggeration and anger. *She'd* believed it, and that was what mattered.

"Do you want to go after her?" Sarah had asked. "I can get Ella and Ruby…"

"Not really." The admission was painful, but I was still throbbing from the wounds my daughter had delivered, too hurt to run after her and play the hero. "I don't think she wants me to, either. I'll text Maria, to see if she's gone home. I think we both need a little space."

It didn't sit well with me, to let Alexa go off when I'd finally found her, but I didn't know what else to do. My daughter didn't want me.

"Who is Maria?" Sarah asked as we walked back to the church, scanning the empty streets for Alexa.

"My nanny. Housekeeper." *Lifesaver*. I remembered what I'd said to her, what felt like so long ago. "She's great."

A text pinged on my phone. Alexa was at home, thank God. *Thank God.* Had I really just thought that?

When we got back to the church, Ella and Ruby were buzzing with energy. Perhaps it was the requisite hot chocolate and cookies they'd scarfed down, or just the excitement of being released from the group, but something seemed a little different tonight. A little lighter.

"Ella spoke," Eloise told me softly, touching my arm. "About the swim team."

"The swim team?" I sounded mystified; I'd been expecting something more relevant and personal. Ella had been on the team for less than two months.

"Yes, she spoke about how proud your wife was of her for making the team. It was very sweet." She smiled and squeezed my arm before moving on.

I turned to Ella, who was nibbling a cookie in the corner of the room. With a jolt, I noticed how thin she looked; standing on the other side of the room, it had taken me a moment to recognize her. I watched as she threw away the rest of her cookie. Maria had mentioned her not eating very much, and I hadn't taken it seriously. Ella had always been the easy one, and I hadn't thought I'd had it in me for that to change.

I walked towards her. "Hey, Ella. Eloise said you spoke in the group?" She nodded cautiously, her gaze downcast. "When's your next race? Shall I take you to it?"

Her startled gaze flew up. "It's on Saturday."

"Okay. It's a date."

"But you usually have to work."

"Not on Saturday." Not that Saturday. I'd make sure of it. "I want to go. I want to see you race."

Ella nodded, but she didn't look entirely pleased, and I tried not to feel hurt.

"Do you want me to go, Ella?" I asked.

"I guess so," she said, and then she turned away, and I told myself not to push. Small, limping steps were still progress.

Sarah came up to me with a hesitant smile. "After the group, we sometimes go get milkshakes," she said. "If you'd like to join us...? Or if you need to get back to Alexa, I understand, of course..."

Right then I really did not want to get back to Alexa. I wasn't even sure I should.

"Milkshakes, Daddy!" Ruby screeched, jumping up and down. "Milkshakes, *please*!"

Ella smiled shyly, waiting for my answer, and I thought of her sipping a thousand-calorie milkshake, color coming into her wan cheeks.

"Milkshakes would be great," I said.

And they were. We chatted, we laughed a little, Ella drank most of hers. It felt normal, and normality was what we all craved. Tomorrow I would tackle Alexa. We could get there. Somehow, we would get there.

The next morning I woke up, determined to be different. I felt energised in a way I hadn't been in months, thanks at least in part, a large part, to Maria. The grief was still there, lodged like a stone beneath my breastbone, but it was a stone I could carry, along with Laura's heart. A weight that was becoming part of me, and that was okay. At least, it could be okay, one day.

With a spring in my step, I got Ruby dressed and I made Ella two pieces of toast for breakfast; she nibbled on one.

"Eat up, Ella," I said as cheerfully as I could. "You'll be hungry later."

"I won't," she said, but at least she took a bite.

I told myself I'd make an appointment with the paediatrician next week, talk about healthy eating. Another step.

As we were heading off, I turned to my oldest daughter.

"Alexa…" I tried to keep my voice gentle but firm, my keys in my hand, my gaze on my daughter. "About last night."

She looked away, feigning boredom, but I could see how twitchy she was, her fingers fluttering and then clenching on the strap on her leather bag. We were in the kitchen while Ella and Ruby brushed their teeth before leaving for school; I'd told Maria I'd take them today, and now she hovered behind us, wiping counters, keeping her head down.

"Look, let's just forget it, okay?" Alexa's voice trembled. "I don't *care*, Dad."

"But I do." I spoke steadily, trying not to cheapen this into some sort of sentimental Hallmark moment. I didn't, and it wasn't.

Alexa hitched her bag higher on her shoulder and flicked her hair. "*Now* you do," she said, and I tried not to let that hurt. She was grieving too. I couldn't lose sight of that.

"Alexa, we can talk about Mom and my work and even God another time, okay? All that stuff. But right now…" I hesitated, weighing the options, wondering what was important. "I just want us to be okay again," I said quietly.

No response, not even a flicker of her heavily made-up eyelids.

"I love you," I said at last, and it felt like the last trick in my bag. Manipulative, even though I meant it.

For a second, I thought I had her. I thought she might even say it back. Her lips trembled, then pursed, as if she were about to speak. But then she just shook her head, hair flying, and pushed past me, out the door.

I stood there for a moment, fighting disappointment, and then I lifted my head and caught Maria's gaze.

"That didn't go so well," I said, trying for a wry note.

"It was not too bad." She smiled sadly. "You told her you loved her. That is important, however she responds."

I sighed, the familiar weariness already rushing back. I'd managed one morning and it felt like too much. "How did you get so wise, Maria?"

She looked surprised, and then she shook her head. "I am not so wise."

"Wiser than me, I think."

"Perhaps," she answered with a small smile, and when I realized she was actually teasing me, I let out a laugh.

Small steps. I had to keep remembering that.

That weekend I took Ella to her swim meet, while Maria stayed home with Ruby, and Alexa was out with her friends. When I'd asked what friends, because I'd never met any, she rolled her eyes, looking annoyed.

"Friends from school, Dad," she'd said. "Duh."

Right. Duh. Friends I didn't know, friends that might not even exist, or if they did, I might not want them to be her friends. Once again I was all too aware that I had no idea what Alexa got up to. Still, I could hardly hold her back, force her to stay at home. I let her go, both the easy option and a harder choice.

The day was crisp and cold, with the tiniest hint of spring in the air, just to fool us. I hoped Ella would be excited about her meet, and even the fact that I was going with her, although I realized that was a bit self-centered of me. Instead she seemed more withdrawn than usual, her face full of focus, striding down the sidewalk with far too much purpose for a ten-year-old.

"What's the rush, Ella?" I asked lightly. "There's plenty of time. We're not in a hurry."

"I want to get there early. I like to wait by the pool, so I'm ready."

"You're sounding like a real pro," I teased gently. "How many times have you done this before?"

"One." She scowled at me; clearly I was hitting all the wrong notes. "This time it's going to be different."

"Ella..." I tried to stay her with one hand on her shoulder, but she wasn't having it, and she flung it off. "This doesn't have to be so important, you know," I said gently.

She looked at me with wounded incredulity. Yet another wrong thing to say. Even when I tried, I got it wrong. I told myself that didn't matter; the trying was what did. Wasn't that what Maria had said? Had she been right? In that moment, looking at Ella's hurt face, I wasn't sure anymore.

"I didn't mean that it isn't important," I tried again. "Only that you don't need to be worried about it."

She just shook her head and kept walking.

When we got to the pool, Ella disappeared into the girls' locker rooms while I drifted over to a stand of bleachers where parents were sitting. After exchanging a few awkward smiles, I realized pretty much everyone here knew each other except for me. People were sharing stories, talking about the world of competitive junior swimming, a universe I hadn't realized had existed until this moment, when the acronyms and swimming speak about categories and levels and licensed meets flew around me as I settled onto the metal bleacher, the chlorine-heavy air stinging my eyes. All I'd known before today was that Ella swam. I'd been picturing something friendly and easy, akin to splashing around in a baby pool, but not quite. Obviously. Ella was ten. I felt the depth of my ignorance now, as a conversation with Laura that I may or may not have had surfaced in my consciousness.

Ella's been picked for the junior swim team.
Oh?
It's kind of a big deal.
Great.

I just don't want her to feel pressured. She's only ten.

She'll be fine, Laura.

Except maybe Laura hadn't said all that. Maybe she had, and I'd said something else.

Although, on second thought, I probably hadn't.

I leaned forward, bracing my elbows on my knees, as the teams came out. Ella was racing in one event, the butterfly. I knew that much, at least.

Something in me jolted at the sight of my normal dreamy daughter with her hair scraped back and hidden by a tight, white swim cap, striding down the length of the pool as she adjusted her goggles. Her body looked positively bony when all she was wearing was a black racing-back Speedo suit, all sharp points and uncomfortable angles. She definitely needed more milkshakes, and mentally I moved the appointment with the paediatrician to the top of my list.

I tensed as the girls, all looking so determined and so *little*, got ready. It wasn't Ella's race, but I was still nervous. A whistle blew. All the parents around me were straining forward, watching with equal parts eagerness and apprehension. One of them had a clipboard and a stopwatch. This was all far more intense than I'd ever realized. These little girls were twelve at the most, eight at the youngest, and they were all completely focused on what they were doing.

I sat through several races, the tension ratcheting higher with each one, until it was Ella's turn. My heart was pounding, actually pounding, as she lined up in her lane at the end of the pool, toes curled over the concrete edge, body poised and ready.

The shrill piercing sound of the whistle made me jolt. Ella dove, her body arcing elegantly into the water, before she started cutting through it, arms windmilling, head bobbing up and down.

"Go, Ella! You can do it! Go!" I was yelling without even realizing what I was doing, half-rising from my chair. When the other parents had cheered and screamed, I'd looked at them a bit askance. *Isn't that a little much? They're ten.* Now I grew hoarse with yelling, even though I doubted Ella could hear any of it.

Yet as the race progressed, I started to realize she wasn't going to come first. She wasn't even going to come second. Even though she was trying her hardest, even though she looked amazing to me, Ella was going to come in fourth. I sat back down as the race ended, my heart sinking not because Ella hadn't won, but because I had a terrible feeling she would take it badly.

I didn't know how badly, until she hauled herself out of the pool, ripped off her swim cap and goggles, throwing them aside, and stalked towards the locker room. A coach followed her, and around me murmurs rippled like the tide.

Oh dear... it's so difficult... poor sport... No, don't say that. She's only little.

The coach was trying to keep Ella by her, but I could see, even from the other side of the pool, that my daughter was falling apart. Her face was red, her hands clenched as she struggled between rage and grief. I didn't understand why this race had been so important, only that it had been, and I wasn't going to let my daughter deal with the fallout alone.

Quickly I rose from my seat and made my way down to the side of the pool, even though parents weren't supposed to enter the pool area, and there was a large sign proclaiming boldly that no shoes were allowed. I didn't care. I just wanted to get to Ella.

"Excuse me, sir..." One of the pool staff caught up with me, reaching for my arm.

"My daughter's racing."

"Parents are requested to—"

I shook her off and walked faster, my heart sinking as Ella shrugged off her coach yet again and ran into the female changing rooms. Of course, I couldn't go into the changing rooms, and so

I stood in front of the door, one hand pressed to the moisture-beaded wood, wishing I could break the door down, calling her name as loudly as I dared.

"Ella… *Ella*. It's Dad. Daddy." My voice caught on a ragged edge as I heard the sound of her choked cries from behind the door. My little girl was falling apart and she *needed* me. "Please come out, sweetheart. It's going to be okay, I promise…"

"Excuse me, sir?" Another staff member hovered by me. "We really can't have parents in the pool area."

"Look," I said, trying to sound reasonable and failing, "my daughter's in there and she's upset, okay? And her mother died three months ago." Yes, I would pull that card if I had to.

"Why don't I go get her," the staff member murmured, and she went inside the locker rooms.

I waited, feeling helpless, everyone eyeing me askance, not that I cared at all. I was so tempted to storm through the doors myself, rules be damned, but some thread of common sense kept me tethered.

A few tense minutes later, Ella came out, her face blotchy and red, her hair in a damp tangle. She averted her gaze from me, shoulders slumped.

"Oh, Ella." I dropped to my knees right there on the wet concrete and pulled her into my arms. She resisted at first, but then she came, her tense little body melting into mine as she burrowed her wet head into my shoulder, a shudder running through her. "Ella, sweetheart, love," I said, the threat of tears thick in my throat, stinging my eyes. "It's okay. It's *okay*."

"It isn't." Her voice was caught between a sob and a howl of rage. "It *isn't*."

There was a lot more going on here than swimming. I wasn't so emotionally ill-tuned not to see that, although I knew I should have realized it earlier. Standing in the pool area, in the middle of a swim meet, with about a hundred spectators, I knew, was not the time to hash it all out.

"Ella, why don't you get dressed," I said as I eased back. "And then we'll go out for milkshakes."

Her lips trembled. "I don't want a *milkshake*."

"Something else, then. We'll talk, Ella, but not here. I want to understand what's going on. Please."

She stared at me for a moment, her body still trembling, and then, finally, she nodded. I let out a quiet sigh of relief as she turned back towards the locker rooms.

I was conscious of the curious as well as censorious stares of the staff and swimmers, parents and coaches, as I stood there, my hands in my pockets, and waited for my daughter. Clearly we'd broken a million rules, and this was not the done thing. I didn't care for myself, but I hoped it wouldn't make things more difficult for Ella.

She came out of the locker room a few minutes later, dressed in her clothes and looking subdued. I put my arm around her shoulders, and she let me.

"Let's go."

"I'm meant to stay till the end of all the races..."

"I'm sure we can make an exception this time, Ella." The woman who had tried to stop me before smiled down at her. "We'll see you at practice on Monday, okay?"

I wasn't sure about that, but I kept silent as Ella nodded miserably. The woman patted her clumsily on the shoulder and then we were thankfully walking out of the pool area, the air cold and fresh as we left the muggy, chlorine-heavy atmosphere behind.

We didn't talk until we got to a diner a few blocks away, sliding into a well-worn vinyl booth and taking the laminated menus from the waitress that were nearly as tall as Ella.

"What would you like, Ella?" I asked, trying to inject a note of cheer into my voice that I knew neither of us were feeling. "You can have anything. Waffle a la mode? Cookies and cream milkshake?" I had a desperate urge to give her something full of cream and sugar, to put a little meat on her scrawny bones.

Ella just shook her head.

"Ella." I put down the menu and looked at her directly. "Why was it so important for you to win that race?"

She shrugged and stared down at the menu. I waited, wishing I could read her mind. Ella had always been the dreamiest and most distant of children, in a way that was so different from Alexa's deliberate sullenness. Ella was so often in a world of her own, happy to amble along. Her teachers had always said the same thing—*Ella is a happy child but she doesn't have any particular friends.* Laura had sometimes worried about it, but I hadn't troubled myself too much.

I was a bit of a loner at school, and I'm fine.

It was different for you, Nathan. You moved schools so often, you had to be that way. Ella doesn't. Besides, wasn't the whole point of this to give our children something different?

This. What had she meant by that? Was I imagining the frustrated tone creeping into her voice? Was I imagining the entire conversation? I had no idea. All I knew was I wanted to reach Ella now.

The waitress came to take our order, and Ella said she wasn't hungry.

"Two chocolate milkshakes," I said firmly. "And waffles with ice cream."

"Daddy, I don't want it." Ella sounded angry.

"Then I'll eat yours." I tried to smile, but I felt too anxious. Why hadn't I noticed what was going on with Ella before now? And what *was* going on with her? "Ella, will you tell me about the race?"

She shrugged, picking at a peeling corner of the Formica table. "I didn't win."

"Why was it so important to win?"

Another shrug.

"Ella."

A long silence as Ella stared at the table, her damp hair falling in front of her face like a curtain. "Mom was so proud of me," she finally whispered. "For being on the team."

"She was," I said after a second, feeling my way through the dark. "But she was always proud of you, Ella, whatever you did or didn't do. And she'd be proud of you now, whether you came in first or fiftieth. I *know* that."

Ella shook her head slowly. "I wanted to win. For her."

A lump was forming in my throat, hard and heavy. I could barely speak past it. "I know you did, sweetheart, and I understand that. If you'd won, Mom would have been thrilled. Just as thrilled if you hadn't. It's you she loves, not your accomplishments, your grades or your races or anything like that." I'd slipped into the present tense without even realizing it, and I felt it painfully now.

Laura was in the past. She wasn't here, couldn't be proud. She was *gone*. How could it still feel so surprising? How could it hurt as much now as it had in the beginning?

Gently I reached over and squeezed Ella's hand. "Mom wants you to be happy, Ella. Happy and healthy and whole. That's the most important thing. Not whether you win at swimming or not."

Ella looked up at me, blinking back tears. "Do you think she sees me, Daddy? Can she see me swimming?"

I held onto her hand, my throat working as I tried to find the right words to say. Words Ella could hold onto, and words I could believe. "I don't know," I said finally. It felt like a big admission, and it was followed by an even bigger one, one that filled me with a humble longing. "I hope so."

A tear trickled down Ella's cheek as she tried to smile. "So do I."

The waitress came with our milkshakes and waffles, and I ate all of mine, hoping to encourage Ella, but she had only a few sips of milkshake, not nearly enough. When I pressed her, she just shook her head. No easy fixes, then, but more small, limping steps. We were getting somewhere, even if I wasn't sure where. That felt like as much as I could hope for. It was enough.

CHAPTER TWENTY-TWO

MARIA

The next two weeks passed without incident. That is a funny word, incident—it was how they first described Laura's murder. But those two weeks in February, when spring hovered in the air, like a promise or perhaps a taunt, we had no *incidents* at all.

I look back on them as if they were a dream, and yet at times they have felt like the most real part of my life. Ruby snuggling with me in the mornings. Sunlight streaming through the windows as we all ate breakfast. Board games at the dining room table after school. Ella slowly losing that pinched look—Nathan had taken her to the paediatrician, who gave her a meal plan and recommended a child psychologist that Ella had started meeting once a week. And Alexa… was I mistaken in thinking she had begun to soften? Sometimes she would slink into the dining room to watch us, forgetting her phone for a little while. At dinner once in a while she would say something, nothing much, but so much better than her sullen silence. I told myself these were steps forward, but I wonder now if I was fooling myself because I so wanted to believe there was a happy ending for all of us.

It all felt so hopeful, and that was something I had not felt in a long, long time. We were on the cusp, I was sure of it… I just didn't realize of what.

Then, at the end of February, right before Laura's parents were going to take the girls skiing, it changed in an instant. Ruby was at preschool and I was making *sarma* for dinner, the stuffed cabbage rolls the girls had discovered they liked. I remember how the sunshine slanted through the window and pooled on the floor, and how I was humming under my breath. I thought it was warm enough to take Ruby to the park after preschool; I thought I might even bring a picnic. If I did not feel happy, then at least I felt something close to it—a lightness I'd never thought to experience again.

Then my phone rang.

I did not recognize the officious-sounding voice on the other end of the line, a woman who asked for me by name.

"Is this Maria Dzino?"

"Yes…"

"I'm calling from The Walkerton School. I've been trying to reach Nathan West, but he's been unavailable."

"He's at work. Is something wrong…"

"Alexa West has been suspended from school," the woman stated in a flat voice. "She needs to be picked up from the premises immediately."

A jolt ran through me, like a current, sharp and electric. "Suspended…" I was not entirely sure what this meant, but I knew it could not be good.

"The headmistress, Miss Faber, can give you more information. May I assume you will be able to collect her?"

"Yes, of course." It was still over an hour until I had to pick up Ruby. "I'll come right now."

I walked hurriedly to the school, my mind in a daze of worry. I tried calling Nathan twice, but his phone was switched off. I finally sent a text: *Alexa is in trouble at school. Please come.*

The receptionist knew who I was as soon as I walked through the school's double doors, into its elegant lobby; she rose from her desk and ushered me into an office adjoining the lobby, a large, sunny room with polished wood, an imposing desk, and a thick carpet. There were several framed pictures on the wall, mostly of diplomas.

Alexa was sprawled in a chair in front of the desk, her bag in her lap. My heart sank as I saw the expression on her face—deliberately sullen and bored.

The headmistress rose from her seat behind the desk as I came in.

"Ms. Dzino? Please have a seat."

I sat down opposite Alexa, glancing at her, but she looked away and refused to meet my gaze. I turned back to the headmistress, Miss Faber.

"What has happened here?" I asked.

"I'm afraid Alexa has been suspended." I did not want to betray my ignorance of that word, so I just waited. After an uneasy moment where Miss Faber clearly expected something from me, she continued, "She will be suspended from school for one week."

"She will not be able to come?"

Miss Faber's expression tightened. "Yes, that is what suspended means."

"Why has this happened?"

Miss Faber glanced at Alexa. "Alexa, would you like to tell Ms. Dzino why you are being suspended?"

Alexa shrugged.

After an arctic pause the headmistress continued, "Alexa was discovered skipping class, smoking and… congregating… with some boys from a nearby school."

Congregating? That was another word I did not know, but again I knew it couldn't be good. "And for this she is suspended?"

"Yes, Ms. Dzino, she is. We have high expectations of our young women at Walkerton. Very high expectations. Now, the staff here are aware, of course, of Alexa's family situation, and we are very, very sorry for it." Her face tightened. "You might recall our PTA organised a schedule of meals to be delivered to the West family." I did not see how that had any relevance, and so I remained silent. "But no matter what her family's situation," Miss Faber continued after another tense pause, "her behavior cannot and will not be tolerated at this school." She turned to Alexa, who was staring at the wall. "I hope, Alexa, that a week at home will give you time to think about your actions. I am very sorry for your loss, my dear. But acting out in this way isn't helpful to you or your peers."

Alexa, of course, did not respond.

Miss Faber turned back to me. "Do you have any other questions?"

I shook my head. I did not know enough to ask questions. If Nathan were here, perhaps he would protest, demand Miss Faber reconsider. As it was, all I could do was murmur thanks—for what, I did not know—and slink out of the office with Alexa behind me.

Outside, I gazed up at the bright blue sky, felt the hint of warmth in the air that had seemed so promising earlier. I turned to Alexa.

"I suppose we should go home." She shrugged. "Do you want to tell me what happened?" No reply. "We'll talk when we get home," I decided, although I did not know what either of us would say, or if Alexa would say anything at all.

I could not keep from feeling disappointed, and rather stupidly hurt. I had thought Alexa had been coming along these last few weeks. Warming up to me, to everyone. I had thought we were moving forward, and shamefully, I had thought it had been, at least a little, up to me. But now all of it seemed like a lie, a mirage. False hope, which was worse than no hope at all.

Back at the apartment, Alexa headed towards her room. "Wait." I barked out the word, although I hadn't meant to. "Alexa, we should talk."

She let out a long, drawn-out sigh and turned around. "What about?"

"This… suspended."

"Suspension." The sneer in her voice made me blink.

"Suspension," I repeated. My English had never failed me so noticeably before. "You were not in school? You were smoking?"

She put her hands on her hips, her chin tilted at a defiant angle. "Yeah, so what?"

"And… with boys?"

"I was hanging out with boys, yeah." She rolled her eyes. "Miss Faber can't even say it. *Congregating*." She snickered, a sound I found I hated.

"What does it mean? Congregating?" I asked.

"I was hooking up with them, Maria," Alexa drawled. "Obviously."

This too was a term I was not familiar with, but I could imagine. I pressed one hand to my throat, trying to stay calm even though all sorts of feelings were jolting through me, current after awful current. "With more than one boy?" I asked faintly.

"With three." She smirked. "Now does that shock you, Saint Maria? The woman who never does anything wrong?"

"I do many things wrong, Alexa. So many things. But why would you do this? Why would you…" My throat was tight, and spots danced before my eyes. "Why would you lower yourself so much?"

"I wasn't *lowering* myself." She snorted. "What, are you just jealous? You probably wish you could get off with my dad, don't you? Get off with anyone, even? Do you have a life, or are you just like some sort of parasite on ours? Have you ever even had *sex*?"

I had walked the two steps towards her before I knew what I was doing. My hand was in the air, moving towards her face before I could even think to stop myself, though distantly I knew I should. Of course I should. *Crack*.

We stared at each other, Alexa and I, the terrible, vivid red print of my hand on her cheek. She looked too shocked to cry, or say anything, or move. I stared at her in horror. I could not believe myself. I could not believe I had been capable of such an act of violence.

"Alexa... I..." I stared at her helplessly, appalled by my actions, shocked by the sudden rage that had gripped me when I thought of the things she had said and done.

For a second I had been completely consumed by it, so I could almost imagine it coming out of me in lightning bolts from my fingers and toes, my eyes and mouth. I thought if someone touched me they would burst into flames, or I would. It had led me to slap her, but now, looking at the mark of my hand on Alexa's cheek, I did not feel angry, I felt shame—as well as sorrow and fear. How could I have done such a thing?

"I'm sorry," I whispered, but Alexa just stared at me for an awful, frozen moment, and then, without a word, she wheeled around and ran into her bedroom, slamming the door so hard behind her, the whole apartment rattled.

I stood there, dazed and horrified, unsure what I should do. Was there any way to make this better? Should I apologise again? Explain, even, about how her words had touched memories and emotions inside me I could not bear to recall or feel? I did nothing; I felt too shaken to move. To act.

After some time, I didn't know how long, my phone pinged. A text from Nathan.

I'm so sorry. I was in a meeting with my phone switched off. Are you at school?

For a second my rage swelled again, big enough for him, as well. Why had he switched his phone off? Why had it all been up to me?

With shaking fingers, I texted him back. *We are back at home. Should I come?*

He needed to ask me? He needed my *permission*? When was he going to decide for himself what kind of father he would be, what kind of *man*?

I did not answer that text. I could not, because I was still angry, and I was also afraid. What would happen when Alexa told Nathan what I had done? How could I make this better?

I realized I needed to get Ruby; I left a note for Alexa that I doubted she would read, and then I hurried towards The Garden School, everything in me still reeling from what had happened.

My mind was a blur as I fetched Ruby, who started happily babbling away as soon as she saw me, blissful in her innocence. The mothers and other nannies still didn't really talk to me, although they might murmur hello. Today, they just looked away. Perhaps they sensed my disquiet; perhaps they saw it in my face.

"Can we go to the park, Maria?" Ruby asked as she skipped next to me, yanking on my hand. "Please? It's so warm. They might even have the sprinklers on."

"Ruby, it is February, they will not have the sprinklers on." The plans I'd had for a picnic seemed ridiculous now. I removed my hand from hers to keep her from yanking on it.

"Please?"

My head was starting to clear, and also to pound. I felt sick to my stomach, nausea swirling around, threatening to rise. What could I do? How could I make this better?

"Maria?" Ruby asked hopefully.

I put one hand to my head, dazed, the world seeming to spin around me. "Yes," I said finally. I dreaded returning to the apartment, to Alexa. "Yes, we will go to the park."

I sat on a bench in the chilly sunshine as Ruby raced through the concrete pyramids of the Ancient Playground, next to the Metropolitan Museum of Art. I listened to the calls and squeals of the children in the park, sitting a little bit apart from a bevy of nannies who were chatting at a picnic table. I wondered where they came from, what their stories were. What had brought them to this country? What had they seen and had to forget? I had no idea, just as they had no idea about me. No one did.

Eventually I forced myself to think about the present, which was pushing into my brain like someone forcing open the doors of an elevator and squeezing inside. *No room, no room.* But they came anyway, because they were so important.

I would be fired. This was the thought that squeezed in first and took up all the air in that cramped little space. I would be fired, because I had slapped Alexa. I had slapped her *face*. How could I have done such a thing? Even now I could hear the crack of my hand against her cheek, like a gunshot.

A *gunshot*.

I closed my eyes. I was so filled with regret, it felt like a swamp inside me, miring me in its murky, muddy depths. And yet, even so, I still had the rage. My hand tingled. I did not know how to feel.

"Maria, why are you closing your eyes?"

Like the petals of a flower, Ruby's little hands cupped my face. I opened my eyes and smiled down at her sweetness, even though my lips trembled.

"I am just tired, *koka*. That is all."

She studied me for a few seconds, a crinkle in the middle of her forehead, and then she leaned forward and kissed me on my cheek. "I love you, Maria," she said, before skipping away.

I bowed my head, humbled by her words, by the sweet simplicity of it, wishing it was all that easy and pure. But of course it wasn't.

I would be fired. Perhaps I would even be arrested. Had I committed a crime? Maybe Nathan was home already, and Alexa was telling him what had happened, showing him her reddened cheek. Would there be a bruise? I cringed inwardly at the thought, horrified and appalled all over again. How had it come to this? How had I let it?

We stayed in the playground until it was time to pick Ella up, and then we walked hand in hand back to Walkerton, although I dreaded that place now. Ruby was tired from playing, and so she was quiet as we walked, her head pressed against my hip.

Ella came out smiling; she'd had a good day, and the teacher quietly told me she'd eaten two-thirds of her lunch. Progress, even if she still looked too thin and she still talked about racing. Today she was happy, and she held my other hand as we headed towards home.

Home. Would it still be my home? I had not even realized I'd let myself think of it that way.

Inside the apartment, all was quiet. I saw Nathan's messenger bag in the hall, and I wondered why he was not waiting, his face filled with fury as he demanded to know how I could have raised a hand to his child.

Ella and Ruby ran into the living room, squealing when they saw him.

"Daddy, you're home so early!"

"Will you play with me, Daddy?"

"Can I have a snack?"

Wearily, I brought their school bags into the kitchen, checking for any letters or forms that had been sent home. There was nothing. Mindlessly, I started cutting up fruit for their snack, waiting for Nathan.

"Thank you, Maria."

I stiffened at the sound of his voice, turning in shock to see him smiling tiredly in the doorway of the kitchen.

"Alexa isn't talking to me, surprise, surprise." He shook his head. "I thought we were past this. Stupid me, I suppose. Two steps forward, one step back. Or is it the other way around?"

"You've talked to her?" I asked cautiously.

"Yes, briefly. She wouldn't say much, just that she's been suspended for skipping school." And smoking, and the boys. I stayed silent. "A whole *week*… that's not going to look good on the transcript."

I thought that should be the least of his concerns now, but I did not say so. I was realizing that Alexa had not told him I'd slapped her. Was she waiting? Or was she ashamed?

My mind whirling, I brought the bowls of fruit to Ella and Ruby in the living room; they were watching their precious hour of TV, already absorbed in the luridly colored cartoon on the screen in front of them.

Back in the kitchen, Nathan leaned against the counter.

"Do you mind having her at home for the week?" he asked.

I shook my head. "No. It is fine." How could I say anything else?

"I'm wondering if she needs more counselling. Someone else to talk to, the way Ella has… How did she do today, by the way? Did she eat her lunch?"

"Most of it, I think."

"I'm not sure I want her to race next weekend." He sighed, raking a hand through his hair. "What do you think?"

I shook my head helplessly. "I do not know."

Nathan must have sensed my disquiet for he leaned forward, craning his head to look at me. "Maria, is everything all right?"

I hesitated, because part of me—oh, such a large part—wanted to say yes, of course, everything was absolutely all right. Alexa wouldn't tell, and life could go on as it had been, these last few weeks so simple and pleasant, on and on.

But I knew I could not do that. These weeks had been neither simple nor pleasant; they had just *seemed* so, ever so briefly. I could not go forward with this lie so heavy inside me, weighing me down with its guilt.

"No," I said to Nathan. "Everything is not all right."

Nathan frowned, straightening where he stood. "What's wrong, Maria? What's going on?"

I took a deep breath and I looked him full in the face. "I have done something wrong," I said. "Something I must tell you about."

CHAPTER TWENTY-THREE

NATHAN

Maria was looking at me so seriously, I had that strange, buzzing sensation of being outside my body, looking in. The same sensation I'd had when the policewoman had come to my office. But surely whatever she said couldn't be as bad as that. Nothing could.

"What happened?" I asked her. "What do you need to tell me?"

She glanced behind her, at the girls. "Perhaps I should tell you later," she murmured. "When everyone is in bed. It is not something I wish to speak of in front of the little ones."

So it was serious, then. My heart felt as if it were clenching in my chest even as I told myself I had to be overreacting. "Okay," I said.

The next few hours felt endless. I helped with homework while Maria made dinner; Alexa came to the table when called, and stayed silent all the while, looking at no one and eating nothing. I gave Ruby a bath while Maria folded laundry; I read to Ella while she tucked Ruby in. We'd become adept, her and I, at sharing the load, moving quietly around each other.

Finally, a little after nine, having wrestled Alexa's phone off her and with the little girls in bed, I confronted Maria. She looked so resigned, I had the urge to comfort her. I had no idea what she intended to say to me.

"I am very sorry, Nathan," she began, perched on the edge of the sofa, her hands clasped tightly on her lap. "I am so very sorry."

She was starting to scare me now. "Maria, please tell me what's happened."

"I was angry with Alexa," she said. "We argued after she came home. I was so angry..." She shook her head, biting her lips, and I stared at her in bemused confusion.

"I've been angry with Alexa," I ventured. "Plenty of times."

"This was different." Maria kept biting her lip, leaving a deep indent in it, as she shook her head.

"So what happened?" I asked eventually.

"I slapped her. Across the face." Maria looked up at me, her eyes filled with both fear and resignation.

"You slapped her..." I spoke dazedly, because I could not picture it. Maria was so gentle. She never even raised her voice. "You slapped her," I said again, seeking confirmation, and she nodded.

"I'm so very sorry. I didn't mean to. It just..." She shook her head helplessly. "I'm sorry," she said again.

"Maria..." I hesitated, because I wasn't sure what to say, what tone to take. She'd *slapped* my daughter. I couldn't make sense of it. And what was I supposed to do now? Fire her? I knew I didn't want to, slap or not, and yet... she'd been violent to my child. "I have trouble imagining you doing something like that," I said at last. "You never even lose your temper."

"I did then," she said, her head bowed. "I'm so sorry."

"Alexa didn't even mention it." Which begged the question why not. "Why did she make you so angry, Maria?" I still had trouble picturing it. Alexa had tested both of our patience many times. What about this time had made Maria break?

"It does not matter."

"I think it does." I had a growing conviction that there was more going on here than I realized. "You don't usually get angry. What happened?"

Maria's gaze skittered back to mine; she looked frightened. "She said some things…"

"What things?"

Another shake of her head, and I felt myself growing both impatient and anxious. What could she be possibly hiding?

"*Maria*. Please tell me what's going on. What did Alexa say?"

"It is not my place. You should ask her…"

"As if she'd tell me, and I'm asking you, the person I've hired to care for her, who was in the wrong." I was sounding strident now, and I could see Maria shrinking into herself. *How had we got here*? "Please, Maria."

"She skipped school to smoke," she finally said in a small, squeezed-out voice. "And to… be… with boys."

Be with boys? Words to freeze a father's heart, and yet I didn't want to believe it. "What do you mean, be with boys?"

Maria shook her head. "Please, ask her."

"Trust me, I will." I was getting angry now, angry and afraid, just like Maria. Then realization trickled in. "But why did this make you so angry?" I asked. She'd taken plenty of back talk and bad behavior from Alexa before; we both had. Why had she been angry enough to *slap* her? I still could not picture Maria raising her hand and hitting someone. *My daughter*.

"Please," Maria said.

I didn't know what she was asking for, but I wasn't going to give it to her.

"Tell me. Considering what happened, I have a right to know."

Maria closed her eyes briefly, the way I used to. When she spoke, her voice was so low, I strained to hear it. "Because… because she made me remember."

"Remember?" I was nonplussed. "Remember what?"

Maria just shook her head. Again.

"Maria, what did she make you remember?"

"Please," she whispered, her eyes still closed.

I stared at her for a long moment, caught between concern, compassion, and a morbid curiosity. "Whatever this is… have you ever spoken to anyone about this?" I finally asked. I sensed something far deeper and more complex happening here than a single slap. "Because I don't think it's healthy to—"

"Healthy?" She opened her eyes, and they flashed nearly golden with anger. Suddenly I believe she could slap Alexa, or even me, and I was taken aback by the change. "Healthy?" she repeated with an incredulous sneer. "This was not about being healthy. It was about surviving."

We stared at each other, her wild-eyed and me having no idea where this conversation might lead, or even how it had got here. We weren't talking about Alexa anymore. "What happened to you, Maria," I said quietly, half-statement, half-question.

She stared at me for another long moment; it was as if there was a furnace blazing behind her eyes.

"You want to know what happened to me, Nathan?" she finally asked. "You really want to know?"

Did I? "If you want to tell me," I said, backtracking a bit.

"If I *want* to tell you." She let out a high, wild sound; I think it was meant to be a laugh.

"Maria, if you've been keeping this inside for who knows how long…"

"Twenty-six years. Since I was fourteen. *Fourteen*," she emphasised, as if I might not realize that was the same age as Alexa.

"Fourteen," I agreed. "Perhaps it's time for you to talk about it." I sounded so sanctimonious. I heard it, I knew it, and yet I couldn't keep myself from it. I didn't know how else to be. "You might feel better, getting it all out in the open."

I registered Maria's wild expression and started to regret making such an offer. Did I really want to hear what she had to say? Could I handle it? I had so much to deal with already… what was I supposed to do with yet another person's pain? And yet how could I leave it here, when I'd been the one to encourage her to speak?

"What happened?" I asked gently. "What happened when you were fourteen?"

"It doesn't begin there. It ends there." A shudder went through her and she sank back against the sofa, her gaze turning inward and distant.

"Where does it begin?"

"Where? In Sarajevo, I suppose. In my family's apartment on Logavina Street." She let out a huff of sound. "We had an apartment a bit like this one. Big rooms. A fireplace. My father's bookcases with glass doors…" She trailed off and I waited. Already I found the details jarring; Maria had lived in an apartment like this one? Had had a *life* like this one? Why did that surprise me? "We were happy," she said quietly. "My mother, my father, my brother and me. It was a simple, quiet life, but we were happy."

"Tell me about your family." I wasn't sure if I was asking because I was genuinely interested or simply as a stalling technique. Both, perhaps.

"My father was a school inspector. My mother worked in a dentist's office. My brother loved music." She fell silent, lost in thought. "It sounds so little, as if that is all I can say about them."

Yet with just a few simple sentences, she had painted a vivid picture. I found I could envision the apartment, with its homely, slightly shabby, Old World feel; I could see Maria's brother, with eyes and hair like hers, a slight figure, lost in his music. Her mother making *krofne*. Her father reading. And Maria… there in the middle, telling one of her stories, enlivening everyone with her laugh. What had happened to her?

"The siege started in April 1992," she said flatly. "I was twelve. It felt very sudden, at least to me. There were murmurings of things happening—people leaving the city, soldiers seen nearby.

Civil wars erupting in countries all around us, after Communism fell. But no one thought it could happen to *us*. We weren't like those in Croatia, who seemed to be fighting over nothing, a squabble over who was who, and who belonged where. We wouldn't be so foolish. We all got along." She sighed heavily. "But, of course, you know something about the war."

"A little," I said, which was the truth. I knew a very little, a few photos, an item on the news, not much more. Bosnians, Serbs, and Croats all fighting for their own place—or something like that. I wasn't really sure, and now was hardly the time to ask.

"Sarajevo was surrounded by the Serb Army. They were extremists, radicals—they hated Bosniaks." At my blank look, she clarified, "Bosnian Muslims. It lasted for years—no one getting in or out, food limited, electricity and water constantly disrupted, if they were on at all. And worse, far worse… snipers hiding in the hills, shooting at anyone, even children. And mortar shells whistling through the air… you could hear them coming, you *knew*. We all slept in the kitchen, away from the windows. We couldn't go out… sometimes for days, weeks. And always someone was being hurt, being killed. Every day."

"I can't imagine…" I murmured, because of course I couldn't, not remotely. It sounded like something out of a film.

"My father died in April of 1993, a mortar shell flew into our sitting room. He'd been reading the newspaper. I heard him turning the pages, and then that awful whistling." She shook her head. "After that, nothing but silence." I opened my mouth to speak, but found I had no words. Maria continued with her story, her voice flat and determined. "Then, one day in June, after my father had died, our apartment was hit again, worse this time. None of us were hurt, but my mother decided we should try to leave Sarajevo."

This surprised me, after all she'd just described. "I thought you said no one could get out?"

"Not many could. We were surrounded. But there were ways… you could pay people…" Her throat moved convulsively. "Some people were lucky, and were taken as part of a humanitarian convoy, to somewhere safe. Others…"

The silence lengthened and stretched into something else. "And what about you?" I asked finally.

"We were not so lucky. We paid someone to hide us in the back of his truck. We wanted to get to Mostar, to where my father's sister and her husband lived. My mother thought it would be safe there, but I learned later that it wasn't. It wasn't safe anywhere." A sort of stillness came over her, her expression so distant it seemed as if she wasn't there anymore.

I felt a sense of dread creeping up on me. "Did you get to Mostar?"

Maria shook her head. I didn't think she was going to say anything more, as if that were the end of the story, when I knew it had to be only the beginning.

I leaned forward, my heart thudding strangely. I reached out one hand to her but didn't touch her. "What happened, Maria?" I asked softly.

"The soldiers found us, outside Mostar." Her voice was so quiet, I could barely hear it. "They took us to a camp." Her face hardened. "We never should have been in that camp. It was meant for men, for the military. There shouldn't have been any women or children there at all." The raw, jagged note in her voice had me tensing where I sat. I didn't know what question to ask, and I was afraid asking any would break Maria. Her head was bowed, her body shuddering with the effort of holding back.

I waited, staying silent, unsure if she would say any more. Unsure if I wanted her to. *Whatever happened in that camp…*

"The camp was filthy," Maria said after a long moment. "There was no clean water, not enough food, rooms made like cages. No beds, no blankets." She drew a shuddering breath, seeming to draw the air from right down in her toes. "It was awful, like nothing I'd ever seen before, and yet I could have stood it. I could have." She looked up at me, the expression in her eyes both blank and fierce. "My mother became very ill. My brother..." Her voice wavered. "My brother broke. The things they made him see and do... but we could have stood it, I think we could have. They made us cook and clean for them. We were useful." Her face contorted. "*So* useful."

"You don't have to tell me, Maria." I didn't know why I said that then, perhaps because I felt a towering sense of something dark looming, something that could not be unsaid or unheard, and I was afraid to know it.

"No, I will tell you now." Maria's voice was flat and firm. "You have asked, Nathan," she reminded me, and it sounded like a warning. "I will tell you."

I fell silent, waiting, wary.

"There were perhaps fifty women and children in that camp, among all the men."

Briefly I closed my eyes before I forced them open. I made myself look at Maria, as she was looking at me. She wasn't shuddering any longer; she looked very steady and sure, and it scared me.

"They took the girls and women out in twos and threes," she said, and everything in me thought *no*. "To a room—a shabby bedroom. With a padlock on the door. And the smell of beer. There was an orange bedspread. I remember that."

"Oh, Maria..." I could barely get the words out.

"There were four men."

"No..."

"I didn't even know what they wanted from me. Not at first." She paused, her breathing ragged and I fought the urge to say something, to make her stop. "Still, I was one of the lucky ones, really. It only happened a few times. There were others..." She shook her head. "They did not fare so well. Many times, even more men. They lost their souls in that room."

Oh, God. *Oh, God.* I didn't know whether I was cursing or praying. Perhaps both. I opened my mouth to say something, but I had no words.

"None of us spoke of it. We came back from that room and no one ever said a word. My mother was too weak to be taken there, thank God. But she started to wonder, to suspect. Before she died, she asked me. She asked me what had happened, and I said nothing. Nothing happened, I told her. I could not have her die knowing. And I so wanted to believe it as well." She drew a quick, hard breath. "She made me promise and I did."

"I'm sorry…" So feeble, but what else could I say?

"My brother, the last time I saw him, asked me as well. *Maria, did they?* That was all he was able to say. I looked away as he was dragged off by the soldiers. I heard a gunshot. I never saw him again."

I shook my head helplessly.

"Before I went into that room, I had never been touched by a boy. One had never even held my hand."

I felt tears well in my eyes, but I could not let myself cry. This was Maria's pain, not mine. I could not take it from her, even if I wished to.

Finally she sagged back against the sofa; it felt as if a gust of wind had blown through the room. "In twenty-six years, I have not told anyone that. Even the immigration officers, in order to come to this country. I told them I was at the camp at Vojno, that was all. Though perhaps they knew what that meant. But I never said a word—not to friends, not to my aunt and uncle, whom I lived with after, although my aunt suspected." Maria let out a harsh laugh. "She was shamed by me, and I never said a word."

"How could she be ashamed of you?" I demanded. "It wasn't your fault."

"Even so." Maria shrugged this pain away, heaped on all the others. "But even after all that..." She paused. "I thought to myself, I will forget. I can make myself forget. I told my mother it didn't happen. I didn't answer my brother. I will forget." She turned back to look at me, her gaze focused once more. "But I could not forget. I lived in Mostar, and I saw one of those men in the street. He was the butcher, where my aunt shopped. He stood behind the counter with his white apron smeared with blood... he didn't even remember me."

I gaped at her. "But how could that be? He must have been arrested..."

"No. That was not how it happened. Everyone made peace and went back to their homes. Everyone went back to their lives."

"But..."

"And I could not forget." She drew herself up. "That was why I came to America. I could not stand it anymore. I could not live in that city, in that country, and see those men. I felt like a ghost, but I wanted to live again."

"I'm glad you came here," I managed. It felt like so little, but I didn't know what else I could offer her.

"But I have still been a ghost. All these years..." Her voice cracked. Her lips trembled. The steady force of her gaze faltered as she struggled, finally, to keep from crying.

"Maria..."

"All these years," she gasped out, and then she was crying, the sounds pulled from deep within her, racking her whole body, her hands hiding her face. I had never cried like that. I had never let myself. And I didn't think Maria had, either.

"Maria," I said softly, and then, clumsily, afraid to scare or hurt her, I put my arms around her. She tensed for a second and I waited, ready to move back if I needed to. If I should have. But then she leaned into me, her face pressed against my shoulder, the sobs torn from her body like they'd been part of herself for all these years and were only now wrenching free.

I didn't know how long we sat like that, how many tears Maria shed. I felt my shirt grow damp and my arms ached and still I held her. Finally she drew back.

"You should fire me," she said as she wiped her eyes.

"Maria, I'm not going to fire you." Of that I was sure.

"I should not have let myself become so angry. It wasn't Alexa's fault."

It wasn't Maria's, either. I knew that much. "Look, we'll sit down, the three of us, okay? We'll hash it out. You can apologise to Alexa. We'll make it work."

She stared at me, her expression clear yet desolate. "How can you trust me?"

How could I not? She'd been through so much, and yet she'd still had love to give. A slap couldn't discount that. "I trust you, Maria," I said, and she bowed her head, overcome.

CHAPTER TWENTY-FOUR

MARIA

The morning after—another *after*, such a different one—I woke up feeling heavy-limbed and foggy-minded, as if I had drunk too much rakia, although in my whole life I have never touched a drop. I imagined that was how it must feel, as if my head was full of cotton wool, my tongue thick, my arms and legs uncoordinated.

I swung my legs from my bed, blinking in the sunlight streaming through my window. I looked at the clock and saw it was after eight. I should have been up hours ago; breakfast had to be made, and Ella and Alexa needed to go to school very soon. Although, I remembered, not Alexa. Alexa was suspended.

Still, I should have been up. I wondered why someone had not woken me. I could not remember the last time I had slept this late.

All these thoughts tumbled through my mind as I sat on the edge of my bed, and then I remembered last night, and all the things I had said, and I did not feel as I had expected. I did not feel a rush of regret, a flood of shame. I felt… at peace. Fragile, tentative, barely there, but still. And yet even so I worried about going into the kitchen, and seeing Nathan.

Last night, after I had wept as I never had before, and he had told me he would not fire me, that he trusted me, I'd mumbled some sort of thanks, wiped my eyes, and, feeling wrung out and

empty, I had gone to bed, all without being able to look at him.
I did not know how he was going to look at me today.

This was why the women at Vojno, and so many girls and
women in Bosnia, did not ever speak of what happened. Because
we did not want people to look at us differently. We did not want
people to look at us and see only *that*.

But I couldn't stay in my bedroom, hiding away; I needed to
face Nathan. I needed to get the girls ready. And so I rose, and
dressed quickly, and stepped into the kitchen.

The room was filled with sunlight, so it was hard to see;
everything looked bright and blurry. I blinked and the world came
into focus—Nathan at the stove, flipping pancakes. *Pancakes*.

Ruby was helping him, standing on a stool. Ella stood nearby,
on her tiptoes. Alexa was by the door, leaning against it, arms
folded. She glanced at me as I came in, and then looked away. I
thought of my hand on her cheek and then I pushed that thought
away. I would deal with that later. I would apologise again, as
much as I needed to, until it was all right once more.

"I am so sorry I slept," I said, and Ruby skipped up to me,
her mouth sticky with syrup.

"Are you feeling better, Maria?" she asked.

"Better…" I glanced at Nathan, a question.

"I told them you were a bit under the weather," he explained,
and I pictured myself bowed beneath dark clouds, stooped
beneath the heavy weight of them, and then, wonderfully, the
skies clearing.

"I am not under the weather," I told Ruby. "Not anymore."

"I made you a card." Shyly, Ella handed me a piece of folded
paper with bright writing on the front. *Get Well, Maria*.

I smiled at that. Get well. Yes, perhaps, for the first time, I
actually would. Perhaps we all would, together, a miracle borne
out of grief and sorrow, like the sunlight streaming through the
clouds.

I look back on that morning and I think of it as the last time. The last time of sitting simply in sunshine, of listening to Ruby's chatter, of feeling that weightlessness inside that was so new to me, and yet so wonderful. The last time of allowing myself to hope.

"I should get Ella to school," Nathan said apologetically, and quickly I rose from the table.

"Yes, it is late. I can…"

"You stay there," he insisted. "Enjoy your coffee." He glanced at Alexa, sternness and compassion tangled in his gaze. "Be good today, Alexa. Be helpful…"

Of course, Alexa would be home all day. I was determined to make it into something good.

"We will do the shopping together," I told Nathan. "Alexa, you can help me make *cevapi*." She shrugged in response, which I chose to take as assent. When we were alone, I would apologise. I would make it better.

Nathan and Ella left soon after, and Ruby danced around while I cleared the dishes and Alexa drummed her fingers on the table top; Nathan had taken her phone off her for the week, and she was clearly restless as a result. Still, it would be good. Today would be good.

Then, as the door was closing behind Nathan, my phone, left on the counter, rang.

Alexa rose to snatch it before I could even turn. I didn't mind; I had no secrets. Not anymore. Still, I was a bit taken aback by her presumption.

"Alexa…"

"It's the police." She thrust the phone out at me and I took it automatically. "Why are they calling you?"

"I don't know," I said. I didn't recognize the number, and I wondered how Alexa had.

"Maria Dzino?" The sound of Lisa's voice, sounding so formal, made me tense. Instinctively, I angled my body away from Alexa. "This is Detective Lisa Allan from the New York Police Department."

"Yes."

"I wasn't sure this was your number. Nathan West gave it to me, but…" A pause. "I didn't realize you'd become a nanny to his children."

"Yes." Why did I sound defensive?

"Nathan didn't inform me of that," Lisa continued. "I learned it from a friend of yours at Global Rescue…? Selma…?"

"Right." I hadn't seen Selma since I'd come to work for the Wests. I hadn't seen anyone from there, shedding my former life, such as it had been, like an old skin.

"It's an interesting connection," Lisa remarked, and I had no idea what that was supposed to mean.

"Was there a reason you called?"

"Yes, in fact there was. We'd like you to come down to the station, to answer a few questions that have arisen."

I felt Alexa standing behind me, bristling with curiosity. "Why?" I asked, trying to hold onto my polite tone. "I've told you everything I know." It took effort to keep my voice steady.

"Even so," Lisa said, sounding both equable and firm. "It would help us in our inquiries."

"All right." What else could I say? "When should I come?"

"As soon as possible."

As soon as possible? I swallowed, the sound audible even over the phone. "I need to take one of the West children to preschool," I said. "And I have the oldest with me…"

"That's fine," Lisa assured me. "Why don't you come after you drop the littlest one off?"

After I'd disconnected the call, I turned slowly to face Alexa, bracing myself.

She was glaring at me, her hands on her hips. "The police want to talk to you?"

"Yes, they have some questions." I resumed loading the dishwasher, trying to hold onto the sense of peace I'd had only moments ago.

"Why do they want to talk to you?" Alexa asked, sounding aggressive. "What could you possibly know?"

"I volunteered with your mother, Alexa," I said. "I might have seen someone." I thought of that photo Nathan had seen, the man—whoever he was—walking behind me. I'd tried not to think of it. I'd told myself it had nothing to do with me. And yet, right now, it did. I was going to the police station, after all. "You should get dressed," I told her. "We need to take Ruby to preschool, and then we'll have to go to the station."

Alexa looked as if she wanted to argue, but then, with a shrug, she strode off to her room.

I thought, briefly, of calling Nathan. He'd offered to accompany me, but I knew it would be a hassle for him, having to leave work, and there was a panicky part of me that did not want him there. I could not even say why.

"Come on, Ruby," I called. She was sprawled on her stomach in the dining room, playing with some little plastic figurines. "Time to go."

I knew I still needed to apologise to Alexa, but with the police visit pressing down on me, I told myself it could wait till after. We'd talk properly then.

I held onto that after as I walked into the police station downtown, having dropped off Ruby at preschool, Alexa sullen and silent by my side.

"She can wait here," one of the desk sergeants said when I told them who I was. She smiled at Alexa. "Would you like a hot chocolate?"

While she fetched Alexa her drink, I followed another officer to a small interview room in the back with a metal table and a couple of chairs. It felt far more official and formal than when I'd been interviewed at Global Rescue.

I sat down, trying not to feel nervous, while the sergeant murmured that Lisa and Tom would be with me soon.

Had Nathan been in a room like this? Had he felt nervous the way I did, my heart starting to pound, my palms slick? *What was I so scared of?*

I took a deep breath and let it out again.

The door opened and Lisa came in, followed by Tom. They both looked serious.

"Thank you for coming in, Maria," Lisa said.

Tom put a recorder on the table and I stared at it with apprehension. This conversation needed to be recorded? What was going on?

"That's just routine," Lisa assured me when she saw my nervous glance towards the little black machine. "Would you like a drink? Coffee? Tea?"

"Just water, please."

A few minutes later, they settled in front of me, their chairs creaking as they sat down, while I clutched a plastic cup of lukewarm water and took a tiny sip.

"What do you need to ask me?" I finally said when no one spoke.

"When did you become nanny to Nathan West's children?" Lisa asked, her tone not quite conversational.

"He asked me just before the New Year."

"I didn't realize you knew each other."

"He came to the center, to Global Rescue. He wanted to talk to someone who knew Laura. We went for coffee…"

"And from that he asked you to be his children's nanny?" Lisa raised her eyebrows.

I found myself blushing. "Yes, more or less."

"More… or less?" I heard a slight edge to her voice then and something flared to life inside me.

"Why are you asking me things? What does it matter?"

Tom leaned back in his chair, affecting a pose of relaxation. "It's just strange, that's all. Surely you can see that. Maria."

I didn't like the way he said my name, like an afterthought.

"Stranger things have happened," I said. "I thought you had some questions about the… the incident?"

"Yes, as a matter of fact we do." Lisa took a photo from a file and placed it on the table in front of me. "This is the suspect. He's walking right behind you." It had to be the photo Nathan had seen, and though I'd been expecting it, it still jolted me.

There I was, in grainy black and white, walking along the sidewalk. I recognized my bag, my coat. And there behind me, his back to the camera, was a man. I searched his form, the rangy length of it, the shaggy hair, but I knew no more than I had at the beginning.

I looked up at Lisa and Tom, shrugging helplessly. "I don't know what to say."

"You don't recognize him?"

I stiffened. "Of course I don't."

"Why don't you look again," Tom said.

"I don't need to," I returned sharply, more sharply than I would have usually dared. "It's the back of his head. There are dozens, hundreds, of people on the street. *I don't recognize him.*"

We stared at each other for a long, tense moment. Finally Lisa shifted in her seat, folded her arms. "We've had some new information about the suspect," she said. "He flew to New York from London in September of last year." Two months before Laura had been shot. I said nothing. "And before that, he flew to London from Tirana." A heavy silence.

"Tirana…" I stared at them blankly. "That is the capital of Albania." More silence. "What does that have to do with me?" A shrug. "Tirana is hundreds of kilometres from Sarajevo, and I haven't been back to Sarajevo in twenty years," I reminded them, my voice not quite steady. "You know that from my records."

"We have some other pictures of the assailant, taken from various CCTV cameras," Lisa said as she reached for more photos from her folder. "Why don't you take a look at them?"

Wordlessly, I held my hand out. Lisa gave me several sheets of paper—black and white print-outs, magnified to blurriness, all of the same man. I studied them each in turn, willing my heart rate to slow. This had nothing to do with me. I had nothing to be afraid of. I kept telling myself that, chanting it silently like a prayer.

On the third photo, I paused. Unwillingly, I brought it a little closer. The silence in the room grew as thick as smoke. I studied the photo until it blurred before my eyes. The raggedy hair. The thin face. A scar on the left cheekbone, near the eye, no more than a nick.

"Maria?" Lisa's voice was sharp. Tom stayed silent, watchful. "Do you know that man?"

I looked at the next photo, another close-up. Peaked eyebrows. A pointy chin. *That scar.*

"*Maria.*"

"I just want to be sure," I murmured. "You know this is the man who shot Laura West?"

"Yes." Lisa spoke firmly. "Without a doubt. Do you recognize him?"

I looked through all of them again, each one in turn, deliberate, thorough. Then I shuffled them into a neat pile. I looked up at Lisa, and when I spoke my voice was steady. "I do not know that man."

"You took your time."

I kept her gaze; I didn't even blink. "As I said, I wanted to be sure."

"And are you sure?" Lisa pressed. "Quite, quite sure?"

A pause in which a lifetime unfolded in front of me—a matter of seconds, and yet I saw it all. Ruby losing her first tooth. Ella coming out of her shell, eating properly. Alexa starting to smile, finally coming to peace with her anger. A lifetime I feared I would no longer be part of, because how could I now? *How could I?* "Yes," I said, my voice firm. "I am very sure."

Lisa stared at me for a long moment; Tom did, too. I didn't move, I didn't even blink.

Then Lisa nodded slowly. "We'll call you if we need you to come in again," she said.

"I am free to go?"

"This was only a request, Maria," Lisa answered. "You were always free to go."

Back in the waiting room, Alexa had finished her drink and was looking bored, tossing aside an old magazine as I came through the door.

"Are you done?"

"Yes," I said in the same firm voice I'd used with Lisa, and I started towards the door. Alexa hurried to keep up with me.

"What did they ask you?"

"They had some new photographs. They wished to know if I recognized the man."

"And did you?"

"No." I walked faster, down the street, towards the subway.

"Slow down," Alexa complained, but I couldn't. I was fighting the urge to run, although where? I did not even know.

"We need to get Ruby," I said, even though it was still over an hour to her pickup time.

As the train rattled uptown, Alexa brought it up again. "Did they have information about him? The... the man?"

I shook my head. "No."

"Not that they'd tell you," she muttered, and I nodded in agreement. That much was certainly true.

Thankfully, she lapsed into silence then, and I stared at the wall opposite, the windows looking onto black tunnels, my face reflected in the dark glass. I looked like a ghost.

Above the doors, there was a poster with a poem on it, just a few short words: *So much depends upon a red wheelbarrow glazed with rain water beside the white chickens.*

It did not seem like much of a poem to me, and yet at the same time I thought it so beautiful, I could weep. I imagined the wheelbarrow, the chickens, just as I imagined the sunny kitchen this morning, pancakes and sticky syrup, and both seemed completely beyond my reach, glimpses of a world I would never know.

I bowed my head, closing my eyes against the rattle of the train, the beauty of the poem, the dark windows and a sunlit kitchen. I closed my eyes against a scar by an eyebrow, a pointy chin, peaked eyebrows.

Because when Lisa had handed me those photos, when I'd looked at those grainy images of a man I had been so sure I couldn't possibly know, I'd realize who they were of. Who had, at least according to the police, shot Laura West.

My brother Petar.

CHAPTER TWENTY-FIVE

NATHAN

I used to think life was like a house. You made a plan, you laid the foundation, and you built it as you wanted. Simple. But after Laura died, and after Maria told me all that had happened to her, I realized life wasn't like that at all.

You might have a plan, but you weren't given the material or tools that you needed. Or perhaps you were, but then a massive wrecking ball smashed into the side of that lovely house, and you were left trying to figure out how to rebuild it all over again, or even if you could, with what broken tools and poor materials you had.

The night after Maria told me her story, I lay in bed and wondered how she could have endured so much. I wondered how I could be allowed my grief when hers was so much greater, and yet I knew she wouldn't give credence to that type of thinking for a moment. *Grief is grief*, she might have said.

And it was her grief that had drawn me to her in the first place—that sense of calm stillness and contained emotion. She might have called herself a ghost, but she'd still *survived*.

And I wanted to survive—I wanted to do more than survive, three and a half months on from Laura's death. I wanted to thrive. I wanted the girls to thrive. Not yet, not even in the next few weeks or months, but eventually. I wanted to see it in our future someday. And I knew that meant taking steps towards it now. More steps than I'd been willing to take before, more than a support group or a sunny morning, a milkshake or a swim meet.

So I texted Frank to let him know I'd be a little bit late, and I got up with Ruby and we made pancakes, just as we had once before, except this time the egg landed in the bowl and Ella didn't burn herself and I even laughed. This time I wasn't just going through the motions. I wasn't full of joy, not yet, not even close, but I could see it hovering on the horizon, tomorrow's sunrise, whenever tomorrow came.

I knew things needed to change. *I* did.

That day, after I left the apartment, after I told Alexa I loved her, I dropped Ella off at school and I went to work. I told Frank I was going to adjust my schedule to four days a week. He looked at me in horrified amazement.

"Nathan, are you serious? We've got so much work coming in. We need you…"

"And I'll still be here. But I've got a family, Frank. I've got daughters who need me. Right now I need to work four days a week, and I need to leave the office every day by six."

"Six…"

It was not an outrageous request. Plenty of people, even in Manhattan, even in the most demanding industries, left work at six.

"We can review it in six months," I said. "And see how things are going then."

After that, I called my in-laws. Paul answered, his voice full-bodied and firm as usual. "Nathan. I was going to call you, make sure the girls had their all their ski stuff ready—"

"The girls aren't going skiing with you, Paul." My tone, surprisingly, was almost gentle.

An electric pause. "We've already booked the condo."

"I'm sure you can find someone to take it. Or I'll pay you for it, if you can't."

"It's not about the money—"

"No, it never was about the money, was it?" I said. "It just felt like it was."

Another pause, this one bristling. "Look, Nathan, whatever it is—"

"I'm not going to do this," I said firmly. "I'm not going to have you take my daughters from me every holiday. I want them to have a relationship with you. Believe it or not, I recognize how important that is. I know Laura would have wanted it."

"Then…" For the first time, Paul sounded uncertain.

"You can't cut me out of the picture. I know I was never what you wanted for Laura. I didn't have the right background, the right breeding, all that. But she loved me, and I loved her, and we had three beautiful girls together. And like you said, they are what matter now. And for their sakes, we can't trade them between us. They feel the tension, Paul, and it's not good for them. Don't make them choose. Don't put them in the middle."

A long silence followed. I waited, feeling more certain than I had in a long time. Finally Paul spoke, gruffly. "What are you suggesting?"

"I'll bring them to visit you. We'll do it together. Skiing, Cape Cod—"

"You never wanted to come to Cape Cod." He practically spat the words.

"No, that's true. I didn't. But I do now. I want us to get along, Paul. For Alexa, Ella, and Ruby's sakes." I paused, my throat thickening. "And for Laura's."

"Do we have a choice?" he finally asked, sounding bitter. I hadn't expected some heart-warming reconciliation, but his tone and words still stung. I was trying; why couldn't he?

"I'd rather not think about it in terms of choices."

"How would you like to think of it, then?"

"I'd like us to work together. To want to."

"Yet you just cancelled our vacation. Elaine was looking forward—"

"I'm sorry, I didn't mean it as some sort of penalty. I just think the girls need to be at home with me right now."

"You mean with your *nanny*." He said nanny as if it were a rude word.

"With all of us. I'm going to take some time off—"

"That would be a first."

I heard the hurt and anger in Paul's voice, and I understood it. I felt something I hadn't felt for him before—compassion. "Yes, it will be," I agreed. "I'm trying to change. I'm trying to do the right thing."

"Nathan…" My name was a warning, but I wasn't heeding it.

"I'll let you think about it," I said, and then I disconnected the call.

I sat in my office, my hands flat on the table, everything in me both peaceful and buzzing. I was taking steps, and they didn't feel so limping. I was moving forward. We all were, even if it hurt.

That afternoon, Alexa called from the home phone.

"Alexa, sweetheart? Is everything okay?"

"We went to the police station." Her voice was low, almost frightened.

"The police…?"

"They called Maria. They asked her to come in."

"I thought they might." I wasn't really worried. "They must have realized she was in that photo."

"What photo?" Alexa's voice sounded high and thin, with a ragged edge.

"Just a photo from CCTV…" I hadn't shared the details of the investigation with Alexa, although she'd asked on occasion. I'd just told her they were pursuing some leads. "It doesn't really matter, Alexa. It was just a photo of the street. Maria was walking and there was a man behind her."

"The man who…"

My stomach clenched at the thought. "Yes."

"She seems weird," Alexa said after a moment. "All afternoon, she's seemed really weird."

"Weird?" I still wasn't alarmed, not then. I was holding onto that feeling of hope; I wasn't going to let anything shake it. "It's just that she doesn't like going to the police, Alexa."

"Why not?"

"It… it brings back memories, I think." I didn't want to tell any more than I had to. "Why don't I talk to her?"

"I don't know…"

"Please."

After a moment, Alexa mumbled her assent and the phone clattered onto some surface. I waited, and then a few seconds later I heard Maria's voice, small and tense.

"Nathan?"

"Hi, Maria. Alexa told me the police called you."

"Yes."

"I'm sorry if it was distressing for you. You should have called me. I would have come with you."

"It was okay." She did sound strange, sort of blank, as if she wasn't really listening.

"Are you sure? Were they asking you about that photo?"

"Yes. And they were… suspicious, I think. Because I now work for you."

I frowned. "Why would that make them suspicious?"

"I don't know. They said it was… an odd connection."

Looking back, I knew it had been odd, that I'd asked a virtual stranger to take care of my children, and yet I couldn't regret it for a moment. We'd come so far, together.

"I don't know why they would suspect you of anything," I said. "You weren't involved." It was so obvious, I felt uncomfortable even having to say it.

"No," Maria agreed after a pause. "I was not involved." Her voice sounded heavy, and I didn't understand it. Perhaps I didn't want to.

"So you're okay? Because Alexa was a bit worried…"

"I am fine. Please, do not worry yourself."

"Okay." I still felt a little bit uneasy, unsure, although about what I didn't know. "I'll be back for dinner."

"All right."

"And we should talk… the three of us. You, me, and Alexa. Get it all straight…"

"Yes."

I couldn't judge her tone, but I knew it felt off. I felt the need to say something more, but I didn't know what. "Take care, Maria," I said finally, although that didn't feel like the right thing.

She let out a choked sound—so small I thought I might have misheard or even imagined it—and then she disconnected the call.

The conversation lingered with me all afternoon, although I tried not to think about it. Not to worry about it. And when Sarah texted me a few hours later, asking if I'd like to go out for a coffee one afternoon this week, as we both worked near Madison Square, I pushed those concerns away and focused on the present that was unfolding in front of me.

Maria seemed mostly back to her usual self that evening, although perhaps a little quiet. I read Ruby a story and listened to Ella play piano, and later I coaxed Alexa out of her bedroom to watch TV with me. Small but important triumphs.

Maria went to bed early, saying she had a headache, postponing the reconciliation chat I'd been planning, but that was okay. I told myself she would feel better tomorrow.

When the girls were all in bed, I walked through the quiet rooms of the apartment, savouring the peace, even as I made notes to myself. Over President's Day weekend, we could strip the wallpaper in the dining room. I'd sand the walls and paint them a nice mellow cream. We'd do the same with the living room; perhaps I'd let the girls choose the color. And I'd start to box up Laura's things.

The thought brought me a pang of grief, but I knew it was the right time. I'd go through her jewelry and pick something for each of my girls. Laura had never been one for expensive stuff, although I'd given her a few pieces over the years. A sapphire and diamond bracelet from Tiffany's for our tenth anniversary. A diamond eternity ring for our fifteenth, just a few months before she'd died. We'd been planning to go to Paris this summer to celebrate, just the two of us, a trip of a lifetime. Perhaps I'd go now with Alexa, Ella, and Ruby.

The future wasn't what I'd thought and hoped it would be, but it still *was*.

In the kitchen, I glanced at the calendar; March, in just a week's time, had none of Laura's handwriting, no appointments she'd made, no reminders she'd needed. It was a blank slate, a fresh start. At least, I was trying to look at it that way. I was trying to find the good amidst all the grief and loss. *Was it even there?*

I stood in the kitchen, the apartment quiet all around me, the night so dark. Was I still searching for meaning when there wasn't any to be found? Was making sense of all this even possible?

I thought of Maria, of how she'd cried in my arms like with no one else. I thought of Ella, sobbing about swimming, needing to let it go. I thought about Alexa, sitting silent next to me as we watched a repeat of *Designated Survivor*. Perhaps that was what we all were. Perhaps that was where the meaning lay.

I left the kitchen, switching off the light, and walked in darkness to my bedroom.

CHAPTER TWENTY-SIX

MARIA

I do not remember much about those days after I saw the photograph of Petar. Everything felt as if it were happening far away; as if there was static between me and the world, a constant crackle so I couldn't hear or speak or even think.

And yet my thoughts circled and circled, a flock of crows with nowhere to land. How could it be Petar? *How*? He was dead. He'd been dead for twenty-six years. I'd heard the gunshot; he *had* to be dead.

And even if he hadn't died, why would he be in New York? Had he really shot Laura West, and if he had, *why*? *How had he been walking right behind me and he had not seen me, told me? How had I not known*?

I thought I might go crazy with the questions, I might tear my hair or claw my skin. There was a scream inside me trying to get out, and every time I opened my mouth, I feared it would emerge. It would start and never stop.

I thought of how I'd been afraid of what would happen after I slapped Alexa's face; that seemed like so little compared to this. So ridiculously unimportant, and yet it still lay unresolved between the two of us, because I did not know how to apologise to Alexa with this scream in my chest. I did not how to do anything.

And yet somehow I made it through the days, step by step, one foot in front of the other. I picked up Ruby from preschool,

I picked up Ella from school, I spoke to Nathan, I made dinner. I could not tell how I sounded; I could not judge the expression on my face. I felt frozen, my circling thoughts trapped now, forever stuck in flight. I did not want them to land. I did not want to think about what this meant, what would happen if I told Nathan, if I told the police.

Because I knew that was what I should do. Of course it was. How could I do anything else?

And yet I was so afraid. They would find Petar. They would arrest him, if he really did this terrible thing, and I knew in my heart, in my leaden gut, that he had. Perhaps they would even arrest me. And everything would be over, forever this time. I couldn't bear any of it, and so for those few fragile days, I stayed silent.

I told myself it didn't matter that I knew him, that he was my brother. I hadn't known he was in the country. I hadn't even known he was alive. It didn't make any difference to anything. But I knew that these things didn't work that way. I knew if I told the police who he was, they would suspect me too. Lisa's tone would lose that conversational bent and all would be accusation.

Are you telling me you did not recognize your own brother? Are you saying that he never once contacted you? Did you tell him to kill Laura West?

Who knew what conclusions they would jump to, what they would let themselves think. Perhaps they'd think I planned it all—I was living in her home, after all. I was practically taking her place.

For three days, I did not sleep. I lay in bed the whole night long and stared at the ceiling. I was trying not to think about the future, and so it was the past that claimed me.

I thought of Petar as a child—his dark hair, his blue eyes, his slender hands. He had always been so quiet, so gentle. I hadn't realized it until I was a bit older, but he'd been teased at school, for being too shy. Too soft.

Lying on my bed, I recalled my father's arm slung about his shoulders, the murmured words. *Don't pay any attention to them, Petar. Don't pay any attention at all.*

I remembered the faint smile on his face as I capered about the room, being my silly self. The friendly glint in his eyes.

How had that man, that gentle, lovely boy, come to shoot a stranger on the subway?

But then, of course, I remembered other things. I remembered Petar at the camp, the men hustling him away, one taking each arm.

I remembered the blank, deadened look in his eyes the last time I saw him.

Where was he now? Lisa had said the assailant had been in the country since September. All this time, and Petar had not found me? Yet he had been so close. He had walked right behind me.

What if he *had* found me… and chosen not to reveal himself?

I could not think about it. I could not let myself. And so I went through the days, step by painstaking step, just trying to survive. To get through this, even though I could see no end in sight. *How* would it end? They would find Petar, or they wouldn't. Neither option was a solution, not for me.

That week of blurred days, I remember Alexa watching me. She was at home all day, phoneless, going out with me wherever I went, and always I felt her eyes on me. Ever since I'd answered the call from Lisa, I had felt her eyes. I hadn't thought I had something to feel guilty about, but now I knew I did.

Still, I tried to keep going. I made myself speak to her, stumbling through an apology for that terrible slap. She shrugged me off, refusing to speak of it, or to me at all. When I looked at her, I wondered how, just weeks before, we had shown each other our scars, we had shared each other's pain. Where had that healing gone?

Ella and Ruby didn't seem to notice the tension between us or the strangeness in myself; neither did Nathan. One afternoon he came home from work early and, with the girls' help, he put all of Laura's things in boxes. I watched from the kitchen as he let them each pick out a piece of her jewelry, an item of her clothing, for keepsakes. Ella was tearful, Ruby excited, Alexa silent but willing.

Afterwards, he put his arms around them all, and they stood there in the bedroom in a tableau of both grief and acceptance. I turned away.

Nathan was full of vigour, those days, buoyed by a hope he'd never shown before. He told me of his plans for the weekend—no more skiing, instead they would all work together to redecorate the dining and living rooms.

"I should have done it ages ago," he said. "But I'm doing it now. You'll help, won't you?"

I nodded, because I did not know what else to do.

And then, on Wednesday I went to the greengrocer's around the corner, more just to get away from Alexa's watchful eyes than anything else, and as I rounded the corner with a paper bag of apples, I felt someone's hand on my shoulder.

"Maria." The voice was low, gravelly, a smoker's rasp, and yet I still recognized it. I always would.

Even so, I did not want to turn. The hand was heavy on my shoulder, and I stilled beneath it. I bowed my head.

"Maria," Petar said again.

I turned to face him. His face jolted me; even now, I had been expecting the boy I remembered, not from Vojno, but from before. *Always before.* The boy with the quiet eyes and the slender hands and the faint smile.

The man in front of me had a face hatcheted with deep lines, blue eyes sunk into weathered skin. He wore a woolly hat over wild, unkempt hair, a mishmash of baggy clothes. Dirt rimmed his nails as he lifted one hand as if to touch my cheek, and then dropped it again before he did.

"It really is you," he said in Bosnian.

I clutched the bag of apples to my chest, my head whirling and my heart thudding. Here was Petar, my brother. Here was Petar, the man who had shot Laura West, who had made three girls I'd grown to love motherless. I could not reconcile the two; worlds collided inside me and then broke apart again, spinning into the void.

"Petar…" I whispered. "How… what…" I did not even know what to ask. Part of me just wanted to run away, even as I ached to hug him.

He shook his head slowly. "After all this time."

"*Petar*." I glanced around, fear rising like a hydra inside me, its many heads writhing. "What are you doing here? How did you find me?"

"I found you months ago, Maria. Back at that center." He spoke with a sort of weary despair, as if it was of no consequence anymore; it was all finished.

"Back at the center…" The bag of apples slipped from my hands, the paper bag tearing. Apples bounced and rolled around us. Petar crouched down to pick one up. "No." I glanced around again, and then up, at the living room of the Wests' apartment, that faced this street corner. The windows glinted in the sun, bright and blank.

I grabbed Petar by the arm and pulled him around the corner, nearly tripping on one of the fallen apples. Petar didn't protest, following me docilely without a word.

I drew him to the side of a building, near an alley, the only shelter I could find. People walked past in a busy stream, barely sparing us a glance.

My mind was racing, racing. Petar had always known where I was. He knew where I *lived*. Were the Wests in danger from my *brother*? What could I do?

"Why didn't you talk to me?" I demanded. "Why didn't you let me know you were alive?"

"For a long time, I didn't know you were."

"I was in Mostar for five years after the war ended." I did not know whether I was angry at him or just afraid. "Surely you could have found me then?"

Petar shook his head. A broken, blank look had come over his face that scared me. It was as if there was nothing behind those eyes.

"What happened at Vojno?" I asked. "I heard a gunshot…"

"Yes, what happened at Vojno?" Petar asked me, his voice turning hard and unfamiliar. "What happened to *you* at Vojno, Maria?"

My mouth dried as I recognized the knowledge in his eyes. "How did you find out?" I whispered.

"A guard was bragging about it in the camp."

Nausea churned in my stomach. I couldn't bear the bitter look on my brother's face. "Why didn't you die?" I cried, and Petar's lips twisted.

"Is that what you wanted?"

"No!" And yet yes, because look what had happened. Laura was dead. I pressed my forehead against the rough brick wall, grinding my skin into it until I felt it burn. I took a deep breath and turned back to face him. He was standing there loose-limbed, hands spread, as if the fight had all gone out of him. And yet he'd shot Laura. "What happened after they took you away? The last time I saw you?"

Petar stared at me for a long moment. "They gave me a gun," he finally said. "And they told me it was either me or him."

I pressed one hand to my mouth. "You shot another prisoner?"

Petar shrugged. "It was either me or him."

I closed my eyes, squeezing them shut, longing only to block all of this out. "Why didn't I see you after that?"

"They kept us separate, and then you were released."

I opened my eyes, stared at him hard. "And what happened to you?"

He shrugged. "More of the same."

"Oh, Petar…" I shook my head. "Why didn't you find me in Mostar?"

"I couldn't."

"You knew I was there?"

He shrugged. Behind the blankness in his eyes, I saw far too much despair.

"Were you ashamed of me?" I asked. "Because…?"

"I was ashamed of me." His voice broke and then firmed again. "I couldn't stand to be back there, staring at all those faces…"

"I know," I whispered. "I felt the same. But where did you go? Where have you been all these years?" *And how did you come to America? And why did you shoot Laura?*

He hesitated, and I felt myself tense.

"Petar…"

"I worked in Doboj for a while," he said finally. "For the railway."

"And then…?"

Another awful pause. "I went to Syria," he said at last, and I sagged against the wall as the full meaning of that slammed into me. Syria… to fight. Why else would he go?

"Oh, Petar. Oh, no. *No*."

"A few of us joined up. You know what they did, Maria, to us during that forsaken war, just because we were Bosniak. The injustice of it… I wanted to fight back—"

I wanted to put my hands over my ears. As it was, I kept shaking my head. "No. No, no, no."

"But they were just the same," he said after a moment. "Just as bad, everyone, no matter who or what. I couldn't make sense of any of it," he said, his voice broken now, nothing but jagged splinters of sound. "All I saw was cruelty. No one was right. No one was good, on any side. I went back to Bosnia, and then to Albania, to find work there. And then I thought I'd find you, that finding you might be something good—that was when they told me you'd gone to America."

"Who did?"

"Tetka Emina and Ujak Daris. I wrote to them." My aunt and uncle.

"So you came…?"

"Yes. I came. And I found you."

"But you never even spoke to me…" I practically whimpered.

"I didn't know how. You looked so different… so *clean*. And I was…" He shook his head helplessly.

Tears gathered in my eyes.

"But why Laura?" I whispered. "Why did you shoot her, Petar?" I could hardly believe I was asking such a question.

He shook his head again, tears spilling down his weathered cheeks. "I don't know. I don't know. I saw her touching you… *grabbing* you, pushing you…"

"What!" I could not believe it, until I remembered that awkward little dance we'd done, the morning Laura had left, how she'd moved me out of the way. She'd held onto my shoulders, and I'd been a little surprised by the physicality of it, and yet…

Who could have ever anticipated this?

"For that, you *shot* her?" I demanded, and Petar shrugged.

"For everything. You deserved more, Maria, you deserved so much more. And I was able to do nothing…" He let out a choked cry.

"But that doesn't have anything to do with Laura West." I stared at him hopelessly, because none of it mattered anymore. Who knew what had gone through my brother's shattered mind when he'd seen Laura manhandling me, what torturous memories that moment had stirred? Who knew what twisted and terrible logic had led him to shoot a woman he'd never even known?

The man in front of me was not my brother. The man in front of me was a broken wreck, any semblance of the brother I knew beaten out by cruelty and suffering, by the things that had been done to him as well as the things he had done.

And yet he'd *killed* Laura. Even now, with everything he had said, everything that had happened, I struggled to believe it.

"How could you do such a thing to an innocent woman?" I whispered.

"No one is innocent." And then he began to weep, great, heaving sobs that tore from his chest and made people pause and look before hurrying on.

"Petar…" I reached one hand out to him, but I could not touch him. "Petar, you must turn yourself into the police."

"The *police*?" He lifted his head, his face tear-streaked, his eyes blazing. "You want me to give myself up?"

"You killed an innocent woman." My voice trembled. "She didn't deserve to die, you had no reason to do anything to her at all."

"I'm sorry…" he mumbled, as if that made it better.

"They will find you anyway," I persisted. "They already have photographs of you, from cameras… they know when you entered the country…"

Petar shook his head, again and again, back and forth. "No. No."

"Petar, please. For my sake. The police think I am connected with you. They have asked me questions—"

"You had nothing to do with it, Maria. They must know this."

"She didn't deserve to die!" My voice rose, and someone looked over. I lowered it, drawing closer to Petar. "Please."

"Do you know what they will do to me if they find me?"

"This is not Bosnia, Petar. This is not Syria."

"I'll go to *prison*—"

"And isn't that what you deserve?" I cried.

Petar drew back. "Is that what you think? After Vojno? After everything?"

"If you don't go to prison, then how can any of the men who tortured you? How can there be justice for one and not the other?" We both knew how few war criminals had been brought to justice over the years. How everyone wanted to look away, because it was easier. Because it was over.

"It's different, Maria—"

"But you killed her." Tears were running down my cheeks. "She was nobody to you. She was *innocent*. She had three little girls—" I stopped, because I realized I did not want Petar to know about Laura's girls.

Petar bowed his head. "I am sorry. I don't expect you to believe me, but it is true."

"Then tell the police that. Perhaps, considering your history, they will go lightly on you…"

"Lightly." He sneered the word. I stared at him despairingly.

"Where are you staying, Petar?" I asked. I did not know if I asked because I cared, or because I wanted information. My mind felt like a tangle, a hopeless knot. "Are you safe?" I continued. "Do you have a place to sleep?"

"As if I'd tell you." He stepped back from me then, and it felt like a chasm opening between us, one that would never be crossed. He stood two feet away from me, but I knew he was already gone.

"Please," I whispered. "Please, Petar."

"I only wanted to see you," he said. "Just once. Just so you'd know."

"Know what?"

"That I am sorry. For all of it." His face contorted as he drew a ragged breath. "God help me." And then he was half-stumbling, half-walking away from me, and I stared at him, the remnant of the torn bag still clutched to my chest, as he disappeared down the street.

I didn't call out. I didn't say a word. And after what felt like an age, I turned and walked back around the corner, into the apartment building, and up to where Alexa waited for me.

"What took you so long?" she demanded as I came in the house. Her arms were crossed, her eyes narrowed, her body nearly vibrating with tension. When I spoke my voice was calm.

"There was a line."

"*What*?" Alexa stared at me incredulously.

It took me several stunned seconds to realize I was still speaking in Bosnian.

"A line," I said in English. "There was a line."

"You didn't even buy anything," she scoffed, still looking so suspicious, and I glanced at the bit of bag I was still holding.

"The bag split. The apples rolled into the gutter. I didn't want to go back." I turned away from her, bracing my hands on the counter as I took several deep breaths, willing myself not to break down. Not to let that scream out.

A silence ticked on and on, like a rope being drawn tighter and tighter.

"Figures," Alexa said quietly, and then she walked out of the room.

CHAPTER TWENTY-SEVEN

NATHAN

I was full of such optimism that week. Such determination and hope. On Wednesday evening after work, I took the girls to the hardware store on York Avenue and let them pick out paint colors; Ruby wanted pink, Ella wanted green.

"We can't have a pink living room," Ella said. "It's too babyish."

"Pink is *not* babyish."

I smiled at Alexa, willing her to join in. "What do you think, Alexa?"

She glanced at us all, standing there in the paint aisle with a rainbow of sample cards behind us, as if only noticing us now for the first time. "What? Oh, I don't care."

I frowned, because she sounded as if she really didn't care, not her usual determined-to-be-indifferent routine.

"I thought you didn't like the apartment the way it was," I said lightly. "Aren't you glad we're finally doing something about it?"

She shrugged and walked off a little bit. I tried not to feel hurt, and more importantly, not to feel annoyed. I wasn't going to go down that tired old route anymore.

"All right, girls," I said cheerfully as I turned back to Ella and Ruby. "Let's try again. What about that nice sage green for the living room, and the pale rose for the dining room?"

"See," Ruby said, glee audible in her voice. "Pink is not babyish."

Alexa was quiet on the way home, a different, more thoughtful type of silence than her usual resolute sulk. I fell into step beside her, Ruby holding my hand, Ella walking a little bit behind.

"Back to school next week," I said, trying for an upbeat tone, and she just shrugged. I hadn't yet confronted her about the smoking and, more importantly, the boys. I was waiting for the right moment even as I realized it probably would never come. I had to make it. "Alexa… we should talk."

The sudden look she threw me was surprised, even frightened. "What about?"

"About the suspension," I clarified gently. "And the reason for it."

"Oh." She sounded strangely relieved. "That."

"Yes, that." Annoyance crept into my tone and I strove to moderate it. "Very much that. I'm not angry, Alexa, but I am concerned about the ways you are trying to cope with what happened—"

She shook her head. "Dad, please don't. You're just embarrassing yourself."

"Then I'll embarrass myself." I quickened my stride to match hers, pulling Ruby along. "Now is not the time, but I just want you to know there's a conversation ahead of us, and I want it to be a good one."

"Whatever," Alexa muttered, and walked faster. I let her go, because I was out of ideas about what to say and in any case poor Ruby's little legs couldn't go any faster.

The next afternoon, I met Sarah from the support group for coffee downtown, near both of our offices. I was still determinedly buoyant, telling her all my plans.

"I feel like I'm finally doing something," I said as we huddled over our lattes, a chilly breeze gusting into the tiny café every time the door opened. "Talking to my father-in-law… even painting the living room. I'm finally doing this." I smiled at Sarah, only to register that she was looking at me with a sympathetic sort of pity. "What?"

"I'm so happy for you, Nathan," she said. "Truly."

"But…?" Because there was obviously a but.

"But just keep in mind that this is another stage," she said after a moment. "It's not the end. You're not finished with grief."

"I know that." I was stung by her words even as I recognized the truth of them. I wanted to be done with grief. I wanted to move on; I wanted to feel joy. I didn't want to forget Laura, of course I didn't, but I wanted to remember her a little less.

"It's just, I've been where you are," Sarah said gently. "You feel like you've passed a hurdle. You start looking towards the future, and it feels *good*."

"Yes." My cheeks were warm; I was embarrassed. I'd been practically bragging about my progress.

"And it is good. It's an important step. But that's what it is—a step."

"I know—"

"Don't be surprised if next week, or next month, or even tomorrow, you find yourself back where you started, or even in a worse place. Six months on and the grief can feel even fresher than it did at the start. I'm not trying to be a downer, really, I'm not. I suppose I just wish someone had given me the warning."

"Right." The thought of ending up in a worse place than where I'd already been appalled me. I didn't think I could survive that.

"I'm sorry." She grimaced an apology. "I think I am being a downer. Never mind me. I've had a bad week."

"You have?" I felt guilty for going on about my own upbeat mood. "What's happened?"

"Nothing, which is so annoying. Will is actually doing okay in school, work is good. Nothing's gone wrong, and yet a few days ago I felt as if the wheels were coming off." She gave a shaky laugh and took a sip of her coffee; I could see that she was near tears.

"I'm sorry, Sarah. I suppose I thought you had it all together."
I tried for a smile. "I was looking forward to when I was more
like you."

"Sorry to disappoint you."

"No, you haven't. Not at all." I shook my head. "I know I'm
being unrealistic about all of this. I just want to see an endpoint,
something to work towards."

"I know."

"And there isn't one, is there?"

She smiled sadly. "I haven't found it yet. But in the meantime… enjoy the little things, Nathan. Painting your living room.
Seeing Ruby smile. Whatever it is… enjoy it."

I nodded slowly. I felt, strangely, both heavier and lighter
from our conversation. "Thanks for giving me the heads-up," I
said finally, even though it wasn't something I'd wanted to hear.

On Friday, with the girls out of school for the long weekend, I
took the day off and we started stripping wallpaper from the
dining room. It was easy; the faded paper with its old-fashioned
pattern of cabbage roses was already hanging off in long, curling
peels in some places. I couldn't believe I'd let it go this long.

"Can we really do this, Daddy?" Ruby asked as she gave one
of the peels a cautious tug. "Because Mommy always said not to
pull on it, or we'd make it worse."

"She told me once that maybe we should," Ella said with a
hearteningly mischievous grin. "She said then maybe you would
do something about it."

"Ouch." I smiled at them to show them I didn't mind. "Well,
I think Mom was right. I should have done something about this
ages ago." I forced myself past the inevitable regret. "But we're all
doing it now. Together."

"Whee!" Ruby gave the strip of wallpaper a hearty tug, and it came away from the wall with a flurry of dried paste and flakes of plaster.

"That's the way, Ruby," I encouraged. "Do it again."

With a squeal of delight, she stood on her tiptoes and pulled again, the wallpaper coming away from the wall with a loud rip and another puff of plaster dust and dried paste.

"You too, Ella," I encouraged. "Come on. Let's get into this."

I reached for a curling edge of wallpaper high up on the wall and felt the satisfaction of it pulling away easily, leaving bare, old wall. It would need a lot of work to be ready to be painted, but I was up for the job.

"Alexa?" I called.

She was standing in the doorway, her arms folded, a remote expression on her face. What, I wondered for what felt like the thousandth time, would it take to reach her? Crack that impossible shell?

"Come on, Alexa," Ella implored softly. "It's fun."

"Okay, fine." She sauntered forward and half-heartedly tugged at a piece of wallpaper. It came away only a little bit.

"Give it a bit more oomph," I advised and Alexa threw me an indecipherable look before pulling harder. A faint smile flickered across her face as the strip of wallpaper came away in her hand. "Oh. Gross. What is all this dried yellow stuff?" she exclaimed as she dropped the thing.

"It's old paste. This wallpaper has probably been on these walls for about seventy-five years." For a moment we were silent, absorbing the longevity of it, and then with a grin, Ruby seized another piece. I laughed out loud. "That's the spirit!"

Soon enough the air was full of dust, and I opened the window to let in the air as the floor became littered with long strips of old paper.

"It's going to look so pretty," Ruby exclaimed. "Can we start painting now, Daddy?"

"Sorry, Rubes. I have to prepare the walls first. But keep peeling."

I looked around for Maria, surprised to realize she wasn't here with us. I poked my head into the kitchen and saw her sitting at the little table by the window, her hands cradled around a cup of tea.

"Maria? Won't you come join us?"

Her head jerked up as if she'd been startled, and for a second I thought I saw panic in her eyes. I took a step forward.

"Maria?"

"No, no, you go ahead." She fluttered her fingers. "You are having so much fun."

"You can be part of it, too."

"Come on, Maria," Ella said as she appeared in the kitchen doorway. "It's fun." Her eyes were alight as she added, "It feels like you should get in trouble but you don't."

Maria gave Ella a strained smile. "That sounds pretty good to me."

"Come on, then." I held out a hand and she rose from the table, taking her tea to the sink. "Is everything all right?" I asked quietly. "You seem a bit..." I paused, unsure how she did seem. Worried? Distracted? Unhappy?

"I am fine." She turned to me with a brighter smile, but I could still see the crow's feet of strain by her eyes. "Fine," she said again and walked into the dining room.

Alexa threw her a sharp look as she came into the room, and I wondered if that was what this was about. Was Alexa still angry about the slap? I'd been meaning to sit us all down for a talk, but it hadn't happened yet, another moment I would have to make.

"Where should I...?" Maria began, and I gestured grandly to the tattered wallpaper.

"Take your pick."

She tugged on a thin strip, half-heartedly, and it came away, revealing a sliver of yellowed wall. "There."

"Do some more, Maria," Ruby called. "Watch me!"

Ruby leaped up high to catch the top, ragged edge of a strip of wall paper and then pull it, satisfyingly, all the way to the bottom.

"Very good, Ruby," Maria said with a smile and a nod. "Already this room looks better."

We kept at it for another hour, until the walls were mostly clear, and I used a scraper to get the stuck bits off.

"Can we do the living room next?" Ruby asked eagerly, and I laughed and shook my head.

"One room at a time, Rubes. Otherwise we'll be living in complete chaos."

"I should make dinner…" Maria, having been pretty quiet the whole time, edged towards the kitchen.

"Why don't we have takeout?" I suggested. "To celebrate being rid of this wallpaper."

"Pizza!" Ruby cried. "Can we please have pizza?"

"I think that sounds like a good idea."

"If you're sure," Maria said. She did not sound entirely pleased. I really needed to get us all to sit down and talk. Part of me dreaded the conversation, even as I recognized its necessity.

"I'll call for pizza," I said. "What topping does everyone want?" I glanced around, noticing that Alexa had made an exit without me realizing. When had she gone? I still had her phone, so I knew she couldn't be on that, so where was she? And why didn't she want to be with us?

I found her in her room, huddled on her bed, picking at a ragged fingernail as she stared into space.

"Alexa?"

She didn't look at me as she answered. "What?"

"Why don't you come out and join us again?"

She shook her head as she chewed on her nail. "No thanks."

"What's going on, Alexa?" I stepped into the room, dim and messy, clothes littering the floor. In other words, a pit. "Is this about Maria?"

"What?" It came out nearly as a screech as she jerked around to look at me.

"She told me about what happened."

"She did?" Alexa sounded disbelieving.

"Yes, about the argument you had, and how she… slapped you." When I said it out loud, it sounded worse.

"She told you?" Alexa sounded vaguely impressed by this news, but then she shrugged. "Whatever."

"Are you still angry at her?"

"Oh, Dad." She let out a sigh and slumped back against the pillows. "You really have no clue about anything, do you?"

I didn't let that sting as I answered. "I guess I don't, unless you tell me."

She shook her head. "You wouldn't believe me."

"Why wouldn't I?"

Alexa looked away, still picking at her fingernail. "It doesn't matter," she said, but I thought it did.

I just had no idea how much.

An hour later, the pizza had arrived. As the dining room was an utter mess of dust and paper, we ate in the living room, the pizza boxes spread out on the coffee table, everyone happily slurping on their slices, even Alexa.

I felt happy. Despite everything, *because* of it, I actually felt happy. It was fragile, faint, and most certainly fleeting, but it was there. And that was enough; it was a lot more than I'd had before, at least in that moment, for in the next my entire world upended for a second time.

A sharp knock sounded on the door, followed by the unexpected and incredible sound of it being forced open, then banging against the wall. I remember hot pizza sauce on my hand, a bolt of shock running through me at the sound even as I struggled to make sense of it.

"What the..."

"Police!" A gruff voice shouted, and then they were streaming into the living room like something out of a bad action movie, policemen with bulletproof vests and drawn pistols. Ruby started screaming, a continuous high-pitched wail. I flung my pizza away as I raised my hands in the air.

"What do you... why are you here?" I could barely stammer out the words. I fought a bizarre urge to laugh, even as terror gripped my insides, turning them liquid. This couldn't be happening. This simply couldn't be happening.

The policemen—there were three of them, which seemed like far too many—advanced into the room, still with their guns drawn.

"Maria Dzino?" one of them said, and he pointed his gun at her.

She rose carefully, her hands in the air, her face full of resignation. "Yes, that is me," she said softly.

"*Maria!*" Ella wailed, tears streaking down her face. Ruby kept screaming.

"What do you want with Maria?" I demanded. My voice wavered at the end, because these were policemen and they had actual guns.

"Maria Dzino," the policeman began, and now he really sounded as if he were in a bad movie, "you are under arrest."

"For what?" I blustered, trying in my pointless, pathetic way, to take charge of the situation.

The man didn't even look at me as he kept his gaze and his gun trained on Maria. "For accessory to murder."

I turned to Maria, and my stomach bottomed out at the expression on her face. She didn't even look surprised.

"What…" The word came out of me like air from a deflating balloon. I stared at Maria, willing her to say something. To explain. To protest, at least. "Maria," I began, and then couldn't finish.

Her gaze flicked to me for only a second. "I am sorry, Nathan," she said quietly. "I am so very sorry."

"What?" I stared at her in disbelief, not wanting to process what that apology meant. "*What?*"

Ruby had stopped screaming and was now simply staring in incomprehension, her mouth a rounded O, while Ella wept softly. Wildly, I looked around for Alexa, and when I saw her standing in the corner, her face pale, her arms crossed, I realized she didn't look surprised either.

"Alexa…" I began, and again I had to stop. I had no words, no thought, my mind nothing but a buzzing, blank screen.

"She knew him," Alexa said defiantly. "She *knew* him, Dad. I saw them together."

"What…"

I looked back at Maria, who was now being handcuffed, although I hardly thought she needed the restraint. She was utterly docile, almost lifeless.

"You knew him?" I whispered. Of course I knew who *him* was.

"He is my brother," she answered in a voice laden with sorrow. "I am so sorry."

Her *brother?* Petar, I remembered, who loved music, who was quiet and shy. Petar Dzino had killed my wife? And Maria had known?

I put my hands to the sides of my head, as if to keep myself from exploding. The policemen began to lead Maria out.

"Daddy." Ruby tugged on my arm, her face streaked with tears. "Daddy, don't let them. Don't let them take her."

I just shook my head silently as four policemen escorted Maria out of the apartment, and out of our lives.

CHAPTER TWENTY-EIGHT

MARIA

So it came to this. I sat in the cell, staring at the grey concrete walls, the little metal toilet, and thought, *I know what to do in a place like this. I know how to be.*

I did not feel scared, which surprised me; I did not even feel worried. I had a strange, heavy sort of peace, a resignation that was also relief. It was over. I had no more secrets to carry, to keep. The worst had happened, and I had got through it.

The policemen had not spoken to me as they'd taken me to a station somewhere in the city, I did not know where. I'd sat in the back of a van, a policeman crouching near me, looking at me as if I were someone dangerous. I could tell from the curl of his lip that he assumed the worst—accessory to murder, must have planned it all, perhaps even a terrorist. Who knew? I had stared at the inside of the van and let my mind empty out. I did not want to think about Ruby looking so terrified, Ella so heartbroken, Nathan so betrayed. And Alexa… she must have seen Petar and me from the windows. She must have called the police. I did not blame her. I did not blame anyone.

At the station, they fingerprinted and photographed me and then locked me in this room. They said I could have a lawyer, and so I called Cathy at Global Rescue, because I knew she could recommend someone.

"Maria, you've been *arrested*?" She sounded shocked.

"It is a long story." I felt so tired, wanting only to get through these necessary steps. Needing to have it all be over. Whatever sentence they gave me, I knew I would accept it. How could I not?

I was only in the cell for an hour or so when Lisa and Tom, those old friends, summoned me to an interrogation room, just as before, except now of course it was so different. Now they informed me I could wait until my lawyer came, and I said I did not need to. Perhaps that was foolish, but I was afraid that waiting for a lawyer would make me look guilty, and I was not guilty. I was not.

Yet I *felt* guilty as I sat in front of them; now there were no conciliatory smiles, no conversational tone. They were both giving me stony looks as I waited for them to speak, my head slightly bowed.

"Where is your brother, Maria?"

"I do not know."

"And I don't believe you." In all of our interviews, she'd never sounded so hard.

"I am sorry. If I knew, I would tell you."

"Really? Because you didn't tell us when you recognized the photo. You didn't tell us when he found you near the Wests' apartment, and spoke to you."

"I know. I should have. I wanted to…"

"Yeah, right." This from Tom, a sneer. "I think that's a load of crap, Maria. I think you've known Petar Dzino was in this country all along." He leaned forward, one elbow on the table, so he could thrust his face near mine. "I think you planned this the whole time, together."

I shook my head, feeling the futility of it all. "No."

"Then how did you end up in the Wests' apartment? In Laura's *life*?"

Again I shook my head, over and over, knowing it was useless. "No. I did not. I never would."

"Then it's a pretty strange coincidence, isn't it? Pretty damn strange."

I straightened, lifting my head to gaze at them both. "I will tell you the truth, if you want me to."

They stared back at me, looking distinctly nonplussed, and wearily I realized, as with so many others, they did not want to know the truth. They wanted to shape and twist the facts to fit their own story, the one where they captured two killers, assigned motives, wrapped it all up so neatly. I could even understand that. How often we want things in this world to be neat.

"All right, Maria," Lisa said in an equable tone that managed to convey her utter skepticism. "Why don't you tell us the truth?"

And so I did, explaining about how Petar had been taken away from me back at Vojno, how I had never seen him again, never recognized him in any of the sketches or photos they had shown me, until less than a week ago. Monday. It was Friday, and it had only been on Monday that I had seen that terrible photograph and known who it was. Five days, and yet a lifetime.

"Why didn't you say anything at the time?" Lisa asked. "Instead you assured us you didn't recognize him. You lied."

"I was scared," I said as I looked down at my hands. "I didn't know what to do."

"The obvious thing to do would have been to—"

"I know that," I cut her off, raising my voice a little. "Of course I know that. But what you do in the moment and what you know you should do are often two different things."

"There was time later," Lisa persisted.

"I know that too. All I have been thinking about these last five days has been Petar, and what I should do."

"And when he approached you, as you say he did? Why didn't you call the police then?"

"I begged him to turn himself in."

"Not good enough, Maria."

Of course it wasn't. I shook my head yet again. "I made a mistake," I said. "I realize that, and I will pay for it. But I did not have anything to do with my brother killing Laura West." My voice trembled.

"Why did he kill Laura West, if not for you?" Tom asked.

My shoulders slumped at this. "It was for me, but not in the way you think. He saw me with Laura." The admission brought a rush of pain as well as guilt. "She was leaving to go home, I was in the way. She grabbed me by my shoulders…"

Tom snorted in disbelief. "Are you saying your brother killed a woman he didn't know because she *touched* you?"

"It seems crazy, I know, but that is what he said. It seemed to spark something inside him, some memory…" Of Vojno. Those old ghosts rising up again, and yet I longed to lay them to rest forever. "My brother… he is a broken man. You do not know the things that were done to him, that he was made to do…"

"Oh, we know all about Petar Dzino," Tom informed me. "We know the false name he was traveling under, we know he spent three years in Syria, we know he has links to—"

"Do you know he was beaten and tortured in Vojno?" I cried. "Do you know they made him shoot another prisoner?" My voice broke. "Do you know he pulled me on a sled, or that he liked to play piano, Mozart, always Mozart…" And then I began to weep, my shoulders shaking, as I mourned my brother. I did not know what would happen to him, only that he was already lost. I couldn't save him; I couldn't save anyone. Not Laura, not the Wests, not even myself.

Eventually, they led me back to my cell, still seeming unconvinced, unimpressed, by either the truth or my tears. I sat on the thin mattress and stared at the wall, my mind tired and drifting.

It hurt too much to think about Nathan or the girls, and so I let my mind wander back to Sarajevo; I found myself picturing my childhood bedroom in minute detail—the pink bedspread, the soft rabbit toy I'd had since I was a baby, the row of Matry-oshka dolls on my shelf, fat and rosy-cheeked and smiling.

When I opened my eyes, I was startled to see the concrete walls of the cell. Like the camp in Vojno, where this all began, and where, perhaps, it would end.

Eventually I slept, and the next morning I was escorted to yet another room, where my lawyer was waiting for me. I recognized him from Global Rescue, a dark-skinned man with warm eyes and an efficient manner. He wore a nicely pressed button-down shirt in the same pink as my old bedspread.

"Maria. Damien Banks." I shook his hand before sitting down. "I'm so sorry you're in this situation. I understand you spoke to the police last night?"

"I told them the truth."

"It would have been better if you had waited until I could be there."

"I am sorry." Again, for everything.

"Why don't you tell me what happened, from the beginning?"

And so I did, sparing nothing. I stared at the wall as I recited the facts. Damien took notes, interrupting me to clarify a few points, and when I finished there was a heavy silence. I felt drained and empty.

"Will I go to jail?" I asked and he sighed; that was a heavy sound too.

"The thing is, Maria, this case has blown up already. It was on the front page of three newspapers this morning."

"What?" I straightened. "Why?"

"Because it seems sensational. Refugees... terrorists... con-spiracies..." He shrugged, an apology.

"But it wasn't like that."

"It doesn't matter."

So the papers were saying the same things Lisa and Tom had been—that I'd planned it all, that I'd been involved from the beginning, in such a terrible crime.

"The police are going to interview Nathan West. What he says will, of course, help to determine your case and what they decide to charge you with, if anything."

And what would Nathan say? Would he believe like all the rest? I hoped not. I prayed not; my fledgling prayers rising like vapor to the sky. Would he remember that he had asked me to come into his home, and not the other way round? Or would he rewrite the past, because that could be so easy and tempting to do?

"When will you know more?" I asked Damien.

"They're interviewing Nathan this morning. I should know more later today."

And so, I waited some more in my cell, the hours drifting by with surprising speed as my mind wandered back to the past, lingering in the rooms of my childhood. I could hear Petar playing the piano, my father's dry chuckle. The kitchen smelled of spicy *cevapi*. It was such a pleasant place to be.

Then I was called back, and Damien told me all that had happened.

"I'm so sorry to tell you they found Petar this morning."

Found. It did not sound good.

"He'd killed himself. I'm so sorry, Maria."

I nodded slowly, strangely unsurprised, the grief too old to hurt. I had mourned my brother years ago. I realized some part of me had been expecting this since he had walked away from me.

"I'm very sorry for your loss. Unfortunately, that means he can't answer any questions about your involvement, or lack thereof," Damien continued.

"What about Nathan?" I asked quietly, steeling myself for whatever Damien said next.

"That is much more positive, I'm happy to say. Nathan has told the police he does not believe you had any involvement in his wife's killing. He said he was the one who sought you out on every occasion and also made the suggestion that you become his family's nanny, which he said was a great shock to you at the time. That's all very much in your favor."

I nodded, a wave of bittersweet relief going through me, making me shudder with the force of it. "That is good."

"Actually, he wishes to see you. To talk with you."

"He does?"

"Yes. I'll see if I can arrange it. He's petitioning for the accessory charges to be dropped. Considering all the negative press, I'm not sure if that'll be possible, but I will keep you updated."

"Thank you."

"In the meantime, they have applied to be able to hold you for a total of thirty-six hours until they decide whether to charge you."

I nodded my acceptance; I did not mind. If they released me, where would I go? I could not go back to the Wests. I would probably never see Alexa, Ella, or Ruby ever again. That brought more pain than I could bear, and so I did not think about it. I could not.

"Maria, there is another possibility I feel I have to mention to you." Damien sounded so hesitant, I wondered what on earth he could be worried about telling me.

"What is it?"

"You are not a U.S. citizen…"

"I am a permanent resident."

"I'm afraid that doesn't matter in these circumstances."

"What are you saying?"

"Even if the charges are dropped, there is a chance you could be deported back to Bosnia."

Bosnia. I sank back against my seat, my mind reeling all over again. What would I do there? Where would I go? How would I live? "What would that mean? Would I be charged in Bosnia? Would I go to prison there?"

"It depends what they put on your deportation sheet." He paused. "If they do decide to deport you, it will happen very quickly."

"How quickly?"

"Most likely you'd be removed to a detainment center within the next few days."

A shiver of shocked realization went through me. It sounded as if this were a very real possibility, perhaps the likeliest. *Deported.*

"Your case would be referred to the U.S. Citizenship and Immigration Service. I'll know more soon. In the meantime, I'll talk to the authorities and see if Nathan can visit with you," Damien murmured, and then I was being escorted back to my cell again.

My mind did not drift so much this time. I sat very still and let the realizations filter through me, one at a time—Petar's death, Nathan's trust, *Bosnia.* With each one, I felt something in me, something that had been rusted and weary, start to strengthen. I did not want to become a ghost again. I would not. This time it was a choice I would make, that I would live out day by day. I did not yet know how, only that I would. I would not let myself be mired in the past yet again, drifting through my days, wherever I ended up.

That evening, Damien returned to visit, looking tired as he smiled. "You have some friends," he said, and I looked at him in surprise.

"Friends?"

"Nathan West and Cathy Trainor, from Global Rescue. They are both arguing against you being deported, citing your record and reputation."

I felt my spirits lift, just a little. "What does it mean?"

"I don't know. So often these cases become emotional, and reason doesn't always win out. I'll know more soon."

"Can I leave here?"

"I'm sorry, but not until they've decided. I hope to have news tomorrow."

Yet again I was taken back to my cell, and this time my mind drifted once more back to Sarajevo. I wondered if our old apartment on Logavina Street was still standing. Had it been repaired after it had been hit by a mortar shell? Who lived there now? If I was deported, would I see it again? And what if I wasn't? I could not go back to the Wests. I felt that deep within, a door softly closing shut. The association would be too painful for all of us; that period of our lives was surely over. There were some things you could not come back from, no matter how much healing happened, no matter how hard you fought for hope.

And yet what would my future be? Would I go back to my small studio in Astoria, resume working with Neriha, volunteering at Global Rescue, another twenty years of the same, on and on? No. I could not go back to that, either. I didn't want to. I wanted, I realized with a wave of shock, a ripple of rightness, to go home.

Imperceptibly my heart stirred, like something worn and wounded flickering back to life. *Home.* Could I go there? Did that place exist for me, after all these years?

There was only one way to find out.

CHAPTER TWENTY-NINE

NATHAN

In the aftermath of Maria's arrest, I felt as if an earthquake had shaken our apartment—the sauce-splattered pizza boxes, the dusty dining room littered with peels and shreds of wallpaper… the silence that seemed to go on and on.

Then, as if some invisible hand had pressed pause and now pushed play again, everyone sprang back to life.

"Daddy, what's going on? Why are they taking Maria?" Ella asked, grabbing at my sleeve.

"What's happened?" Ruby cried. "When will she come back?"

"*Daddy…!*"

I turned to Alexa. "Tell me what you saw."

Her face was pale, her lips trembling. "She was talking to the man from the photos."

"What?" I stared at her, uncomprehending. "How… how could she have been? How did you know? How did you see?"

"I recognized him." Alexa's voice was high and thin. "The photos from CCTV have been online all over the place. He was wearing the same clothes, he looked the same. I'm not *dumb*, Dad."

"Alexa…" I pressed my thumb and forefinger to my eyes, hard enough to see flashes of light. "I'm just trying to figure out what happened."

"What man, Daddy?"

"What photos?"

I knew I couldn't have this conversation with Alexa with Ella and Ruby in the room. I also wanted to call the police, a lawyer, *someone*. I was reeling almost as much as I had after Laura's death. Where was the manual for this situation? What were the three or five or ten easy steps?

"Everybody just hold on," I said. "We'll figure this out." Because one thing I was sure of, one conviction I could and would not let myself shake, was that Maria was innocent. She *had* to be innocent. I couldn't contemplate any alternatives.

Reluctantly, Ruby and Ella allowed themselves to be fobbed off with TV. I ushered Alexa into the kitchen and closed the door, determined to get to the bottom of this, even if that was a low, low place.

"Alexa, what exactly did you see?"

And so she told me, her voice and body both trembling, about how a man had approached Maria, how he'd looked familiar. How they'd talked, and then gone around the corner. How Alexa had followed them from upstairs, going to Maria's bedroom and peering out from the fire escape, so she could see them four stories below, huddled against the wall. They were arguing. The man hurried off.

"And Maria was acting so strange," Alexa continued. "Like she was in a daze, but also like she was scared. Didn't you notice, Dad? Didn't you see how weird she was being?"

"She was quiet," I admitted numbly. "I thought she was just quiet."

"She was always quiet. It was more than that."

I drew a long, steadying breath. "So you called the police?"

"I called Lisa. You had her card. I saw it on your dresser."

"And what did you tell her?"

"That I thought I recognized the man. That Maria had been talking to him. I didn't do it right away. I wanted to be sure, and I was." She looked at me anxiously. "I was, Dad. I saw the pictures online, and he was wearing the same clothes. And when I talked to Lisa, she said they already had a lead. They said I was helping."

And from that, they'd decided to arrest Maria. To break into our home and terrify my children. Couldn't there have been a better way?

I was furious with the police, but I was also scared. What if there was more to this story than I knew or understood? There had to be, based on everything Alexa had told me, as well as Maria herself. *I am so sorry*, she'd said.

Why, Maria?

"I need to talk to the police," I said. "I need to figure this out."

"I did the right thing, didn't I, Dad?" Alexa said. She was clenching her fists, biting her lips. "Didn't I do the right thing?"

"Oh, Alexa, sweetheart." I didn't know what to tell her. "You didn't do the wrong thing," I said finally. "Of course not. If you were worried, if you suspected something, you were right to act on it. I'm just sorry you were dealing with all this alone. I wish you'd felt you could tell me. We could have talked about it, asked Maria…"

"Asked Maria?" Alexa's voice rose on a shriek. "But she would have lied! She *knew* him, Dad. All this time she knew him. He was her brother. You heard her admit it. Her *brother*."

Her words thudded through me. *No, Maria. No, surely not…*

The next morning, I asked Sarah to watch the girls while I went to the station. I didn't know if we knew each other well enough for that, but this was an emergency, and she was both kind and willing, giving me a quick hug before I left the apartment.

As I walked to the street corner to hail a cab, I saw the papers, their lurid headlines. They'd condemned Maria already, hinted at some great conspiracy, seeming to relish the torrid drama of it, and yet everything in me resisted such a melodramatic version of events, and continued to resist as I spoke to Lisa and Tom.

"Your wife was killed by Petar Dzino, the brother of your nanny, Maria Dzino," they informed me. "We believe they had been in contact for some time."

"For some time? Since when?" I sounded aggressive; I realized I was angry, and not at Maria.

"Perhaps since he arrived in New York in September."

"But you have no proof of that."

Lisa's eyebrow rose. "Do you not find it suspicious, that she ended up in your home?"

"No, I don't find it *suspicious*, because I was the one who asked her to come there." I thought of the first time I saw Maria at Laura's funeral, how the director of Global Rescue had introduced her. And again, when I'd gone to the center, and looked for her, and asked her to have coffee. I initiated everything. Maria never orchestrated anything. Of that I was absolutely sure. "What is Maria saying happened?" I demanded and when, rather reluctantly, they told me, I nearly exploded. "That's the truth, then! Why can't you see it? She didn't know it was her brother until less than a week ago." It made so much sense.

"She still didn't come forward," Lisa pointed out. "She withheld crucial information that could have led to his capture."

"She was scared." Of course she was. With her history, all that was at stake? She most likely had no idea what to do. I wished I'd seen it. I wished she'd trusted me enough to confide in me.

"Petar Dzino was seen near your home," Tom pointed out in his gravelly voice. "He could have been a risk to your family..."

"Maria would never have let that happen." I spoke firmly, but the words still chilled my heart. Petar Dzino had held a gun to my wife's head and pulled the trigger. I could never forget that. Was I being naïve because I couldn't handle any more pain? Or was I being right, for once? Standing up for something I believed in, fighting for someone I cared about?

"Or a risk to someone else," Tom continued. "He was a known killer."

"But Maria isn't." I was sure of that, with every fibre of my being. "I want the charges dropped."

"That is not within your remit, Mr. West."

We were back to Mr. now, were we? "The newspapers would be very interested to hear my side of the story, I think…" I began meaningfully.

Lisa and Tom exchanged looks. They hadn't expected me to make it difficult for them. They'd counted on me being on their side, and I realized I wasn't. I absolutely wasn't.

"I also want to see Maria," I said, and my tone did not allow for disagreement.

I saw her that afternoon. It had been an endless few hours, talking to officials, experts, lawyers, police. Trying to care for my girls, all of whom were grieving now for Maria too.

"Will Maria come back, Daddy?" Ruby asked as she scrambled into my lap. "Will they let her come back?"

I'd just had a phone call from Maria's lawyer, and my heart was heavy, so heavy. Maria's brother, Laura's killer, was dead, and deportation seemed likely for her, but I'd still fight it, for my own sake as well as hers. "I don't know, Rubes. I hope so."

"I want her to come back."

"I know. I do, too." I didn't realize quite so much until this moment, when her absence felt like a gaping hole in our lives. I wrapped my arms around Ruby. "Sometimes things don't work the way we want them to. But no matter what happens, Maria loves you. I know that. And I love you, too."

I glanced up to see Alexa standing in the doorway, looking stricken. My poor daughter hadn't thought through this part of the story, how it would actually end. She'd acted out in anger and fear, and I didn't blame her for it. She was a child, and she saw things in black and white, not the endless shades of gray I saw and understood.

"What's going to happen to her?" she asked in a whisper.

"She might have to go back to Bosnia," I said quietly. "But I'm trying to get it reversed, along with some other people who know Maria. If we vouch for her, maybe that won't have to happen."

"Bosnia? *Why?*" This from Ella.

"Because… the police want her to."

"But what did she do?" Ella cried. "What did she do wrong?"

"Maria made a mistake," I said slowly. "Because she was scared. She didn't say something when she should have…"

Alexa let out a little squeak, and then pressed her lips together, shaking her head back and forth.

"I'm going to see her tomorrow. Maybe you could make her a card, Ruby? Ella?" I glanced at Alexa, but her lip curled, defiant again, yet still tearful, and she disappeared into her bedroom.

"Yes, let's make her a card," Ruby said, sniffing, as she wiped away her tears. "I'm going to make her the bestest card ever." Her voice wobbled as she ran to the craft cupboard in the kitchen for paper and markers, glitter and glue, with Ella following behind, both of them eager to get started.

The next morning, with Sarah watching the girls again, I headed to the station, my heart like a stone within me. But when I arrived, I was told, rather abruptly, that Maria was no longer there.

"Where is she?" My voice rose. "What have you done with her?"

"We haven't done anything with her," a voice from behind me said. I turned to see Lisa. "The charges against her have been dropped, and the immigration service decided against deportation. She's free."

Free. I stared at Lisa in shock, unable to absorb it. "Just like that?"

She smiled wearily. "I don't know if Maria sees it that way, but yes. Just like that."

"Why? I mean, how…?" I realized how much I'd been bracing myself for the worst, because lately the worst had always happened. I didn't feel ready for good news.

"The judge wasn't convinced of any wrongdoing on her part. And, in the end, neither were we." She paused. "I'm sorry for any undue strain we put you through. We had to investigate all possibilities…"

I accepted her apology with a nod. "You were just doing your job. I know that. But… do you know where Maria is? Has she left?"

"I'm here."

I turned, shocked again to see Maria walking towards me from the waiting area. Lisa excused herself, but I was barely aware of her.

"Maria…"

She stood before me, looking smaller somehow, her hair stranded with grey, her eyes the same startling blue-green as always. She bowed her head. "I'm so sorry for everything, Nathan."

"You don't need to be sorry." My voice was thick. "None of this was your fault."

"I should have said something," she murmured. "I know that. I always knew that. I was just so afraid."

"I understand, Maria. Please believe me, I understand."

"Thank you," she murmured. "You are so kind."

"I'm not," I blurted, and suddenly I felt as if I could break down, right there in the police station waiting room, with an indifferent sergeant at the desk and Maria in front of me, looking so sad and yet somehow peaceful. The way Laura had been, according to witnesses. "I'm not, Maria," I said, my voice turning ragged. It felt like a confession.

"Nathan…"

"I've been so lousy about so many things," I continued, reckless now, needing to say it all. "I've been so ambitious and arrogant and lazy and stupid… and now this…" Before I knew what was happening, a sob tore out of me, followed by another.

The grief that I thought had hardened inside me softened and spilled out as my shoulders shook helplessly and tears streamed from my eyes. I had never cried like this before; I'd kept myself from it, all these months. *All these years.* And now it was happening here, in a police station, with Maria. Because of Maria.

I was crying for her, and for Laura, and for my three daughters who were struggling on and on, and would have to for a long time. I was crying for myself, for the mistakes I'd made all along and the life I would no longer live, now that Laura was gone, and even for the boy I'd been, bounced from school to school, always looking for a home. Thinking I could carve one out myself, with ambition and hard work, and failing so badly, so many times.

And as I cried, Maria put her arms around me, her voice a soothing murmur. "It is good to cry," she said. "It is good to cry. To cry is to heal."

I wanted to believe her as I wept; I wanted to believe that something good could come of all this, even now. Especially now.

After a few moments, I eased back, wiping my cheeks, embarrassment rushing in. "I'm so sorry. I don't know what happened… I've never…"

"I know you've never," Maria said with a small smile. "Trust me, Nathan, I know. You don't need to be sorry."

I gave a little laugh of acknowledgement as I wiped the last of the tears from my face. "Alexa…" My daughter's name bottled in my throat. Did Maria know she'd been arrested because of Alexa?

"Alexa," she repeated softly. "Yes. I have a letter for her here, and also for Ruby and Ella. If you would give them to them. If you would be so kind?"

"Letters…" I shook my head slowly. "Maria, aren't you coming back with us?" I could not conceive of anything else. She hesitated, and in her face I saw her answer. "But why not?"

"Nathan, it was my brother." Her voice was gentle, sad.

"I know, but…" I trailed off helplessly. I didn't really know anything.

"I have been thinking," Maria said quietly. "When I thought I was going to be deported, I was thinking that perhaps it is time for me to return home."

"To Bosnia?" I felt numb.

"Yes, to Bosnia. I ran away, all those years ago, because I could not face it all. I could not bear it, but perhaps now I can. I know I do not want to keep running."

"But you have a life here." *You have us*, I wanted to say, but I didn't, because she was already shaking her head.

"No, I have never had a life here. Not really. I haven't tried to have one."

"But…" I didn't want to tell Ruby and Ella and even Alexa that Maria wasn't coming back, that they would experience yet another loss. "You aren't going *now*?" I said.

"No, not now. But soon." She smiled sadly. "I am so sorry, Nathan. For everything."

"Can you at least come and see the girls?" My voice cracked. "Talk to them? They miss you…"

"Of course. If they want me to."

"They do." I thought of Alexa's stricken face. "They do," I said again.

We took a cab uptown, and when I opened the door of our apartment, I felt as if I'd been gone for two lifetimes. Sarah came to the door, looking concerned, her eyes widening when she saw Maria.

"I'll just get my things," she murmured, and she slipped out as the girls came running.

"Maria!" Ruby's voice was full of joy as she threw herself at Maria, wrapping her arms around her waist. "You're back."

"Yes, for now." She stroked Ruby's hair tenderly, and then held one arm out, beckoning to Ella who was holding back as usual. "Come here, *koka*. Come here."

I watched them embrace, my chest throbbing with both the sweetness and the pain.

"Why did you go, Maria?" Ruby asked. "Why did the police take you?"

"You're staying now, aren't you?" Ella sounded anxious. "You'll stay with us."

Maria glanced back at me. "For now, yes."

While Maria shepherded Ella and Ruby to the living room, I went in search of Alexa.

"Maria's here?" she asked, her voice fearful, when I found her in her bedroom. I'd explained how Maria hadn't had any part in Laura's death, and she'd nodded in acceptance, tearful and resigned. Now she bit her lips, looking anxious. "Is she... is she angry with me?"

"No, not at all, Alexa." I paused. "Are you angry with her?"

"No." Alexa's lips trembled and she pressed them together. "I thought she was guilty. I wanted her to be guilty."

"Why, Alexa?" I asked softly. I closed the door and came to sit with her on the bed.

"Because... because then somehow it made sense. There was a reason, even if it wasn't a good one. There was..." She gulped. "There was someone to blame."

I understood that impulse; I'd struggled with it myself. Alexa bit her lip, tears filling her eyes.

"Alexa," I said, and I put both my hands on her shoulders, making her look at me. "Alexa," I said again, the words coming from deep within me, "whatever you're feeling now... whatever you've been struggling with... Mom loved you, and I love you. No matter what. That will never change. I love you," I said again, because some things, I'd discovered, could never be said too much.

A tear trembled on her lash and then slipped down her cheek. "Dad," she said, and she started to cry, the same kind of wrenching sobs I had experienced earlier with Maria. "Dad," she gasped out again, and then my arms were around her, and I was murmuring I knew not what, telling Alexa I loved her, that it was okay. It really was okay.

"I was mad at Mom the morning she died," Alexa managed to gasp out between choking sobs. "I told her I hated her. That was the last thing I ever said to her. The very last thing."

"Oh, Alexa." My poor, heartsick, guilt-stricken daughter. Had she been feeling guilty all this time? How had she lived with that burden for all these months, let it eat her up from the inside? "If you were feeling guilty about that, Alexa, you didn't need to. None of this was your fault. At all. And you couldn't have done anything to change what happened. Mom knew you loved her. Of course she did, always. *Always.*"

"It was all over a phone," Alexa continued, her voice breaking on the words. "All over a stupid phone." And then she was sobbing in my arms as if her body were being wrenched out, and like Maria had said, I knew it was good. It would heal.

We all would. It would take time, tears, striving, and pain. But it would happen. I felt sure of that, as I held my daughter in my arms.

"I need to tell Maria I'm sorry," she finally said, wiping her cheeks, and I nodded.

"I think that would be a good thing to do."

*

Three days later, Maria said goodbye. The girls had begged her to stay, and with tears in her eyes Maria had hugged and kissed them all, as she shook her head and explained that she had to go. I think they understood, just as I did; after all that had happened, we all needed to move on in some way.

I'd found a nanny; the agency had done a rush job. Maria had booked her ticket. Part of me railed against it, but another part understood. We couldn't go back—not to when Laura was alive, not to when Maria had lived with us. There was never any going back.

We took her to the airport, all four of us, the girls still tearful but accepting. Maria hugged them in turn; she'd already given me letters for each of them, of everything she remembered Laura saying about them, as keepsakes. I knew they would be treasured.

"You must write me letters," Maria said as she squeezed their hands. "Lots of letters. Perhaps I'll figure out email. It would be about time."

She lifted her head to smile at me, her eyes still filled with sorrow.

"I don't regret it, you know," I said, needing to say it. Needing her to believe me. "You coming into our lives. No matter why or what happened… that was a good thing, Maria, for us, and I hope, for you. I don't regret it, I promise. You've done so much for me. For all of us." I put my arms around Alexa and Ella, Ruby pressing her back against my knees. "We'll all miss you."

"As I will you." She smiled at each of the girls in turn. "All of you, so much."

"I wanted to give you something." I fumbled in my pocket for the necklace I'd found when I'd been going through Laura's things. "It was Laura's… I was just going to put it away in a box, but I want you to have it. I think… I think she would too." Carefully, I lifted the necklace out of my pocket and handed it to Maria. It wasn't anything particularly special or expensive—no diamonds or sapphires, just a single silver shape on a chain, that I'd given her years ago, for her birthday.

"A heart," Maria murmured as she held up the pendant with its simple silver heart. "It's beautiful."

"Because you carry all of our hearts, just like you said before. *Dilbere*."

"Oh, Nathan." Tears sparkled in Maria's eyes as she looked at me. "Thank you, all of you." She fastened the pendant around her neck. "Let me teach you another word in my language," she said. "Another word that you do not have quite the same in English. *Halaliti*. It means many things, all in one. It means to forgive, to make peace with, to accept, and to say goodbye. This is our *halaliti*."

"But we will see you again," Ruby said, her voice wobbling. "Won't we?"

"Yes, *koka*, one day. I hope so." She looked at me. "I hope."

And I knew I did too—that somehow, in the midst of all this grief and sadness, we'd both found hope. I smiled at her as she turned and started to walk away, towards the departure gates. Ruby, Ella, Alexa, and I all stood there silently, watching her walk out of our lives, knowing that something was ending, and yet something else was beginning. Something new, and maybe even beautiful.

That was six months ago now. Six long, hard, painful, *good* months. Maria is back in Sarajevo. She has written us to let us know how she is doing; the first few weeks were strange and difficult, but she is working at a hairdresser's now, and volunteering with a charity that supports victims of the Bosnian genocide, especially women. Women like her. She is, in her own words, no longer a ghost.

We've even talked, the girls and I, about taking a trip to Sarajevo someday, perhaps next summer. I would like to see Maria's city. I would like to see Maria.

In the last six months, we've made many changes. I work four days a week still; the girls are now in the local public school, with Ruby at a government-funded pre-K program. The living room is sage green, the dining room a lovely rose. I've finished the bathroom as well, and next up is Alexa's room.

We have a nanny, a young woman from Denmark named Sofie. She is friendly and helpful and she spends the weekends visiting her boyfriend in Boston. She is nothing like Maria, and that is okay.

Alexa isn't angry, and Ella is eating better, but there are bad days as well as good days, days when Ruby falls apart and Ella won't eat and Alexa slams into her room, and even that has been okay. Small steps. We are taking small steps.

And now we are here, in a grassy field outside Boston, headstones all around us. We've come up for the weekend, the girls and I, to see Laura's headstone. We've come to Boston a few times over the last six months, and to Cape Cod over the summer, and while it hasn't always been easy, it's been good. So much has been, strangely, surprisingly, *sweetly*, good.

As I stand in front of Laura's headstone, Ruby slips her hand in mine. "Daddy, what does it say?"

I stare at the words graven on the slab of granite, words I'd chosen five months ago, with Paul and Elaine's blessing, and then I tell them to Ruby. "It says 'Laura West, beloved wife, mother, and daughter. *Dilbere*.'"

"*Dilbere*," Ruby repeats softly, because she knows what it means.

Gently, with a little smile, Elaine takes Ruby by the hand, and she leads her and Ella and Alexa a bit away, to give me a moment with Laura, even though I know she's not really here.

It is a beautiful September day, the sun shining, the air full of birdsong and promise. In the distance, a child's laughter drifts on the breeze. I crouch down, close to Laura's grave, as a thousand memories tumble through my mind: Laura throwing her arms around me when I asked her to marry me. Her feet in my lap as we sat on the sofa and watched TV. The moment Alexa was born and teasingly Laura told me not to drop her. Her laughter ringing out on Christmas morning, or while running through the park, or flipping pancakes with Ruby. Her smiling at me, an easy, uncomplicated love shining from her eyes, her face.

These memories, I know, are real. I'm not rewriting our history, or casting it into a sentimental, sepia tint. It was real, just as the harder memories were real, the ones I've had to accept and forgive myself for.

I've accepted the hard along with the good, I've seen how one can give birth to the other, hope rising from the ashes, purpose emerging from the pain—for me, for Laura, for the girls, and for Maria. Amidst the grief and the loss, the confusion and even the evil, there can be a reason.

As I crouch there, I ask a silent question, a question that comes from up the depths of me, that matters more than anything, and then I strain to hear its answer.

In the stillness, and then in the gentle whispering of the breeze, in the green leaves of the trees around me and in my oldest daughter's hand slipping into mine, I hear it. I hear it and I smile as we turn for home.

EPILOGUE

Eighteen months earlier

It's my first day, and I'm nervous. What am I doing here, really? It's all a bit cliché, isn't it, the bored Upper East Side housewife playing Lady Bountiful downtown?

But I needed to come. I couldn't even say why, only that I felt drawn to this place, with a desire to make a difference, even if it's just to one person. Of course, I don't even know yet who that will be, if anyone, but I'm glad I'm here.

The foyer of Global Rescue is buzzing with people as classes empty out and fill up again; I've been smiling randomly at strangers for ten minutes, waiting for my own class to begin. Forty-five minutes teaching English to refugees and immigrants—it's not much, but it's something. And who am I to say it won't make a difference to someone? I hope it will. I hope I'm here for a reason, because it feels like I am, even if Nathan would roll his eyes at such a notion.

Nathan. My stomach clenches as I think of him, even as my heart swells with love. He tries so hard, and yet somehow he is still missing something. I don't know how to help him to find it, or even if I can… which is part of the reason why I'm here. Because I think I need to find something too, even if I don't yet know what it is.

Just then, from across the room, a woman with blue-green eyes catches my attention. She stands a little bit off by herself, composed and still, seeming serene even as I sense a sorrow emanating from her that feels almost tangible, and I find myself walking towards her.

"Hi," I say, keeping my voice cheerful. "I'm new here. What's your name?"

She looks startled, and then she gives me a fleeting, tentative smile that doesn't reach her eyes. "My name is Maria."

"I just started volunteering here," I confide, stepping closer. "I'm about to teach my first class, and I'm kind of nervous."

"Oh?" She looks at me with shy surprise. "You don't need to be nervous."

"Have you been helping out here for very long?"

"Almost twenty years."

"Wow." I am impressed. "That's a long time."

"What made you volunteer?" Maria asks, and I shrug, self-conscious now, because it sounds so silly, so small.

"I want to make a difference, I suppose, in some little way. And be a good example to my girls." Even if they don't know I'm here yet. One day they will.

"You have children?"

"Three daughters." I hear the pride in my voice, and I picture my girls—Ruby, snuggled in my lap; Ella, her head on my shoulder as she stands next to me, Alexa rolling her eyes at me before she can't help but dissolve into laughter. "They're wonderful," I say, and Maria nods.

"That is good."

"What about you?"

She shakes her head. "There is no one."

She speaks matter-of-factly, but I still hear such loss in her voice; I see it in her eyes, and I wish I could do something about it. I wonder what her story is, if she'll ever trust me enough to tell me. I want to help her, which seems ridiculous, because I don't even know how, and yet…

I'm here. Maybe I'll find a way; maybe we'll be friends. It's only my first day, after all, and anything could happen.

For a moment, standing there on the cusp of this new step I've taken, I feel as if I am brimming with possibility, with wonderful hope. Anything could happen, and that seems like a beautiful promise.

"Sorry, I don't think I told you my name," I tell Maria as I hold out my hand for her to shake. She takes it cautiously, a fragile smile blooming across her face, and I realize I'm glad I sought her out. This feels like a beginning. "I'm Laura," I say, and I smile.

A LETTER FROM KATE

Dear Reader,

Thank you so much for reading *No Time to Say Goodbye*. If you are interested in learning about my upcoming releases, you can sign up for my newsletter here. Your email address will never be shared and you can unsubscribe at any time.

www.bookouture.com/kate-hewitt

The idea for *No Time to Say Goodbye* came to me a long time ago, while I was living in New York as a mother of young children. Back then, I hadn't enough experience of writing or of life to attempt the story, but ten years later (and older), I felt ready to try to write about so many serious things—death and grief, war and crime. Weighty issues aside, however, at its heart this story is about finding hope amidst the pain and tragedy of life.

Someone recently asked me if there was a common theme in my books, and I answered that all my stories explore the question "what do you do when the worst happens?" The worst might be different in every book, and for every person, but as someone who has struggled through my own losses and sorrows, as everyone must do eventually, I do believe hope can be found even amidst the deepest sorrow or the wildest grief, and I try to communicate that through my writing.

While writing *No Time to Say Goodbye*, I researched the terrible atrocities of the Bosnian War, and how far reaching they are for the women who must continue to live in Bosnia, sometimes seeing their attackers every day, with no real way to bring justice. It's an issue that remains largely ignored by the wider world, and I hope that my story might raise awareness of this terrible time in modern history. If you'd like to support charitable efforts to help women survivors of war crimes, Women for Women (www.womenforwomen.org.uk) is a wonderful charity that supports efforts to help women victims of war rebuild their lives and choose their own futures.

I hope you have enjoyed *No Time To Say Goodbye*. If you did, I would be very grateful if you could write a review. I'd love to hear what you think, and it makes such a difference helping new readers to discover one of my books for the first time.

I also love hearing from my readers—you can get in touch on my Facebook page, through Twitter, Goodreads or my website.

Thanks again and happy reading,
Kate

 @katehewitt1

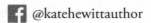 @katehewittauthor

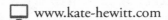 www.kate-hewitt.com

ACKNOWLEDGEMENTS

Every book I write needs a lot of help along the way, and I'm so thankful to all the people who give me their time, advice, thoughts, expertise, and listening ears!

In particular, I'd like to thank Slavko Hadzic, who shared his experiences of living through the Bosnian War with me, as well as making my daughter Charlotte laugh—a lot!

I'd also like to thank my dear family members who offered advice when I felt stuck in the middle of the story—Cliff, for listening to me go on and on about refugees and war; Ellen, for listening to me vent about not knowing how to end the story while she was practicing driving (she gave me a good idea and she passed her driving test!); Caroline, for reading my books and then actually wanting to discuss them with me; and Charlotte, Anna, and Teddy for generally being patient with a mother who is half-living in an alternate reality while she's writing.

As ever, I must thank my fabulous editor, Isobel, who has made every story I've written for Bookouture a hundred percent better, and all the wonderful team at Bookouture who work so hard to bring our books into the world.

And lastly, thank you to all my wonderful readers who buy and read my books, and then so very kindly take the time to let me know how much they enjoyed them. Thank you so very much!